Simon Beckett is a freelance journalist and writes for national newspapers and colour supplements. He lives in Sheffield. His new book, *Written in Bone*, is also published by Bantam Books.

For more information on Simon Beckett and his books, visit his website at www.simonbeckett.com

THE CHEMISTRY OF DEATH

Simon Beckett

BANTAM BOOKS

LONDON • TORONTO • SYDNEY • AUCKLAND • JOHANNESBURG

THE CHEMISTRY OF DEATH
A BANTAM BOOK: 9780553817492

Originally published in Great Britain by Bantam Press,
a division of Transworld Publishers

PRINTING HISTORY
Bantam Press edition published 2006
Bantam edition published 2007

23

Copyright © Simon Beckett 2006

Set in 10.5/12pt Sabon by
Falcon Oast Graphic Art Ltd.

Bantam Books are published by Transworld Publishers,
61–63 Uxbridge Road, London W5 5SA,
a division of The Random House Group Ltd,
in Australia by Random House Australia (Pty) Ltd,
20 Alfred Street, Milsons Point, Sydney, NSW 2061, Australia,
in New Zealand by Random House New Zealand Ltd,
18 Poland Road, Glenfield, Auckland 10, New Zealand
and in South Africa by Random House (Pty) Ltd,
Isle of Houghton, Corner of Boundary Road & Carse O'Gowrie,
Houghton 2198, South Africa.

Penguin Random House is committed to a sustainable future for
our business, our readers and our planet. This book is made from
Forest Stewardship Council® certified paper.

MIX
Paper from
responsible sources
FSC® C018179

Printed and bound in Great Britain by Clays Ltd, St Ives plc

For Hilary

1

A human body starts to decompose four minutes after death. Once the encapsulation of life, it now undergoes its final metamorphoses. It begins to digest itself. Cells dissolve from the inside out. Tissue turns to liquid, then to gas. No longer animate, the body becomes an immovable feast for other organisms. Bacteria first, then insects. Flies. Eggs are laid, then hatch. The larvae feed on the nutrient-rich broth, and then migrate. They leave the body in orderly fashion, following each other in a neat procession that always heads south. South-east or south-west sometimes, but never north. No-one knows why.

By now the body's muscle protein has broken down, producing a potent chemical brew. Lethal to vegetation, it kills the grass as the larvae crawl through it, forming an umbilical of death that extends back the way they came. In the right conditions – dry and hot, say, without rain – it can extend for yards, a wavering brown conga-line of fat yellow grubs. It's a curious sight, and for the curious what could be more natural than to follow this phenomenon back to its source? Which was how the Yates boys found what was left of Sally Palmer.

Neil and Sam came across the maggot trail on the edge of Farnham Wood, where it borders the marsh. It was the second week of July, and already the unnatural summer seemed to have been going on for ever. The heat seemed eternal, leaching the colour from the trees and baking the ground to the hardness of bone. The boys were on their way to Willow Hole, a reed pond that passed as the local swimming pool. They were meeting friends there, and would spend the Sunday afternoon bombing into the tepid green water from an overhanging tree. At least, so they thought.

I see them as bored and listless, drugged by the heat and impatient with each other. Neil, at eleven three years older than his brother, would be walking slightly ahead of Sam to demonstrate his impatience. There's a stick in his hand, with which he whips the stalks and branches he passes. Sam trudges along behind, sniffing from time to time. Not from a summer cold, but from the hay fever that also reddens his eyes. A mild antihistamine would help him, but at this stage he doesn't know that. He always sniffs during summer. Always the shadow to his bigger brother, he walks with his head down, which is why he and not his brother notices the maggot trail.

He stops and examines it before shouting Neil back. Neil is reluctant, but Sam has obviously found something. He tries to act unimpressed, but the undulating line of maggots intrigues him just as much as it does his brother. The two of them crouch over the grubs, pushing dark hair out of similar faces and wrinkling their noses at the ammoniac smell. And though neither could later remember whose idea it was to see where they were coming from, I imagine it to be Neil's. Having walked past the maggots himself, he would be keen to assert his authority once more. So it's Neil who sets off first, heading towards the yellowed tufts of marsh grass from which the larvae are flowing, and leaving Sam to follow.

Did they notice the smell as they approached? Probably. It would be strong enough to cut through even Sam's blocked sinuses. And they probably knew what it was. No city boys, these, they would be familiar with the cycle of life and death. The flies, too, would have alerted them, a somnolent buzzing that seemed to fill the heat. But the body they discovered was not the sheep or deer, or even dog, they might have expected. Naked but unrecognizable in the sun, Sally Palmer was full of movement, a rippling infestation that boiled under her skin and erupted from mouth and nose, as well as the other less natural openings in her body. The maggots that spilled from her pooled on the ground before crawling away in the line that now stretched beyond the Yates boys.

I don't suppose it matters which one broke first, but I think it would be Neil. As ever, Sam would have taken his cue from his big brother, trying to keep up in a race that led them first home, then to the police station.

And then, finally, to me.

As well as a mild sedative, I also gave Sam antihistamine to help his hay fever. By this time, though, he wasn't the only one to have red eyes. Neil too was still shaken by their discovery, although now he was beginning to recover his juvenile poise. So it was he rather than Sam who told me what had happened, already starting to reduce the raw memory to a more acceptable form, a story to be told and retold. And later, when the tragic events of that preternaturally hot summer had run their course, years later Neil would be telling it still, forever identified as the one whose discovery had started it all.

But it hadn't. It was just that, until then, we had never realized what was living among us.

2

I came to Manham in the late afternoon of a wet March, three years earlier. I arrived in the train station – little more than a small platform in the middle of nowhere – to find a rainswept landscape that seemed as empty of human life as it was of contour. I stood with my suitcase and took in the surrounding scenery, barely noticing the rain that dripped down the back of my collar. Flat marshland and fens spread out around me, a linear topography broken only by patches of bare woodland as it stretched to the horizon.

It was my first time in the Broads, my first time in Norfolk. It was spectacularly unfamiliar. I took in the sweeping openness, breathed in the damp, cold air, and felt something, minimally, begin to unwind. Unwelcoming as it might have been, it wasn't London, and that was enough.

There was no-one to meet me. I hadn't arranged any transport from the station. I hadn't planned that far ahead. I'd sold my car, along with everything else, and not given a thought to how I would get to the village. I still wasn't thinking too clearly, back then. If I'd thought about it at all, with the arrogance of a city-dweller I'd assumed there would be taxis, a shop, something. But there was no taxi rank, not even a phone box. I briefly regretted giving away my mobile, then picked up my suitcase and headed for the road. When I reached it there were just two options, left or right. Without hesitating I took the left. No reason. After a few hundred yards I came across a junction with a faded wooden road sign. It leaned to one side, so that it seemed to be pointing into the wet earth to some point underground. But at least it told me I was heading in the right direction.

The light was fading when I finally reached the village. One or two cars had passed as I'd walked, but none had stopped. Other than those, the first signs of life were a few farms set well back from the road, each isolated from the other. Then ahead of me in the half-light I saw the tower of a church, apparently half-buried in a field. There was a pavement now, narrow and slick with rain but better than the verge and hedgerows I'd been using since leaving the train station. Another bend in the road revealed the village itself, virtually hidden until you stumbled across it.

It wasn't quite a picture postcard. It was too lived in, too sprawling to fit the image of a rural English village. On the outskirts was a band of pre-war houses, but these soon gave way to stone cottages, their walls pebbled with chunks of flint. They grew progressively older as I drew nearer to the heart of the village, each step taking me further back in history. Varnished with drizzle, they huddled against each other, their lifeless windows reflecting back at me with blank suspicion.

After a while the road became lined with closed shops, behind which more houses ran off into the wet dusk. I passed a school, a pub, and then came to a village green. It was ablaze with daffodils, their yellow trumpets shockingly colourful in the sepia world as they nodded in the rain. Towering over the green, a gigantic old horse chestnut spread its bare black branches. Behind it, surrounded by a grave-yard of canted, moss-covered stones, was the Norman church whose tower I'd seen from the road. Like the older cottages, its walls were encrusted with flint; hard, fist-sized stones that defied the elements. But the softer mortar surrounding them was weathered and worn by age, and the church windows and door had subtly warped as the ground it stood on had shifted over the centuries.

I stopped. Further on I could see that the road gave way to more houses. It was obvious that this was pretty much all there was to Manham. Lights were on in some of the windows, but there was no other sign of life. I stood in the rain, unsure which way to go. Then I heard a noise and saw two gardeners at work in the graveyard. Oblivious to the rain and dying light, they were raking and tidying the grass around the old stones. They carried on without looking up as I approached.

'Can you tell me where the doctor's surgery is?' I asked, water dripping down my face.

They both stopped and regarded me, so alike despite the disparity in their ages that they had to be grandfather and grandson. Both faces held the same placid, incurious expression, from which stared calm, cornflower-blue eyes. The older one motioned towards a narrow, tree-lined lane at the far side of the green.

'Straigh' up there.'

The accent was another confirmation I was no longer in London, a coiling of vowels that sounded alien to my city ears. I thanked them, but they'd already turned back to their work. I went up the lane, the sound of the rain amplified as it dripped through the overhanging branches. After a while I came to a wide gate barring the entrance to a narrow drive. Fixed to one of the gateposts was a sign saying 'Bank House'. Beneath it was a brass plaque that said 'Dr H. Maitland'. Flanked by yews, the drive ran gently uphill through well-kept gardens, then dropped down to the courtyard of an imposing Georgian house. I scraped the mud from my shoes on the worn cast-iron bar set to one side of the front door, then raised the heavy knocker and rapped loudly. I was about to knock again when the door was opened.

A plump, middle-aged woman with immaculate iron-grey hair looked out at me.

'Yes?'

'I'm here to see Dr Maitland.'

She frowned. 'The surgery's closed. And I'm afraid the doctor isn't making home visits at the moment.'

'No . . . I mean, he's expecting me.' That brought

no response. I became aware of how bedraggled I must look after an hour's walk in the rain. 'I'm here about the post. David Hunter?'

Her face lit up. 'Oh, I'm *so* sorry! I didn't realize. I thought . . . Come in, please.' She stood back to let me in. 'Goodness, you're soaked. Have you walked far?'

'From the station.'

'The train station? But that's miles!' She was already helping me off with my coat. 'Why didn't you call to tell us when your train was in? We could have had someone pick you up.'

I didn't answer. The truth was it hadn't occurred to me.

'Come through into the lounge. The fire's lit in there. No, leave your case,' she said, turning from hanging up my coat. She smiled. For the first time I noticed the strain evident in her face. What I'd taken earlier for terseness was just fatigue. 'No-one'll steal it here.'

She led me into a large, wood-panelled room. An age-worn leather chesterfield faced a fire on which a pile of logs were glowing. The carpet was Persian, old but still beautiful. Surrounding it were bare floorboards burnished to a deep umber. The room smelled appealingly of pine and wood smoke.

'Please sit down. I'll tell Dr Maitland you're here. Would you like a cup of tea?'

It was another sign I was no longer in the city. There it would have been coffee. I thanked her and stared into the fire when she had gone out. After the cold, the heat made me drowsy. Outside the French

17

window it was now completely dark. Rain pattered against the glass. The chesterfield was soft and comfortable. I felt my eyelids begin to droop. I stood up quickly, almost panicking as my head began to nod. All at once I felt exhausted, physically and mentally drained. But the fear of sleep was even greater.

I was still standing in front of the fire when the woman came back. 'Do you want to come through? Dr Maitland's in his study.'

I followed her down the hall, shoes creaking on the floorboards. She tapped lightly on a door at the far end, opening it with an easy familiarity without waiting for an answer. She smiled again as she stood back for me to enter.

'I'll bring the teas in a few minutes,' she said, closing the door as she went out.

Inside, a man was sitting at a desk. We regarded each other for a moment. Even sitting down I could see he was tall, with a strong-boned, deeply lined face and a thick head of hair that was not so much grey as cream. But the black eyebrows contradicted any suggestion of weakness, and the eyes beneath them were sharp and alert. They flicked over me, receiving what sort of impression I was unable to say. For the first time I felt faintly disturbed that I wasn't exactly at my best.

'Good God, man, you look drenched!' His voice was a gruff but friendly bark.

'I walked from the station. There weren't any taxis.'

He gave a snort. 'Welcome to wonderful Manham.

You should have let me know you were coming a day early. I'd have arranged a lift from the station.'

'A day early?' I echoed.

'That's right. I wasn't expecting you till tomorrow.'

For the first time the significance of the closed shops dawned on me. This was a Sunday. I'd not realized how badly skewed my sense of time had become. He pretended not to notice how thrown I was by my gaffe.

'Never mind, you're here now. It'll give you more time to settle in. I'm Henry Maitland. Pleased to meet you.'

He extended his hand without getting up. And it was only then I noticed his chair had wheels on it. I went forward to shake his hand, but not before he'd noticed my hesitation. He smiled, wryly.

'Now you see why I advertised.'

It had been in the appointments section of *The Times*, a small notice that was easy to overlook. But for some reason my eyes had fallen on it straight away. A rural medical practice was looking for a GP on a temporary contract. Six months, accommodation provided. It was the location that attracted me as much as anything. Not that I particularly wanted to work in Norfolk, but it would take me away from London. I'd applied without much hope or excitement, so when I'd opened the letter a week later I'd been expecting a polite rejection. Instead I found I'd been offered the job. I had to read the letter twice to take in what it was saying. At another time I might have wondered what the catch was. But at another time I would never have applied for it in the first place.

I wrote back to accept by return of post.

Now I looked at my new employer and belatedly wondered what I'd committed myself to. As if reading my mind, he clapped his hands on his legs.

'Car accident.' There was no embarrassment or self-pity. 'There's a chance I'll recover some use in time, but until then I can't manage by myself. I've been using locums for the past year or so, but I've had enough of that. A different face from one week to the next; that's no good for anyone. You'll learn soon enough they don't like change around here.' He reached for a pipe and tobacco on his desk. 'Mind if I smoke?'

'Not if you don't.'

He gave a laugh. 'Good answer. I'm not one of your patients. Remember that.'

He paused while he held a match to the pipe bowl. 'So,' he said, puffing on it. 'Going to be quite a departure for you after working in a university, isn't it? And this certainly isn't London.' He looked at me over the top of the pipe. I waited for him to ask me to enlarge on my previous career. But he didn't. 'Any last-minute doubts, now's the time to speak up.'

'No,' I told him.

He nodded, satisfied. 'Fair enough. You'll be staying here for the time being. I'll get Janice to show you to your room. We can talk more over dinner. Then you can make a start tomorrow. Surgery kicks off at nine.'

'Can I ask something?' He raised his eyebrows, waiting. 'Why did you hire me?'

It had been bothering me. Not enough to make me turn it down, but in a vague way nevertheless.

'You looked suitable. Good qualifications, excellent references, and ready to come and work out in the middle of nowhere for the pittance I'm offering.'

'I would have expected an interview first.'

He brushed aside the comment with his pipe, wreathing himself in smoke. 'Interviews take time. I wanted someone who could start as soon as possible. And I trust my judgement.'

There was a certainty about him I found reassuring. It wasn't until long afterwards, when there was no longer any doubt that I'd be staying, that he laughingly confided over malt whiskies that I'd been the only applicant.

But right then such an obvious answer never occurred to me. 'I told you I don't have much experience in general practice. How can you be sure I'm up to it?'

'Do you think you are?'

I took a moment to answer, actually considering the question for the first time. I'd come here so far without thinking very much at all. It had been an escape from a place and people it was now too painful to be around any longer. I thought again about how I must look. A day early and soaking wet. *Not even sense enough to come in out of the rain.*

'Yes,' I said.

'There you are then.' His expression was sharp,

but there was an element of amusement. 'Besides, it's only a temporary post. And I'll be keeping an eye on you.'

He pressed a button on his desk. A buzzer rang distantly somewhere in the house. 'Dinner's usually around eight, patients permitting. You can relax till then. Did you bring your luggage or is it being sent on?'

'I brought it with me. I left it with your wife.'

He looked startled, then gave an oddly embarrassed smile. 'Janice is my housekeeper,' he said. 'I'm a widower.'

The warmth of the room seemed to close in on me. I nodded.

'So am I.'

That was how I came to be the doctor at Manham. And how, three years later, I came to be one of the first to hear what the Yates boys had discovered in Farnham Wood. Of course, no-one knew who it was, not straight away. Given its evident condition the boys couldn't even say if the body was that of a man or a woman. Once back in the familiarity of their home, they weren't even sure if it had been naked or not. At one point Sam had even said it had wings, before lapsing into uncertainty and silence, but Neil just looked blank. Whatever they had seen had overwhelmed any terms of reference they were familiar with, and now memory was baulking at recalling it. All they could agree on was that it was human, and dead. And while their description of the abundant sea of maggots implied wounds, I knew only too well

22

the tricks the dead can play. There was no reason to think the worst.

Not then.

So their mother's conviction was all the stranger. Linda Yates sat with her arm around her subdued youngest son, huddled against her while he half-heartedly watched the garishly coloured TV in their small lounge. Their father, a farm worker, was still at work. She'd called me after the boys had run home, breathless and hysterical. Even though it was a Sunday afternoon, there was no such thing as off-duty in a place as small and isolated as Manham.

We were still waiting for the police to arrive. They clearly saw no reason to rush, but I felt obliged to stay. I'd given Sam the sedative, so mild as to be almost a placebo, and reluctantly heard the story recounted by his brother. I'd tried not to listen. I knew well enough what they would have seen.

It wasn't anything I needed reminding of.

The lounge window was wide open, but no breeze came through to cool the room. Outside was dazzlingly bright, bleached to whiteness by the afternoon sun.

'It's Sally Palmer,' Linda Yates said, out of the blue.

I looked at her in surprise. Sally Palmer lived alone on a small farm just outside the village. An attractive woman in her thirties, she'd moved to Manham a few years before me after inheriting the farm from her uncle. She still kept a few goats, and the blood-tie made her less of an outsider than she might otherwise have been; certainly less than I was, even

23

now. But the fact she made her living as a writer set her apart, and made most of her neighbours regard her with a mixture of awe and suspicion.

I hadn't heard any talk of her being missing. 'What makes you say that?'

'Because I had a dream about her.'

It wasn't the answer I expected. I looked at the boys. Sam, calmer now, didn't seem to be listening. But Neil was looking at his mother, and I knew whatever was said here would be spread around the village the moment he got out of the house. She took my silence as scepticism.

'She was standing at a bus stop, crying. I asked her what was wrong, but she didn't say anything. Then I looked down the road, and when I turned back she was gone.'

I didn't know what to say.

'You have dreams for a reason,' she went on. 'That's what this was.'

'Come on, Linda, we don't know who it is yet. It could be anyone.'

She gave me a look that said I was wrong, but she wasn't going to argue. I was glad when the knock came on the door, announcing the arrival of the police.

There were two of them, both solid examples of rural constabulary. The older man was florid-faced, and periodically punctuated his conversation with a jovial wink. It seemed out of place under the circumstances.

'So, you think you've found a body, do you?' he announced cheerily, shooting me a look, as if to include me in an adult joke that was over the boys' heads. While Sam huddled against his mother, Neil mumbled responses to his questions, cowed by the uniformed authority in their home.

It didn't take long. The older police officer flipped his book closed. 'Right, we'd better go and take a look. Which one of you boys is going to show us where it was?'

Sam burrowed his head into his mother. Neil said nothing, but his face paled. Talking was one thing. Going back there was another. Their mother turned to me, worried.

'I don't think that's a good idea,' I said. In fact, I thought it was a lousy one. But I'd dealt with the police enough to know diplomacy was usually better than confrontation.

'So how are we supposed to find it when neither of us know the area?' he demanded.

'I've got a map in the car. I can show you where to go.'

The policeman didn't try to hide his displeasure. We went outside, squinting in the sudden brightness. The house was the end one of a row of small stone cottages. Our cars were parked in the lane. I took the map out of my Land Rover and opened it on the bonnet. The sun glanced off the battered metal, making it hot to the touch.

'It's about three miles away. You'll have to park up and cut across the marsh to the woods. From what they said the body should be somewhere round here.'

I pointed to an area on the map. The policeman grunted.

'I've got a better idea. If you don't want one of the boys to take us, why don't you?' He gave me a tight smile. 'You seem to know your way around.'

I could see by his face that I wasn't going to have any choice. I told them to follow me and set off. The inside of the old Land Rover smelled of hot plastic. I wound both windows down as far as they would go. The steering wheel burned my hands as I gripped it. When I saw how white my knuckles were, I made myself relax.

The roads were narrow and meandering, but it wasn't far. I parked in a rutted semicircle of baked earth, the passenger door brushing against the yellowed hedge. The police car bumped to a halt behind me. The two officers climbed out, the older one hitching up his trousers over his gut. The younger, sunburned and with a shaving rash, hung back a little.

'There's a track across the marsh,' I told them. 'It'll take you to the woods. Just keep following it. It can't be more than a few hundred yards.'

The older policeman wiped the sweat from his head. The armpits of his white shirt were dark and wet. An acrid waft came from him. He squinted at the distant wood, shaking his head.

'It's too hot for this. Don't suppose you want to show us where you think it is?'

He sounded half-hopeful, half-mocking.

'Once you reach the woods your guess is as good as mine,' I told him. 'Just keep an eye out for maggots.'

The younger one laughed, but stopped when the other looked at him balefully.

'Shouldn't you let a scene of crime team do this?' I said.

He snorted. 'They'll not thank us for calling them out for a rotting deer. That's all it usually is.'

'The boys didn't think so.'

'Well, I think I'd rather see it for myself, if you don't mind.' He motioned to the younger man. 'Come on, let's get this over with.'

I watched the two of them clamber through a gap in the hedge and make their way towards the woods. He hadn't asked me to wait, and I couldn't see any point in staying. I'd brought them as far as I could; the rest was up to them.

But I didn't move. I went back to the Land Rover and took a bottle of water from under my seat. Tepid, but my mouth was dry. I put my sunglasses on and leaned against the dusty green wing, facing towards the woods where the police officers were heading. The flatness of the marsh had already swallowed them from sight. The heat gave the air a steamy, metallic taint, full of the hum and chirrup of insects. A pair of dragonflies danced past. I took another drink of water and looked at my watch. There was no surgery today, but I had better things to do than stand around on a roadside waiting to see what two rural policemen found. They were probably right. It could have just been a dead animal the boys had seen. Imagination and panic had done the rest.

I still didn't move.

A while later I saw the two figures heading back. Their white shirts bobbed against the bleached grass stalks. Even before they'd reached me I could see the pallor of their faces. The younger one had a wet stain of vomit on his front that he seemed unaware of. Wordlessly, I handed him the bottle of water. He took it gratefully.

The older one wouldn't meet my eye. 'Can't get a bloody signal out here,' he muttered as he went to their car. He was trying for his earlier gruffness, but not quite making it.

'It wasn't a deer then,' I said.

He gave me a bleak look. 'I don't think we need keep you any longer.'

He waited until I was in the Land Rover before he made his call. As I drove away he was still on the radio. The younger police officer was staring at his feet, the bottle of water dangling from his hand.

I headed back to the surgery. Thoughts were buzzing away in my head, but I'd erected a screen, keeping them out like flies behind mesh. I kept my mind blank by an effort of will, but the flies were still whispering their message to my subconscious. The road leading back into the village and the surgery came up. My hand went to the indicator and then stopped. Without thinking about it, I made a decision that would echo down the weeks to come, one that would change my own life as well as that of others.

I went straight on. Heading for Sally Palmer's farm.

3

The farm was bordered by trees on one side and marshland on the others. The Land Rover threw up dust as it jolted along the rutted track that led to it. I parked on the uneven cobblestones that were all that was left of the courtyard and got out. A tall corrugated-metal barn shimmered in the heat. The farmhouse itself was painted white, peeling and fading now, but still blindingly bright in the sun. Bright green window boxes were fixed either side of the front door, the only shot of colour in a bleached-out world.

Usually, if Sally was in, her Border collie Bess would set off barking before you had chance to knock. Not today, though. There was no sign of life through the windows, either, but that didn't necessarily mean anything. I went to the door and knocked. Now I was here my reason for coming seemed pretty stupid. I stared out towards the horizon as I waited, trying to think of what I should say if she answered. I supposed I could always tell her the truth, but that would make me look as irrational as Linda Yates. And she might misconstrue it, take the reason for my visit as something more than a nagging disquiet I couldn't explain.

Sally and I had, if not exactly a history, then at least something more than a casual acquaintance. There had been a time when we'd seen quite a lot of each other. Not too surprising, really: as outsiders who'd both moved to the village from London, we had our past metropolitan lives in common. Plus she was around my age, and the outgoing sort who made friends easily. And attractive. I'd enjoyed the few times we'd met in the pub for drinks.

But that was as far as it had gone. When I began to sense she might want more I backed off. She'd seemed puzzled at first, but as things had never really had a chance to develop between us there had been no ill feeling or embarrassment. When we bumped into each other we still chatted easily enough, but that was all.

I'd made sure of that.

I knocked on her door again. I remember I actually felt relieved when she didn't open it. She was obviously out, which meant I wouldn't have to explain why I was there. Come to that, I didn't even know myself. I wasn't superstitious, and unlike Linda Yates I didn't believe in premonitions. Except she hadn't said it had been a premonition, not exactly. Just a dream. And I knew all about how seductive dreams can be. Seductive and treacherous.

I turned away from the door, and the direction in which my thoughts had started to travel. It was just as well she wasn't here, I thought, annoyed with myself. What the hell had I been thinking of? Just because some hiker or birdwatcher had died was no reason to let my imagination run away with me.

I was halfway back to the Land Rover when I stopped. There was something bothering me, but until I turned around again I didn't know what it was. It still took me a few moments before I realized. It was the window boxes. The plants in them were brown and dead.

Sally would never let them get that way.

I went back. The soil in the boxes was baked hard. No-one had watered them for days. Perhaps longer. I knocked on the door, called her name. When there was no answer I tried the handle.

It wasn't locked. It was possible she'd got out of the habit of locking her door since she'd lived here. But she was from a city, like me, and old habits died hard. The door stuck as I opened it, caught on the mound of envelopes that lay behind. They slithered in a mini-avalanche as I pushed my way in and stepped over them into the kitchen. It was as I remembered: cheerful lemon walls, solid rustic furniture and a few touches that showed she hadn't been able to leave behind all traces of the city – an electric juicer, stainless-steel espresso maker and large, well-stocked wine-rack.

Other than the build-up of post, at first glance there was nothing wrong. But the house had a musty, unaired smell, overlaid with the sweet scent of decaying fruit. It came from an earthenware bowl on the old pine dresser, a still-life memento mori of blackened bananas, apples and oranges furred white with mould. Dead flowers, now unrecognizable, hung limply over a vase on the table. A drawer by the sink was half-open, as if she'd been disturbed as she was about to take something from it. I automatically went to close it, but left it as it was.

She could be on holiday, I told myself. Or been too busy to bother throwing out old fruit and flowers. There were any number of possible explanations. But I think at that point, like Linda Yates, I knew.

I considered checking the rest of the house, but decided against it. Already I was starting to think of it as a potential crime scene, and I knew better than to risk contaminating any evidence. Instead I went back outside. Sally's goats were in a paddock around the back. One glance confirmed that something was badly wrong. A few were still standing, emaciated and feeble, but most were lying prone, either unconscious or dead. They'd almost stripped the paddock of grass, and when I went to the water trough it was bone dry. A hose was lying nearby, obviously used to fill it. I hung it over the edge of the trough and followed the other end back to a stand-pipe. As water spluttered into the metal trough one or two of the goats tottered over and began to drink.

I would get the vet over here, just as soon as I'd called the police. I took out my phone but there was no signal. Reception around Manham was notoriously patchy, which made mobile phones unpredictable at the best of times. I moved further from the paddock and saw the signal bars stutter into life. I was about to dial when I noticed a small, dark shape half-hidden behind a rusting plough. With a tense, oddly certain feeling of what it would be, I went over.

The body of Bess, Sally's Border collie, lay in the dry grass. It looked tiny, its fur dusty and matted. I batted away the flies that left it to inspect my fresher meat and turned away. But not before I'd seen how the dog's head had been almost severed.

The heat seemed suddenly to have intensified. My legs automatically took me back to the Land Rover. I resisted the urge to get in and drive away. Instead, putting it between me and the house, I continued with my call. As I waited for the police to answer I stared at the far green smudge of the woods I'd just come from.

Not again. Not here.

I realized a tinny voice was coming from the phone. I turned away from both the distant wood and the house.

'I want to report a missing person,' I said.

The police inspector was a squat, pugnacious man called Mackenzie. Perhaps a year or two older than me, the first thing I noticed about him were his abnormally large shoulders. The lower part of his body seemed out of proportion in comparison; short legs tapered to absurdly dainty feet. It would have given him the appearance of a cartoon bodybuilder if not for the blurring line of his gut, and a threatening aura of impatience that made it impossible to take him anything less than seriously.

I'd waited by the car while Mackenzie and a

plain-clothed sergeant had gone to look at the dog. They'd seemed unhurried, almost unconcerned as they strolled over. But the fact that a chief inspector from the Major Investigation Team was here instead of uniformed officers was a sign this was being taken seriously.

He'd come back over to me while the sergeant had gone inside the house to check the rooms. 'So tell me again why you came.'

He smelled of aftershave and sweat, and, faintly, of mint. His sunburned scalp flamed through his thinning red hair, but if he felt any discomfort at standing out in the sun he didn't show it.

'I was near by. I thought I'd call round.'

'Social call, was it?'

'I just wanted to make sure she was all right.'

I wasn't going to bring Linda Yates into it unless I had to. As her doctor I had to suppose she'd told me what she had in confidence, and I didn't think a policeman would put much stock in a dream anyway. I should have known better myself. Except that, irrational or not, Sally wasn't here.

'When was the last time you saw Miss Palmer?' Mackenzie asked.

I thought back. 'Not for a couple of weeks.'

'Can you narrow it down more than that?'

'I remember seeing her in the pub for the summer barbecue about two weeks ago. She was there then.'

'With you?'

'No. But we spoke.' Briefly. *Hi, how are you? Fine, see you later.* Hardly meaningful, as last words go. If

34

that's what they were, I reminded myself. But I no longer had any doubt.

'And after not seeing her since then you suddenly decided to come round today.'

'I'd just heard a body had been found. I wanted to check that she was all right.'

'What makes you so sure the body is a woman's?'

'I'm not. But I didn't think it would hurt to make sure Sally was OK.'

'What's your relationship?'

'Friends, I suppose.'

'Close?'

'Not really.'

'You sleeping with her?'

'No.'

'Been sleeping with her?'

I wanted to tell him to mind his own business. But that's what he was doing. Privacy didn't count for much in these situations, I knew that well enough.

'No.'

He stared at me without saying anything. I looked back at him. After a moment he took a packet of mints from his pocket. As he unhurriedly put one in his mouth I noticed the odd-shaped mole on his neck.

He put the mints back without offering me one. 'So you weren't in a relationship with her? Just good friends, is that it?'

'We knew each other, that's all.'

'But you still felt compelled to come out to see if she was all right. No-one else.'

'She lives out here by herself. It's pretty isolated even by our standards.'

'Why didn't you phone her?'

That stopped me. 'It didn't occur to me.'

'Does she have a mobile?' I told him she did. 'Do you have her number?'

It was in my phone memory. I scrolled to it, knowing what he was going to ask and feeling stupid for not having thought of it myself.

'Shall I ring it?' I offered, before he could say anything.

'Why don't you?'

I could feel him watching me as I waited for the connection to be made. I wondered what I would say if she answered. But I didn't really think she would.

The bedroom window opened in the house. The police sergeant leaned out.

'Sir, there's a phone ringing in a handbag.'

We could hear it faintly from behind him, a tinkling electronic tune. I rang off. In the house the notes stopped. Mackenzie nodded to him. 'All right, it was just us. Carry on.'

The sergeant disappeared. Mackenzie rubbed his chin. 'Doesn't prove anything,' he said.

I didn't answer.

He sighed. 'Christ, this bloody heat.' It was the first sign he'd given that it bothered him. 'Come on, let's get out of the sun.'

We went to stand in the shadow of the house.

'Do you know of any family?' he asked. 'Anyone who might know where Miss Palmer is?'

'Not really. She inherited this place, but as far as I know she doesn't have any more family in the area.'

'How about friends? Apart from yourself.'

36

There might have been a barb there, but it was difficult to tell. 'She knew people in the village. But I don't know of anyone in particular.'

'Boyfriends?' he asked, watching for my reaction.

'I wouldn't know. Sorry.'

He grunted, looking at his watch.

'So what happens next?' I asked. 'Will you check if the DNA from the body matches a sample from the house?'

He regarded me. 'You seem to know a lot about it.'

I could feel my face reddening. 'Not really.'

I was glad when he didn't pursue it. 'We don't know this is a crime scene yet anyway. We've got a woman who may or may not be missing, that's all. There's nothing to link her to the body that's been found.'

'What about the dog?'

'Could have been killed by another animal.'

'From what I could see the wound in its throat looks like a cut, not a tear. It was made by a sharp edge.'

Again he gave me that appraising look, and I kicked myself for saying too much. I was a doctor now. Nothing else. 'I'll see what the forensic boys say,' he told me. 'But even if it was, she could have killed it herself.'

'You don't really think that.'

He seemed about to retort, then thought better of it. 'No. No, I don't. But I'm not going to jump to conclusions, either.'

The house door opened. The sergeant emerged,

giving a shake of his head. 'Nothing. But the lights had been left on in the hallway and lounge.'

Mackenzie nodded, as if that were what he'd expected. He turned to me. 'We'll not keep you any longer, Dr Hunter. Someone'll be around to get your statement. And I'd appreciate it if you didn't talk about this to anyone.'

'Of course not.' I tried not to feel annoyed that he'd even asked. He was turning away, speaking with the sergeant. I started to go, then hesitated.

'Just one thing,' I said. He glanced at me, irritably. 'That mole on your neck. It's probably nothing, but it might not hurt to get it checked out.'

I left them staring after me as I went back to the car.

I drove back to the village feeling numbed. The road cut past Manham Water, the shallow lake or 'broad' that each year lost a little more of itself to the encroaching reedbeds. Its surface was mirror still, fragmented only by a flight of geese that descended onto it. Neither the lake nor the choked creeks and dykes that cut through the marshes to it were navigable, and with no river close to the village Manham was bypassed by the boat and tourist traffic that descended on the rest of the Broads during summer. Although only a few miles separated it from its neighbours, it seemed to belong to a different part of Norfolk, older and less hospitable. Surrounded by woodland, bog-like fens and poorly drained marsh-land, it was a literal as well as figurative backwater. Apart from the occasional birdwatcher the village was left to itself, sinking further into its isolation like an antisocial old man.

Perversely, this evening Manham looked almost cheery in the sunshine. The flowerbeds in the church and village green were like punches of colour, so bright they hurt. They were one of Manham's few sources of pride, scrupulously maintained by old George Mason and his grandson Tom, the two gardeners I'd met when I'd first arrived. On the edge of the green, even the Martyr's Stone had been garlanded with flowers by the local schoolchildren. It was an annual event, decorating the old millstone where in the sixteenth century a woman had supposedly been stoned to death by her neighbours. The story went that she'd cured an infant of some palsy, only to be accused of witchcraft. Henry joked that only Manham could martyr someone for doing a good turn, and claimed there was a lesson there for both of us.

I didn't feel like going home, so I headed for the surgery. I often went there, even when I didn't have to. At times my cottage could feel lonely, whereas at the big house there was always at least the illusion of work, if nothing else. I let myself into the back door that led into the self-contained clinic. An old conservatory, dense and humid with plants that Janice lovingly tended, served as a reception and waiting room. Part of the ground floor had been converted into Henry's private living quarters. But that was at the other end of the house, which was more than big enough to accommodate all of us. I'd taken over his old consulting room, and as I closed the door behind me the scent of old wood and beeswax was calming. Even though I'd been using it almost every day since I'd arrived it was still more a distillation of Henry's personality than mine, with its old hunting oil, roll-top desk and leather-seated captain's chair. The bookshelves were filled with his old medical books and journals, as well as less obvious subjects for a village GP. There were texts by Kant and Nietzsche, and an entire shelf given over to psychology – one of Henry's hobby-horses. My only contribution to the room was the computer monitor that hummed quietly on the desk, an innovation Henry had disgruntledly acquiesced to after months of persuasion.

He never had recovered enough to return to work full-time. Like his wheelchair, my temporary contract had developed into something more permanent. It had been first extended, then changed into a partnership when it became apparent that he would no longer be able to run the practice solo. Even the old Land Rover Defender I now drove had once been his. It was a battered old automatic, bought after the car crash that had left him a paraplegic and killed his wife Diana. Buying it had been a statement of intent, when he still clung to the hope of being able to drive – and walk – again. But he never had. Or ever would, the doctors had assured him.

'Idiots. Put someone in a white coat and they think they're God,' he'd scoffed.

Eventually, though, even Henry had to accept that they were right. And so I'd inherited not just the Land Rover, but bit by bit most of the practice as well. We'd split the workload more or less equally to begin with, but increasingly more and more of it had been left to me. That didn't stop him remaining 'the proper doctor' in most people's eyes, but I'd given up minding long ago. I was still a newcomer as far as Manham was concerned, and probably always would be.

Now, in the late-afternoon heat, I tried visiting a few medical websites, but my heart wasn't in it. I stood up and went to open the French windows. The fan on my desk whirred, noisily stirring the turgid air without cooling it. Even with the windows open, the difference was purely psychological. I stared out across the neatly tended garden. Like everything else it was parched; shrubs and grass almost visibly withering in the heat. The lake ran right up to the garden's border, with only a low embankment as protection from the inevitable winter flooding. Moored to a small jetty was Henry's old dinghy. It was little more than a glorified rowing boat, but Manham Water wasn't deep enough for anything else. It was hardly the Solent, and there were still areas that were too shallow or clogged with reeds to venture into, but both of us enjoyed going out on it even so.

There was no chance of raising a sail today, though. The lake was so still there was no movement at all. From this angle there was only a scribble of distant reeds separating it from the sky. All was flatness and water, an emptiness that, depending on your mood, could be either restful or desolate.

I didn't find it restful now.

'Thought I heard you.'

I turned as Henry wheeled himself into the room. 'Just sorting out a few things,' I said, pulling my thoughts back from where they'd wandered.

'Like a bloody oven in here,' he muttered, stopping in front of the fan. Except for the non-use of his legs he looked the picture of health; creamy-white hair over a tanned face and keen dark eyes.

'So what's this about the Yates boys finding a body? Janice was full of it when she brought my lunch.'

Most Sundays Janice would deliver a covered plate with whatever she'd cooked for herself. Henry insisted he was capable of cooking Sunday lunch himself, but I noticed he rarely put up much of a struggle. Janice was a good cook, and I suspected her feelings for Henry went beyond those of house-keeper. Unmarried herself, I guessed her disapproval of his late wife stemmed mainly from jealousy, although she'd hinted more than once at some old scandal. I'd made it clear I didn't want to know. Even if Henry's marriage hadn't been the idyllic affair he now seemed to recall, I'd no interest in raking over the bones of gossip.

But I wasn't surprised that Janice knew about the body. Half the village would be buzzing with the news by now.

'Over by Farnham Wood,' I told him.

'Some birdwatcher, probably. Yomping around with a backpack in this heat.'

'Probably.'

His dark eyebrows went up at my tone. 'What,

then? Don't tell me we might have a murder? That'd liven things up a bit!' His smile faded when I didn't join in. 'Something tells me I shouldn't joke about it.'

I told him about my visit to Sally Palmer's house, hoping talking about it might make it seem less of a possibility. It didn't.

'Good Christ,' Henry said heavily, when I'd finished. 'And the police think it might be her?'

'They didn't say one way or the other. I don't suppose they can, yet.'

'God, what a bloody thing to happen.'

'It might not be her.'

'No, of course not,' he agreed. But I could see he didn't believe it any more than I did. 'Well, I don't know about you, but I could do with a drink.'

'Thanks, but I'll give it a miss.'

'Saving yourself for the Lamb later?'

The Black Lamb was the village's only pub. I often went there, but I knew that this evening the main topic of conversation wouldn't be one I wanted to join in.

'No, I think I'll just stay at home tonight,' I told him.

My house was an old stone cottage on the outskirts of the village. I'd bought it when it became obvious I'd be staying longer than six months after all. Henry had told me I was welcome to stay with him, and God knows Bank House was certainly big enough. Its wine cellar alone could have swallowed my cottage. But I'd been ready to move into my own place, to feel I was putting down permanent roots rather than continue as a lodger. And as much as I enjoyed my new work, I didn't want to live with it. There were times when it was still good to be able to close the door and walk away, and hope the phone didn't ring for a few hours at least.

This was one of them. A few people were drifting up the churchyard path for the evening service as I drove by on my way home. Scarsdale, the vicar, was in the church doorway. He was an elderly, dour man I couldn't pretend to like very much. But he'd been here for years and had a loyal, if small, congregation. I raised my hand to acknowledge Judith Sutton, a widow who lived with her adult son Rupert, an overweight hulk who always trudged along two paces behind his overbearing mother. She was talking to Lee and Marjory Goodchild, a prim couple of hypochondriacs who were regulars at the surgery. They regarded me as on-call twenty-four hours a day, and I hoped I wouldn't be flagged down now for an impromptu consultation.

But this evening neither they nor anyone else stopped me. I parked on the baked earth at the side of the cottage and let myself in. It was stuffy inside. I opened the windows as wide as they'd go and helped myself to a beer from the fridge. I might not have wanted to go to the Lamb, but I still needed a drink. In fact, realizing just how badly I needed one, I put the beer back and poured myself a gin and tonic instead.

I broke some ice into the glass, added a wedge of lemon and drank it at the small wooden table in the back garden. It looked out across a field onto woods, but if the view wasn't as spectacular as from the surgery, neither was it quite such a daunting landscape. I took my time over the gin, then cooked myself an omelette and ate it outside. The heat was finally ebbing from the day. I sat at the table as the sky slowly deepened and the stars began making their first hesitant appearance. I thought about what was going on a few miles away. The activity there would now be around the once peaceful stretch of country where the Yates boys had made their discovery. I tried to visualize Sally Palmer safe and laughing somewhere, as if thinking about it would make it so. But for some reason I couldn't hold a picture of her in my mind.

Putting off the moment when I would have to go to bed and face sleep, I stayed there until the sky had darkened to velvet indigo, pierced by the brilliant flickering of stars, a random semaphore of long-dead flecks of light.

I jerked awake, sweat-drenched and gasping. I stared around, with no idea where I was. Then awareness draped itself on me again. I was naked, standing by the open bedroom window, its lower edge pressing into my thighs as I leaned out into space. I backed away, unsteadily, and sat on the bed. Its crumpled white sheets were almost luminous in the moonlight. The tears dried slowly on my face as I waited for my heart to slow back to normal.

I'd had the dream again.

It had been a bad one. As always, it had been so vivid that waking seemed like the illusion, my dream the reality. That was the cruellest part. Because in the dreams Kara and Alice, my wife and six-year-old daughter, were still alive. I could still see them, speak to them. Touch them. In the dreams I could believe we still had a future, not just a past.

I dreaded them. Not in the sense that you would fear a nightmare, because there was nothing fearful about them in themselves. No, it was exactly the opposite.

I dreaded them because I had to wake up.

Then the shock of grief, of loss, would be just as fresh as when it first happened. Often I would wake to find myself somewhere else, my somnambulent body having operated without any awareness on my part. Standing, like now, by the open window, or at the top of the steep and unforgiving stairs, with no memory of getting there or what subconscious urge might have steered me.

I shivered, despite the cloying warmth of the night air. From outside came the lonely barking of a fox. After a while I lay down and stared at the ceiling until the shadows faded and the dark ebbed away.

4

The mist was still rolling off the marshes when the young woman closed the door behind her and set off on her morning run. Lyn Metcalf ran with an easy athleticism. The pull in her calf muscle was healing nicely, but she still took it easy at first, falling into relaxed, loping strides as she ran along the narrow lane from her house. Partway down she cut off onto an overgrown track that led across marshland to the lake.

Long grass stalks whipped at her legs as she ran, still wet and cold with dew. She took a deep breath, savouring the feeling. Monday morning or not, she couldn't think of a better start to a new week. This was her favourite time of day, before she had to worry about balancing the accounts of farmers and small businesses who resented her advice, before the day developed a less optimistic shape, before other people had a chance to sully it. All was fresh and sharp, reduced to the rhythmic thump of her feet on the track and the even rasp of her breathing.

At thirty-one Lyn was proud of her condition. Proud of the discipline that kept her in shape, and meant she still looked good in the tight shorts and cropped top. Not that she would be smug enough to admit that to anybody. Besides, she enjoyed it, and that made it easier. Enjoyed pushing herself, seeing how far she could go, and then trying for that extra bit further. If there was a better start to the day than pulling on a pair of running shoes and putting in the miles while the world came alive around her she'd yet to find it.

Well, OK, except sex, of course. And the edge had gone from that lately. Not that it wasn't still good – just the sight of Marcus showering off the day's plaster dust, the water flattening the dark hair on his body to an otter's pelt, could still produce a coiling in her belly. But when there was a point behind it besides pleasure it tended to blunt the enjoyment for both of them. Especially when it had come to nothing.

So far.

She leapt over a deep rut in the track without breaking stride, careful not to lose her rhythm. *Lose my rhythm*, she thought, sourly. *I wish.* When it came to rhythms her body was regular as clockwork. Every month without fail, almost to the day, the hated flow of blood would begin, signalling the end of another cycle and a fresh disappointment. The doctors had said there was nothing wrong with either of them. For some people it just took longer than others; no-one knew why. Keep trying, they said. And they had, eagerly at first, laughing at being given medical approval for doing something they both enjoyed anyway. Almost like getting it on prescription, Marcus had joked. But the jokes had gradually petered out, replaced by something that wasn't quite desperation, not yet. But the embryonic beginnings of that, if nothing else, were forming. And it was starting to colour everything else, to taint every aspect of their relationship.

Not that either of them admitted it. It was there, though. She knew Marcus found it hard enough that she earned more from her small accountancy practice than he did as a builder. The recriminations hadn't started yet, but she was frightened they might. And she knew she was as capable of hitting out as Marcus. Outwardly, they'd reassured each other that there was nothing to worry about, that there was no rush. But they'd been trying for years, and in another four she'd be thirty-five, the age she'd always claimed would be her cut-off point. She did a quick sum. *That's forty-eight more menstruations*. It seemed frighteningly close. Forty-eight more potential disappointments. Except that this month was different. This month the disappointment was three days late.

She quickly closed down the burst of hope she felt. It was too soon for that. She'd not even told Marcus that her period hadn't started. No point raising his hopes for nothing. She would give it a few more days, then take a test. That thought alone was enough to send a flutter of nerves through her stomach. *Run, don't think*, she told herself, firmly.

The sun was coming up now, burnishing the sky

directly ahead. The track ran along an embankment by the lake, cutting through reedbeds as it headed for a dark expanse of woods. Mist curled slowly on the water, as if it were about to combust. The sound of a fish jumping broke the silence with an invisible slap. She loved this. Loved summer, loved the landscape. Even though she'd been born here, she'd still been away to university, travelled abroad. But she'd always come back. God's own country, her dad always said. She didn't believe in God, not really, but she knew what he meant.

She was coming to her favourite part of the run now. A path forked off into the woods, and Lyn followed it. She slowed her pace as the trees closed in overhead, closeting her in shadows. It was all too easy to trip over a root in the dim light. It had been a stumble over one of them that had made her pull the muscle in her leg, and she'd gone almost two months before she could run again.

But the low sun was already starting to pierce the gloom, turning the canopy of leaves into a glowing latticework. The woodland here was ancient, a wilderness of creeper-strangled trunks and swampy, treacherous ground. Cutting through it was a warren of meandering paths that could lure the unwary into its depths. When they'd first moved into the house Lyn had made the mistake of exploring it during one of her morning runs. It had been hours before she'd emerged onto a familiar stretch by pure luck. Marcus had been frantic – and furious – when she'd finally made it back home. Since then she'd kept to the same path going both in and out.

The halfway point for her six-mile route was a small clearing, in the centre of which was an old standing stone. It might have been part of a stone circle once, or just a gatepost. No-one knew any more. Overgrown with lichen and grass, its history and secrets were long forgotten. But it was a convenient marker, and Lyn had fallen into the habit of patting its rough surface before setting off back. The clearing wasn't far now, a few minutes at most. Breathing deeply but steadily, Lyn thought about breakfast to goad herself to run faster.

She wasn't sure when the unease started. It was more a growing awareness, a subliminal itch that finally tipped into conscious thought. Suddenly, the woods seemed unnaturally quiet. Oppressive. The thud of her feet on the path sounded too loud in the stillness. She tried to ignore the feeling, but it persisted. Grew stronger. She fought the temptation to look around. What the hell was the matter with her? It wasn't as if she hadn't done this run most mornings for the past two years. She'd never been bothered before.

But she was now. The back of her neck prickled, as though something was watching her. *Don't be stupid*, she told herself. But the urge to look back was growing. She kept her eyes on the path. The only other living thing she'd ever seen here was a deer. This didn't feel like a deer, though. *That's because it isn't. It's nothing. Just your imagination. Your period's three days late and you're letting it get to you.*

The thought distracted her, but only briefly. She

risked a quick glance, had time to see only dark branches and the path twisting out of sight before her foot stubbed against something. She stumbled, windmilling her arms for balance, heart thumping as she just managed to keep upright. *Idiot!* The clearing was just ahead of her now, an oasis of dappled sunbeams in the choked woodland. She put on an extra spurt of speed, slapped her hand onto the rough surface of the standing stone and quickly turned around.

Nothing. Just the trees, shadowed and brooding.

What did you expect? Pixies? But she didn't leave the clearing. There was no birdsong, no whisper of insects. The wood seemed to hold its breath in pensive silence. Lyn was suddenly afraid to break it, loath to leave the clearing's sanctuary and feel the trees close in around her again. *So what are you going to do? Stay here all day?*

Without giving herself time to think, she pushed off from the stone again. Five minutes and she'd be back out in the open. Open fields, open water, open sky. She pictured it in her mind. The unease was still there, but less urgent. And the shadowy woods were growing lighter, the sun throwing its light ahead of her now. She began to relax, and that was when she saw something on the ground ahead of her.

She stopped a few feet away. Splayed out on the centre of the path like an offering was a dead rabbit. No, not a rabbit. A hare, its soft fur matted with blood.

It hadn't been there before.

Lyn quickly looked around. But the trees offered

no clue as to where it had come from. She stepped around it, then broke into a run again. A fox, she told herself, as she settled back into her rhythm. She must have disturbed it. But a fox wouldn't have left its prey behind, disturbed or not. And the hare didn't look as if it had been just dropped. The way it was laid out looked . . .

Looked deliberate.

That was stupid, though. She pushed the thought from her mind as she pounded down the path. And then she was out of the wood and back in the open, with the lake spread out before her. The anxiety she'd felt a few minutes before sloughed away, fading with every step. In the sunlight it seemed absurd. Embarrassing, even.

Later, her husband Marcus would remember that the local news was on the radio as she came in. As he put bread in the toaster and chopped a banana he told Lyn that a body had been found only a few miles away. It must have sparked a connection, even then, because she told him about finding the dead hare. But she'd laughed about it, making a joke of how it had spooked her. As the bread popped out of the toaster the incident already seemed insignificant to both of them.

When she came back from the shower, it wasn't mentioned again.

5

I was halfway through the morning surgery when Mackenzie arrived. Janice brought the news along with the next patient's notes. Her eyes were wide with intrigue.

'There's a policeman here to see you. A Chief Inspector Mackenzie.'

For some reason I wasn't surprised. I looked down at the patient's notes. Ann Benchley, an eighty-year-old woman with chronic arthritis. A regular.

'How many more are there to see?' I asked, stalling.

'Another three after this.'

'Tell him I won't be long. And tell Mrs Benchley to come through.'

She looked surprised, but said nothing. By now I doubted there was anyone in the village who didn't know that a body had been found the day before. But so far no-one seemed to have made the connection with Sally Palmer. I wondered how long it would stay that way.

I pretended to study the notes until Janice had gone. I knew Mackenzie wouldn't have come unless it was important, and I doubted any of that morning's patients were urgent cases. I wasn't sure why I was keeping him waiting, other than a deep reluctance to hear whatever he had to say.

I tried not to think what it might be as I saw my next patient. I looked sympathetic as Mrs Benchley displayed her gnarled hands, made the soothing and ultimately useless noises expected of me as I wrote her another prescription, and smiled vaguely as she hobbled out, satisfied. After that, though, I couldn't put it off any longer.

'Send him in,' I told Janice.

'He doesn't look very happy,' she warned me.

No, Mackenzie didn't look very happy. There was an angry flush to his face, and his jaw jutted truculently.

'Good of you to see me, Dr Hunter,' he said, his sarcasm barely concealed. He carried a leather folder. He held it on his lap as he sat down opposite me, uninvited.

'What can I do for you, Inspector?'

'Just a couple of points I'd like to clarify.'

'Have you identified the body?'

'Not yet.'

He took out the packet of mints and popped one in his mouth. I waited. I'd known enough policemen not to be discomforted by the games they played.

'I didn't think places like this were around any more. You know, small, family doctor, home visits, all that sort of thing,' he said, looking around. His eyes settled on the bookshelves. 'Lot of stuff on psychology, I see. That an interest of yours?'

'They're not mine, they're my partner's.'

'Ah. So how many patients do the two of you have?'

I wondered where this was going. 'Five, six hundred altogether, perhaps.'

'As many as that?'

'It's a small village but a big area.'

He nodded, as if this were just a normal conversation. 'Bit different to being a GP in a city.'

'I suppose so.'

'Miss London, do you?'

I knew then what was coming. Again, no real surprise. Just a sense of a weight settling onto my shoulders. 'Perhaps you'd better tell me what you want.'

'I did some research after we spoke yesterday. My being a policeman and all.' He gave me a cool stare. 'You've an impressive CV, Dr Hunter. Not the sort of thing you'd imagine for a village GP.'

Unzipping the folder, he made a show of leafing through the papers in it. 'Took your medical certificate then switched to a PhD in anthropological science. Quite a high-flier, according to this. Followed that with a stint in the States at the University of Tennessee before coming back to the UK as a specialist in forensic anthropology.'

He cocked his head. 'You know, I wasn't even sure what forensic anthropology was, and I've been a policeman for nearly twenty years. I could manage the "forensic" bit, of course. But anthropology? I always thought that was studying old bones. Bit like archaeology. Shows how things can slip by you.'

'I don't like to rush you, but I've got patients waiting.'

'Oh, I won't take any longer than I have to. But while I was on the internet I also found some papers you'd written. Interesting titles.' He picked up a sheet of paper. ' "The Role of Entomology in Time-Since-Death Analysis". "The Chemistry of Human Decomposition".'

He lowered the paper. 'Pretty specialist stuff. So I phoned a friend of mine in London. He's an inspector with the Met. Turned out he'd heard of you. Surprise, surprise, it looks like you've worked as a consultant for various police forces on quite a few murder investigations. England, Scotland, even Northern Ireland. My contact said you were one of the few registered forensic anthropologists in the country. Worked on mass graves in Iraq, Bosnia, the Congo. You name it. According to him you were pretty much the expert when it came to human remains. Not just identifying them, but how long they'd been dead, what they'd died of. He said you picked up where pathologists left off.'

'Is there a point to this?'

'The point is I can't help but wonder why you didn't mention any of this yesterday. When you knew we'd found a body, when you found evidence it could be a local woman, when you knew we would want to identify who it was as soon as bloody possible.' He kept his voice level, though his face had grown redder than ever. 'My friend at the Met thought it was highly amusing. Here am I, the senior investigating officer of a murder inquiry, with one of the country's leading forensic experts in front of me pretending to be a GP.'

I didn't let the fact he'd finally called it a murder distract me. 'I am a GP.'

'But that's not all you are, is it? So why the big secret?'

'Because what I used to do doesn't matter. I'm a doctor now.'

Mackenzie was studying me as if trying to decide if I was joking or not. 'I made some other phone calls after that one. I know that you've only been practising as a GP for three years. Packed in forensic anthropology and came out here after your wife and daughter died in a car crash. Drink-driver in the other car survived unhurt.'

I sat very still. Mackenzie had the grace to look uncomfortable. 'I don't want to open old wounds. Perhaps if you'd been straight with me yesterday I wouldn't have had to. But the bottom line is we need your help.'

I knew he wanted me to ask how, but I didn't. He went on anyway.

'The condition of the body's making it difficult to identify. We know it's female, but that's all. And until we've got an ID we're pretty much hamstrung. We can't start a proper murder investigation unless we know for certain who the victim is.'

I found myself speaking. 'You said "for certain". You're already pretty sure, aren't you?'

'We still haven't been able to trace Sally Palmer.'

It was only what I'd been expecting, but it still shook me to hear it confirmed.

'Several people remember seeing her at the pub barbecue, but so far we haven't found anyone who can recall seeing her since,' Mackenzie continued. 'That's nearly a fortnight ago. We've taken DNA samples from the body and the house, but it'll be a week before we get any results.'

'What about fingerprints?'

'Not a chance. We can't say yet if that's down to decomposition or if they've been deliberately removed.'

'Dental records, then.'

He shook his head. 'There aren't enough teeth left to get a match.'

'Someone broke them?'

'You could say that. Could have been done deliberately to prevent us identifying the body, or just a by-product of the injuries. We don't know yet.'

I rubbed my eyes. 'So it's definitely murder?'

'Oh, she was murdered, right enough,' he said, grimly. 'The body's too badly decomposed to know if she was sexually abused as well, but the assumption is that she probably was. And then somebody killed her.'

'How?'

Without answering, he took a large envelope from the folder and dropped it on the desk. The shiny edges of photographs peeped out. My hand was reaching for them before I realized what I was doing.

I pushed the envelope away. 'No thanks.'

'I thought you might want to see for yourself.'

'I've already told you I can't help.'

'Can't or won't?'

I shook my head. 'I'm sorry.'

He regarded me for a moment longer, then abruptly stood up. 'Thank you for your time, Dr Hunter.' His voice was cold.

'You've forgotten this.' I held out the envelope.

'Keep it. You might want to look at them later.'

He went out. I still had the envelope in my hand. All I had to do was slide out the photographs. Instead I opened a drawer and dropped it inside. I closed the drawer and told Janice to send in the next patient.

But the envelope's presence stayed with me for the rest of the morning. I could feel its tug throughout every conversation, each examination. After the last patient had closed the door I tried to distract myself by writing up his notes. Those finished, I went and stared out of the French doors. Two home visits, and then I had the afternoon to myself. If there had been a breath of wind I could have taken the dinghy out on the lake. But as it was I'd only be as becalmed on the water as I felt now, on dry land.

I'd felt curiously numb as Mackenzie had dredged up my past. He might have been talking about someone else. And in a way he was. It was a different David Hunter who had immersed himself in the arcane chemistry of death, seen the end product of countless incidents of violence, accident and nature combined. I'd looked on the skull beneath the skin as a matter of course, priding myself on knowledge that few other people were even aware existed. What happened to the human body when life had left it held little mystery for me. I was intimate with decay in all its forms, could chart its progress depending on the weather, the soil, the time of year. Grim, yes, but necessary. And I took a magician's satisfaction in identifying when, how, who. That these were individuals I was dealing with I never forgot. But only in an abstract sense; I knew these strangers only in death, not in life.

And then the two people I cherished more than anything else in this world had been snatched from me. My wife and daughter, snuffed out in an instant by a drunk who had walked away from the crash unscathed. Kara and Alice, both transformed in a moment from living, vital individuals to dead organic matter. And I knew – I *knew* – exactly what physical metamorphosis they would be undergoing, almost to the hour. But that failed to answer the single question that had come to obsess me, and to which all my knowledge couldn't even begin to find an answer. Where were they? What had happened to the life that had been within them? How could all that animation, that spirit, simply cease to exist?

I didn't know. And that not knowing was more than I could bear. My colleagues and friends were understanding, but I hardly noticed. I would have gladly plunged myself into my work, except that was a constant reminder of what I'd lost, and the questions I couldn't answer.

And so I ran. Turned my back on everything I'd known, relearned my old medical training and hid away out here, miles from anywhere. Given myself, if not a life, exactly, then a new career. One that dealt with the living rather than the dead, where I could at least try to delay that final transformation, even if I was no closer to understanding it. And it had worked.

Until now.

I went to my desk and opened the drawer. I took out the photographs, keeping them face down. I would look, then give them back to Mackenzie. I still wasn't committing to anything, I rationalized, and turned them over.

I hadn't known how I'd feel, but what I hadn't banked on was the familiarity of it all. Not so much because of what the images showed – God knows that was shocking enough. But the fact of looking at them was like taking a step back in time. Without even realizing it, I began studying them for what they might tell me.

There were six photographs, taken from different angles and viewpoints. I leafed through them quickly, then went back to the start and looked at each one again in more detail. The body was naked and lying face down, arms stretched out above it as though it were in the act of taking a dive into the long stalks of marsh grass. It was impossible to tell its sex from the photographs. The darkened skin hung off the body like badly fitting leather, but that wasn't what caught the eye. Sam had been right. He'd said that the body had wings, and so it had. Two deep cuts had been sliced into the flesh either side of the spine.

Thrust into them, giving the body the look of a fallen, decaying angel, were white swan wings.

Set against the decaying skin, the effect was shockingly obscene. I looked at them for a while longer, then studied the body itself. Maggots spilled like rice from the wounds. Not just the two large ones on the shoulder blades but from numerous smaller gashes on the back, arms and legs. The decomposition was well advanced. Heat and humidity would have accelerated the process, and animals and insects speed it further. But each factor would have its own story to tell, each one helping to provide a timetable of how long it had lain there.

The last three photographs were of the body after it had been turned over. There were the same small cuts on the body and limbs, and the face was a shapeless mess of splintered bone. Below it the exposed cartilage of the throat, harder and slower to decompose than the softer tissue that had covered it, gaped wide where it had been slashed open. I thought about Bess, Sally's Border collie. The dog's throat had also been cut. I went through the photographs one more time. When I found myself looking for anything recognizable about the body, I put the photographs down. I was still sitting there when a rap sounded on the door.

It was Henry. 'Janice told me the police had been. Locals been buggering the livestock again?'

'It was just about yesterday.'

'Ah.' He sobered. 'Any problem?'

'Not really.'

Which wasn't really the truth. I felt uncomfortable

63

keeping anything from Henry, but I hadn't gone into all the details about my background. While he knew I'd been an anthropologist, it was a broad enough field to cover any number of sins. The forensic aspect of my work, and my involvement in police investigations, I'd kept to myself. It hadn't been something I'd wanted to talk about.

It still wasn't.

His eyes went to the photographs lying on the desk. He was too far away to make out any detail, but I felt as though I'd been caught out, all the same. He raised his eyebrows as I put them back in the envelope.

'Can we talk about it later?' I said.

'Of course. I didn't mean to pry.'

'You weren't. It's just . . . there are a few things I need to think about right now.'

'Are you OK? You seem a little . . . preoccupied.'

'No, I'm fine.'

He nodded, but the look of concern didn't fade. 'How about taking the dinghy out some time? Bit of exercise will do us both good.'

Although he needed help getting in and out of the boat, Henry's disability didn't prevent him from rowing or sailing once he was on board. 'You're on. But give me a few days.'

I could tell he wanted to ask more, but thought better of it. He wheeled himself back to the door. 'Just say the word. You know where I am.'

When he'd gone I sat back in the chair and closed my eyes. *I didn't want this.* But then, nobody did. Least of all the dead woman. I thought about the pictures I'd just seen, and realized that, like her, I didn't have a choice.

Mackenzie had left his card with the photographs. But I couldn't reach him on either his office number or mobile. I left messages to call me on both and hung up. I couldn't say I felt better for reaching a decision, but some of the weight seemed to lift from me.

After that, there were the morning's visits to do. Only two, and neither was serious; a child with mumps, and a bedridden elderly man who was refusing to eat. By the time I'd finished it was lunchtime. I was on my way back, debating whether to go home or to the pub, when my phone rang.

I grabbed it, but it was only Janice to tell me that the school had called. They were worried about Sam Yates, and could I go to see him? I said I would. I was glad to do something constructive while I waited for Mackenzie to call.

Back in Manham, the presence of police officers on the streets was a sobering reminder of what had happened. Their uniforms were a stark contrast to the gaiety of the flowers brightening the churchyard and green, and there was a sense of muted but unmistakable excitement about the village. But the school, at least, seemed normal. Although the older children had to travel five miles to the nearest comprehensive, Manham still had its own small primary school. A former chapel, its playground was colourfully noisy in the bright sunshine. This was the last week of term before the long summer holiday, and the knowledge seemed to give an extra edge to the usual lunchtime hysteria. A little girl bounced off my legs as she dodged another who was chasing her. Giggling, they ran off, so preoccupied in their game that they barely noticed my presence.

I felt the familiar hollowness as I went into the school office. Betty, the secretary, gave me a bright smile as I knocked on the open door.

'Hello, there. You here to see Sam?'

She was a tiny, warm-faced woman who'd lived in the village all her life. Never married, she lived with her brother and treated the schoolchildren as her extended family.

'How is he?' I asked. She wrinkled her nose.

'Bit upset. He's next door in the sick bay. Just go straight in.'

'Sick bay' was a rather grand title for what was in effect a small room with a sink, a couch and a first-aid cabinet. Sam was sitting on the couch, head down and feet dangling. He looked peaky and close to tears.

A young woman was sitting next to him, talking in soothing tones as she showed him a book. She broke off, looking relieved when I walked in.

'Hi, I'm Dr Hunter,' I said to her, then gave the boy a smile. 'How you doing, Sam?'

'He's a bit tired,' the young woman answered for him. 'Apparently he had bad dreams last night. Didn't you, Sam?'

She sounded matter-of-fact, calm without seeming condescending. I guessed she was his teacher, but I hadn't seen her before and her accent was too slight for her to be local. Sam had dropped his chin onto his chest. I squatted down so I was on his eye level.

'That right, Sam? What sort of nightmares?' After seeing the photographs, I could guess. He kept his head down, saying nothing. 'OK, let's take a look at you.'

I didn't expect there to be anything physically wrong with him, and there wasn't. Temperature a little high, perhaps, but that was all. I ruffled his hair as I stood up.

'Strong as an ox. Will you be OK while I have a word with your teacher?'

'No!' he said, panicked.

She gave him a reassuring smile. 'It's all right, we'll be right outside. I'll even leave the door open, and then I'll come right back. OK?'

She gave him the book. After a second he took it, sullenly. I followed her into the corridor. She left the door ajar, as promised, but stood far enough away so we were out of earshot.

'Sorry you had to come out. I didn't know what else to do,' she said in a low voice. 'He got completely hysterical earlier. Not like him at all.'

I thought again about the photographs. 'I suppose you've heard about what happened yesterday?'

She grimaced. 'Everybody's heard. That's the trouble. All the other kids wanted to hear about it. It just got too much for him.'

'Have you sent for his parents?'

'Tried to. Can't get hold of them at any of the contact numbers we have.' She shrugged, apologetically. 'That's why I thought we'd better send for you. I was really worried about him.'

I could see she meant it. I'd have put her in her late twenties or early thirties. Her short-cropped blond hair looked natural, but it was several shades lighter than the dark eyebrows that, at the moment, held an anxious crease. Her face was lightly dusted with freckles, brought out by a faint tan.

'He's had a bad shock. It might take him a while to get over it,' I said.

'Poor Sam. Just when he's got the school holidays coming up as well.' She glanced towards the open door. 'Do you think he's going to need counselling?'

I'd been wondering that myself. If he was no better in a day or two then I'd have to refer him. But I'd been down that route myself, and knew that sometimes picking at a wound only made it bleed all the more. Not a fashionable view, perhaps, but I'd rather give Sam a chance to recover by himself.

'Let's see how he goes. By the end of the week he might be up and running again.'

'I hope so.'

'I think the best thing for now is to get him home,' I told her. 'Have you tried his brother's school? They might know how to get in touch with their parents.'

'No. No-one thought of that.' She looked annoyed with herself.

'Can someone stay with him till they get here?'

'I will. I'll get someone to cover my class.' Her eyes widened. 'Oh, sorry, I should have said! I'm his teacher!'

I smiled. 'I sort of guessed that.'

'God, I've not introduced myself at all, have I?' A

blush made her freckles more prominent. 'Jenny. Jenny Hammond.'

She held out her hand, self-consciously. It was warm and dry. I remembered hearing that a new teacher had started earlier that year, but this was the first I'd seen of her. Or so I thought.

'I've seen you in the Lamb once or twice, I think,' she said.

'That's more than possible. The night-life's a bit limited around here.'

She grinned. 'I noticed. Still, that's why you come somewhere like this, isn't it? Get away from it all.' My face must have registered something. 'Sorry, you don't sound local, so I thought . . .'

'It's all right, I'm not.'

She looked only slightly relieved. 'I'd better get back to Sam, anyway.'

I went back in with her to say goodbye to him and make sure he didn't need a sedative. I would check on him that evening, tell his mother to keep him off school for a few more days, until the raw memory of what he'd seen had sufficiently scabbed over to resist the pokings of his schoolmates.

I was back at the Land Rover when my phone rang. This time it was Mackenzie.

'You left a message,' he said, bluntly.

I spoke in a rush, in a hurry to get rid of the words. 'I'll help you identify the body. But that's all. I'm not going to get involved beyond that, OK?'

'Whatever you like.' He didn't sound exactly gracious, but then neither was my offer. 'So how do you want to play it?'

'I need to see where they found the body.'

'It's already been taken to the mortuary, but I can meet you there in an hour—'

'No, I don't want to see the body itself. Just where it was found.'

I could feel his exasperation down the line. 'Why? What good's that going to do?'

My mouth was dry. 'I'm going to look for leaves.'

6

The heron drifted lazily above the marsh, sliding across the gelid air. It looked too big to be able to stay aloft, a giant compared to the smaller waterfowl its shadow passed over. Angling its wings, it banked down towards the lake, giving two breaking flaps as it landed. With an arrogant shake of its head it picked its way deliberately across the shallows before standing immobile, a fossilized statue on its reed-thin legs.

I turned reluctantly away from it as I heard Mackenzie approach. 'Here,' he said, holding out a sealed plastic bag. 'Put these on.'

I took the white paper overalls from the bag and stepped into them, careful not to rip the flimsy fabric as I tugged them over shoes and trousers. As soon as I zipped them up I could feel myself beginning to sweat. The humid discomfort was disturbingly familiar.

It was like stepping back in time.

I'd been unable to shake a sense of déjà vu ever

71

since I'd met Mackenzie at the same stretch of road where I'd brought the two policemen the day before. Now it was lined with police cars and the big trailers that functioned as mobile incident rooms. After I'd put on the overalls and paper shoes, we walked in silence on the track across the marsh, our route marked by parallel ribbons of police tape. I knew he wanted to ask what I was planning to do, knew also that he thought it was a sign of weakness to let me see his curiosity. But I wasn't holding back out of any misplaced desire to play power games. I was just putting off the moment when I'd have to face up to why I was here.

The area where the body had been found was cordoned off with more tape. Inside it crime scene investigators swarmed over the grass, anonymous and identical in their white overalls. The sight brought another unwelcome jolt of memory.

'Where's the bloody Vicks?' Mackenzie asked no-one in particular.

A woman held out a jar of vapour rub. He put a smear under his nose and offered it to me.

'It's still a bit ripe in there even though the body's gone.'

There had been a time when I was so used to the smells inherent in my work I no longer worried about them. But that was then. I daubed the menthol-smelling Vicks on my top lip and wriggled my hands into a pair of surgical rubber gloves.

'There's a mask if you want it,' Mackenzie said. I shook my head automatically. I'd never liked wearing masks unless I had to. 'Come on then.'

He ducked under the tape. I followed him. The officers on the crime scene team were combing the ground inside. A few small markers stuck into the earth indicated where potential trace evidence had been found. I knew most would turn out to be irrelevant – sweet wrappers, cigarette ends and fragments of animal bone that would have nothing to do with what they were looking for. But at this stage they had no idea what was important and what wasn't. Everything would be bagged and taken away for examination.

We received one or two curious glances, but my attention was on the patch of ground in the centre. The grass here was blackened and dead, almost as if there had been a fire. But it wasn't heat that had killed it. And now something else was noticeable: an unmistakable smell that cut through even the concealing smear of menthol.

Mackenzie flipped a mint into his mouth, put the packet away without offering it. 'This is Dr Hunter,' he told the other officers, teeth cracking the sweet. 'He's a forensic anthropologist. He's going to help us try to identify the body.'

'Well, he's going to have to try harder than this,' one of them said. 'It isn't here.'

There was laughter. This was their job, and they resented anyone else encroaching on it. Especially a civilian. It was an attitude I'd encountered before.

'Dr Hunter's here at the request of Detective Superintendent Ryan. You'll obviously give him any assistance he needs.' There was an edge to Mackenzie's voice. I could see from the suddenly closed faces that it hadn't been well received. It didn't bother me. I was already crouching down by the patch of dead grass.

It held the vague shape of the body that had been lying on it, a silhouette of rot. A few maggots still squirmed, and white feathers were scattered like snowfall on the black and flattened stalks.

I examined one of the feathers. 'Were the wings definitely from a swan?'

'We think so,' one of the crime scene officers said. 'We've sent them to an ornithologist to find out.'

'How about soil samples?'

'Already at the lab.'

The iron content of the soil could be checked to see how much blood it had absorbed. If the victim's throat had been cut where the body was found, the iron content would be high; if not, then either the wound had been made after she was dead, or she'd been killed somewhere else and her body dumped here later.

'What about insects?' I asked.

'We have done this before, you know.'

'I know. I'm just trying to find out how far you've got.'

He gave an exaggerated sigh. 'Yes, we've taken insect samples.'

'What did you find?'

'They're called maggots.'

It raised a few snorts. I looked at him.

'What about pupae?'

'What about them?'

74

'What colour were they? Pale? Dark? Were there empty shells?'

He just blinked at me, sullenly. There was no laughter now.

'How about beetles? Were there many on the body?'

He stared at me as though I were mad. 'This is a murder inquiry, not a school biology project!'

He was one of the old school. The new breed of crime scene investigators were keen to learn new techniques, open to any knowledge that might help them. But there were still a few who were resistant to anything that didn't fit into their proscribed experience. I'd come across them every now and again. It seemed there were still some around.

I turned to Mackenzie. 'Different insects have different life-cycles. The larvae here are mainly blowfly. Bluebottles and greenbottles. With the open wounds on the body we can expect insects to have been attracted straight away. They'll have started laying eggs within an hour if it was daylight.'

I poked about in the soil and picked up an unmoving maggot. I held it out on my palm. 'This is about to pupate. The older they are the darker they get. By the look of this I'd say it was seven or eight days old. I can't see any husk fragments lying about, which mean no pupae have hatched yet. The blowfly full life-cycle takes fourteen days, so that suggests the body hasn't been here that long.'

I dropped the pupa back into the grass. The other officers had stopped work to listen now.

'OK, so from basic insect activity you're looking at

a preliminary time-since-death interval of between one and two weeks. I take it you know what this stuff here is?' I asked, indicating the traces of yellow-white substance clinging to some of the grass.

'It's a by-product of decomposition,' the crime scene officer said, stiffly.

'That's right,' I said. 'It's called adipocere. Grave wax, as it used to be known. It's basically soap formed from the body's fatty acids as the muscle proteins break down. That makes the soil highly alkaline, which is what kills the grass. And if you look at this white stuff you'll see it's brittle and crumbly. That suggests a fairly rapid decomposition, because if it's slow the adipocere tends to be softer. Which fits in with what you'd expect for a body lying outdoors in hot weather, and with a lot of open wounds for bacteria to invade. Even so, there isn't much of it yet, which again fits with a time-since-death of less than two weeks.'

There was silence. 'How much less?' Mackenzie asked, breaking it.

'Impossible to say without knowing more.' I looked at the decaying vegetation and shrugged. 'Best guess, even allowing for a rapid rate of decomposition, I'd say perhaps nine, ten days. Much longer than that in this heat and the body would have been full skeletonized by now.'

As I was talking I'd been scanning the dead grass, trying to see what I hoped would be there. 'Which way was the body orientated?' I asked the crime scene officer.

'Which way what?'

'Which end was the head?'

He pointed, sullenly. I visualized the photographs I'd seen, how the arms had been outstretched above the head, and moved to examine the ground around that area. I couldn't find what I wanted on the area of dead grass, so I began to extend my search beyond, carefully parting the grass stalks to see what lay at their base.

I was beginning to think nothing was there, that some scavenging animal had discovered it, when I saw what I'd been looking for.

'Can I have an evidence bag?'

I waited till one was produced, then reached into the grass and gently lifted out a wizened brown scrap. I put it into the bag and sealed it.

'What's that?' Mackenzie asked, craning his head to look.

'When a body's been dead for a week or so you start getting skin slippage. That's why it looks so wrinkled on a corpse, like it doesn't fit properly. Particularly the hands. Eventually the skin will slough completely off, like a glove. It's often overlooked because people don't know what it is and mistake it for leaves.'

I held up the see-through plastic bag containing the parchment-like scrap of tissue.

'You said you wanted fingerprints.'

Mackenzie drew his head sharply back. 'You're joking!'

'No. I don't know if this is from the right or left hand, but the other should be around here as well, unless an animal's had it. I'll leave you to find it.'

The crime scene officer snorted. 'And how are we supposed to get prints off that?' he demanded. 'Look at it! It's like a bloody crisp!'

'Oh, it's easy enough,' I told him, beginning to enjoy it. 'Like it says on the packet, just add water.' He looked blank. 'Soak it overnight. It'll rehydrate and you can slip it onto your hand like a glove. Should give you a decent enough set of prints to get a match from.'

I held the bag out to him. 'I'd get someone with small hands, if I were you. And put rubber gloves on first.'

I left him staring at the bag and ducked under the tape. Reaction was beginning to set in. I stripped off the overalls and protective shoes, glad to be rid of them.

Mackenzie came over as I was wadding them up. He was shaking his head. 'Well, you live and learn. Where the hell did you pick that up from?'

'Over in the States. I spent a couple of years at the anthropology research facility in Tennessee. The Body Farm, as it's called unofficially. It's the only place in the world that uses human cadavers to research decomposition. How long it takes under different conditions, what factors can affect it. The FBI use it to train in body recovery.' I nodded over at the crime scene officer, who was bad-temperedly snapping instructions to the rest of the team. 'We could use something like it over here.'

'Fat chance.' Mackenzie struggled out of his own overalls. 'I hate these bloody things,' he muttered, brushing himself down. 'So you

78

reckon the body's been dead for about ten days?'

I peeled off my gloves. The smell of latex and damp skin brought back more memories than I cared for. 'Nine or ten. But that doesn't mean it's been here all that time. It could have been moved from somewhere else. But I'm sure your forensic boys will be able to tell you that.'

'You could help them.'

'Sorry. I said I'd help you identify the body. This time tomorrow you should have a better idea who it is.' Or isn't, I thought, but kept that to myself.

Mackenzie obviously saw through me. 'We've started serious inquiries now to try and find Sally Palmer,' he said. 'No-one we've spoken to so far has seen her since the pub barbecue. She'd got a grocery order she was supposed to be picking up the next day that she never appeared for. And she usually called into the newsagent's every morning for her papers. Avid *Guardian* reader, apparently. But she stopped collecting that as well.'

A dark, ugly feeling was beginning to grow in me. 'Nobody reported this till now?'

'Apparently not. Seems like nobody missed her. Everyone thought she must have gone off somewhere, or be busy writing. The newsagent told me it wasn't like she was a local. So much for living in a close-knit community, eh?'

I couldn't say anything. I'd not noticed her absence either. 'It doesn't mean it's her. The barbecue was almost two weeks ago. Whoever you found here hasn't been dead for that long. And what about Sally's mobile phone?'

'What about it?'

'It was still working when I called it. If she'd been missing for all that time, the battery would be dead.'

'Not necessarily. It's a new model, with a standby time of four hundred hours. That's about sixteen days. Probably exaggerated, but just sitting in her bag without being used, it could have lasted.'

'This could still be somebody else,' I persisted, not believing it myself.

'Perhaps.' His tone implied there was something he wasn't going to share with me. 'But whoever it is we need to find who killed her.'

There was no arguing with that. 'Do you think it's somebody local? From the village?'

'I don't think anything yet. Victim could be a hitch-hiker; killer could have just dumped her here as he was passing through. Too soon to say one way or the other.' He drew in a breath. 'Look—'

'The answer's still no.'

'You don't know what I'm going to ask yet.'

'Yes, I do. Just one more favour to help you out. Then it'll be another, and another.' I shook my head. 'I don't do this any more. There are other people in the country who do.'

'Not many. And you were the best.'

'Not any more. I've done what I can.'

His expression was cold. 'Have you?'

Turning, he walked away, leaving me to make my own way back to the Land Rover. I drove away, but only until I was out of sight. My hands were shaking uncontrollably as I pulled into the side of the road. All at once I felt I couldn't breathe. I rested my head on the wheel, trying not to gulp air, knowing if I hyperventilated that would only make it worse.

Finally, the panic attack subsided. My shirt was sticking to me with sweat, but I didn't move until there was a blare of horn from behind me. A tractor was chugging up towards where I was blocking the road. As I looked the driver gestured angrily for me to get out of the way. I held up my hand in apology and set off again.

By the time I reached the village I was beginning to feel calmer. I wasn't hungry but I knew I should eat something. I stopped outside the store that was the closest thing the village had to a supermarket. I was planning to buy a sandwich and take it back home, snatch an hour or two trying to put my thoughts in order before evening surgery started. As I passed the chemist's a young woman came out and almost bumped into me. I recognized her as one of Henry's patients, one of the loyal number who still preferred to wait until they could see him. I'd treated her once, when Henry hadn't been working, but still had to search for her name.

Lyn, I thought. Lyn Metcalf.

'Oh, sorry,' she said, clutching a parcel to her.

'That's all right. How are you, anyway?'

She gave me a huge grin. 'I'm great, thanks.'

As she went off up the street I can remember thinking it was good to see someone so obviously happy. And then I didn't give her another thought.

It was later than usual when Lyn reached the
embankment that ran through the reedbeds, but the
morning was even mistier than the day before. A
white smudge overlaid everything, swirling into aim-
less shapes that remained just out of sight. It would
burn off later, and by lunchtime it would have
become one of the hottest days of the year. But right
now all was cool and damp, and the idea of sun and
heat seemed far away.

She felt stiff and out of sorts. She and Marcus had
stayed up late the night before to watch a film, and
her body was still protesting about it. She'd found it
uncharacteristically hard to force herself out of bed
that morning, grumbling to Marcus who merely
grunted unsympathetically as he locked himself in the
shower. Now she was out her muscles felt stiff and
grudging. *Run it off. You'll feel better for it afterwards.*
She grimaced. *Yeah, right.*

To take her mind off how hard the run was proving, she thought about the parcel she'd hidden in the

chest of drawers under her bras and pants, where it was a safe bet Marcus wouldn't find it. The only interest he took in her underwear was when she was wearing it.

She hadn't intended to buy the pregnancy testing kit when she went into the chemist's. But when she'd seen them on the shelves, impulse had made her put one into her basket along with the extra box of tampons she hoped she wouldn't be needing. Even then she might have had second thoughts. It was hard enough keeping anything secret in this place, and buying something like that could well mean the entire village would be giving her knowing looks before the day was out.

But the shop was empty, and there had only been a bored young girl on the checkout. She was new, indifferent to anyone over the age of eighteen, and unlikely to even notice what Lyn was buying, let alone care enough to gossip. Face burning, Lyn had stepped forward and busied herself rummaging in her bag for the money as the teenager listlessly rang the testing kit through on the till.

She'd been grinning like a kid when she hurried out, only to bump straight into one of the doctors. The younger one, not Dr Henry. Dr Hunter. Quiet, but not bad-looking. Caused quite a stir among the younger women when he arrived, though he didn't seem to notice it. God, she'd felt so embarrassed; it had been all she could do not to laugh. He must have thought she was mad, beaming at him like an idiot. Or thought she fancied him. The thought of it made her smile again now.

The run was doing its work. She was finally starting to loosen up, kinks and aches easing as the blood
began to pump. The woods were just ahead now,
and as she looked at them some dark association
stirred in her subconscious. At first, still distracted
by the memory of what had happened at the chemist,
she couldn't place it. Then it came to her. She'd forgotten about the dead hare she'd found on the path
the day before until now. And the sense of being
watched she'd felt when she'd entered the woods.

Suddenly the prospect of going into them again –
especially in this mist – was strangely unappealing.
Stupid, she thought, doing her best to dismiss it. Still,
she slowed a little as she approached them. When
she realized what she was doing she clicked her
tongue in irritation and picked up her speed. Only
when she had almost reached the treeline did she
think about the woman's body that had been found.
But that hadn't been near here, she told herself.
Besides, the killer would have to be some sort of
masochist to be out this early, she thought wryly.
And then the first of the trees closed around her.

It was a relief when the foreboding she'd felt the
day before failed to materialize. The woods were just
woods again. The path was empty, the dead hare no
doubt part of the food chain by now. Just nature,
that was all. She glanced at the stopwatch on her
wrist, saw she'd lost a minute or two on her usual
time, and picked up her pace as she approached the
clearing. The standing stone was in sight now, a dark
shape ahead of her in the mist. She was almost on
top of it before it registered that something about it

was wrong. Then light and shadow resolved themselves, and all thoughts of running went out of her mind.

A dead bird had been tied to the stone. It was a mallard, bound with wire around its neck and feet. Recovering, Lyn quickly looked around. But there was nothing to see. Only trees, and the dead mallard. She wiped sweat from her eyes and looked at it again. Blood darkened its feathers where the thin strand bit into it. Uncertain whether or not to untie it, she leaned forward to examine the wire more closely.

The bird opened its eyes.

Lyn cried out and stumbled backwards as it began to thrash about, head jerking against the wire pinning its neck. It was damaging itself even more, but she couldn't bring herself to go near the wildly beating wings. Her mind was beginning to function again, making the connection between this and the dead hare, laid on the path as though for her to find. And then that was swept away by a more urgent realization.

If the bird was still alive it couldn't have been here long. Someone had done this recently.

Someone who knew she'd find it.

Part of her insisted that was just fantasy, but she was already sprinting back down the path. Branches whipped her as she pounded past, no thought of pacing herself now, just *get out get out get out* yelling again and again in her head. She didn't care if she was being stupid or not, wanted only to escape from the woods to the open landscape beyond. Only one more twist in the path and she'd be able to see it. Her breath rasped as she ran, eyes flitting to the trees at either side, expecting someone to appear out of them at any second. But no-one did. She gave a half-moan, half-sob as she neared the final bend. *Not far*, she thought, and as she felt the first stirrings of relief something snatched her foot out from under her.

There was no time to react. She pitched forward onto the ground, the impact forcing the air from her lungs. She couldn't breathe, couldn't move. Stunned, she managed one breath, then another, sucking the damp scent of loam into her throat. Still dazed, she looked back at what had tripped her. At first what she saw made no sense. One leg was stretched out awkwardly, the foot twisted at an odd angle. There was a thin gleam of fishing line snagged around it. No, she realized, not fishing line.

Wire.

Understanding came too late. As she tried to scramble to her feet a shadow fell across her. Something pressed into her face, smothering her. She tried to rear back from the cloying, chemical stink, fighting with all the strength in her legs and arms. It wasn't enough. And now even that was ebbing. Her struggles grew weak as the morning swam away from her, light bleeding to black. *No!* She tried to resist, but she was already sinking further into darkness, like a pebble dropped into a well.

Was there a last sense of disbelief before consciousness winked out? Possibly, though it wouldn't have lasted long.

Not long at all.

For the rest of the village, the day broke as any other. Perhaps a little more breathless, excited by the continued presence of the police and speculation about the identity of the dead woman. It was a soap opera come to life, Manham's very own melodrama. Someone had died, yes, but for most people it was still a tragedy at arm's length, and therefore not really a tragedy at all. The unspoken assumption was that it was some stranger. If it had been one of the village's own, wouldn't it have been known? Wouldn't the victim have been missed, the perpetrator recognized? No, far more likely that it was an outsider, some human flotsam from a town or city who had climbed into the wrong car, only to wash up here. And so it was regarded almost as an entertainment, a rare treat that could be savoured without shock or grief.

Not even the fact that the police were asking about Sally Palmer was enough to change that. Everyone knew she was a writer, often travelled to London. Her face was too fresh in people's minds to associate with what had been found on the marsh. So Manham was unable to take any of it seriously, slow to accept the fact that, far from being an onlooker, its role was far more central.

That would change before the day was out.

It changed for me at eleven o'clock that morning, with the phone call from Mackenzie. I'd slept badly, gone into the surgery early to try and shake the vestiges of another night's ghosts from my mind. When the phone on my desk rang and Janice told me who was on the line I felt a renewed tension in my gut.

'Put him through.'

The hiatus of connection seemed endless, yet not long enough.

'We've got a fingerprint match,' Mackenzie said as soon as he came on. 'It's Sally Palmer.'

'Are you sure?' Stupid question, I thought.

'No doubt about it. The prints match samples from her house. And we've got hers on record as well. She was arrested during a protest when she was a student.'

She hadn't struck me as the militant type, but then I hadn't really got to know her. And never would now.

Mackenzie hadn't finished. 'Now we've got a firm ID we can get things moving. But I thought you might be interested to know we still haven't found anyone who can remember seeing her after the pub barbecue.'

He waited, as if I should find some significance in that. It took me a moment to drag my thoughts back. 'You mean the maths don't add up,' I said.

'Not if she's only been dead for nine or ten days. It's looking likely now that she went missing almost a fortnight ago. That leaves several days unaccounted for.'

'That was only an estimate,' I told him. 'I could be wrong. What does the pathologist say?'

'He's still looking into it,' he said, dryly. 'But so far he isn't disagreeing.'

I wasn't surprised. I'd once come across a murder

victim who'd been stored in a freezer for several weeks before the killer finally dumped the body, but usually the physical processes of decay worked to an ordered timetable. It might vary depending on the environment, be slowed down or speeded up by temperature and humidity. But once they were taken into account then the process was readable. And what I'd seen at the marsh the day before – I still hadn't made the emotional jump to connecting it with the woman I'd known – had been as irrefutable as the hands on a stopwatch. It was just a matter of understanding it.

That was something few pathologists were comfortable with. There was a degree of overlap between forensic anthropology and pathology, but once serious decomposition started most pathologists tended to throw up their hands. Their area of expertise was cause of death, and that became increasingly difficult to determine once the body's biology started to break down. Which was where my work started.

Not any more, I reminded myself.

'You still there, Dr Hunter?' Mackenzie asked.

'Yes.'

'Good, because this is going to leave us with a predicament. One way or another we need to account for those extra days.'

'She might have been holed up writing. Or just have gone off somewhere. Been called away without having time to tell anyone.'

'And been killed as soon as she got back, without anyone in the village seeing her?'

'It's possible,' I said stubbornly. 'She could have surprised a burglar.'

'She could,' Mackenzie conceded. 'In which case we need to know one way or the other.'

'I don't see where I come into it.'

'What about the dog?'

'The dog?' I repeated, but I could already see what he was getting at.

'It makes sense to assume that whoever killed Sally Palmer killed her dog as well. So the question is, how long has the dog been dead?'

I was torn between being impressed at Mackenzie's sharpness, and irritation that I hadn't seen it myself. Of course, I'd been trying hard not to think about it at all. But there was a time when I wouldn't have needed it pointing out.

'If the dog's been dead roughly the same length of time,' Mackenzie went on, 'then that gives more credence to your burglar. She's either here all the time writing or arrives back from wherever, her dog disturbs an intruder, he kills them both and then dumps her body on the marsh. Or whatever. But if the dog's been dead longer that puts a different complexion on it. Because that means whoever murdered her didn't do it straight away. He kept her prisoner for a few days before getting bored and carving her up with a knife.'

Mackenzie paused to let the impact of his words hit home. 'Now, I'd say that was something we'd need to know, wouldn't you, Dr Hunter?'

Sally Palmer's house had been transformed since the last time I'd seen it. Then it had been silent and empty; now it was host to grim-faced and uninvited visitors. The courtyard had filled with police vehicles, while uniformed and white-boiler-suited forensics officers went about their business. But the activity only seemed to underline the atmosphere of abandonment, transforming what had once been a home into a pathetic time capsule of the recent past, to be picked apart and pored over.

There seemed nothing left of Sally's presence as I walked across the courtyard with Mackenzie.

'The vet came for the goats,' he told me. 'Half of them were already dead, and he had to destroy a couple of others, but he says it's amazing any survived at all. Another day or two would have finished them. Goats are tough buggers, but he reckoned they must have been a couple of weeks without being fed or watered to get to that state.'

The area at the back of the house where I'd found the dog had been taped off, but other than that it was as I'd found it. No-one was in as much of a hurry to move a dog, and either the forensics team had already finished or felt there were other priorities to examine first. Mackenzie stood back and popped a mint into his mouth as I crouched down beside the body. It looked noticeably smaller than I remembered – not necessarily a trick of memory as by this time the decay would be waging an almost visible war of attrition on what was left.

The fur was misleading, disguising the fact that the dog had largely been reduced to bone. Tendons and cartilage remained, like the open tube revealed by the wound in its throat. But there was hardly any soft tissue left. I used a stick to lightly poke in the earth around it, took in the empty eye sockets, and then stood up.

'Well?' Mackenzie asked.

'It's difficult to say. You've got to take into account the smaller body mass. And its fur will have some effect on the rate of decay. I'm not sure what, exactly. The only comparative work I've done on animals was with pigs, and they have a hide, not a pelt. But I'd guess it'd make it harder for insects to lay their eggs, except in open wounds. So that'll probably slow things down.'

I was talking to myself more than him, rapidly brushing through cobwebs of memory, sifting through the knowledge that had been lying dormant.

'What soft tissue was exposed has had animals picking at it. See this here, around the eye sockets? The bone's been gnawed. Too small for foxes, so it's probably rodents and birds. That probably happened quite early on, because once it gets too ripe they'll leave it alone. But that means less soft tissue, and so less insect activity. And the ground here is much drier than the marsh where you found the woman.' I couldn't quite bring myself to say Sally Palmer. 'That's why it looks dried up. In this heat, without moisture it'll mummify. It changes the way the body decays.'

'So you don't know how long it's been dead?' Mackenzie prompted.

'I don't *know* anything. I'm just pointing out that there are a lot of variables here. I can tell you what I think, but bear in mind it's only a preliminary estimate. You're not going to get any hard and fast answers just from a quick look.'

'But . . . ?'

'Well, there still aren't any empty pupae husks, but some of these look about ready to hatch. They're darker than those we found around the body, obviously older.' I pointed at the open wound in the dog's throat. On the ground around it, a few shiny black carapaces could be seen crawling in the grass. 'There are a few beetles here as well. Not many, but they tend to come later. Flies and maggots are the first wave, if you like. But as the decay progresses the balance changes. Less maggots, more beetles.'

Mackenzie was frowning. 'Were there beetles where Sally Palmer was found?'

'Not that I saw. But beetles aren't as reliable an indicator as maggots. And, like I say, there are all the other variables to take into account.'

'Look, I'm not asking you to swear under oath. I just want some idea of how long the damn thing's been dead.'

'Rough guess.' I looked at the scrap of fur and bone. 'Twelve to fourteen days.'

He chewed his lip, scowling. 'So it was killed before the woman.'

'That's how it looks to me. Comparing this with what I saw yesterday, the decomposition is perhaps three, four days more advanced. Take off the extra day and night this has been lying outside and you're still looking at around three days. But like I say, it's only guesswork at this stage.'

He eyed me, thoughtfully. 'Do you think you're wrong?'

I hesitated. But he wanted advice, not false modesty. 'No.'

He sighed. 'Shit.'

His mobile rang. He unclipped it from his belt and moved away to answer it. I stayed by the dog's body, scrutinizing it for anything that might cause me to revise my opinion. Nothing did. I bent down to take a closer look at its throat. Cartilage lasted longer than soft tissue, but animals had been here too, chewing the edges. Even so, it was still evident that it was a cut, not a bite. I took a pencil light from my pocket, reminding myself to disinfect it before I examined anyone's tonsils again, and shone it inside. The cut extended all the way to the cervical vertebrae. I played the light on a pale line gouged across the bone. No animal had caused that. The blade had gone so deep it had cut into the spine as well.

That made it a big knife. And a sharp one.

'Seen something?'

I'd been too engrossed to hear Mackenzie return. I told him what I'd found. 'If the bone's marked clearly enough you might be able to tell if the blade was serrated or not. In any event, it would have taken strength to cut that deeply. You're looking for a powerful man.'

Mackenzie nodded, but he seemed distracted. 'Look, I've got to go. Take as long as you like here. I'll tell forensics not to disturb you.'

'No need. I'm done.'

'You won't change your mind?'

'I've told you as much as I can.'

'You could tell us more if you wanted to.'

I was beginning to feel angry at the way he was trying to manipulate me. 'We've already been through this. I've done what you asked.'

Mackenzie seemed to be weighing something up. He squinted into the sun. 'The situation's changed,' he said, reaching a decision. 'Someone else has gone missing. You might know her. Lyn Metcalf.'

The name hit me hard. I remembered seeing her outside the chemist's the evening before. Thinking how happy she'd looked.

'Went running this morning and didn't come back,' Mackenzie went on, relentlessly. 'Could be a false alarm, but right now it doesn't look like it. And if it isn't, if this is the same man, then the shit's really going to hit the fan. Because either Lyn Metcalf's already dead, or she's being held somewhere. And given what was done to Sally Palmer, I wouldn't wish that on anybody.'

I almost asked why he was telling me all this, but even as the question formed I knew the answer. On the one hand he was putting more pressure on me to co-operate; on the other, Mackenzie was simply being a policeman. The fact that I'd reported Sally Palmer as missing had put me low on the list of potential suspects, but if there was now a second victim then everything was up in the air again. No-one could be discounted.

Including me.

Mackenzie had been watching to see how I would react. His expression was unreadable. 'I'll be in touch. And I'm sure I needn't ask you to keep this to yourself, Dr Hunter. I know you're good at keeping secrets.'

With that he turned and walked away, his shadow chasing him across the grass like a black dog at his heels.

If Mackenzie had been serious about my keeping Lyn Metcalf's disappearance to myself he needn't have bothered. Manham was too small a place for something like that to remain secret for long. Word had already spread by the time I'd got back from the farm. It came at roughly the same time as news broke that the murdered woman was Sally Palmer, a double blow that was almost too much to take in. Within hours the mood of the entire village had changed from febrile excitement to one of shock. Most people clung to the hope that the two events would prove unconnected, and that the supposed second 'victim' might yet turn up safe and sound.

But it was a hope that faded every hour.

When Lyn didn't return from her run, her husband Marcus had set out to look for her. He admitted later he wasn't unduly worried to start with. At that point, before Sally Palmer's name had been released, his main concern was that his wife might have decided to try a different route and become lost. It had happened before, and as he followed the track towards the lake, it was with a degree of irritation that he called her name. Lyn knew he had a busy day, and now her stupid insistence on an early-morning run was making him late.

He still wasn't too anxious as he crossed the reedbeds and cut into the woods. When he found a dead mallard tied to the standing stone, his first reaction was anger at the senseless cruelty. He'd lived all his life in the country and had no time for sentiment where animals were concerned, but neither did he like casual sadism. Only as he thought of it in those terms did the first chill of fear begin to enter his mind. He told himself that the dead bird couldn't possibly have any connection with Lyn being late. But once there, the fear was impossible to dislodge.

It continued to grow, fed by his echoing shouts that rang unanswered in the trees. By the time he began making his way out of the woods he was fighting to remain calm. Hurrying back towards the lake, he told himself she would probably be waiting for him back at home. And then he saw something that blew away his false hopes like so much dust.

Half-hidden by a tree root was Lyn's stopwatch.

He picked it up, took in the broken strap and cracked face. Fear now giving way to panic, he looked around for some other sign of her. There was nothing. Or, at least, nothing he recognized as such. He saw the thick wooden stake hammered into the ground nearby without realizing its significance. It would be several hours before the police forensic team confirmed it as the remains of a snare, and several more before splashes of Lyn's blood were identified on the path.

But of Lyn herself, there was no trace.

8

It seemed like most of the village turned out to help
with the search. At another time, or in different
circumstances, it might have been thought that Lyn
Metcalf could have left of her own accord. Oh, she
and Marcus seemed happy enough, it was generally
agreed. But you could never tell. Coming when it
did, though, on the heels of the murder of another
woman, her disappearance immediately took on a
far more sinister aspect. And while the police con-
centrated their efforts on the woods and area where
she'd gone running, virtually everyone who was fit
and able wanted to help find her.

It was a beautiful summer evening. As the sun
lowered in the sky and swallows dipped and swooped,
the atmosphere could almost have been festive, a rare
sense of communal unity and resolve. But no-one
could forget for long the reason for them being there.
And with that came another unpalatable fact.

Whoever had done this was one of Manham's
own.

It was no longer possible to blame an outsider. Not any more. It could hardly be an accident, and certainly no coincidence, that the two women came from the same village. No-one could believe that an outsider would have either stayed around after killing Sally Palmer, or come back to claim a second victim. Which meant that whoever had hacked one woman to death and strung wire across a path to snare another had to be local. There was a chance it was someone from a neighbouring village, but that begged the question of why Manham had been the site for both attacks. The other possibility was both more likely and more frightening: that not only did we know the two women, we also knew the animal responsible.

That realization was still taking root as people set out to look for Lyn Metcalf. And although it hadn't yet begun to flower, it was already beginning to put up shoots. It revealed itself as a slight distance in the way people responded to each other. Everyone knew of murders where the killer had taken part in the search. Where they had publicly expressed revulsion and sympathy, even shed reptilian tears, when all the while the victim's blood was barely dry on their hands, the final screams and entreaties locked away to fester in their heart. And even as Manham showed its solidarity as a community, kicking aside long grass and peering under bushes, suspicion was already undermining it from within.

I'd joined the search myself as soon as I finished evening surgery. Its epicentre was the police trailer set up as near to the woods where Marcus Metcalf had found his wife's stopwatch as the road allowed. It was on the outskirts of the village, and cars were pulled into the hedgerows for quarter of a mile either side of it. Some people had just struck off by themselves, but the majority had come here, drawn by the glut of activity. There were a few journalists, but only from the local press. At that point the nationals still hadn't picked up on the story, or perhaps felt that one woman murdered and another abducted wasn't particularly newsworthy. That would soon change, but for the moment Manham was still able to go about its business with relative anonymity.

The police had set up a table to help co-ordinate the public search. It was as much a PR exercise as anything; giving the community a sense that it was doing something and making sure the volunteers didn't get in the way of the professional teams. But the countryside around Manham was so wild that it would be impossible to cover all of it anyway. It could soak up searchers like a sponge without ever giving up its secrets.

I saw Marcus Metcalf standing with a group of men, yet slightly apart from them. He had the undefined muscle bulk of a manual worker, and a face that, under normal circumstances, was pleasant and cheerful under a shock of blond hair. Now he looked haggard, a pallor yellowing his tanned features. With him was Scarsdale, the reverend finally finding a situation that suited the severity of his features. I'd considered going over to express . . . what? Sympathy? Condolences? But the hollowness of anything I could say, and memory of how little I'd appreciated the awkward utterances of near strangers myself, prevented me. Instead, leaving him to the reverend's ministrations, I went straight to the table to be told where to go.

It was a decision I would come to regret.

I spent an unproductive few hours trudging across a boggy field as part of a group that included Rupert Sutton, who seemed glad of the excuse to be out without his domineering mother. His bulk made it hard work for him to keep up with the rest of us, but he persevered, breathing heavily through his mouth as we slowly made our way across the uneven land-scape, trying to skirt the wetter patches of ground. Once he slipped and stumbled to his knees. His perspiring body gave off an animal whiff of exertion as I helped him up.

'Bugger,' he panted, his face colouring with embarrassment as he stared at the mud coating his hands like black gloves. His voice was surprisingly light, almost girlish. 'Bugger,' he kept repeating, blinking furiously.

Other than that, few people spoke. When the growing dusk made it impractical to search any longer we abandoned the attempt and made our way back. The general mood was as sombre as the darkening landscape. I knew many of the searchers would stop off at the Black Lamb, seeking company more than alcohol. I almost went straight home. But I didn't feel like being alone any more than anyone else did that night. I parked outside the pub and went in.

Apart from the church, the Lamb was the oldest

building in the village, and one of the few in Manham that had a traditional thatched roof. Anywhere else in the Broads it would have been smartened into twee respectability, but with only the locals to please no real attempt had been made to halt its slow decay. The reeds on its thatch were slowly mouldering, while the unpainted plaster of its walls was cracked and stained.

Tonight, though, it was doing good business, but it was far from a party atmosphere. The nods I received were solemn, the conversation low and subdued. The landlord lifted his chin in silent enquiry as I reached the bar. He was blind in one eye, the milky cast emphasizing the resemblance to an ageing Labrador.

'Pint, please, Jack.'

'You been out on the search?' he asked as he set the glass in front of me. When I nodded he waved away my money. 'On the house.'

I barely had time to take a drink before a hand fell on my shoulder. 'Thought you might come in tonight.'

I looked up at the giant who'd materialized beside me. 'Hi, Ben.'

Ben Anders topped six feet four, and seemed half as broad again. A warden at Hickling Broad nature reserve, he'd lived in the village all his life. We rarely saw much of each other, but I liked him. He was easy company, someone I felt as comfortable maintaining a silence with as talking to. He had a pleasant, almost dreamy smile in a heavy-boned face that looked as though it had been screwed up and only partially smoothed out again. Set in its tanned leather, his eyes seemed incongruously bright and green.

Normally they held a twinkle of good humour, but there was no humour in them now. He propped an elbow on the bar. 'Bad business.'

'Lousy.'

'I saw Lyn a couple of days ago. Not a care in the world. And then Sally Palmer, as well. It's like being struck by lightning twice.'

'I know.'

'I hope to Christ she's just buggered off some-where. But it's not looking good, is it?'

'Not very, no.'

'God, poor Marcus. Doesn't bear thinking about what the poor bastard must be going through.' He pitched his voice lower so it wouldn't carry. 'There's a rumour going around that Sally Palmer was cut up pretty bad. If it's the same man who took Lyn ... Jesus, makes you want to break the fucker's neck, doesn't it?'

I looked down into my glass. Obviously word hadn't got out that I'd helped the police. I was glad, but it made me feel awkward now, as if keeping quiet about my involvement were making me a liar.

Ben slowly shook his massive head. 'You think there's any chance for her?'

'I don't know.'

It was as honest an answer as I could give. I remembered what Mackenzie had said earlier. If I was right, then Sally Palmer hadn't been killed until around three days after she'd disappeared. I wasn't a psychological profiler but I knew that serial killers followed a pattern. Which meant, if this was the same man, there was a chance that Lyn might still be alive.

Still alive. God, could she be? And if she was, for how long? I told myself I'd done what I could, given the police as much as could reasonably be expected of me. But it felt like a cheap rationalization.

I realized Ben was looking at me. 'Sorry?'

'I said are you OK? You look pretty bushed.'

'It's just been a long day.'

'You can say that again.' His expression soured as he looked towards the doorway. 'And just when you think it can't get any worse . . .'

I turned to see the dark figure of Reverend Scarsdale blocking out the light as he entered. Conversations died away as he advanced stern-faced to the bar.

'Don't suppose he'll be getting them in,' Ben muttered.

Scarsdale cleared his throat. 'Gentlemen.' His eyes drifted disapprovingly over the few women in the pub, but he didn't bother to acknowledge them. 'I thought you should know that I will be holding a prayer service tomorrow evening for Lyn Metcalf and Sally Palmer.'

His voice was a dry baritone that carried effortlessly.

'I'm sure all of you' – he let his gaze run around the pub – '*all* of you will be there tomorrow evening to show your respect for the dead and support for the living.' He paused before stiffly inclining his head. 'Thank you.'

As he headed for the door he stopped in front of me. Even in summer there seemed an odour of mildew about him. I could see the white dusting of dandruff on the black wool of his jacket, smell the mothball taint of his breath.

'I trust I'll see you as well, Dr Hunter.'

'Patients allowing.'

'I'm sure no-one will be selfish enough to keep you from your duty.' I wasn't quite sure what he meant by that. He favoured me with a humourless smile. 'Besides, I think you'll find most of them will be at the church. Tragedies draw communities like this together. Coming from the city you'll probably find that strange. But we know where our priorities lie here.'

With a final terse nod, he left. 'There goes a real Christian,' Ben said. He raised his empty glass, more like a half-pint in his big hand. 'Ah, well, you ready for another?'

I declined. Scarsdale's appearance hadn't improved my mood. I was about to finish my drink and go home when someone spoke behind me.

'Dr Hunter?'

It was the young teacher I'd met at the school the day before. Her smile faltered at my expression. 'Sorry, I didn't mean to intrude . . .'

'No, that's OK. I mean, no, you aren't.'

'I'm Sam's teacher. We met yesterday?' she said, uncertainly.

Normally I'm bad at remembering names, but I recalled hers straight away. Jenny. Jenny Hammond.

'Sure. How is he?'

105

'OK, I think. I mean, he didn't come to school today. But he seemed better by the time his mother collected him yesterday afternoon.'

I'd meant to check on him, but other things had intervened. 'I'm sure he'll be fine. There's no problem with him being off, is there?'

'Oh, no, not at all. I just thought I'd . . . you know, say hello, that's all.'

She looked embarrassed. I'd assumed she'd come over to ask something about Sam. Belatedly, it occurred to me she might just be being friendly.

'So, are you with some of the other teachers?' I asked.

'No, I'm by myself. I went on the search and then . . . well, my housemate's out, and it just didn't feel like a night for sitting in alone, you know?'

I knew. There was a silence for a while.

'Can I get you a drink?' I asked, just as she said, 'Well, I'll see you later.' We laughed, self-consciously. 'What would you like?'

'No, it's all right, really.'

'I was just going to get myself another.' I realized as I said it that my glass was still half-full. I hoped she wouldn't notice.

'A bottle of Becks, then. Thanks.'

Ben had just finished getting served as I leaned on the bar. 'Changed your mind? Here, let me.' He started putting his hand in his pocket.

'No, it's all right. I'm getting someone else's.'

He glanced behind me. His mouth twisted in a smile. 'Fair enough. See you later.'

I nodded, conscious of my face burning. By the

time I was served I'd finished the rest of my beer. I ordered myself another and took the drinks over to where Jenny was standing.

'Cheers.' She raised the bottle in a little toast and took a drink. 'I know the landlord doesn't like you doing it, but it just doesn't taste the same from a glass.'

'And it's less to wash up, so you're actually doing him a favour.'

'I'll remember that next time he tells me off.' She grew more serious. 'I just can't believe what's happened. It's so awful, isn't it? I mean, two of them, from here? I thought places like this were supposed to be safe.'

'Was that why you came?'

I didn't mean it to sound as intrusive as it did. She looked down at the bottle she was holding. 'Let's just say I was tired of living in a city.'

'Where was that?'

'Norwich.'

She had started to peel the label from the bottle. As if realizing what she was doing she suddenly stopped. Her expression cleared as she smiled at me.

'Anyway, how about you? We've already established you're not a local either.'

'Nope. London, originally.'

'So what made you come to Manham? The bright lights and scintillating night-life?'

'Something like that.' I saw that she was expecting more. 'Same as you, I suppose. I wanted a change.'

'Yeah, well, it's that all right.' She smiled. 'Still, I quite like it. I'm getting used to living out in the middle of nowhere. You know, the quiet and every-thing. No crowds or cars.'

'Or cinema.'

'Or bars.'

'Or shops.'

We grinned at each other. 'So how long have you been here?' she asked.

'Three years.'

'And how long did it take you to be accepted?'

'I'm still working on it. Another decade and I might be thought of as a permanent visitor. By the more progressive elements, obviously.'

'Don't say that. I've only been here six months.'

'Still a tourist, then.'

She laughed, but before she could say anything there was a commotion in the doorway.

'Where's the doctor?' a voice demanded. 'Is he here?'

I pushed my way forward as a man was half-supported, half-carried into the pub. His face was contorted in pain. I recognized him as Scott Brenner, one of a large family who lived in a ramshackle house just outside Manham. A boot and the bottom of one trouser leg were soaked in blood.

'Sit him down. Gently,' I said, as he was lowered into a seat. 'What happened?'

'He stepped in a snare. We were going up to the surgery but we saw your Land Rover outside.'

It was his brother Carl who'd spoken. The Brenners were a clannish lot, ostensibly farm workers but not averse to poaching as well. Carl was the eldest, a wiry, truculent individual, and as I eased back the blood-soaked denim from Scott's leg I entertained the uncharitable thought that this had happened to the wrong brother. Then I saw the damage that had been done.

'Do you have a car?' I asked his brother.

'Don't think we walked here, do you?'

'Good, because he needs to go to hospital.'

Carl swore. 'Can't you just patch him up?'

'I can put a temporary dressing on, but that's all. This needs more than I can do.'

'Am I going to lose my foot?' Scott gasped.

'No, but you're not going to be doing much running for a while.' I wasn't as confident as I sounded. I considered taking him up to the surgery, but by the look of him he'd been manhandled enough. 'There's a first-aid kit under a blanket in the back of my Land Rover. Can somebody fetch it?'

'I will,' Ben said. I gave him the car keys. As he went out I asked for water and clean towels and began mopping the blood from around the wound.

'What type of snare was it?'

'Wire noose,' Carl said. 'Tightens once anything's got its foot in it. Cut through to the bone, it will.'

It had done that all right.

'Whereabouts were you?'

Scott answered, face averted from what I was doing. 'Over on the far side of the marsh, near the old windmill—'

'We were looking for Lyn,' Carl cut in, giving him a look.

I doubted that. I knew where they meant. Like most windmills in the Broads, the one outside

Manham was actually a wind-powered pump, built to drain the marshes. Abandoned decades before, it was now an empty shell that lacked sails or life. The area was desolate even by Manham's standards, but it was ideal for anyone wanting to hunt or trap animals away from prying eyes. Given the Brenners' reputation, I thought that was a more likely reason for them to be out there at this time of night than any sense of public duty. As I wiped the blood from the wound I wondered if they'd managed to blunder into one of their own snares.

'Wasn't one of ours,' said Scott, as though he'd read my mind.

'Scott!' his brother snapped.

'It wasn't! It was hidden under grass on the path. And it was too big for rabbit or deer.'

The announcement was met by a silence. Although the police hadn't yet confirmed it, everyone had heard about the remains of the tripwire that had been found in the woods where Lyn had disappeared.

Ben returned with the first-aid box. I cleaned and dressed the wound as best I could. 'Keep the foot elevated and get him to casualty as soon as you can,' I told Carl.

Roughly, he hauled his brother to his feet and half-supported, half-hauled him out. I washed my hands and then went back to where Jenny stood with my drink.

'Will he be all right?' she asked.

'Depends how much damage has been done to the tendon. If he's lucky, he'll just end up with a limp.'

She shook her head. 'God, what a day!'

Ben came over and handed me my car keys. 'You'll be needing these.'

'Thanks.'

'So what do you think? Reckon that's anything to do with what's happened to Lyn?'

'I don't know.' But, like everyone else, I had a bad feeling about it.

'Why should it have?' Jenny asked.

He seemed unsure how to answer. I realized they didn't know each other.

'Ben, this is Jenny. She teaches at the school,' I told him.

He took it as approval to continue. 'Because it seems like too much of a coincidence. Not that I've any sympathy with any of the Brenners, bunch of poaching bast—' He broke off with a glance at Jenny. 'Anyway, I hope to God that's all it is. A coincidence.'

'I don't follow.'

Ben looked at me, but I wasn't going to say it. 'Because if not it means it's somebody from around here. From the village.'

'You don't know that for sure,' Jenny objected.

His face said otherwise, but he was too polite to argue. 'Well, we'll see. And on that note, I think I'll say good night.'

He drained his glass and started for the door. As if as an afterthought, he turned to Jenny. 'I know it's none of my business, but did you come in a car?'

'No, why?'

'Just that it might be a good idea not to walk home alone, that's all.'

111

With a last look at me to make sure I'd got the message, he went out. Jenny gave an uncertain smile. 'Do you think it's that bad?'

'I hope not. But I suppose he's right.'

She shook her head, incredulously. 'I don't believe this. Two days ago this was the quietest place on the planet!'

Two days ago Sally Palmer had still been dead, and the animal responsible was probably already turning his gaze towards Lyn Metcalf. But I didn't say that.

'Is there anyone here you can go with?' I asked.

'Not really. But I'll be fine. I can look after myself.'

I didn't doubt it. But beneath the defiance I could see she'd been unnerved.

'I'll give you a lift,' I said.

When I got home I sat outside at the table in the back garden. The night was warm, without a breath of wind. I put my head back and stared up at the stars. The moon was approaching full, an asymmetrical, haloed white disc. I tried to appreciate its dappled contours, but my eyes were drawn lower until I was looking at the shadowed wood across the field. Normally it was a view I enjoyed, even at night. But now I felt uneasy as I looked at the impenetrable mass of trees.

I went into the house, poured myself a small whisky, and took it back outside. It was after midnight and I knew I'd be up early. But I grasped any excuse to put off sleep. Besides, for once I had too much to think about to be tired. I'd walked with

Jenny to the small cottage she rented with another young woman. We hadn't bothered with my car after all. It was a warm, clear night, and she only lived a few hundred yards away. As we walked she'd told me a little about her job, and the children she taught. Only once had she spoken about her past life, mentioning working at a school in Norwich. But she'd quickly brushed past it, burying the lapse in a flurry of words. I'd pretended not to notice. Whatever it was she was avoiding, it was none of my business.

As we walked up the narrow lane towards her house a fox suddenly cried out nearby. Jenny grabbed my arm.

'Sorry,' she said, quickly letting go as if burned. She gave an embarrassed laugh. 'You'd think I'd be used to living out here by now.'

There'd been an awkwardness between us after that. When we reached her house she stopped by the gate.

'Well. Thanks.'

'No problem.'

With a last smile she'd hurried inside. I'd waited until I heard the snick of the lock before turning away. All the way back through the dark village I could feel the pressure of her hand on my bare arm.

I could still feel it now. I sipped my drink, wincing at the memory of how flustered I'd become just because a young woman had accidentally touched me. No wonder she'd gone quiet.

I finished the whisky and went inside. There was something else pricking my subconscious, a nagging sense of something I had to do. I thought for a moment before I remembered. Scott Brenner. I wasn't confident his brother would let him tell the police about the wire snare. It might be nothing, but Mackenzie needed to know about it. I found his card and dialled his mobile. It was almost one o'clock, but I could leave a voicemail message for him to get first thing.

He answered straight away. 'Yeah?'

'It's David Hunter,' I said, caught off-guard. 'Sorry, I know it's late. I just wanted to make sure Scott Brenner had got in touch.'

I could hear his irritation and fatigue in the pause. 'Scott who?'

I told him what had happened. When he spoke, the tiredness had gone. 'Where was this?'

'Near an old windmill a mile or so south of the village. You think it might be connected?'

There was a sound it took me a moment to identify – the rasp of his whiskers as he rubbed his face.

'Ah, what the hell. We're going to have to go public with this tomorrow anyway,' he said. 'Two of my officers were injured tonight. One got caught by a wire snare, the other stepped in a hole someone had stuck a sharpened stick in.'

There was no mistaking the anger in his voice.

'So I think we've got to assume that whoever took Lyn Metcalf expected us to come looking for him.'

There was no shock of transition from the dream that night. I simply found myself awake, eyes open and staring at the spill of moonlight falling through the window. For once I was still in bed, my nocturnal wandering this time confined to the dream. But the memory of it remained with me, as vivid as if I'd just walked from one room into another.

It was always in the same setting. A house I'd never seen in my waking life, a place I knew didn't exist but that nevertheless felt like home. Kara and Alice were there, vibrant and real. We would talk about my day, about nothing in particular, just as we had when they were alive.

And then I would wake, and confront again the stark fact that they were dead.

I thought again about what Linda Yates had said. *You have dreams for a reason.* I wondered what she would make of mine. I could imagine what a psychiatrist would say, or even an amateur psychologist like Henry. But the dreams defied any neat rationalization. There was a logic and reality to them that was far from dreamlike. And, although I could barely acknowledge it even to myself, a part of me didn't want to believe that's all they were.

If I let myself believe that, though, it would be the first step on a road I was scared to take. Because there was only one way I could ever be with my family again, and I knew taking it would be an act of despair, not love.

What scared me even more was that sometimes I didn't care.

9

Next morning two more people were injured in traps. They were separate incidents, neither of them anywhere near those of the previous night. I knew because our surgery lacked a permanent nurse, so I treated them both. One, a policewoman, had impaled her calf on a stick embedded point up in a concealed hole. As with Scott Brenner, I did what I could and sent her to hospital for stitches. The other injury, to Dan Marsden, a local farmhand, was more superficial, the wire noose having only partially cut through his tough leather boot.

'Christ, I'd like to get my hands on the bastard who put it there,' he said through gritted teeth as I dressed the wound.

'Was it well hidden?'

'Bloody invisible. And the size of it! God knows what they were hoping to catch with something that big.'

I didn't say anything. But I thought it was likely the traps had caught exactly what had been intended.

So did Mackenzie. He called a temporary halt to the search for Lyn Metcalf and had a first-aid station set up outside the mobile incident room. He also issued a statement warning everyone else to stay out of the woods and fields around the village. The result was predictable. If the mood before had been largely one of numb shock, news that the countryside around Manham was no longer safe brought the first touch of real fear.

Of course, there were those who refused to believe it, or stubbornly insisted they weren't going to be scared away from land they'd known all their lives. That lasted until one of the loudest objecters, fuelled by an afternoon's drinking in the Lamb, put his foot into a hole that had been covered with dried grass and snapped his ankle. His yells drove home the point far more effectively than any police warning.

As more police were drafted in and the national press finally woke up to what was going on, descending on the village with their microphones and cameras, Manham began to feel like a place under siege.

'There's just the two different kinds of trap so far,' Mackenzie told me. 'The wire one is pretty much a basic snare, same sort of thing any poacher might know how to make. Except these are big enough to take an adult's foot. The stakes are even worse. Could be ex-military or one of these survivalist buffs. Or just someone with a nasty imagination.'

'You said "so far"?'

'Whoever laid them knows what he's doing. There's real thought been put into this. We can't assume he hasn't planted some more surprises.'

'Couldn't that be what he wanted? To disrupt the search?'

'I daresay. But we can't afford to take the chance. The ones we've found have only caused injuries. We carry on blundering through the woods and next time someone might get killed.'

He broke off as we came to a junction, drumming the steering wheel impatiently as he waited for the car in front to pull out. I looked out of the window, my anxiety returning in the silence.

I'd called Mackenzie first thing that morning to tell him I would examine Sally Palmer's remains if he still wanted me to. The knowledge had been with me from the moment I'd woken, as if the decision had been made while I was asleep. Which, in a way, I suppose it had.

Realistically, I didn't know how much use I would be. At best I might be able to give a more precise idea of the time-since-death interval, assuming my rusty knowledge hadn't deserted me. But I was under no illusions that it would do much to help Lyn Metcalf. It was just that doing nothing was no longer an option.

That didn't mean I was happy about it.

Mackenzie had sounded neither surprised nor greatly impressed when I'd told him. Just said he'd check with his superintendent and get back to me. I hung up feeling left in limbo, wondering if I'd made a misjudgement.

But he'd rung back within half an hour to ask if I could make a start that afternoon. Mouth dry, I'd said I could.

'The body's still with the pathologist. I'll pick you up at one and take you over,' he'd told me.

'I can make my own way.'

'I've got to go back to the station anyway. And there's one or two things I'd like to talk about.'

I'd wondered what they might be as I went to ask Henry if he would cover for me during that evening's surgery.

'Of course. Something come up?'

He'd looked at me expectantly. I still hadn't got round to telling him why Mackenzie had been to see me in the first place. I felt bad about that, but it would have meant more explanations than I'd been ready to go into. I knew I couldn't put it off much longer, though. I owed him that much, at least.

'Give me till the weekend,' I'd said. By then I should have finished what I had to do, and there wouldn't be a surgery to worry about. 'I'll tell you everything then.'

He'd studied me. 'Everything all right?'

'Fine. It's just . . . complicated.'

'Things generally are. This time last week no-one expected we'd have bloody journalists crawling all over the place and police asking everybody questions. Makes you wonder where it's all going to end.'

He'd made an effort to brighten. 'OK. Come for Sunday lunch. I fancy cooking, and I've got a nice Bordeaux I've been looking for an excuse to open. Talking's always easier on a full stomach.'

Grateful to be able to put that much off for a little longer, at least, I'd agreed.

The traffic streamed past as Mackenzie came to a roundabout. The interior of the car smelled of menthol air freshener and his aftershave. It was as neat as if it had been newly valeted. Outside the roads and streets were all confusion and noise. It seemed familiar and strange at the same time. I tried to remember when I'd last been in a city, and realized with a shock that this was the first time I had been outside Manham since the rainy afternoon when I'd arrived. I felt warring emotions, torn between wishing I'd stayed there and amazement that I had buried myself away for so long.

Life outside had gone on, regardless.

I watched a crowd of schoolchildren jostling each other as a teacher tried for order outside school gates. People hurried by, intent on their own affairs. All of them with their own lives, untouched by mine. Or each other's.

'The wire from the snares is the same type as was used to bring down Lyn Metcalf,' Mackenzie said, bringing me back to the here and now. 'And that was used to tie the bird to the stone. Don't know if it's from the same batch, but I think it's a safe assumption.'

'What do you make of that? The bird, I mean.'

'Not sure yet. Could have been to panic her. Could be some sort of statement or signature.'

'Like the wings found on Sally Palmer's body?'

'It's possible. We heard back from the ornithologist about those, by the way. Mute swan. Common enough round here, 'specially this time of year.'

'You think there's a connection between the swan's wings and the mallard?'

'I can't believe it's a coincidence, if that's what you mean. Perhaps he's just got a thing against birds.' He overtook a slow-moving van. 'We've got psychologists on it now, to give us some idea what sort of mindset we're dealing with. And every other type of specialist you'd care to think of, in case it's part of some pagan ritual, or Satanism. Some bollocks like that.'

'But you don't think so?'

He didn't answer at first, clearly debating how much to say. 'No, I don't,' he said at last. 'The wings on Palmer's body got everybody all excited. There was talk about the killer using religious or classical symbolism, everything from angels to God knows what. Now, though, I'm not so sure. If the mallard had been sacrificed or mutilated, then perhaps. But just tied up with wire? No, I think our boy just likes hurting things. Showing off, if you like.'

'Like with the traps.'

'Like with the traps. Fair enough, it slows us up. We can't just concentrate on the search when we've got to worry about what else he might have left behind. But why bother? Anybody sussed enough to go to all this trouble will know how to cover their tracks. Instead, we've got the bird left for us to find, the stakes used to trip his victim left in place, and now all this. He's either not worried about us finding anything, or he's just, I don't know . . .'

'Marking his territory?' I offered.

'Something like that. Showing us he's in charge.

Doesn't even take that much effort. He just leaves a few traps dotted around at strategic points, then stands back to watch the fun.'

I was quiet for a while, thinking about what Mackenzie had said. 'Couldn't it be more than that?'

'How do you mean?'

'He's made the woods and marshes a no-go area. People are going to be scared to go for a walk in case they step in one of his traps.'

He was frowning. 'So?'

'So perhaps he doesn't just like hurting things. Perhaps he likes frightening them as well.'

Mackenzie stared thoughtfully through the windscreen. It was dappled with the squashed remains of dead insects. 'Could be,' he said at last. 'Mind telling me where you were between six and seven o'clock yesterday morning?'

The sudden change of tack threw me. 'At six o'clock I was probably in the shower. Then I had breakfast and went to the surgery.'

'What time?'

'Perhaps quarter to seven.'

'Early start.'

'I didn't sleep well.'

'Anyone vouch for those times?'

'Henry. I had a cup of coffee with him when I arrived. Black, no sugar, in case you need to know that as well.'

'It's just routine, Dr Hunter. You've been involved in enough police inquiries in the past to know how it works.'

'Pull over.'

'What?'

'Just pull over.'

He seemed about to argue, then flicked on the indicator and pulled into the side of the road.

'Am I here as a suspect or because you want my help?'

'Look, we're asking every—'

'Which is it?'

'All right, I'm sorry, perhaps I shouldn't have come out with it like that. But they're questions we've got to ask.'

'If you think I had anything to do with it then I shouldn't be here. You think I'm looking forward to this? I'd be more than happy if I never had to see another dead body in my life. So if you're not going to trust me I might as well get out now.'

Mackenzie sighed. 'Look, I don't think you had anything to do with it. If I did, then you can take my word for it we wouldn't be using you. But we're asking everyone in the village the same thing. I just thought I'd get it over and done with, OK?'

I still didn't like the way he'd sprung the question on me. He'd wanted to surprise me, to see how I would react. I wondered if the rest of our conversation had been a similar test. But, whether I liked it or not, that was his job. And I was starting to realize that he was good at it. Grudgingly, I nodded.

'Can I carry on now?' he asked.

I had to smile. 'I suppose so.'

He pulled out again. 'So how long is this likely to take? The examination,' he asked after a while, breaking the silence.

'Difficult to say. A lot depends on the condition of the body. Has the pathologist come up with anything?'

'Not much. Although we can't tell if there was a sexual assault, given that she was found naked it's pretty likely. There's what seem to be numerous small cuts on the torso and limbs, but they're only superficial. He's not even able to say for sure whether it was the throat wound or the head injuries that killed her. Any chance you'll be able to shed any light on that?'

'I don't know yet.' Having seen the crime scene photographs, I already had some ideas, but I didn't want to commit myself until I was sure.

Mackenzie gave me a sideways glance. 'I know I'm probably going to regret asking, but what exactly is it you're going to do?'

I'd been deliberately trying not to think about it. But the answers came automatically. 'I'll need to X-ray the body, if it hasn't been already. Then I'll take samples of the soft tissue to find the TSD, and—'

'The what?'

'Time-since-death interval. You can analyse changes in the body chemistry to find out how long it's been dead, basically. Composition of amino acids, volatile fatty acids, the level of protein break-down. After that I'll have to remove any soft tissue that's left so I can examine the skeleton itself. See what sort of trauma it suffered, what type of weapon caused it. That sort of thing.'

Mackenzie had a frown of distaste. 'How do you do that?'

124

'Well, if there's not much soft tissue left you can either use a scalpel or forceps. Or you boil the body for a few hours in detergent.'

Mackenzie pulled a face. 'Now I know why you wanted to be a GP.' I could see the moment when he remembered my other reasons. 'Sorry,' he added.

'Forget it.'

We drove in silence for a while. I noticed Mackenzie scratching his neck.

'Have you had it looked at yet?' I asked.

'Had what looked at?'

'The mole. You were scratching it.'

He hurriedly lowered his hand. 'Just an itch.' He turned into a car park. 'Here we are.'

I followed him into the hospital. We took a lift from the ground floor to the basement. The mortuary was at the end of a long corridor. The smell of it hit me as soon as I went inside, a sweetly pungent chemical blanket that seemed to coat the lungs after a single breath. Inside was an essay in white, stainless steel and glass. A young Asian woman in a white lab coat stood up from behind a desk as we walked in.

'Afternoon, Marina,' Mackenzie said, easily. 'Dr Hunter, Marina Patel. She's going to be around to help you.'

She smiled as we shook hands. I was still trying to get my bearings, adjust to once again being back in a setting that was both so familiar and strange.

Mackenzie looked at his watch. 'Right, I'd better get to the station. Just ring me when you've finished and I'll get you a lift back.'

After he'd gone the young woman looked at me expectantly, waiting for instructions. 'So . . . are you the pathologist?' I asked, putting off the moment for a little longer.

She grinned. 'Not yet. Just a graduate student. But I have hopes.'

I nodded. Neither of us moved.

'Do you want to see the body?' she asked, eventually.

No. No, I didn't. 'Fine.'

She gave me a lab coat and led me through a pair of heavy swing doors. Behind them was a smaller room, like an operating theatre. It was cold inside. The body was laid out on a stainless-steel table, incongruous on the dulled metal surface. Marina switched on the bright lights fixed overhead, showing it in its pathetic entirety.

I looked down at what had been Sally Palmer. But there was nothing of her left here now. The relief I felt was fleeting, quickly replaced by a clinical detachment.

'OK. Let's get started,' I said.

The woman had seen better days. Her face was pockmarked and worn, her features beginning to lose any distinction they might once have held. With her bowed head, she seemed to bear the weight of the world on her shoulders. Yet there was something noble about her resignation, as though, unwelcome as it was, her lot was one she nevertheless accepted.

The statue of the unknown saint drew my attention during the church service. I couldn't say what there was about it I liked. Mounted on its stone pillar, it was roughly hewn, and even to my unschooled eye the sculptor had a poor sense of proportion. Yet whether it was the softening effect of age or something less definable, there was something about it that appealed. It had endured for centuries, seen countless days of joy and tragedy played out beneath it. It would still be there, watchful and silent, long after everyone else had faded from memory. It was a reminder that, good or bad, everything passes.

Right now that was a comforting thought. The old church was cool and musty, even on a warm evening. Light fell through the stained-glass window in blues and mauves, the ancient glass warped and uneven in its leaded frames. The central aisle was flagged with uneven stone slabs now worn smooth, interspersed with ancient gravestones. The one nearest me was engraved with a skull, beneath which some medieval stonemason had inscribed a sombre message.

As you are now, so I once was
As I am now, so will you be

I moved my weight from side to side on the hard wooden pew as Scarsdale's insidious baritone echoed off the stone walls. What had supposedly set out to be a prayer service had predictably become an excuse for the reverend to inflict his own brand of piety on a captive audience.

'Even as we pray for the soul of Sally Palmer, and for the deliverance of Lyn Metcalf, there is undoubtedly a question all of us want answered. Why? Why should this have happened? Is it judgement that these two young women have been taken from us so brutally? But judgement for what? And on who?'

Gripping the aged wooden pulpit in both his hands, Scarsdale glowered down at his congregation. 'Judgement can fall upon any of us, at any time. It is not for us to question it. It is not for us to cry that it isn't fair. God is merciful, but we have no right to expect His mercy. And God's mercy is delivered in ways we may not understand. It does not fall to us to decry it, simply because of our ignorance.'

Flashbulbs popped silently as Scarsdale paused for breath. He'd allowed the press inside the church, which added to the unreality of the situation. Its normally meagre congregation had swollen to over-flowing. By the time I'd arrived the pews were full, and I'd been forced to ease my way through to a small space at the back.

I'd forgotten about the service until I'd seen the glut of people in the churchyard. Mackenzie had arranged for me to be driven back to Manham by a taciturn plain-clothed police sergeant, who clearly resented being forced into taxi duties. The inspector's phone had been switched off when I'd called to tell him I'd finished for the day. But I'd left a voicemail message and he'd rung back almost immediately.

'How did it go?'

'I've sent off samples for gas chromatograph tests. When they're back I'll be able to give you a more accurate time-since-death,' I'd told him. 'Tomorrow I'll be able to start examining the skeleton. That might give us a better idea of what sort of weapon was used.'

'You've not got anything yet, then?' He'd sounded disappointed.

'Only that Marina told me the pathologist thinks the cause of death was probably the head injuries rather than the throat wound.'

'And you don't agree?'

'I'm not saying they wouldn't have been fatal. But she was still alive when her throat was cut.'

'Are you sure?'

'The body's prematurely desiccated. Even in the heat we've been having it wouldn't have dried out this quickly unless there was major blood loss. That doesn't happen after death, even with a cut throat.'

'The soil samples from where the body was found showed a low iron content,' Mackenzie had pointed out.

That meant not much blood had soaked into the ground where the body had been found. With the amount that would have gushed out of a severed jugular, the soil's iron content should have been sky high.

'Then she was killed somewhere else.'

'What about the head injuries?'

'Either they didn't kill her or they were caused post-mortem.'

He was silent for a while, but I could guess what he was thinking. Whatever Sally Palmer had gone through, the same was now facing Lyn Metcalf. And if she wasn't dead already, it was only a matter of time.

Barring miracles.

Scarsdale was beginning to wind down. 'Some of you may still be asking what those two poor women did to deserve this. What our community has done to deserve this.' He spread his hands. 'Perhaps nothing. Perhaps the modern consensus is right; perhaps there is no reason, no prevailing wisdom behind our universe.'

He paused, dramatically. I wondered if he were deliberately playing to the cameras.

'Or perhaps we have just allowed ourselves to be too dazzled by our own arrogance to see it,' he went on. 'Many of you here have not set foot in this church for years. Your lives are too busy to share with God. I cannot claim to have known either Sally Palmer or Lyn Metcalf. Their lives and this church did not often intersect. That they are tragic victims, however, I have no doubt. But victims of what?'

Now he leaned forward, thrusting his head at us.

'We should all of us, every one, look into our hearts. Christ said, "As ye sow, so shall ye reap." And today we are doing just that. Reaping the fruit not just of the spiritual blight of our society, but of turning a blind eye to it. Evil doesn't cease to exist just because we choose to ignore it. So where should we look to lay the blame?'

He levelled a bony finger and slowly swept it around the packed church.

'At ourselves. We are the ones who have permitted this Serpent to move freely among us. No-one else.

And now we need to pray to God for the strength to cast it from our midst!'

There was an uneasy silence as people tried to digest his words. Scarsdale didn't give them a chance. He lifted his chin and closed his eyes, as the camera flashes cast shifting shadows on his face.

'Let us pray.'

Outside the church there was none of the milling around that normally follows a service. A police trailer had been set up by the village square, and its white, bulky presence seemed both incongruous and intimidating. Despite the attempts of the press and TV cameras, few people felt inclined to provide interviews. This was all still too raw, too private for that. It was one thing watching coverage of other communities that had been struck by tragedy. Being part of one yourself was another matter.

So the journalists' fevered questions were met with a stony response that was no less impenetrable for being polite. With only one or two exceptions, Manham turned its collective back to the eyes of the outside world. Surprisingly, Scarsdale was one of those who allowed himself to be interviewed. He wasn't the sort you would normally expect to have much truck with publicity, but he'd obviously felt it was permissible to sup with the devil, just this once. Given the tone of his sermon, he seemed to regard what had happened as a vindication of his calling. In his jaundiced eyes he had been proved right, and he was going to grasp the moment in both gnarled fists.

Henry and I watched him preaching to soundbite-starved journalists in the churchyard, while behind him excited children scrambled over the Martyr's Stone, trampling the wilted flowers that still decorated it as they hoped to get in shot. His voice, if not his actual words, carried to the green where we waited under the horse chestnut. I'd found Henry there when I'd emerged after the service. He'd given me a skewed smile when I went over.

'Couldn't you get in?' I asked.

'I didn't try. I wanted to show my respects, but I'll be damned if I'm going to pander to Scarsdale's ego. Or listen to his bile. What was it, God's judgement on our sins? We've brought this on ourselves?'

'Something like that,' I admitted.

Henry snorted. 'Just what Manham needs. An invitation to paranoia.'

Standing behind Scarsdale as he continued his impromptu press conference, I noticed that the ranks of his hard-line parishioners had been swelled by new converts. The likes of Lee and Marjory Goodchild and Judith Sutton and her son Rupert had been joined by many less regular church-goers. They looked on like a mute, approving chorus as the reverend raised his voice to drive home his point to the cameras.

Henry shook his head in disgust. 'Look at him. In his element. Man of God? Hah! This is just his chance to say "I told you so".'

'Still, he has a point.'

He gave me a sceptical look. 'Don't tell me you've been converted.'

'Not by Scarsdale. But whoever's behind this must be local. Someone who knows the countryside around here. Knows us.'

'In that case God help us, because if Scarsdale gets his way things are going to get a lot worse before they get any better.'

'What do you mean?'

'You ever seen *The Crucible*? Play by Arthur Miller about the Salem witch-hunts?'

'Only on TV.'

'Well, that's going to be nothing to what goes on in Manham if this carries on much longer.' I thought he was joking, but the look he gave me was entirely serious. 'Keep your head down, David. Even without Scarsdale stirring things up, the mud-slinging and finger-pointing is going to start soon. Make sure you don't walk into any of it.'

'You're not serious?'

'No? I've lived here a lot longer than you have. I know what our good friends and neighbours here are like. The knives are going to be sharpened already.'

'Come on, don't you think that's stretching it a bit?'

'Is it?'

He was watching Scarsdale, who was turning back towards the church having finished whatever he had to say. As the more persistent of the journalists tried to follow, Rupert Sutton stepped to block them with his arms outstretched, a vast barrier of flesh none of them felt inclined to pass.

Henry gave me a meaningful look. 'Something like this brings out the worst in everyone. Manham's a small place. And small places breed small minds. Perhaps I'm being overly pessimistic. But if I were you I'd watch my back all the same.'

He held my gaze for a moment to make sure I'd got the message, then glanced over my shoulder. 'Hello. Friend of yours?'

I turned to find a young woman smiling at me. Dark-haired and plump, I'd seen her around occasionally but didn't know her name. It was only when she moved to one side slightly that I saw she was with Jenny. By contrast, her expression was far from happy.

Ignoring the look Jenny shot her, the other young woman stepped forward. 'Hi. I'm Tina.'

'Pleased to meet you,' I said, wondering what was going on. Jenny gave me a brief smile. She looked flustered.

'Hello, Tina,' Henry said. 'How's your mum?'

'Better, thanks. The swelling's nearly gone now.' She turned to me. There was an unmistakable glint in her eye. 'Thanks for walking Jenny home last night. I share the house with her. Nice to see there's some courtesy left.'

'Uh, it wasn't a problem.'

'I was just saying you'll have to come round some time. For a drink or a meal, or something.'

I glanced at Jenny. Her face was crimson. I felt my own beginning to match it.

'Well . . .'

'How about Friday night?'

'Tina, I'm sure he's got—' Jenny began, but her friend didn't take the hint.

'You're not busy then, are you? We could always make it another night.'

'Uh, no, but—'

'Great! See you at eight o'clock.'

Still grinning, she took Jenny's arm and marched her away. I stared after them.

'What was all that about?' Henry asked.

'No idea.'

He looked amused.

'I haven't!' I insisted.

'Well, you can tell me all about it over Sunday lunch anyway.' The smile left his face as he looked at me, serious again. 'Just remember what I said. Be careful who you trust. And watch your back.'

With that he began to wheel himself away.

10

The music floated through the shadowed room, its off-key notes dancing through the objects hanging from the low ceiling. Moving almost in counterpoint to it, the bead of dark liquid traced a crooked line, gaining momentum as gravity finally claimed it. As it fell it formed a perfect sphere, only for its short-lived symmetry to end as it burst against the ground.

Lyn starred dumbly at the blood as it ran down her arm, dripping off her fingers to spatter onto the floor. It had formed a small but spreading puddle, already beginning to thicken and clot at the edges. The pain from the cut had merged with that from all the others, the hurt from one becoming indistinguishable from the rest. The blood from them smeared her skin in an abstract pattern of cruelty.

She wobbled unsteadily on her feet as the discordant music slowed to a stop. Thankful it had ended, she leaned against the rough stone of the wall for support, becoming aware once again of the bite of the rope tied around her ankle. Her fingertips were torn from the futile hours spent trying to untie it as she lay in darkness. But the knot remained as unyielding now as ever.

She had passed beyond the initial feelings of disbelief and betrayal to a state almost of resignation. There was no pity for her in this dark room, she knew that much. No chance of mercy. Still, she had to try. Shielding her eyes from the harshness of the light focused on her, she tried to see into the shadows where her captor sat and watched.

'Please . . .' Her voice was a parched croak she barely recognized. 'Please, why are you doing this?'

Her question was met by silence, broken only by the sound of his breathing. The smell of burning tobacco hung in the air. There was rustling, an indistinct sound of movement.

Then the music began to play again.

11

Thursday was the day when the chill began to set into Manham. Not a physical chill – the weather remained as hot and arid as ever. But regardless of whether it was an inevitable reaction to recent events or a result of Scarsdale's sermon, the psychological climate of the village seemed to undergo a marked change overnight. Now that it was no longer possible to lay blame for the atrocities on an outsider, the village had little choice but to turn its scrutiny on itself. Suspicion stole in like an airborne virus, not apparent at first, but already carried unknown by the first victims.

Like any contagion, there were those who were more vulnerable than others.

I was unaware of this as I came back from the lab in the early evening. Henry had agreed to cover for me again, waving away my suggestion of bringing in a locum. 'Take as long as you want. Do me good to get my finger out for once,' he'd said.

I drove with the windows full down. Once I was

away from the busiest roads, the air was scented with pollen, a tickling sweetness that overlay the faintly sulphurous scent of drying mud from the reedbeds. It was a welcome counter to the chemical stink of detergent that still seemed to coat the back of my nose and throat. It had been a long day, most of which had been spent working on Sally Palmer's remains. Occasionally I still felt an odd schism if I tried to reconcile my memories of the extrovert, vital woman I'd known with the collection of bones that had been boiled of any last vestiges of flesh. But that wasn't something I wanted to dwell on.

Luckily, there was too much to do for my thoughts to wander.

Unlike skin and flesh, bone retains the impression of anything that cuts into it. In Sally Palmer's case, some of these were little more than scratches, revealing nothing. There were three places, though, where the blade had gone deep enough to leave an ossified record of its passing. Where her back had been cut for the swan wings, the flat bone of both shoulder blades bore matching grooves. About six or seven inches long, each had been made with a single, sweeping stroke. That much was apparent from the way the wounds were shallower at either end than they were in the middle; in both cases the knife had travelled across the scapula in an arc rather than been thrust. Slashed rather than stabbed.

I'd used a tiny electric saw to carefully cut longitudinally along one of the grooves, so it was split down its full length. Marina had hovered curiously nearby as I'd examined the exposed surfaces where the knife had cut through the bone. I motioned her to take a look.

'See how the sides are smooth?' I asked. 'That tells us the knife wasn't serrated.'

She peered at it, frowning. 'How do you know?'

'Because a serrated blade makes a pattern. A bit like when you cut wood with a buzz saw.'

'So these weren't caused by anything like a bread or steak knife.'

'No. It was sharp, though, whatever it was. See how clean and well defined the cuts are? And they're quite deep. Four, five millimetres in the middle.'

'Does that mean it was big?'

'I'd say so. Could be something like a large kitchen or butcher's knife, but I'd guess some sort of hunting knife was more likely. The blades on those tend to be heavier and less flexible. Whatever did this didn't bend or wobble. And the cut itself is quite wide. Meat knives are much thinner.'

A hunting knife also tied in with the killer's obvious woodcraft, though I didn't say that. I'd taken photographs and measurements of both shoulder blades before turning to the third cervical vertebra. This was the section of bone that had sustained most damage, caused when Sally Palmer's throat had been cut. It was a different sort of wound, almost triangular in shape. Stab, not slash. The killer had plunged the knife into her throat point-first, then drawn it across her trachea and carotid artery.

'He's right-handed,' I said.

Marina looked at me.

140

'The depression in the vertebra's deep at the left-hand side, then tapers off to the right. So that's the way he cut.' I pointed at a spot on my own throat and drew my finger across. 'Left to right. Which suggests he's a right-hander.'

'Couldn't it have been done backhanded?'

'That would have made it more of a slash, like on the shoulder blades.'

'From behind, then? You know, to avoid the blood.'

I shook my head. 'Makes no difference. He might have stood behind her to do it, but in that case he'd still reach around, put the knife in, and then pull it back across her throat. Left to right, for a right-hander. If not it would mean pushing the knife rather than pulling it. Too awkward, and it would make a different-shaped mark in the bone.'

She was silent as she went through it in her mind. She gave a nod when she accepted it. 'That's pretty cool.'

No, I thought. Just the sort of thing you pick up when you've seen enough of it.

'Why do you say "he"?' Marina asked, abruptly.

'Sorry?'

'When you're talking about the killer you always talk as if it's a man. But there are no witnesses, and the body's too far gone for us to find any evidence of rape. So I just wondered how you knew.' She shrugged, embarrassed. 'Is it just a figure of speech or have the police found something out?'

I hadn't given it much thought, but she was right. I'd automatically assumed the killer was male.

Everything so far pointed to it – physical strength, female victims. But I was surprised I'd taken something like that for granted.

I smiled. 'Force of habit. It usually is. But no, I don't know for sure.'

She looked at the bones we'd been so clinically examining. 'I think it's a man too. Let's hope they catch the bastard.'

Thinking about what she'd said, I almost missed the final piece of evidence. I'd examined the vertebra under a bright light and low-powered microscope, and it was only as I was about to straighten that I spotted it. A tiny black fleck, lying like rot at the deepest point of the hole carved by the knife. But whatever it was, this was no rot. I carefully scraped it out.

'What's that?' asked Marina.

'No idea.' But I felt a race of excitement. Whatever it was, the only way it could have got there was on the tip of the killer's knife. Perhaps it was nothing.

Perhaps.

I sent it off to the forensic lab for spectroscopic analysis, something I had neither the expertise nor equipment to carry out myself, and started making plaster casts of the knife cuts in the bones. If the weapon that had caused them was ever found, it would be possible to identify it simply by seeing if it fitted – a match every bit as conclusive as Cinderella's slipper.

I was almost done now. It was just a matter of waiting for the lab results, not only on whatever substance I'd just found but for the other tests from the day before. They would give an accurate time-since-death, and once I had that I would be finished. My role in Sally Palmer's death, a far more intimate one than we'd ever shared while she was alive, would be over. I could retreat back to my new life, bury myself away again.

The prospect didn't bring the relief I'd expected. Or perhaps it was that, even then, I knew it wouldn't be as simple as that.

I had just washed and dried my hands when there was a rap on the steel door. Marina went to see who it was, and came back with a young policeman. With a sinking feeling, I eyed the cardboard box he was holding.

'Chief Inspector Mackenzie's sent this.'

He looked for somewhere to put it down. I pointed at the empty stainless-steel table, knowing what would be inside.

'He wants you to carry out tests on it. He says you'll know what he means,' the policeman said. The box didn't look very heavy, but he was still red-faced and breathless from carrying it. Or perhaps he'd just been trying to hold his breath. The smell was already noticeable.

He hurried out as I opened the box. In it, wrapped in plastic, was Sally Palmer's dog. I guessed Mackenzie wanted me to carry out the same analysis on the animal as I had on its owner. If, as seemed likely, it had been killed when she'd been abducted, knowing how long ago it had died would also tell us when its owner had been taken. And how long she had been kept alive. There was no guarantee her killer would do the same for Lyn Metcalf, but it would give some idea of her possible survival window.

It was a good idea. Unfortunately, it wouldn't work. A dog's body chemistry isn't the same as a human's, so any comparative tests would be meaningless. The best I could do was examine the score marks made on its vertebrae. With luck that might show if the same knife had also cut the animal's throat. It was hardly going to change the course of the investigation, but had to be done all the same.

I gave Marina a rueful smile. 'Looks like we'll be working late.'

In the end, though, it hadn't taken as long as I'd expected. The dog was much smaller, which made life easier. I'd taken the X-rays I needed and then put its body to boil in detergent. Tomorrow when I arrived at the lab there would be nothing left but its skeleton to examine. The thought of the remains of both Sally and her dog lying in the same room struck a chord within me, but I wasn't sure if it was a comforting or mournful note.

The low sun lanced off the surface of Manham Water, setting the lake on fire as the road bent and dipped in its approach to the village. Squinting, I pulled my sunglasses down from my forehead. For an instant my vision was obscured by the frame, and then I saw a figure walking towards me on the road edge. I was surprised to see someone so close, but they were back-lit by the blinding sun, and I was almost past before I recognized who it was. I stopped and reversed until my open window was level with her.

'Can I give you a lift home?'

Linda Yates looked up and down the empty road as if considering the question before answering. 'I'm not going your way.'

'Doesn't matter. It'll only take a few minutes. Hop in.'

I leaned across and pushed the door open. When she still hesitated I said, 'It's not far out of my way. I've been meaning to check on Sam anyway.'

The mention of her son's name seemed to decide her. She climbed in. I remember noticing how she sat close to the door, but at the time I didn't think anything of it.

'How's he been?' I asked.

'Better.'

'Has he gone back to school?'

She raised a shoulder. 'Doesn't seem much point. They finish tomorrow.'

That was right. I'd lost track of time, forgotten the school was about to break up for the long summer holiday. 'How about Neil?'

For the first time something like a smile came and went. But it was a bitter one. 'Oh, he's fine. He's like his dad.'

There were domestic undercurrents there it was best to avoid. 'Have you been at work?' I asked. I knew she sometimes cleaned for a couple of the village shops.

'We needed some things from the supermarket.' She lifted the plastic bag she'd been carrying as if to prove it.

'Bit late to go shopping, isn't it?'

145

She glanced at me. By now there was no mistaking her nervousness. 'Somebody's got to do it.'

'Couldn't . . .' I searched for her husband's name. 'Couldn't Gary take you?'

She shrugged. It obviously wasn't an option.

'I don't know that walking home alone is a good idea right now.'

Again, that quick, nervous look. She seemed to press herself up against the door even more.

'Everything all right?' I asked, but I was beginning to see that it wasn't.

'Fine.'

'You seem a bit on edge.'

'Just . . . be glad to be home, that's all.'

She was gripping the edge of the door, where the window was open. She seemed ready to fling herself out of it. 'Come on, Linda, what's wrong?'

'Nothing.' It came out too quickly. And now, belatedly, I began to understand what it was.

She was scared. Of me.

'If you'd rather I stopped so you can walk the rest of the way, just say,' I told her, cautiously.

I could tell from the way she looked at me that I'd been right. I thought back, realized with hindsight how reluctant she'd been to get into the car. But it wasn't as if I was a stranger, for God's sake. I'd been the family's doctor since I arrived, seen Sam through mumps and chickenpox, Neil through a broken arm. It was only a few days earlier that I'd been in her kitchen, when her boys had made the gruesome discovery that had started all this. *What the hell's going on?*

After a moment, she shook her head. 'No. It's all right.' Some of the tension had left her, though not all of it.

'I don't blame you for being wary. I just thought I was doing you a favour.'

'You are, it's just . . .'

'Go on.'

'It's nothing. Only talk.'

Until then I'd been putting her reaction down to a general anxiety, an indiscriminate mistrust in the face of what was happening in the village. Now my own unease began to grow as I began to understand it was something more.

'What sort of talk?'

'There's a rumour going round . . . That you'd been arrested.'

I hadn't known what to expect, but it certainly wasn't that.

'I'm sorry,' she said, as though I might blame her for it. 'It's just stupid gossip.'

'Why the hell would anyone think that?' I asked, stunned.

She was fretting at her hands now, no longer afraid of me, only of having to tell me this: 'You've not been at the surgery. People are saying that the police came to see you, that you'd been driven away with that inspector. The one in charge.'

It was becoming all too clear now. In lieu of any real news, rumour had rushed in to fill the vacuum. And by agreeing to help Mackenzie I'd inadvertently made myself a target. It was so absurd I could have laughed. Except it wasn't funny.

147

I realized I was about to drive past Linda's house. I pulled up, still too stunned to speak.

'I'm sorry,' she said again. 'I just thought . . .' She didn't finish.

I tried to think of what I could say that wouldn't involve dredging up my entire past for the village to examine. 'I've been helping the police. Working with them, I mean. I used to be . . . a sort of specialist. Before I came here.'

She was listening, but I wasn't sure how much sense this was making to her. Still, at least she didn't look as though she wanted to throw herself out of the car any more.

'They wanted my advice,' I went on. 'That's why I haven't been in the surgery.'

I couldn't think of anything else to say. After a moment she looked away. 'It's this place. This village.' She sounded weary. She opened the door.

'I'd still like to look in on Sam,' I said.

She gave a nod. Still shaken, I followed her up the path. Inside, the house seemed misty and dim after the brightness of the evening. The TV was playing in the lounge, a cacophony of sound and colour. Her husband and youngest son were watching it, the man slumped in a chair, the boy lying on his stomach in front of the set. They both looked around when we entered. Gary Yates turned to his wife, silently demanding an explanation.

'Dr Hunter gave me a lift home,' she said, setting down her shopping bags, moving around too quickly. 'He wanted to see how Sam was.'

Yates seemed unsure of how to react. He was a

wiry man in his early thirties, with the pinched, feral look of a tinker about him. He slowly stood up, hands held uncertainly. He decided not to offer them, stuffed them into his pockets instead.

'Didn't know you were planning to call,' he said.

'I didn't know myself. But given what's happened I couldn't let Linda walk home by herself.'

He flushed and looked away. I told myself to ease up. Any points I scored against him would only be extracted from his wife's account after I'd gone.

I smiled at Sam, who'd been watching from the floor. The fact that he was inside on a summer evening like this said he wasn't fully himself, but he seemed better than the last time I'd seen him. When I asked him what he would do during the school holidays he even smiled at one point, showing some of his old animation.

'I think he's doing OK,' I told Linda in the kitchen afterwards. 'He'll probably bounce back soon enough now he's over the initial shock.'

She nodded, but distractedly. She was still ill at ease. 'About earlier . . .' she began.

'Forget it. I'm glad you told me.'

It had never occurred to me that people might get the wrong impression. But perhaps it should have. Only the night before Henry had warned me to be careful. I'd thought he was overreacting, but he obviously knew the village better than I did. It rankled, not so much because of my misjudgement, but because a community I'd considered myself a part of was so readily prepared to think the worst.

I should have known even then that the worst can always surpass expectations.

I glanced over my shoulder to make sure the door to the lounge was shut. There was a question I'd been waiting to ask since I'd stopped to give Linda a lift.

'On Sunday, after Neil and Sam found the body,' I began, 'you said you knew it was Sally Palmer, because you'd dreamed about her.'

She busied herself at the sink, rinsing cups. 'Just coincidence, I expect.'

'That wasn't what you said then.'

'I was upset. I shouldn't have said anything.'

'I'm not trying to trick you out. I just . . .' Just what? I was no longer sure what I was hoping to prove. I ploughed on anyway. 'I wondered if you'd had any more dreams. About Lyn Metcalf.'

She stopped what she was doing. 'I wouldn't have thought somebody like you would have much time for that sort of thing.'

'I was just curious.'

The look she gave me was speculative. Piercing. I felt myself grow uncomfortable under it. Then she gave a quick shake of her head. 'No,' she said. And then she added something so quietly I almost missed it.

I would have asked her more, but at that moment the door opened. Gary Yates regarded us with suspicion.

'I thought you'd gone.'

'I'm just going,' I said.

He went to the fridge, opened its rust-edged door.

150

A skewed fridge magnet on it said 'Start the day with a smile'. It showed a grinning crocodile. He took out a can of beer and opened it. As if I wasn't there he took a long pull, giving a stifled belch as he lowered the can.

'Bye, then,' I said to Linda. She bobbed her head, nervously.

Her husband watched through the window as I went back to the Land Rover. As I drove into the village I thought about what Linda Yates had said. After she'd denied dreaming about Lyn Metcalf, she'd added something else. Just two words, barely loud enough for me to hear.

Not yet.

Ridiculous as the rumours about me were, I couldn't afford to ignore them. It was better to meet them head on than let the whispers get out of hand, but I still felt an unaccustomed apprehension as I headed for the Lamb. The garlands on the Martyr's Stone were limp and dying now. I hoped it wasn't an omen as I drove by the police trailer parked by the village square. Two bored-looking policemen sat outside it in the evening sunshine. They stared incuriously at me as I passed. I parked outside the pub, took a deep breath and pushed open the doors.

When I stepped inside my first thought was that Linda Yates had exaggerated. People glanced my way, but there were the usual nods and acknowledgements. A little subdued, perhaps, but that was only to be expected. No-one was going to be laughing and joking around here for a while yet.

I went to the bar and ordered a beer. Ben Anders was on his mobile in the corner. He held up his hand in greeting before going on with his conversation. Jack pulled my drink as contemplatively as ever, placidly watching the golden liquid chase the suds up the glass. Henry's warning the previous night had been misplaced, I thought with relief. People knew me better than that.

Then someone further along the bar cleared his throat. 'Been away?'

It was Carl Brenner. And as I turned to him I realized that the room had gone quiet.

Henry had been right after all, I realized.

'Hear you've not been around much the last couple of days,' Brenner went on. He had a jaundiced, heavy-lidded look about him that told me he was in his cups.

'Not much, no.'

'How come?'

'There were some things I needed to do.' As much as I wanted to end the rumours about me, I wasn't going to be bullied into anything. Or give the village tongues even more to wag about.

'That's not what I heard.' There was a yellow anger burning in his eyes, waiting only for a target. 'I heard you were with the police.'

The pub seemed very quiet now. 'That's right.'

'So what did they want?'

'Just advice.'

'Advice?' He made no attempt to hide his disbelief. 'About what?'

'You'll have to ask them that.'

'I'm asking you.'

His anger had found its focus now. I looked away from it, around the room. Some people were staring into their drinks. Others stared back at me. Not yet condemning, but waiting.

'If someone's got something to say, say it,' I said, as calmly as I was able. I held their gazes until, one by one, the faces turned away.

'All right, if nobody else is going to, I will.' Carl Brenner had risen to his feet. He aggressively swigged what was left in his glass and banged it down. 'You've been—'

'I'd be careful if I were you.'

Ben Anders had materialized beside me. I was pleased to see him, not just because of his reassuring physical presence, but because it was a welcome sign of support.

'Stay out of this,' Brenner said.

'Stay out of what? Just trying to stop you from saying something you'll regret tomorrow.'

'I won't regret anything.'

'Good. How's Scott?'

The question took away some of Brenner's bluster. 'What?'

'Your brother. How's his leg? The one Dr Hunter fixed up the other night.'

Brenner fidgeted, sullen but deflated. 'It's all right.'

'Good thing the doc here doesn't charge for out-of-surgery hours,' Ben said, affably. His gaze took in the rest of the room. 'I daresay most of us have had cause to be grateful for that some time or another.'

He let his words hang, then clapped his hands

together and turned to the bar. 'Anyway, when you've got a minute, Jack, I'll have another.'

It was as though someone had suddenly opened a window to let in a clean breeze. The atmosphere cleared as people stirred, some of them looking slightly shamefaced as they went back to their conversations. I became aware of sweat damping the small of my back. It had nothing to do with the heat in the airless bar.

'Would you like a whisky?' Ben asked. 'You look as though you could use one.'

'No thanks. But I'll get yours.'

'No need.'

'It's the least I can do.'

'Forget it. The bastards just needed reminding of a few things.' He glanced across at where Brenner was staring moodily into his empty glass. 'And that bastard needs someone to give him a sorting. I'm pretty certain he's been milking nests at the reserve. Endangered ones. Normally once the eggs have hatched we're OK, but we've been losing adult birds as well. Marsh harriers, even bitterns. I haven't caught him yet, but one of these days . . .'

He smiled as Jack set his pint down. 'Good man.' He took a long drink and gave an appreciative sigh. 'So what have you been doing?' He gave me a sidelong glance. 'Don't worry, I'm just curious. But it's obvious something's been taking you away from here.'

I hesitated, but he'd earned some sort of explanation. Without going into too many details, I told him.

'Jesus,' he said.

'Now you see why I don't talk about it. Or didn't,' I added.

'You sure you wouldn't just rather tell people? Get it out in the open?'

'I don't think so.'

'I can spread the word, if you like. Put it about what you've been doing.'

I could see the sense in that. But it still went against the grain. I never used to talk about my work, and old habits died hard. Perhaps I was just being stubborn, but the dead had rights to privacy just as much as the living. Once word got out what I'd been doing there would be no end to the morbid curiosity. And I was far from sure how Manham would feel about its doctor's unorthodox activities. I was well aware that my two vocations might not sit comfortably with each other in some people's eyes.

'No thanks,' I told him.

'Your choice. But there's still going to be talk.'

Although I knew as much, my stomach still sank. Ben gave a shrug.

'They're scared. They know the killer must live around here. But they'd still rather it be an outsider.'

'I'm not an outsider. I've been here for three years.' It rang false even as I said it. I might live and work in Manham, but I couldn't claim to belong. I'd just had proof of that.

'Doesn't matter. You could live here for thirty, you're still from a city. Push comes to shove, people look at you and think "foreigner".'

'In that case it won't matter what I say, will it? But I don't think everyone's that bad.'

155

'No, not everyone. But it only takes a few.' He looked solemn. 'Let's just hope they catch the bastard soon.'

I didn't stay long after that. The beer tasted sour and stale, though I knew it was as well kept as ever. There was still a numbness when I thought about what had happened, like the deadened moment before the pain sweeps in from a wound. I wanted to be in my own house when it finally caught up with me.

As I drove from the pub I saw Scarsdale leaving the church. Perhaps it was my imagination, but he seemed to be striding taller than before. Out of everyone, he was the only person who was flourishing from the events that had overtaken the village. *Nothing like tragedy and fear to make a man of the cloth the man of the moment*, I thought, and straight away felt ashamed. He was only doing his job, the same as me. I shouldn't let my dislike of him colour my thinking. God knew, I should have had enough of prejudice for one night.

A guilty conscience made me raise a hand in acknowledgement as I approached. He looked directly back at me, and for a moment I thought he wasn't going to deign to respond. Then he gave his head a short downward tilt.

I couldn't shake the feeling that he knew what I was thinking.

12

By Friday the press had started to drift away. The lack of any developments meant Manham was already losing its hold on the media's fickle interest. If something else happened they would be back. Until then Sally Palmer and Lyn Metcalf would steadily diminish in airtime and column inches, until their names faded altogether from the public consciousness.

As I drove into the lab that morning, though, my thoughts weren't on the fading media presence or, I'm ashamed to say, the two victims. Even the shock of finding myself regarded with suspicion in the village had been temporarily displaced. No, what fretted away at me was something far more trivial.

Dinner at Jenny Hammond's house that evening.

I told myself it was no big thing. That she, or rather her friend Tina, was just being friendly. When I'd lived in London a dinner invitation had been simply polite currency, offered and accepted without much thought. This was no different, I told myself.

It didn't work.

I wasn't in London now. My social life had become reduced to bland conversations with patients or a beer in the pub. And what were we going to talk about? There was only one subject in the village at the moment, and that would hardly make for light dinner-table chat between strangers. Especially not if they'd also heard the rumours about me. I wished I'd had the presence of mind to say no when the offer was made. I even considered calling with some excuse, offering my apologies.

But, as much as the thought of the meal unsettled me, I didn't make the call. Which was almost as unsettling in itself. Because, underneath it all, I was uncomfortably aware of why I was really so nervous. It was the thought of seeing Jenny again. It stirred up a complex silt of emotions I'd rather have left settled. Right up there among them was guilt.

It felt like I was preparing to be unfaithful.

Of course, I realized how ridiculous that was. I was only going for a meal, and since a drunken businessman had lost control of his BMW that afternoon almost four years ago, I was all too aware that there was no-one for me to be unfaithful to.

But again, that made no difference.

So as I parked the car and took the lift to the laboratory, I wasn't exactly focused. I tried to pull my thoughts together as I pushed open the steel door to the mortuary lab and went in. Marina was there already. The door was still swinging shut behind me when she spoke.

'The results are back.'

Mackenzie frowned down at the report I'd given him. 'You're sure?'

'Pretty much. The tests confirm that Sally Palmer had been dead for around nine days when her body was found.'

We were in the lab's small office. I'd offered to email the results, but when I'd called him he'd said he'd call around instead.

'How reliable is that?' he asked now.

'The amino acid analysis is accurate to twelve hours either way, which is as close as you're going to get. I can't tell you the exact time she was killed, but it was some time between noon on the Friday and Saturday.'

'You can't narrow it down any more than that?'

I resisted the urge to snap. I'd spent all morning working out the time-since-death equations. It was a complicated business, factoring in the test results with the average temperature and other weather data for the days that Sally Palmer's body had lain outside. Life's biggest mystery reduced to a banal mathematical formula.

'Sorry. But taking into account everything else, the maggots and so on, I'd put it pretty well in the middle of that range.'

'Call it midnight Friday, then. And she was last seen three days before that at the barbecue.' Mackenzie frowned at the implications. 'There's no way you can be as specific for the dog?'

'A dog's body chemistry is different to a human's. I could run the analysis but it wouldn't tell us anything.'

'Shit,' he muttered. 'But you still think it was dead longer than that?'

I shrugged. All I had to go on was the condition of the dog's body and the insect activity around it, and that was hardly an exact science. 'Pretty sure, but like I say, the same rules don't necessarily apply to dogs. But two or three days more, at least.'

Mackenzie pulled at his lip. I knew what he was thinking. This was the third day since Lyn Metcalf had disappeared. Even if the killer followed the same pattern as before and was holding her somewhere, we were entering the endgame now. Whatever warped agenda he was following, if it hadn't already run its course it soon would.

Unless she was found first.

'We've also got the analysis on the substance that was in one of the knife marks on Sally Palmer's vertebra,' I told Mackenzie. I read from my own copy of the report. 'It's a hydrocarbon. Fairly complex, but around eighty per cent carbon, ten per cent hydrogen, with small amounts of sulphur, oxygen, nitrogen and a few trace metals.'

'Meaning?'

'Bitumen. Common-or-garden bitumen. The sort of stuff you can buy in any hardware or DIY store.'

'Well, that narrows it down.'

Something flickered faintly in the back of my mind, a synaptic connection sparked by something that had just been said. I reached for it but it remained elusive.

'Anything else?' Mackenzie asked, and whatever almost-thought I'd had had slipped away.

'Not really. I've still got to examine the knife marks on the dog's spine. With luck that'll confirm that the same weapon killed them both. Then I'll be finished.'

Mackenzie looked as though he'd expected as much but hoped for more.

'How about your end? Any more developments?' I asked.

I could see the answer from the way Mackenzie's face closed down. 'We're following up a few leads,' he said, stiffly.

I said nothing. After a moment he sighed.

'We've got no suspect, no witnesses and no motive. So, "no" is the short answer. Door-to-door inquiries haven't turned up anything, and even though we've restarted the search we're still having to go slow to check for traps. And it's going to be impossible to cover an area like this. Half of it's like a bloody swamp, and then there's Christ knows how many bloody woods and ditches.'

He shook his head, frustration getting the better of him again. 'If he's decided to hide her body properly we might never find her.'

'You think she's dead, then.'

The look he gave me was jaded. 'You've been involved with enough murder investigations. How often do we get them back alive?'

'It happens.'

'Yeah, it happens,' he conceded. 'But so does winning the lottery. Frankly, I'd give better odds on that than Lyn Metcalf surviving. Nobody's seen anything, nobody knows anything. Forensic didn't find any useful evidence either where she was snatched or where we found Sally Palmer's body. Nothing's been flagged when we checked criminal records or the Sex Offenders Register. All we've got to go on is that the suspect must be reasonably strong and fit and knows a bit about woodcraft and hunting.'

'Doesn't narrow it down much, does it?'

He gave a sour laugh. 'Not much. It might if this was Milton Keynes, but a country community like this, hunting's a way of life. People don't even notice it. No, whoever he is, so far our boy's been able to stay under the radar.'

'What about profiling?'

'Same problem. We just don't have enough to go on. The only profile the psychologists can come up with is so vague it's useless. We're dealing with an outdoor type who's physically fit and reasonably intelligent, but still reckless or careless enough to have left Sally Palmer's body where it could be found. That could apply to half the men in the village. Extend that to neighbouring villages as well and you're looking at two or three hundred potential suspects.'

He sounded depressed. I couldn't blame him. I was no expert, but I knew from experience that most serial killers were found either by luck or because they made some glaring mistake. They're chameleons, apparently ordinary members of society who hide in plain view. When they're finally exposed the first reaction of friends and neighbours is always disbelief. Only with hindsight are the jagged, saw-toothed edges that have been there all along finally recognized. Regardless of what atrocities they've committed, the single most shocking thing about our real-life monsters is how normal they seem.

Just like you and me.

Mackenzie scratched at the mole on his neck. He stopped when he caught me watching. 'There's one thing that's come up that might be important,' he said, with a casualness that wasn't entirely convincing. 'One witness who spoke to Sally Palmer at the barbecue says she was annoyed because someone had left a dead stoat on her doorstep. She thought it was a sick idea of a joke.'

I thought about the swan wings that had been with Sally Palmer's body, and the mallard tied to the stone on the morning Lyn Metcalf had disappeared. 'You think the killer left it there?'

He shrugged. 'Could have been kids. Or it might have been some sort of marker or warning. Staking a claim, sort of thing. We already know he uses birds as a signature. There's nothing to say he might not use animals as well.'

'What about Lyn Metcalf? Did she find anything like that?'

'She mentioned to her husband about finding a dead hare in the woods the day before she disappeared. But it could just as easily have been killed by a dog or fox. There's no way of knowing now.'

He was right, but I still wondered. Coincidences happen, in murders as in every other facet of life. But given the way the killer had behaved so far, it didn't seem impossible that he was confident enough to have marked out his victims in advance.

'So you don't think there's anything to it?' I asked.
'That's not what I said,' he snapped. 'But at this
stage there's not a lot we can do. We're already looking for anyone with a record of animal cruelty. A
couple of people can remember a spate of cats being
killed about ten, fifteen years ago, but no-one was
ever caught, and— What?'

I'd started shaking my head. 'You said yourself,
this isn't like a town or city. Attitudes are different
here. I'm not saying people are deliberately cruel, but
you don't get much sentiment, either.'

'Meaning no-one would notice a few dead
animals,' he said, flatly.

'If someone set fire to a dog on the village green
there'd probably be a reaction. But this is the
countryside. Animals are killed all the time.'

He reluctantly accepted what I'd said. 'Let me
know what you find out from the dog,' he said,
getting to his feet. 'Anything important you can get
me on my mobile.'

'Before you go,' I said, 'there's something else you
should know.'

I told him about the rumour circulating in the
village that I'd been arrested. 'For God's sake,' he
sighed, when I'd finished. 'Is it going to be a
problem?'

'I don't know. I hope not. But people are getting
twitchy. When they see you coming to the surgery
they're liable to jump to conclusions. I don't want to
have to keep explaining myself.'

'Point taken.'

He didn't seem too worried, though. Or surprised,

come to that. After he'd gone it crossed my mind that he might have been expecting something like this to happen, that it might suit him if I became some sort of stalking horse. I told myself that was ridiculous. But the thought persisted as I went back to my examination of the dog's skeleton.

I worked automatically as I prepared and photographed the score mark where the knife had cut into a cervical vertebra. It was routine stuff, worthwhile only from a plodding, evidentiary point of view rather than any real prospect of finding something worthwhile. As I positioned the vertebra under a low-powered microscope to study it in more detail I already knew what to expect. I was still looking at it when Marina arrived with a cup of coffee.

'Anything interesting?' she asked.

I moved to one side. 'See for yourself.'

She bent over the microscope. After a moment she adjusted the focus. When she straightened she looked puzzled.

'I don't understand.'

'Why not?'

'The cut's rough, not smooth like the other one. The knife's left ridges in the bone. You said only a serrated blade made a pattern like that.'

'That's right.'

'But that doesn't make sense. The cut in the woman's vertebra was smooth. Why isn't this one the same?'

'It's pretty straightforward,' I said. 'It was made by a different knife.'

165

13

The meat was still pale. Beads of fat clung to it like sweat, dripping through the mesh to splash hissing on the hot coals below. Thin curls of smoke drifted lazily up from them, scenting the air with a pungent blue haze.

Tina frowned as she poked at one of the uncooked burgers lying on the barbecue. 'I told you, it's not hot enough.'

'Give it a bit longer,' Jenny said.

'If we give it much longer it'll have gone off. It needs to be hotter.'

'You're not putting any more fluid on.'

'Why? We'll be here all night at this rate.'

'I don't care. That stuff's lethal.'

'Come on, I'm ravenous!'

We were in the back garden of the tiny cottage the two of them shared. It was little more than a yard, really, an untidy scrap of lawn enclosed on two sides by a large paddock. But it was private, overlooked by only the bedroom windows of the house next door, and there was an uninterrupted view of the lake that lay a mere hundred yards away.

Tina gave the burgers one last prod and turned to me. 'What do you think? As a doctor, should we risk poisoning ourselves with barbecue fluid or starving to death?'

'Compromise,' I suggested. 'Take the burgers off while you put the fluid on. They won't pick up the taste that way.'

'God, I love a man who's practical,' Tina said, using a cloth to pick up the wire tray from the coals.

I took another drink from my beer bottle, more to give myself something to do than out of thirst. My offer of help had been turned down – no bad thing, probably, given the level of my cooking skills. But that also left me with nothing to do, and with nothing to take my mind off my nervousness. Jenny seemed equally ill at ease, spending more time over arranging the bread and salads on the white plastic picnic table than was really necessary. She looked tanned and slim in a white vest and denim shorts. Apart from saying hello when I'd arrived, we'd barely spoken a word to each other. In fact, if not for Tina, I doubted there would have been anything said at all.

Luckily, Tina wasn't the sort to leave any uncomfortable gaps in conversation. She'd kept up an almost incessant buzz of talk, a cheerful monologue interspaced with instructions for me to make myself useful by making the salad dressing, fetching the kitchen roll that would double as napkins, and opening more beers for the three of us.

That there would just be the three of us was very obvious. I swung between relief that I wouldn't have to face anyone else, and regret that I couldn't take refuge in numbers.

Tina liberally squirted lighter fluid onto the barbecue. 'Shit!' she yelped, jumping back as the coals billowed into flame.

'I told you not to put any more on!' Jenny laughed.

'Don't blame me, it came out in a rush!'

The barbecue was wreathed in smoke. 'Well, it's hot enough now,' I commented, as the heat from it made us all move away.

Tina whacked me on the arm. 'For that you can get some more beers.'

'Don't you think we should move the food first?' I said.

The smoke had engulfed the plastic picnic table, where the salads were uncovered.

'Oh, bollocks!' Tina darted into the cloud to make a grab for the dishes.

'Be easier if we just moved the whole thing,' I said, starting to drag the table.

'Give him a hand, Jen, I've got my hands full,' Tina said, holding up a bowl of pasta.

Jenny gave her a wry look but said nothing as she took hold of the opposite side of the table. Together we half-dragged, half-carried it out of range of the smoke. As we stopped the table legs at her side gave way. The table lurched, sending dishes and glasses careering towards the edge.

'Watch it!' Tina yelled.

I lunged and managed to right it before anything

fell off. My hand was against Jenny's as I took its weight.

'I've got it if you want to let go,' I said.

She started to lower her side, but quickly took hold of it again when it started to wobble.

'I thought you'd fixed this,' she said, as Tina hurried over.

'I did! I stuck some paper in where the legs were loose.'

'Paper? It needed screwing properly!'

'It's not the only thing around here.'

'*Tina*,' Jenny said, blushing, but she was trying not to laugh.

'Watch it, watch the table!' Tina warned as it began to rock again.

'Don't just stand there, go and get a screwdriver or something!'

Tina hurried through the curtain of glass beads that hung across the kitchen doorway. Left holding the table, we smiled at each other, self-consciously. But the ice had been broken.

'Bet you're glad you came,' Jenny said.

'It's a first, anyway.'

'Yeah. Not everywhere's this sophisticated.'

'No, I can tell that.'

I saw her eyes flick downwards. 'Uh, I don't know how to tell you this. But you're getting wet.'

I looked down to see that a bottle had fallen over on the table, spilling beer that was now soaking into the crotch of my jeans. I tried to move out of its way, but all that accomplished was to let it drip down onto my legs instead.

'Oh, God, I don't believe this,' Jenny said, and then we were both laughing helplessly. We hadn't stopped when Tina came back with a screwdriver.

'What's up with you two?' she asked, then saw the wet patch on my trousers. 'Should I come back later?'

Once the table had been repaired a pair of baggy shorts was produced for me. They'd belonged to an ex-boyfriend of Tina's, she said. 'But you can keep them. He won't be asking for them back,' she added, grimly.

Looking at the loud pattern on them, I wasn't surprised. But they were better than my beer-soaked jeans, so I changed into them. When I went back into the garden both Tina and Jenny started giggling.

'Nice legs,' Tina commented, setting them off again.

The burgers were sizzling over the hot coals now. We ate them with salad and bread and the bottle of wine I'd taken. When I went to top up Jenny's glass she hesitated.

'Just a little.'

Tina raised her eyebrows. 'You sure?'

Jenny nodded. 'I'm fine, really.' She saw my querying look and pulled a face. 'I'm diabetic, so I have to watch what I eat and drink.'

'Type one or two?' I asked.

'God, I keep forgetting you're a doctor. Type one.' I'd expected as much. That was the most common diabetes for anyone her age. 'But it's not bad. I'm only on a low insulin dose. I saw Dr Maitland about getting it on prescription when I first moved here,' she added, apologetically.

I guessed she was embarrassed at seeing the 'proper' doctor instead of me. She needn't have worried. I was used to it.

Tina gave an exaggerated shudder. 'I'd pass out if I had to inject myself every day like she does.'

'Oh, come on, it's not that bad,' Jenny protested. 'It's not even a proper needle, only one of those pen-things. And stop going on about it. You'll make David feel embarrassed to have more wine.'

'God forbid!' Tina declared. 'I need somebody round here to keep up with me!'

I didn't keep up with her, but at Jenny's insistence I let my glass be refilled more often than I'd planned. The next day was Saturday, and it had been a long week. Besides which, I was having a good time. I couldn't remember enjoying myself as much in . . .

In a long time.

The only dampening of the mood came after we'd eaten. Dusk had settled, and in the fading light Jenny sat staring across the garden towards the lake. I saw her face cloud, and guessed what she was going to say before she said it.

'I keep forgetting what's happened. Makes you feel . . . well, a bit guilty, doesn't it?'

Tina sighed. 'She wanted to cancel tonight. Thought we might upset people by having a barbecue.'

'I thought it seemed disrespectful,' Jenny said to me.

'Why?' Tina demanded. 'Are you telling me other people won't be watching TV or having a beer in the pub? It's very sad and scary and all that, but I don't see that we need to wear hair shirts to show sympathy.'

'You know what I mean.'

'Yes, but I know what people round here are like. If they decide to get the knives out for somebody they will, regardless of what they have or haven't done.' Tina paused. 'All right, that wasn't the best way of putting it, but it's true.' She looked pointedly at me. 'You've just found that out, haven't you?'

I realized then that they must have heard the rumours. 'Tina,' Jenny said, warningly.

'Well, it's no good pretending we haven't heard. I mean, of course the police are going to want to talk to the local doctor, but all it takes is one person to raise an eyebrow and suddenly everyone's got you convicted. It's just another example of how small-minded people are around here.'

'And big-mouthed,' Jenny flared. It was the first sign of temper I'd seen from her.

Tina shrugged it off. 'Better to get it out in the open. There's too much whispering goes on in this place as it is. I grew up here, you didn't.'

'Sounds like you don't like Manham very much,' I said, hoping to change the subject.

She gave a thin smile. 'Given the chance, I'd be out of here like a shot. I can't understand people like you two, who come here from choice.'

There was a sudden silence. Jenny stood up, white-faced. 'I'll make some coffee.' She went into the house, causing the bead curtain to swing crazily.

'Shit,' Tina said. She gave an apologetic smile.

172

'Big-mouthed, like she says. And a bit drunk,' she added, putting down her wine.

I'd thought at first that the awkwardness was on my behalf, but I saw now it wasn't. Whatever the reason for Jenny's reaction, it was nothing to do with me.

'Is she all right?'

'Just pissed off by her tactless housemate, I imagine.' She stared into the house as if considering going after her. 'Look, it isn't for me to say anything, but just so you know, she had a bad experience a year or so ago. That's why she came here, to sort of get away from it.'

'What sort of bad experience?'

Tina was already shaking her head. 'If she wants to tell you, she will. I probably shouldn't have said anything. I just . . . well, I thought you should know. Jenny likes you, so . . . Oh, God, I'm making a mess of this, aren't I? Can we forget I said anything? Let's talk about something else.'

'OK.' Still distracted by what she'd just told me, I said the first thing that came to mind. 'So what rumours did you hear about me?'

Tina pulled a face. 'I asked for that, didn't I? Nothing really, just gossip. That you'd been questioned by the police, and that . . . well, that you were a suspect.' She gave a grin that was meant to be cocky, but didn't quite make it. 'You're not, are you?'

'Not as far as I know.'

It was enough for her. 'That's what I mean about this bloody village. People are ready to think the worst at the best of times. When something like this happens . . .' She waved her hand. 'There I go again. Tell you what, I'll go and help with the coffee.'

'Can I do anything?'

She was already heading inside. 'It's all right. I'll send Jen out to keep you company.'

I sat in the night silence when she'd gone, thinking about what Tina had said. *Jenny likes you.* What was that supposed to mean? More to the point, how did I feel about it? I told myself it had been the drink talking, that I shouldn't read too much into it.

So why did I feel so nervous all of a sudden?

I got up and went to the low stone wall that bordered the garden. The last of the light had gone now, and the fields were lost in blackness. The faintest breath of breeze came off the lake, carrying the desolate cry of an owl.

There was a noise behind me. Jenny had come back outside, carrying two mugs. I stepped away from the wall, back into the pool of light thrown from the open door. She gave a start as I emerged from the shadows, slopping coffee onto her hands.

'Sorry, I didn't mean to make you jump.'

'It's all right. I just didn't see you.' She put the mugs down and blew on her hand.

I gave her a piece of kitchen roll. 'You OK?'

'I'll live.' She wiped her hands.

'Where's Tina?'

'Sobering up.' She picked up the mugs again. 'I didn't ask if you took milk and sugar.'

'No to both.'

She smiled. 'Good guess.' She handed me a coffee and moved towards the wall. 'Admiring the view?'

'What I can see of it.'

'It's great if you like fields and water.'

'And do you?'

We stood side by side, looking towards the lake. 'Yeah, I do actually. I used to go sailing with my dad when I was a girl.'

'Do you still go?'

'Not for years. I still like being by water, though. I keep thinking I should hire a boat some time. Just a small one. I know the lake's too shallow for anything very big. But it seems a waste living this close and not going out on it.'

'I've got a dinghy, if that's any good.'

I said it without thinking. But she turned to me, eagerly. I could see her smiling in the moonlight. I became aware of how close we were standing. Close enough to feel the warmth of her bare skin.

'Really?'

'It's not mine, exactly. It belongs to Henry. But he lets me use it.'

'Are you sure? I mean, I wasn't dropping hints or anything.'

'I know. Anyway, I could do with the exercise.'

I felt something like astonishment as I said it. *What are you doing?* I looked out at the lake, glad that the darkness hid my face.

'How about this Sunday?' I heard myself say.

'That'd be great! What time?'

I remembered I'd said I'd have lunch with Henry. 'Make it the afternoon? I'll pick you up about three?'

'Three o'clock's fine.'

I could hear the smile in her voice even though I wasn't looking at her. I busied myself taking a drink of my coffee, barely noticing as it burned my mouth. I couldn't believe what I'd just done. *Tina's not the only one who needs to sober up*, I thought.

I made my excuses and left not long afterwards. Tina made a belated appearance as I was going, grinning as she told me I could let her have the shorts back later. I thanked her but changed back into my damp jeans. My reputation in the village had suffered enough without walking back through it in a pair of lurid surf shorts.

I hadn't gone far from the house when my mobile phone gave a short beep to let me know there was a message. I always carried the phone with me so I could be contacted in an emergency, but when I'd taken off my wet jeans I'd left it in the pocket. I'd forgotten all about it, and the realization that I'd been out of touch for over two hours finally roused me from my preoccupation with Jenny. Guiltily, I called my answer service, hoping I hadn't missed anything serious.

But the message wasn't about any of my patients. It was from Mackenzie.

They'd found a body.

14

The floodlights cast a ghostly brightness onto the area. The surrounding trees were transformed into a surreal landscape of light and dark. In the centre of it the team of crime scene officers went about their business. A rectangular section of ground had been marked out with a gridwork of nylon string, and to the background hum of a generator they painstakingly scraped away at the earth, slowly revealing more of what lay hidden beneath.

Mackenzie stood nearby, crunching on a mint as he watched. The policeman looked tired and drawn, the floodlights leaching the colour from his face and accentuating the shadows under his eyes.

'We found the grave this afternoon. It's only shallow, about two or three feet deep. We thought it might be a false alarm at first, some animal or a badger set. Till we exposed the hand.'

The site was in a wood, about two miles from where Sally Palmer's body had been found. The forensics team had cleared away most of the top layer of earth by the time I arrived, just after midnight. I watched one of the officers sifting soil through a sieve. She paused to examine something, then discarded it and continued.

'How did you find it?' I asked Mackenzie.

'Sniffer dog.'

I nodded. It wasn't only drugs and explosives that the police used specially trained dogs to find. Locating a grave was rarely easy, and the larger the area to be searched the harder it got. If the body had been buried for some time there might be a tell-tale depression as the disturbed earth settled, and long-handled probes could be used to check for any areas that were more yielding than the surrounding ground. I even knew of one forensic scientist in the States who'd had interesting results divining for graves using pieces of bent wire.

But dogs remained the best search tool for discovering where a body was buried. Their sensitive noses could detect the taint of the gases released during decomposition through several feet of soil, and good cadaver dogs had even been known to locate bodies buried over a century before.

The forensics team were scraping the soil from partially exposed remains using small trowels and brushes, working with an almost archaeological precision. The same techniques needed to be used whether the grave was a few weeks or a few hundred years old. The aim in both cases was to uncover the body with a minimum of disturbance, the better to decipher whatever evidence might have been unknowingly entombed with it.

In this case, the most telling piece of information was already apparent. I wasn't taking part in the recovery process, but I was standing close enough to see what mattered.

Mackenzie glanced at me. 'Any comment?'

'Only what I expect you know already.'

'Tell me anyway.'

'It's not Lyn Metcalf,' I said.

He gave a non-committal grunt. 'Go on.'

'This isn't a new grave. Whoever it is, they've been here since long before she went missing. There's no soft tissue left at all, no smell. The dog did well to find it.'

'I'll pass on your congratulations,' he said, dryly. 'So how long would you say it's been here?'

I looked at the shallow excavation. The skeleton was now almost fully exposed, its bones the same colour as the earth. It was an adult's, lying on its side with what looked like a T-shirt and jeans still clinging to its form.

'I can only narrow it down so far without doing more tests. Buried this deep, the decomposition would take much longer than it would on the surface. So for it to get to this stage, say a minimum of a year, fifteen months? But my guess is this has been here a good bit longer than that. Probably nearer to five years.'

'How do you know?'

'The jeans and T-shirt. They're cotton, which takes four to five years to rot. They've not gone completely yet, but they're getting there.'

'Anything else?'

179

'Can I take a closer look?'

'Help yourself.'

It was a different scene-of-crime team from the one I'd met before, at the site where Sally Palmer had been found. They glanced at me as I crouched down at the edge of the dig, but continued with what they were doing without comment. It was already late and they had a long night ahead.

'Any signs of trauma?' I asked one of them.

'Some pretty severe cranial damage, but we've only just started to expose it.' He indicated the upper right side, which was still partly covered by soil. But cracks were already visible, radiating from a section where the bone had caved in.

'Looks blunt rather than sharp or ballistic,' I said, examining it. 'What would you say?'

He nodded. Unlike his colleague I'd met at the previous grave site, he didn't seem to resent any interference. 'Looks like it. But I'm not going to commit myself until we make sure there isn't a bullet rattling around inside the skull.'

An injury to the skull caused by either gunshot or something sharp like a knife produced a different type of trauma from one made with a blunt object. It wasn't usually difficult to recognize them, and the signs so far were that this one, with the bone crushed inwards like an egg, was the latter. But I approved of his caution all the same.

'You think the head injury was the cause of death?' Mackenzie asked.

'Could be,' I said. 'By the looks of it, it would have been fatal, assuming it wasn't made post-mortem.

But it's too soon to say one way or the other.'

'What else can you tell me, then?' he said, disgruntled.

'Well, it's a male. Probably white, in his late teens or early twenties.'

He peered into the grave. 'Seriously?'

'Look at the skull. The jaw shape is different for men and women. A man's flares out more. And see where the ear was, how that bit of bone is projecting? That's the zygomatic arch, and it's always bigger in men than women. As for race, the nasal bones suggest European descent rather than African. Could be Asian, I suppose, but the cranial shape is too lozenge-shaped, so I'd say not. Age . . .' I shrugged. 'Again, only a guess at this stage. But from what I can see of them, the vertebrae don't look too worn. And see the ribs here?' I pointed to where the blunt ends of bone protruded from underneath the T-shirt. 'The ends get more irregular and knobbly the older you get. The edges on these are still pretty sharp, so it's obviously a young adult.'

Mackenzie closed his eyes and kneaded the bridge of his nose. 'Perfect. Just what we needed, an unrelated murder.' He looked up suddenly. 'There's no sign of the throat being cut, is there?'

'Not that I can see.' I'd already checked the cervical vertebrae for any knife marks. 'After being buried for this long any damage is going to be harder to make out without a proper examination. But there's nothing obvious.'

'Thank God for small mercies,' Mackenzie muttered.

181

I could sympathize. It was difficult to say which would complicate things more: having to launch a second murder inquiry, or finding evidence that the same killer had been active for years.

But that didn't concern me, for which I was grateful. I stood up, brushing the dirt from my hands. 'If there's nothing else you need me for, I might as well get back.'

'Can you be at the lab tomorrow? I mean, later today,' Mackenzie added, catching himself.

'Why?'

He seemed genuinely surprised by the question. 'To take a better look at this. We should have finished here by mid-morning. We can have the body with you for lunchtime.'

'You seem to take it for granted I'm going to get involved.'

'Aren't you?'

It was my turn to be surprised. Not so much by his question, as the fact that he seemed to know me better than I did. 'I suppose so,' I said, accepting the inevitability of it. 'I'll be there for twelve.'

I woke up in the kitchen, cold and confused. In front of me, the door to the back garden stood open, revealing the first hint of a lightening sky. The memory of the dream was still fresh in my mind, the voices and presence of Kara and Alice as vivid as if I had just spoken to them. It had been even more disturbing than usual. In it I'd felt that Kara had wanted to warn me of something, but I'd not wanted to know. I'd been too afraid of what I might hear.

I shivered. I'd no recollection of coming down-stairs, or what unconscious motive had led me to unlock the door. I went to close it, but then stopped. Rising like a cliff from the pale sea of mist covering the field was the impenetrable dark of the wood. A sense of foreboding gripped me as I stared at it.

Can't see the wood for the trees. The phrase came into my head from nowhere. For a moment it seemed to have some deeper significance, but it faded even as I tried to grasp it. I was still trying when something touched the back of my neck.

I started and turned around. The empty kitchen confronted me. A breeze, I told myself, even though the morning was still and silent, undisturbed by any whisper of air. I closed the door, trying to dismiss the unease that still persisted. But the sensation of fingertips gently brushing my skin lingered as I went back to bed and waited for the dawn.

I'd got most of the morning to kill before I was due at the lab. With nothing better to do, I strolled up to Henry's for breakfast, as I often did on Saturdays. He was already up and seemed in good form, cheer-fully asking me how it had gone the night before as he briskly fried eggs and grilled bacon. It took me a moment to realize he meant the barbecue at Jenny's rather than the discovery in the wood. News of that hadn't broken yet, and what the reaction would be when it did I couldn't imagine. Manham was already struggling to deal with events as it was. And I still felt too unsettled by the dream to want to dwell on such things myself.

So I didn't mention that a second body had been found. But Henry's good mood was infectious, and by the time I left I was in a much brighter frame of mind. My spirits lifted further as I walked back home to collect my car. It was another beautiful morning, without the stifling heat that would come later. The yellows, purples and reds of the flowers edging the village green hurt the eye with their vibrancy, filling the air with the heavy sweetness of pollen. Only the police trailer parked nearby disturbed the illusion of rural quiet.

Its presence seemed to chastise my sudden optimism, but it had been so long since I'd felt like this I didn't care. Of course, I didn't question the reasons for it too closely. And I was careful not to link my new outlook with Jenny. It was enough just to appreciate the moment while it lasted.

As it turned out, it wasn't about to last much longer.

I was passing the church when a voice called out, 'Dr Hunter. A moment, please.'

Scarsdale was in the graveyard with Tom Mason, the younger of the two gardeners who tended Manham's flowerbeds and lawns. I faced him across the low church wall.

'Morning, Reverend. Tom.'

Tom bobbed his head with a shy smile, without looking up from the rose bush he was tending. Like his grandfather he was happiest left alone to look after his plants, which he did with almost bovine gentleness. By contrast, there was nothing bovine or gentle about Scarsdale. He didn't bother to acknowledge my greeting.

'I'm curious as to your thoughts on the current situation,' he said without preamble. His black suit seemed to absorb the sunlight among the old and uneven gravestones.

It seemed an odd thing to say. 'I'm not sure what you mean.'

'The village faces a difficult time. People all over the country will be watching to see how we acquit ourselves. Don't you agree?'

I hoped this wasn't going to be a repeat of his sermon. 'What is it you want, Reverend?'

'To show that Manham won't tolerate what's happened. This could be an opportunity to forge a stronger community. To unite in the face of this test.'

'I don't see how a lunatic abducting and killing women can be regarded as a "test".'

'No, perhaps you don't. But people are frankly concerned about the damage being done to the reputation of the village. And rightly so.'

'I would have thought they'd be more concerned with finding Lyn Metcalf and catching Sally Palmer's killer. Isn't that more important than worrying about Manham's reputation?'

'Don't play games with me, Dr Hunter,' he snapped. 'If more people had paid attention to what was going on in this community it might not have come to this.'

I should have known better than to argue with him. 'I still don't understand what your point is.'

I was conscious of the gardener's presence in the

background, but Scarsdale was never shy about performing in front of an audience. He rocked back on his heels so that he was looking at me down the length of his nose.

'I've been approached by a number of parishioners. It's felt we need to present a united front. Especially in our dealings with the press.'

'Meaning what, exactly?' I asked, though I was beginning to get an inkling of where this was leading.

'It's felt that the village needs a spokesman. Someone best able to represent Manham to the outside world.'

'That's you, I take it.'

'If anyone else is willing to take on the responsibility, I'll be happy to stand aside.'

'What makes you think there'll be need for anyone to do it?'

'Because God hasn't finished with this village yet.'

He said it with a conviction I found unnerving. 'So what do you want from me?'

'You're a figure of some importance. Your support would be welcome.'

The idea of Scarsdale using this as a public platform for himself was galling. Yet I knew the fear and distrust that pervaded the village would create a receptive audience for him. It was a depressing thought.

'I've no intention of talking to the press, if that's what you mean.'

'It's also a question of attitude. I wouldn't want to

think anyone was undermining the efforts of those acting in the village's best interests.'

'I tell you what, Reverend. You do what you think best for the village, and so will I.'

'Is that supposed to be a criticism?'

'Let's say we just have different views on what constitutes the village's best interests.'

He considered me, coldly. 'Perhaps I should remind you that people here have long memories. They're not likely to forget any transgressions at a time like this. Or forgive them, unchristian as that may be.'

'In that case I'll just have to try not to transgress.'

'You can be as glib as you like. But I'm not the only one who's wondered about your loyalties. People talk, Dr Hunter. And what I've been hearing is quite disturbing.'

'Then perhaps you shouldn't listen to gossip. As a man of the cloth aren't you supposed to give the benefit of the doubt?'

'Don't presume to tell me my job.'

'Then don't try to tell me mine.'

He glared at me. He might have said more, but there was a clatter from behind him as Tom Mason put his tools in the wheelbarrow. Scarsdale drew himself up, his eyes as hard as the gravestones he stood among.

'I won't keep you any longer, Dr Hunter. Good day,' he said, stiffly, and stalked away.

Well, you handled that well, I thought, sourly, as I continued on past the church. I hadn't meant it to turn into a confrontation, but Scarsdale brought out

187

the worst in me. Still brooding about what he'd said, I didn't notice the car until it pulled up alongside.

'You look like you lost a pound and found a penny.'

It was Ben. Sunglasses on, he had a brawny arm propped on the open windowsill of his new black Land Rover. It was dusty, but still made mine look like an antique.

'Sorry. I was miles away.'

'So I noticed. Nothing to do with the Witchfinder General over there, was it?' he said, jerking his head towards the church. 'I saw you talking to him.'

I had to laugh. 'Yeah, it was, actually.' I gave him a brief rundown of the encounter. He shook his head.

'I don't know what God he's supposed to worship, but if the good reverend's any indication I wouldn't like to meet him down a dark alley. You should have told him to bollocks.'

'That would have gone down well.'

'By the sound of it he's got it in for you anyway. You're a threat to him.'

'Me?' I said, surprised.

'Think about it. Until now he's been a dried-up minister with a shrinking congregation. This is his big chance, and as far as he's concerned you're a potential challenge to his authority. You're a doctor, educated, come from the big city. And secular, let's not forget that.'

'I'm not interested in competing with him,' I said, exasperated.

'Doesn't matter. The miserable old bastard's set

himself up as the Voice of Manham. If you're not with him you're against him.'

'As if things aren't bad enough as they are.'

'Oh, never doubt the ability of a righteous man to fuck things up. All in the name of the greater good, of course.'

I looked at him. His normal good humour seemed to have left him. 'You all right?'

'Just feeling cynical today. As you might have noticed.'

'What did you do to your head?'

There was a grazed bump next to one of his eyes, partly hidden by his sunglasses. His hand went to it.

'Got it chasing another bastard poacher in the reserve last night. Someone made a try for a marsh harrier's nest I've been keeping an eye on. I set off after them and went arse over elbow on one of the trails.'

'Did you catch them?'

He gave an angry shake of his head. 'I will, though. I'm sure it's that fucking Brenner. I found his car parked nearby. I waited for him, but he didn't show. Probably hiding, waiting for me to leave.' He gave a hard smile. 'I let the bastard's tyres down, so I hope he was.'

'Taking a chance, aren't you?'

'What's he going to do? Report me?' He snorted derisively. 'You going to the Lamb later?'

'Maybe.'

'Might see you there, then.'

He drove off, the Land Rover's powerful engine leaving a haze of exhaust dissipating in the air behind it. As I set off for my house I thought about what he'd said. There was always a thriving black market for endangered species, and birds in particular. But given the role they'd played in Sally Palmer's mutilation and Lyn Metcalf's abduction it was something the police should know about. The problem was that aspect of the crimes hadn't been made public, so it wasn't something I could suggest to Ben. Which meant it was down to me to tell Mackenzie. I wasn't happy with the idea of going behind Ben's back, especially when it would probably turn out to be nothing. But I couldn't take that chance. Experience had shown me that sometimes even the smallest details could be important.

I didn't know it then, but that was about to be proved in the way I least expected.

15

That night there was another victim. Not at the hands of the man responsible for Sally Palmer and Lyn Metcalf. At least, not directly. No, this was a casualty of the suspicion and hostility that had started to grip the village.

James Nolan lived in a tiny cottage in a cul-de-sac behind the garage. One of my patients, he worked in a shop in a neighbouring village, a quiet man whose reserve hid both a gentle nature and a deep unhappiness. He was in his fifties, single and four stone overweight. He was also homosexual. The latter was something of which he was deeply ashamed. In a backwater like Manham, where such traits were regarded as unnatural, there had been little scope for sexual adventure. Consequently, as a young man he'd found such satisfaction as he could in the public parks and lavatories of nearby towns. On one occasion the man he'd approached had been an undercover police officer. The shame of the encounter lasted far longer than the suspended sentence he received. Inevitably, word of it leaked back into the village. Already marked for ridicule, now he was seen as something far more sinister. While the exact nature of his transgression was never discussed, and probably not even known, the rumour of it was enough to brand him. In the way that small communities have of ascribing roles to its members, he became the village untouchable, the pervert whom children were warned not to go near. And Nolan lived up to his image by retreating further into his isolation. He moved through the village like a ghost, speaking to few people, asking only not to be noticed. For the most part Manham was happy to comply, not so much tolerating as ignoring him.

Until now.

In a way, it was almost a relief to him when it happened. Ever since Sally Palmer's body had been found, he'd lived in fear, knowing that rationality didn't play any part in selecting scapegoats. At night when he returned from work he would hurry into his cottage and shutter himself inside, hoping that invisibility would continue to protect him. That Saturday night, though, it failed.

It was after eleven when the banging started on his door. He had turned off the TV, was preparing to go to bed. His curtains were closed, and for a while he sat in his chair, praying that whoever it was would go away. But they didn't. There were several of them, drunk and laughing at first as they mockingly called his name. Then the shouts grew angrier, the blows to the door more violent. It danced and shook under the assault, and Nolan looked at the telephone, almost giving in and calling the police. But a lifetime of not drawing attention to himself prevented it. Instead, when the callers changed tactics, threatening to break the door down unless he opened it, he did what he'd always done.

He did as he was told.

He'd kept the chain on, trusting to the steel links to protect him. Like everything else, they failed. The door and frame splintered under the renewed assault, knocking Nolan back into the hall as the men surged into his home.

Later, he claimed he hadn't recognized any of them, saying he didn't get a look at their faces. Whether he did or not, I find it hard to believe he didn't know who his attackers were. At the very least they must have been people he'd seen before, perhaps even young men whose parents or grand-parents he had grown up with. They beat and kicked him, and then set about wrecking the house. When they'd smashed everything they could, they set about him again, this time not stopping until he was unconscious. It's possible that some semblance of reason made them stop before they killed him. Then again, his injuries were such they could easily have left him for dead.

It was some time after they had gone when my phone rang. I fumbled for it, still half-asleep, and failed to recognize the whispered voice that told me someone had been hurt. While I was still trying to rouse myself the caller told me which house to go to and then rang off. I stared dumbly at the receiver for a moment or two before I collected myself enough to phone for an ambulance. There was always a chance it was a false alarm, but this hadn't sounded like a prank. And it would take an ambulance long enough to get out here as it was.

On the way to Nolan's I stopped off at the police trailer in the village square. It was manned twenty-four hours a day, and I didn't relish the thought of going to the house by myself. It was a mistake. My call to emergency hadn't been passed on to them, and I wasted valuable time on explanations. By the time one of them agreed to come with me I wished I'd gone alone.

The cul-de-sac where Nolan lived was in darkness. It was easy to see which house was his, because the front door was wide open. I looked at the neighbouring houses as we approached. There was no sign of life, but I had the feeling that we were being watched all the same.

We found Nolan in the wreckage of his home where his attackers had left him. There was little I could do but put him in the recovery position, and then wait for the ambulance. He drifted in and out of consciousness, so I kept talking to him until the paramedics arrived. At one point when he seemed quite lucid, I asked him what had happened. But he only shut his eyes again, blocking out the question.

As he was carried out on a stretcher to the ambulance, one of the police officers who'd arrived with it asked why the caller had phoned me rather than the emergency services. I said I didn't know, but that wasn't really true. I looked at the flashing blue lights reflecting from the windows of the surrounding houses. Despite the disturbance, no-one was visible in them, and no-one had come out to see what was happening. But I knew people were looking. Just as they had looked on, or looked the other way, as first Nolan's door, and then the man himself, was assaulted. Someone's conscience might have been pricked, but not enough to try to stop the attack, or to involve outsiders. This was village business. Calling me, an almost-outsider myself, had been a compromise. There would be no witnesses to this, I was certain, just as no-one would ever admit to making the anonymous call. Even that, it emerged, had been made from the village's only public phone box, making the caller impossible to trace. As the ambulance drove away I looked at the blank windows and closed doors and felt like shouting at them. But what I would have shouted, or what good that would have done, I didn't know.

Instead, I went home and tried to sleep for what was left of the night.

Next morning I woke feeling grainy and ill at ease. I fetched a newspaper, then took it outside with a black coffee. The big weekend story was a train crash, compared to which the discovery of a second body in Manham merited only a few paragraphs on the inside pages. The fact it was unconnected with the more recent murder meant it was worth mentioning only as a curio, for its coincidence value.

I'd spent the previous afternoon and part of the evening working on the young man's remains, and while we'd have to wait for tests on the adipocere in the soil samples to get an accurate time-since-death estimate, I didn't expect any surprises. The good news, if it could be called that, was that it shouldn't be too hard putting a name to the victim. His teeth were intact, complete with fillings, so with luck a match with dental records would provide an ID. I'd also found an old fracture on his left tibia. The shin bone was long healed, but it was another feature that would help establish his identity.

Other than that, all I'd been able to do was confirm what I'd told Mackenzie earlier. The grave's occupant was a young white male in his late teens or early twenties whose skull had been crushed by something blunt and heavy. Probably a large hammer or mallet, given the round, radial shape of the holes punched through the bone. The position and amount of damage suggested he'd been struck repeatedly from behind. It was impossible to say for certain after all this time if that had actually killed him, but my guess would be that it had. An injury like that would have been almost instantly fatal, and while there was no way of knowing now what else might have been done to him beforehand, his bones at least bore no other sign of violence.

There was no reason to think this death had anything to do with the current events in Manham. Our killer was targeting women, not men, and although we wouldn't know for sure until the remains had been identified, it was doubtful this victim was local. The village wasn't big enough to hide a disappearance for all this time. More to the point, the murder bore no similarity to Sally Palmer's. She had been left in the open, not buried, and while the bones of her face had been shattered, either from rage or to conceal her identity, the young man's remained untouched. The likeliest scenario was that both he and his killer were from somewhere else, and that the body had simply been brought out into the wilds to be disposed of.

Even so, I'd spent more time than I could probably justify checking that its cervical vertebrae were unmarked. Perhaps it was just the fact that, until a week ago, the only thing outstanding about Manham was its isolation. Now there were two murders, one recent, one not, and a young woman was missing. It was hard not to feel a sense of un-ravelling. If the village was only now starting to give up its secrets, there was no telling what else might be unearthed before this was done.

It wasn't a comforting thought.

I flipped through the rest of the newspaper, but without much interest. I tossed it onto the table and finished the last of my coffee. Time for a shower, and then I'd have to head over to Henry's for Sunday lunch.

The thought of seeing Jenny afterwards made me feel both nervous and excited. And a little guilty, because I hadn't had a chance to tell Henry about it. He wouldn't mind us borrowing the dinghy, but I knew he'd be expecting me to stay for the rest of the afternoon, and I felt bad that I'd have to cut and run. Perhaps I should have rescheduled one or the other. But I didn't like letting him down, and I'd no idea how long it would be before I'd be able to take the dinghy out again. I didn't want to wait.

Why not? a cynical voice chimed in my head. *Are you really so keen to see Jenny again?* But that wasn't something I chose to think about. So I got up to take a shower, leaving the question hanging unanswered.

A nagging tension headache had developed by the time I reached Henry's. But it wasn't so bad that I didn't appreciate the smell of roast beef as I walked into the house. As usual I didn't knock, just called out as I went in.

'Through here,' Henry's voice came back from the kitchen.

I went through. The kitchen was hot even though the door was open, giving a view onto the secluded back lawn. Henry was whipping batter in a dish for Yorkshire puddings, an empty wine glass close to hand. Not ideal fare for a hot afternoon, perhaps, but Henry was a traditionalist when it came to Sunday lunch.

'Nearly ready,' he said, spooning the batter into a baking tray. The hot fat hissed and sizzled. 'Soon as these are done we can eat.'

'Can I do anything?'

'Pour us both some wine. I've already started some plonk, or there's a bottle of decent stuff I've opened to breathe. Should be OK now. Unless you'd rather have a beer?'

'Wine's fine.'

He was already wheeling himself over to the oven. He opened the door, recoiling a little from the blast of heat, then slid in the baking tray. He didn't cook often, usually quite happy to let Janice take care of his meals, but when he did I was always impressed by how adroit he was. I wondered how well I'd have coped in his position. Still, it wasn't as if he'd had much choice. And Henry wasn't the sort to simply give up.

'There,' he said, slamming shut the oven door. 'Another twenty minutes and we're away. Good God, man, haven't you poured that wine yet?'

'Coming up.' I was looking in a drawer. 'Have you got any aspirin or anything? I'm starting with a headache.'

'If there's nothing in there you'll have to get something from the drugs cabinet.'

The drawer yielded an empty packet of paracetamol but nothing else. I went down the hallway to Henry's study, which doubled as his surgery since I'd taken over his old room. We kept the drugs stored there, as well as much of Henry's other paraphernalia. He was a hoarder and had kept all manner of ancient powders, bottles and medical instruments he'd inherited from the previous doctor. Keeping them probably broke any number of health regulations, but Henry had scant regard for red tape and bureaucracy.

His collection gathered dust in an elegant Victorian glass-fronted bookcase, a marked contrast to the unlovely steel drug cabinet and small fridge where we kept our vaccines. The pair of them looked totally out of place among the fine wood and leather furniture, despite Henry's unsuccessful attempt to camouflage them with framed photographs. There was one of the two of us in the dinghy, taken the year before, but most were of him and his wife Diana. In pride of place on top of the cabinet was a picture taken at their wedding. They made an attractive couple as they smiled at the camera, young and happily oblivious to the fate that awaited them.

I looked at the pair of walking sticks gathering dust in the corner by the desk. When I'd first arrived he'd still tried to use them. I would hear him grunting as he struggled to take a few steps. 'I'll prove those buggers wrong,' he'd said, on more than one occasion. But he never had, and gradually he'd given up trying.

I turned from the reminder of human frailty and unlocked the cabinet. I rummaged through the boxes until I found some paracetamol, then locked the cabinet and went back to the kitchen.

'About time,' he grumbled as I returned. 'Hurry up with that bloody wine. Thirsty work, this.' He fanned himself, moving towards the open door. 'Let's go and cool down a bit.'

'Are we eating outside?'

'Don't be barbaric. Do I look Australian? And bring the bottle with you. The Bordeaux, not the cheap stuff.'

I washed the paracetamol down with water, then did as I was told. The garden was well kept without being fussy. Henry had been a keen gardener, and it was yet another source of frustration for him that he was no longer able to look after it himself. We went over to the old wrought-iron table and chairs that sat under the hanging shade of a laburnum.

Beyond the willow-weave fence, the sparkling lake gave the illusion of relief from the heat. I poured us both a glass of wine.

'Cheers,' I said, raising mine.

'Good health.' He swirled the ruby liquid around before sniffing it critically. Finally, he took a drink. 'Hmm. Not bad.'

'Local supermarket?'

'Peasant,' he scoffed. He took another drink, savouring it before setting it down. 'So, come on. Out with it. How did dinner go the other night?'

'It was a barbecue, actually. Outdoors. You'd have loved it.'

'Eating al fresco is acceptable on a Friday night. Sunday lunch requires proper appreciation. And you haven't answered the question.'

'It was fine, thanks.'

He cocked an eyebrow. 'Fine? That it?'

'What else can I say? I enjoyed myself.'

'Do I detect a little coyness here?' He grinned at me. 'I can see I'm going to have to prise this out of you. Tell you what, let's take the dinghy out this afternoon and you can tell me all about it. Not much breeze, but we can row off some of the lunch.'

I could feel my embarrassment burning my face.

'Of course, if you don't want to it's quite all right,' Henry said, his smile fading.

'It's not that. It's just . . . Well, I told Jenny I'd take her out in it.'

'Oh.' He couldn't hide his surprise.

'I'm sorry, I should have said something sooner.'

But Henry had recovered his poise, concealing his

201

disappointment behind a grin. 'No need to apologize! Good for you!'

'I can always—'

He waved away the offer before I could finish it. 'Sunny afternoon like this, you're much better off going out with a pretty girl than an old fogey like me.'

'Are you sure you don't mind?'

'We'll do it some other time. I'm delighted you've met someone you seem fond of.'

'It's no big deal, really.'

'Oh, come on, David, it's high time you started enjoying yourself! You don't need to justify it.'

'I'm not, I'm just . . .' I trailed off, lost for words.

Henry was entirely serious now. 'Let me guess; you're feeling guilty.'

I nodded, not trusting myself to speak.

'It's been, what? Three years now?'

'Nearly four.'

'It's almost five for me. And you know what? It's long enough. You can't bring the dead back, so you might as well carry on with the business of living as best you can. When Diana died . . . Well, I don't have to tell you.' He gave a half-laugh. 'Couldn't understand why I'd survived and she hadn't. In fact, for a long time after the accident . . .'

He broke off, staring out over the lake. But whatever he had been about to say, he changed his mind.

'Anyway, that's another story.' He reached for his wine. 'Changing the subject, I gather there was a bit of excitement last night.'

There wasn't much about the village that Henry

202

didn't hear. 'You could say that. Some of James Nolan's neighbours paid him a visit.'

'How is he?'

'Not good.' I'd phoned the hospital earlier. 'They gave him quite a beating. He'll be in hospital for a week or two yet.'

'And I imagine no-one saw anything?'

'Apparently not.'

His thick eyebrows knitted in disgust. 'Animals, that's all they are. Bloody animals. Still, I can't say I'm surprised. And from what I've heard you've fallen foul of Manham's rumour mill yourself, haven't you?'

I should have known he'd have heard the talk about me by now. 'At least I've not been beaten up so far.'

'I wouldn't shout about it just yet. I warned you what it could get like. Just because you're Manham's doctor doesn't mean you'll get any favours.'

I could see he was sliding into one of his black moods. 'Come on, Henry . . .'

'Trust me, I know this place better than you. Push comes to shove, the people here will turn on you the same as they did Nolan. Doesn't matter what you've done for them in the past. Gratitude? Not in this bloody place!' He took a gulp of wine, forgetting to savour it in his anger. 'Sometimes I wonder why we bother.'

'You don't mean that.'

'No?' He stared broodingly into his wine. I wondered how much he'd had before I arrived. 'No, perhaps not. But there are times I wonder what either of us is doing here, I really do. Don't you ever ask yourself what the point of it all is?'

'We're doctors. What other point is there supposed to be?'

'Yes, yes, I know all that,' he said, irritably. 'But what *good* do we actually do? Can you honestly tell me you never feel you're wasting your time? Keeping some old wreck alive, just for the sake of it? All we're doing is putting off the inevitable.'

I looked at him with concern, noticing his fatigue. For the first time I saw he was starting to show signs of age.

'Are you OK?' I asked.

He gave a dry chuckle. 'Don't take any notice of me, I'm just feeling cynical today. Or even more so than usual.' He reached for the bottle. 'All this business must be getting to me too. Let's have another glass, and then you can tell me what you've been up to all week that's so mysterious.'

That was something I hadn't been looking forward to, but now I was glad to talk about something else. Henry listened, quizzical at first as I told him the truth about my career before I came to Manham, then incredulous as I gave him a rundown of how I'd been helping Mackenzie.

When I finished he shook his head, slowly. 'Well, I think the phrase "dark horse" springs to mind.'

'I'm sorry. I know I should have told you before, but until this week I really thought it was all past history.'

'You don't have to apologize,' he said. But I could tell I'd upset him. He'd taken me on at a time when I was at my lowest, only to find out now that I'd been less than open with him. All this time I'd let him believe my experience as an anthropologist had been entirely academic. Even though I hadn't actually lied, it was a poor repayment of trust.

'If you'd like me to resign, I will,' I offered.

'Resign? Don't be ridiculous!' He looked at me. 'Unless you're having second thoughts about working here?'

'No, of course not. I didn't want to get involved in the first place. I wasn't deliberately keeping it from you. I just didn't want to think about it myself.'

'No, I can see that. It's just a bit of a surprise, that's all. I'd no idea your career had been so ... rarefied.' He gazed reflectively over the lake. 'I envy you. I always regret not going into psychology. I had ambitions to once upon a time, you know. Didn't work out, obviously. Too much extra training. I wanted to marry Diana, and being a GP brought in the money faster. And it seemed glamorous enough back then.'

'There's nothing glamorous about what I've been doing.'

'Exciting, then.' He gave me a knowing look. 'And don't deny it. There's been a definite change in you over the past week. Even before the barbecue.' He gave a short laugh, fishing his pipe from his pocket. 'One way or another it's been a hell of a week. Any news on who this second body might be?'

'Not yet. But hopefully dental records will provide an ID.'

Henry shook his head, filling and lighting his pipe.

'You live somewhere for all these years, and then . . .' He made a visible attempt to shake off the mood that had descended. 'Well, I'd better go and check how lunch is coming along. Things are grim enough without burning the Yorkshires.'

We kept the conversation lighter after that. But Henry was looking tired by the end of lunch. I reminded myself that he'd been carrying most of my workload for the last few days. I tried to insist on washing the dishes, but he would have none of it.

'I'm fine, really. Most of them'll go in the dishwasher anyway. I'd much rather you get off and meet your friend.'

'There's plenty of time.'

'If you insist on doing them, then so will I. And frankly, what I'd like to do right now is pour myself the last of the wine and perhaps have a nap.'

He regarded me with mock-severity.

'Now, do you really want to ruin my Sunday afternoon?'

I'd arranged to meet Jenny at the Lamb. It was neutral territory, whereas going to her house again would have made seeing her seem like too much of a date. I was still trying to tell myself that we were only going sailing. It wasn't like I was taking her out to dinner, with all the sexual politics that would involve. There would be no worry over picking up or giving out the wrong signals. Nothing to it, really.

Except the anticipation I felt said otherwise.

I'd been careful not to have too much wine with lunch, and although I felt like something stronger I stuck to orange juice now. There were the usual nods as I went to the bar. I couldn't read anything in any of them, but I was glad to see that Carl Brenner wasn't there.

I took my drink outside and leaned against the stone wall at the front of the pub. Nerves made me drink the orange almost straight away. I realized I was looking at my watch every few minutes. Resolving not to do it again, I looked up as a car came down the road. It was an old Mini, and a moment later I recognized Jenny behind the wheel. She parked and got out, and at the sight of her I felt a sudden lift. *What's going on here?* I wondered, then any questions were brushed aside as she came over.

'I thought I'd be idle,' she said, smiling as she pushed her sunglasses up onto her head. But I knew the real reason she'd driven was that few women were prepared to walk any distance alone any more. She wore shorts and a sleeveless blue top. There was a faint scent of perfume, hardly there at all. 'Not been waiting long, have you?' she asked.

'Just got here.' I saw her glance at my empty glass, and shrugged, embarrassed. 'I was thirsty. Would you like something?'

'I'm easy either way.'

I could feel us drifting into that zone of tension that makes every sentence ring false. *Decide. Now,* I told myself, knowing this could set the tone for the rest of the afternoon.

'How about getting something to take out with us?' I asked, surprising myself. But as soon as I'd said it I knew it was the right choice.

Jenny's smile broadened. 'Sounds great.'

She waited outside while I went back into the pub to buy a bottle of wine. I tried to ignore the odd looks as I asked to borrow glasses and a corkscrew, kicking myself for not having thought about this sooner. But I knew why I hadn't. I'd avoided anything that would have made this seem like anything other than a casual outing. And it looked as though Jenny had done the same.

'Hang on,' she said when I returned, and disappeared inside herself. She came back a few minutes later brandishing packets of crisps and nuts. 'In case we get the munchies.' She grinned.

The tension disappeared after that. We left her car in the square and walked back to the lake. We could have walked through Henry's garden to the jetty, but rather than disturb him we followed a little-used access track that ran past the house from the road. The dinghy was motionless on the still water. There wasn't a breath of wind as we climbed aboard.

'Don't think we're going to manage much sailing today,' I said.

'Doesn't matter. It'll just be nice to be out on the water.'

Without bothering with the sail, I took the oars and headed out into the lake. Its surface shone like glass in the sunlight, so bright it hurt. The only sound was the melodic plash of the oars as they dipped in and out of the water. Jenny was sitting facing me. Our knees brushed as I rowed, but neither of us moved away. Jenny let her hand trail over the side as I headed for the opposite shore, her fingers leaving a widening trail in their wake.

The water grew shallower as I approached the far side, made impassable in parts by dense thickets of straw-coloured rushes. A low outcrop of land protruded from them, its banks overhung with the shaggy branches of old weeping willows. I let us drift under one, loosely tying the boat to its trunk. Sunlight dappled through the leaves, turning them a translucent green.

'This is lovely!' Jenny exclaimed.

'Do you want to have a look around?'

She hesitated. 'I don't want to sound like a wuss, but do you think it's safe? I mean, with the traps and everything.'

'I can't see anyone going to that much trouble. Nobody comes out here any more, so there wouldn't be much point.'

We left the wine to cool in the lake and set off to explore. There wasn't very much to the outcrop, just a mound of rocks and trees linked to the shore by a rush-choked strip of land. In its centre were the ruins of a tiny building, roofless and overgrown.

'Do you think this used to be a house?' Jenny asked, stooping to go through a low stone doorway. Old leaves crunched underfoot. Even in the heat there was a mustiness of damp and age.

'It might have. All this used to belong to Manham Hall. Could have been a groundsman's house or something.'

'I didn't know there was a hall around here.'

'There isn't now. It was knocked down just after the Second World War.'

She ran her hand across the mossy lintel of an old fireplace. 'Don't you ever wonder who used to live in places like this? What sort of people they were, what their lives were like?'

'Hard, I imagine.'

'But did they think that themselves, or was it just normal for them? I mean, in a few hundred years from now will people look at what's left of our houses and think, "Poor devils, how did they manage?"'

'More than likely. Everybody always does.'

'I always wanted to be an archaeologist. Before I was a teacher, I mean. All those past lives we know nothing about. And everyone thinking their own is the most important, just like us.' She gave a little shudder and grinned self-consciously. 'Makes me feel all shivery. But it still sort of fascinates me.'

I wondered if she'd somehow heard about my own involvement with past lives. But this wasn't contrived. 'So what stopped you? From becoming an archaeologist, I mean.'

'I can't have wanted to do it badly enough, I suppose. So I ended up in a classroom instead. Don't get me wrong, I enjoy it. But sometimes, you know, you think, "What if . . . ?"'

'You could still train.'

'No,' she said, hand still smoothing the stone lintel. 'That me's gone now.'

It seemed an odd thing to say. 'What do you mean?'

'Oh, you know. You get certain chances at certain times. Crossroads, or whatever. You make your decision, you end up going down one track; you

make the other, you end up somewhere else entirely.'
She gave a shrug. 'Archaeology was one of those
tracks I didn't take.'

'Don't you believe in second chances?'

'They're not second chances, just different ones.
Your life's never going to be the same as it would if
you'd made a different decision first time round.'
Her face had clouded. She pulled her hand from the
stone, suddenly embarrassed. 'God, listen to me.
Sorry,' she laughed.

'No need to be,' I said, but she was already duck-
ing out through the doorway.

I followed her out, giving her time to get over
whatever dark thoughts had surfaced. Under the
blond cap of her hair, the nape of her neck was
tanned and smooth. A whorl of fine white hairs ran
down her neck to disappear into her top. I felt an
impulse to touch them and looked away with
an effort.

When Jenny turned around she was bright again.
'Do you think the wine will be cool enough yet?'

'Only one way to find out.'

We went back to the boat and took the bottle from
the lake. 'Are you OK having this?' I asked. 'I bought
some water as well.'

'No, wine would be perfect, thanks. I've had my
insulin shot this morning. I'll be fine with one glass.'
She grinned. 'Besides, I'm with a doctor.'

We drank it on the bank under the willow. We'd
hardly spoken since coming back from the ruins, but
the silence wasn't uncomfortable.

'Do you ever miss living in a city?' she asked at last.

I thought about my recent trips to the lab. 'Not until recently. Do you?'

'I don't know. I miss some things about it. Not so much stuff like bars and restaurants. More the busyness of it all. But I'm getting used to the country. It's just about changing pace, really.'

'Do you think you'll go back?'

She looked at me, then out at the water. 'I don't know.' She snapped off a grass stem. 'How much did Tina tell you?'

'Not much. Just that you'd had a bad experience, but she didn't say what.'

Jenny smiled, plucking at the grass stem. 'Good old Tina,' she said, dryly but without rancour. I waited, letting her make up her mind whether to say more or not.

'I was attacked,' she said after a while, keeping her eyes on the grass. 'About eighteen months ago. I'd been out with some friends and caught a taxi home. Like you're supposed to. Streets not safe and all that. It had been someone's birthday, and I'd had a bit too much to drink. I fell asleep, and when I woke up the driver had parked and was getting into the back with me. When I put up a struggle he started hitting me. Threatened to kill me, and then . . .'

Her voice had grown unsteady. She paused for a moment before continuing, in control again.

'He didn't actually get to rape me. I heard some people nearby. He'd parked in an empty car park, and this group were cutting across it. Just fluke, really. So I started yelling and kicking on the window. He panicked, pushed me out of the car and drove off. The police said I'd been lucky. And they were right. I'd come out of it with just a few cuts and bruises, it could have been a lot worse. But I didn't feel lucky. I just felt scared.'

'Did they catch him?'

She shook her head. 'I couldn't give them much of a description, and he drove off before anyone could get his number. I didn't even know the name of the taxi company, because I'd flagged him down in the street. So he's still out there somewhere.'

She flicked the grass into the water. It floated on the surface, barely making an impression.

'It got so I was afraid to go out. I wasn't frightened of seeing him again, it was just . . . everything. It was like, if something like that had happened for no reason once, it might again. Any time. And so I decided to get out of the city. Go and live somewhere nice and safe. Saw this job advertised and ended up here.' She gave a crooked smile. 'Good move, hey?'

'I'm glad you did.'

The words were out before I knew it. I quickly looked out across the lake, anywhere but at her. *Idiot!* I fumed. *Why the hell did you say that?*

Neither of us spoke. I turned to find her watching me. She gave me a hesitant smile.

'Want a crisp?' she asked.

The awkwardness passed. Relieved, I reached for the wine.

In the coming days I would look back on this afternoon as one last glimmer of blue sky before the storm.

213

16

The next week passed in a state of limbo. A subdued tension filled the air like ozone, a dull anticipation as everyone waited for something to happen.

Nothing did.

The general mood matched the landscape, flat and becalmed. The weather continued as hot and unblemished as ever, without any hint of gathering clouds. The police investigation ground on, producing no sign of either suspect or victim, and the streets became noisy as every child of school age celebrated the start of their long summer break. I returned to my normal hours at the surgery, and if there were more patients now asking to see Henry, or an element of reserve in many of those I did see, I chose not to notice it. This was my life now, and Manham, for better or worse, my home. Sooner or later even this would pass, and then some sort of normalcy would return.

That was what I told myself, anyway.

I saw Jenny regularly over the following days. One

evening we drove out for dinner to a restaurant in Horning, where the tables had linen cloths and candles, and the wine list was more than a choice between red or white. It already seemed as if we'd known one another for years instead of having just met. Perhaps that was partly because of what we'd each been through. We'd both experienced a side of life that was a foreign country to most people, discovered how tenuous was the line separating the everyday from tragedy. The knowledge bonded us like a private language, unspoken most of the time, but there nevertheless. It had seemed natural to tell her about my history, about Kara and Alice, and about the forensic work I'd been carrying out for Mackenzie. She'd listened without comment, only briefly touching my hand when I'd finished.

'I think you're doing the right thing,' she said, allowing the contact to linger a moment before quickly moving her hand away. And then, without awkwardness or embarrassment, we'd started talking about something else.

Only on the way back was there any tension. Jenny withdrew further into herself the closer we drew to Manham. The conversation that had been effortless first became stilted, then dried up altogether.

'Is everything OK?' I asked as I pulled up outside her house.

She nodded, but too quickly. 'Well, good night,' she said in a rush, opening the car door. But she hesitated before she climbed out.

'Look, I'm sorry, I just . . . I don't want to hurry into anything.'

I nodded, numbly.

'No, I don't mean . . . It's not that I don't want . . .' She drew a deep breath. 'Just not yet, all right?' She gave me an uncertain smile. 'Not yet.'

Before I could answer she'd leaned into the car and given me a kiss, a fleeting brush of her lips, before hurrying into the house. I felt breathless, buoyed and guilty at the same time.

But her words stayed with me for another reason. *Not yet.* That had been the answer Linda Yates had given me when I'd asked if she'd dreamed about Lyn. I saw her again one afternoon, during the lull when the entire village was waiting for something to happen. She was hurrying along the main street, a look of preoccupation on her face, and didn't notice me until she was a few feet away. When she did she pulled up short.

'Hi, Linda. How are the boys?'

'Fine.' I was about to go on, but she called me back. 'Dr Hunter . . .'

I waited. She darted a quick look around, making sure no-one was in earshot. 'The police . . . are you still helping them? Like you said?'

'Sometimes.'

'Have they found anything?' she blurted.

'Come on, Linda, you know I can't tell you that.'

'But they've not found her yet? You know. Lyn?'

Whatever her reason for asking, it wasn't idle curiosity. Her anxiety was unmistakable. 'Not as far as I know.'

She nodded, but didn't seem reassured.

'Why?' I asked, although I was already starting to suspect.

'Nothing. I just wondered,' she mumbled, already scurrying off.

I watched her go, disturbed by the encounter. I had the uneasy impression that she hadn't been looking for news so much as confirmation. And I didn't need to be told why. Like Sally Palmer, Lyn Metcalf had finally made an appearance in her dreams.

But I quickly dismissed the notion. I'd been living in Manham too long if I was starting to believe in premonitions, or attach importance to dreams. Hers or mine. It was easy to be complacent. My own sleep had been undisturbed recently, my waking thoughts ones of Jenny and the future. It was as though I was surfacing into the air again after a long time underground. Selfishly, in spite of everything, it was hard not to feel optimistic.

Then, midway through the next week, the inertia broke. The body of the young man was identified when his dental records provided a match with those of a 22-year-old man. Alan Radcliff had been a postgraduate ecology student from Kent who had disappeared five years earlier. He'd been in the area, studying the countryside around Manham. At some point, he'd become a part of it. When his photograph was released a few people in the village could even remember him: a good-looking young man with an engaging smile. For a few weeks while he camped out on the marshes he'd become a familiar face in the village, brightening the days of the village girls before he moved on.

Except he hadn't gone anywhere.

Manham reacted to this new development almost without comment. With the victim's identity and connection to the area now known, no-one needed to state the obvious: the body's location couldn't be dismissed as a coincidence. The village could no longer distance itself from this very literal skeleton from its past.

Coming on top of everything else, it was another, unlooked-for blow. And then, while this was still being absorbed, came a far worse one.

I was just about to start afternoon surgery when the call came. I'd spoken to Mackenzie only the day before, when the student's body had been identified, and it was a mark of how far I'd let my defences slip that I assumed this would be something relating to that. Even when he said he needed to see me straight away I didn't make the connection.

'Surgery's about to start,' I said, phone tucked under my ear as I signed a prescription form. 'Can it wait until later?'

'No,' he said, and hearing his bluntness I stopped writing. 'I need you out here now, Dr Hunter. As soon as possible,' he added, as a sop to courtesy. But it was clear that politeness wasn't a priority for him right now.

'What's happened?'

There was a pause. I guessed he was weighing up how much he could tell me over a public phone line.

'We've found her,' he said.

* * *

There are around a hundred thousand different species of flies. Different shapes, different sizes, different life-cycles. Blowflies, or blue- and green-bottles as the most familiar types are more commonly known, are part of the Calliphoridae family. They breed on decaying organic matter. Rotting food, faeces, carrion. Almost anything. Most people can't see the point of them. They're disease-carrying irritants, as ready to feed on fresh dung as fine cuisine, which they do in both cases by regurgitating onto it.

But, as with everything else in nature, they play their role. As repulsive as it may seem, flies play an essential part in the breakdown of organic matter, helping to speed the process of dissolution, returning the dead to the raw materials of which they're composed. They're nature's own recycling mechanism. And, as such, there's a certain elegance to their single-minded devotion to their task. Far from being pointless, in the greater scheme of things, they're more important than the hummingbird or deer on which they'll one day feed. And from a forensic perspective, flies are not just an unavoidable evil, they're invaluable.

I hate them.

Not because I find them irritating or disgusting, although I'm no more immune to those aspects than anyone else. Or even because they're a reminder of our ultimate physical fate. I hate them because of the noise.

The flies' music was audible as I made my way across the marsh. At first it was almost felt rather than heard, a low thrumming that seemed part of the heat itself. It grew steadily more pervasive as I approached the centre of activity, a senseless, idiot drone which seemed to constantly waver in pitch without actually changing. The air became busy with darting insects. I waved away those that were drawn by the sweat on my face, but by now they were accompanied by something else.

The smell was at once both familiar and repellent. I'd smeared my top lip with menthol, but it cut right through. I'd once heard it likened to an over-ripe cheese left to sweat in the sun. It wasn't – not really. But that was as close as anything came to describing it.

Mackenzie acknowledged me with a nod. The crime scene team went about their tasks in grim-faced silence, faces flushed and damp in the hot coveralls. I looked down at the object that was the reason for all this activity, from the perspiring police officers to the frenzied swarm of flies.

'We haven't moved it yet,' Mackenzie said. 'I wanted to wait until you got here.'

'How about the pathologist?'

'He's been and gone. Said it was too decomposed for him to tell us anything for the moment, except that it was dead.'

It was that all right. It had been a long time since I'd been to a crime scene and looked on what had until recently been a living, breathing person. Sally Palmer's body had already been taken away by the time I'd arrived, and examining it later, in the sterile environment of a lab, was a far more clinical business. Even the remains of Alan Radcliff had been buried for so long they'd become a mere structural relic, with precious little evidence of humanity left about them. This, though, this was different. This was death in its busiest, awful glory.

'How did you find it?' I asked, pulling on a latex glove. I'd already suited up at the nearby trailer. We were several miles from the village, in a bleak region of drained marsh almost diametrically opposed to where the first body had been found. The lake glinted indifferently a few hundred yards away. This time I'd come prepared, and underneath the coveralls I was wearing only shorts. Even so, I was already slick with sweat, just from walking the short distance.

'The chopper spotted it. Fluke, really. They had some sort of systems glitch, so they were on their way back. They wouldn't have flown over here if not. This area's already been searched.'

'When was the last time?'

'Eight days ago.'

That gave us an upper limit of how long the body had been here. Perhaps also how long it had been dead, although that was less certain. People have been known to move bodies, sometimes more than once.

I snapped my other glove into place. I was ready, but felt no enthusiasm for what I was about to do. 'You think it's her?' I asked Mackenzie.

'Officially, we'll have to wait until a formal identification. But I don't think there's much doubt.'

Neither did I. There had already been one reprieve

when the grave had yielded the long-dead student. Somehow I didn't think there would be another.

Lyn Metcalf was unrecognizable. Her body lay face down, half-hidden by hummocks of marsh grass. She was naked, but on one foot was a single running shoe, incongruous and somehow pitiful. She'd been dead for several days, that much was obvious. Death had wrought its usual grim changes, a reverse alchemy transforming the gold of life into a base and stinking matter. But at least this time her killer hadn't added his own obscene modifications.

There were no swan wings.

I shut down the part of me that kept trying to superimpose a memory of the smiling young woman I'd bumped into only the week before and went to examine the body. There were what looked like several slashes in the darkened skin. But the most obvious wound was to the throat. Although the body lay face down, the extent of it was still all too apparent.

'Can you say how long she's been dead?' Mackenzie asked. 'Just roughly,' he added, before I could say anything.

'There's still soft tissue left, and skin slippage is only just starting.' I gestured at the wounds, now boiling colonies of maggots. 'And with this amount of larval activity, we're probably looking at between six and eight days.'

'Can't you narrow it down?'

I was about to point out that he'd asked for a rough estimate only a second before, but stopped myself. This wasn't pleasant for any of us. 'The

222

weather's been constant, so assuming the body hasn't been moved, to get to this stage I'd say six or seven days in this heat.'

'Anything else?'

'Same sort of wounds as we saw on Sally Palmer, though not quite so many. Severed throat, and the body's pretty desiccated again. Not as much, obviously, because it's not been dead as long. But I'd take a preliminary guess that it bled out.' I examined the blackened vegetation around it, seared by the alkali-rich chemicals released by the body. 'We'll need to test iron content to be sure, but I'd guess she was killed somewhere else and dumped here, like last time.'

'Same person did it, would you say?'

'Come on, I can't tell you that,' I said.

Mackenzie grunted. I could understand his unease. In some respects this was similar to Sally Palmer's murder, but there were enough departures from it to raise doubts that the same man was responsible. From what we could see so far there were no facial injuries. More significantly, the bird or animal fetish that had been evident before was conspicuously absent. From a detection point of view, that presented worrying problems. Either something had happened to force the killer to change his methods, or he was so erratic that there was no pattern to his actions. The third possibility was that the murders were the work of two different people.

None of the options offered much cause for optimism.

The monotone hubbub of the flies provided a

backdrop as I took my samples. By the time I straightened, my joints and muscles were stiff from crouching.

'Finished?' asked Mackenzie.

'Pretty much.'

I moved back. The next step was never a pleasant one. Everything that could be managed without moving the body had been done; photographs taken and measurements made. Now came the moment when we would see what lay underneath. The crime scene officers carefully began to turn the body over. Disturbed, the whine of the flies became more agitated.

'Oh, Christ!'

I don't know who spoke. Everyone there was seasoned in this work, but I don't think any of us could have seen anything like this before. The mutilation had been reserved for the victim's front. The abdomen had been cut open, and several objects spilled from the gaping wound as the body was turned. One of the officers quickly turned away, gagging. For a moment no-one moved. Then professionalism took over again.

'What the hell are they?' Mackenzie asked in a hushed, shocked voice. His normally sun-reddened face had turned white. I looked at them, but still couldn't say. This was outside my experience.

It was one of the crime scene officers who was the first to realize. 'They're rabbits,' he said. 'Baby rabbits.'

Mackenzie came over to where I was sitting in the open back of the Land Rover, a bottle of chilled water in my hand. I'd done as much as I could for now. It had been a relief to finally take off my coveralls. But even though I'd washed myself at the police trailer I still felt unclean, and not just because of the heat.

He sat next to me without saying anything. I took another drink of water as he unwrapped a packet of mints.

'Well,' he said at last. 'At least we know it's the same man.'

'Silver lining to every cloud, eh?' It came out sounding harsher than I'd meant. He glanced at me. 'You OK?'

'Just out of practice at this sort of thing.'

I thought he might apologize for involving me. He didn't. The silence ran for a while before he spoke again. 'Lyn Metcalf's been missing for nine days. If she's been dead for six or seven, like you say, that means he kept her alive for at least two. The same as Sally Palmer.'

'I know.'

He stared off into the distance, where the mercury surface of the lake shimmered in the heat. 'Why?'

'I'm not with you.'

'Why keep them alive for so long? Why take the risk?'

'I'm sure this isn't news to you, but we're not exactly dealing with a rational mind.'

'No, but he's not stupid. So why's he doing it?' He chewed his lip, looking annoyed. 'I can't see what's going on here.'

'In what way?'

225

'Usually when women are abducted and killed the motive's sexual. But this doesn't fit the usual pattern.'

'So you don't think they were raped?' The condition of this second body meant it would be just as impossible to say for certain as it had been with Sally Palmer. But it would have been some small comfort if the victims had been spared that much at least.

'That's not what I said. You find a woman's body without any clothes, it's a fair bet there was some kind of sexual assault, at least. But your run-of-the-mill sexual predator generally kills his victims straight away, as soon as he's got his rocks off. Very occasionally you'll get one who keeps them alive until he's tired of playing with them. But what this one's doing here, it doesn't make sense.'

'Perhaps he needs to build up to it.'

Mackenzie looked at me for a moment without speaking. He shrugged. 'Perhaps. But on the one hand we've got someone who's intelligent enough to snatch two women and disrupt the search by planting snares, and on the other doesn't bother to get rid of the bodies properly. And what about the mutilations? What's the point of those?'

'That's one to ask the psychologists, not me.'

'I will, don't worry. But I don't think they're likely to know either. Is he deliberately showing off or just being careless? It's like we're dealing with two conflicting mindsets.'

'A schizophrenic, you mean?'

He was frowning, worrying at the puzzle. 'I don't think so. Someone obviously mentally ill would have shown up long before now. And I'm not sure they'd be capable of this.'

'There's another thing,' I said. 'He's killed two women in, what, less than three weeks? And the second was only ten, eleven days after the first. That's not . . .' I was about to say 'normal', but that wasn't a word that could be remotely applied to this. 'That's not usual, is it? Even for a serial killer.'

Mackenzie looked tired. 'No. No, it's not.'

'So how come he's suddenly in such a rush? What's triggered him?'

'If I knew that we'd be halfway to catching the bastard.' He stood up, wincing as he kneaded the small of his back. 'I'll have the body brought to the lab. Probably tomorrow, OK?'

I nodded. But as he moved away I called him back. 'What about the dead birds and animals? Are you going to go public about them now?'

'We can't release details like that.'

'Not even if he's using them to mark out his victims in advance?'

'We don't know he is for certain.'

'You told me there was a stoat left on Sally Palmer's doorstep, and Lyn Metcalf told her husband she'd found a dead hare the day before she disappeared.'

'Like you said yourself, this is the countryside. Animals die all the time.'

'They don't tie themselves to stones or climb into a murdered woman's stomach.'

'We still don't know he used them to target his victims beforehand.'

227

'But if there's even a chance don't you think you should warn people?'

'What, and invite all the cranks and practical jokers to waste everyone's time? We'd be swamped with calls every time a bloody hedgehog gets run over.'

'If you don't he could target another victim without them knowing it. If he hasn't already.'

'I know that, but people are scared enough as it is. I'm not going to start a panic.'

But there was an undercurrent of doubt to his voice. 'He's going to do this again, isn't he?' I said.

For a second I thought he would actually answer. Then, without a word, he turned and walked away.

17

News that Lyn Metcalf's body had been found detonated in Manham like a silent bomb burst. Given what had happened to Sally Palmer, few people could have been surprised exactly, but that didn't lessen the shock. And while Sally, for all her popularity, had been an outsider, an immigrant to the village, Lyn had been born here. Gone to school here, married in the church. She was a part of Manham in a way that Sally could never be. Her death – her murder – had a far more visceral impact on people who could no longer pretend that the victim might somehow have imported the seeds of their fate from outside. Now the village mourned for one of its own.

And feared another.

There could no longer be doubt in anyone's mind that something terrible was happening in Manham. For this to happen to one woman was bad enough. For it to happen to two, in so short a space of time, was unprecedented. Suddenly, we were news again.

The village once again found itself caught in the spotlight, a collective traffic accident for the public to gawp at. As all victims do, it reacted first with bewildered disbelief, then resentment.

Then anger.

Lacking any other focus on which to vent it, Manham reacted by rounding on the outsiders attracted by its misfortune. Not the police, although resentment for their impotence was already starting to bubble. But the press had no such immunity. The news-gathering media's breathy excitement seemed to many to evince not just a lack of respect, but also contempt. It was met with hostility, exhibited first by stony faces and closed mouths, but then by more overt means. Over the next few days untended equipment either went missing or sustained mysterious damage. Cables were cut, tyres slashed, petrol tanks spiked with sugar. One persistent reporter, whose tightly lipsticked mouth seemed curled in a permanent and inappropriate smile, needed stitches when a flung stone gashed open her head.

Nobody saw anything.

But all that was only a symptom, an outward expression of the real malaise. After centuries of self-containment, of knowing it could always rely on its own no matter what, Manham could no longer trust itself. If suspicion had been a contagion before, now it threatened to become an epidemic. Old feuds and rivalries developed a more sinister depth. A fight broke out one night between three generations of two different families when smoke from a barbecue drifted over the wrong garden. A woman phoned the police in hysterics, only to find that her 'stalker' was a neighbour walking his dog. And two houses had bricks thrown through their windows; one for a perceived slight, the other for no reason anyone was ever able to determine, or at least admit.

And through it all, one man's presence seemed to grow larger every day. Scarsdale had become the voice of Manham. Where everyone else shunned the media, he showed no such reticence in putting himself before the cameras and microphones. He played all sides off against each other, speaking out against the police failure to catch the killer, the moral complacency that he claimed had led to this situation, and – apparently unaware of the irony – the press for exploiting the tragedy. If it had been anyone else they would have been accused of courting publicity. But, while there were a few mutterings about his willingness to have his sulphurous views broadcast, our good reverend developed a growing support. His voice thundered with the outrage everyone felt, and what it lacked in reason it more than made up for in intensity and volume.

Even so, perhaps naively, I expected him to keep his most vociferous announcements for the pulpit. But I'd underestimated Scarsdale's capacity to surprise, as well as his determination to capitalize on his new-found importance. So I was as unprepared as anyone when he announced he was holding a public meeting in the village hall.

It was held on the Monday after Lyn Metcalf's body had been found. The day before there had been a memorial service for her in the church. I'd been surprised to find that this time Scarsdale had refused to allow the media inside. Cynically, I'd wondered if that was less from consideration for the bereaved family than to make the press feel they were missing out. As I approached the village hall, I saw I'd been right.

The hall was a low, utilitarian building set back from the village square. When I'd driven past that morning on my way to the lab I'd seen Scarsdale outside, imperiously directing Tom Mason in its garden. Now the scent of freshly cut grass sweetened the air, and the yew hedges had been neatly trimmed. Old George and his grandson had been kept busy. Even the already immaculate green in the village square had been mown again, so that the area under the sweeping old horse chestnut and around the Martyr's Stone looked almost park-like in its neatness.

But I doubted it had been for our benefit. Denied access to the memorial service, the press had seized on the public meeting as the next best thing. Except this was less a public meeting than a press conference, I realized as I went into the hall. Rupert Sutton stood at the entrance, sweating and breathing adenoidally as he guarded the door. He gave me a reluctant nod, clearly aware I'd earned Scarsdale's disapproval.

Inside it was already cramped and hot. At the far end was a small stage, on which stood a trestle table and two chairs. A microphone was set in front of one of them. On the floor in front of the stage rows of collapsible wooden seats had been set out, leaving space around the sides and at the back of the hall for the TV crews and journalists.

All the seats were taken by the time I arrived, but I saw Ben standing off in one corner where there was a little more space. I made my way over.

'I didn't think I'd see you here,' I said as we regarded the packed hall.

'Thought I'd hear what the miserable bastard has to say. See what poisonous bullshit he's dreamed up now.'

He stood a good head above most of the other people there. I noticed a few of the TV crews looking over at him, but none seemed inclined to try their luck with an interview. Or perhaps they just didn't want to risk losing their places.

'Doesn't look like any of the police are here,' Ben said. 'You'd have thought they'd show their faces at least.'

'They haven't been invited,' I told him. Mackenzie had admitted as much earlier. He hadn't been happy about it, but a decision had been taken above his head not to interfere. 'Manham residents only.'

'Funny, I don't recognize some of the neighbours,' he said, looking at the assembly of cameras and microphones. He sighed and pulled at the neck of his shirt. 'God, it's hot in here. Fancy a pint afterwards?'

'Thanks, but I can't.'

'Got some late visits?'

'Uh, no, I'm seeing Jenny. You met her in the pub.'

'I know, the teacher.' He grinned. 'Been seeing quite a bit of each other, haven't you?'

233

I was conscious that my face had coloured like a teenager's. 'We're just friends.'

'Right.'

I was glad when he changed the subject. He looked at his watch. 'Might have guessed he'd keep everybody waiting. What do you think he's up to?'

'Soon find out,' I said, as a door on the stage opened.

But it wasn't Scarsdale who appeared. It was Marcus Metcalf.

The room instantly quietened. Lyn Metcalf's husband looked awful. He was a big man, but grief seemed to have reduced him. His suit was crumpled and he walked in slowly, as though favouring some deep injury. When I'd visited him shortly after the police had broken the news he seemed to have been barely aware of me. He hadn't wanted a sedative, for which I couldn't blame him. Some wounds can't be dulled, and trying only makes them worse. But looking at him now I wondered if he hadn't taken something anyway. He looked dazed and in shock, a man caught in a waking nightmare.

In the silence, Scarsdale followed Marcus out onto the stage. Their footsteps echoed on the wooden boards. As they approached the table the reverend placed his hand supportively – proprietorially, I couldn't help but think – on the younger man's shoulder. I felt a prickle of apprehension, knowing that the presence of the latest victim's husband would give far more credibility to whatever our reverend had in mind.

Scarsdale steered him towards one of the chairs.

The one without a microphone, I noticed. He waited until Marcus was seated before sitting down himself. He tapped the microphone once, making sure it was working, then unhurriedly surveyed the people in front of him.

'Thank you all for—' A faint whine of feedback made him draw back, frowning sharply in displeasure. He slid the microphone further away before continuing. 'Thank you for coming. This is a time of mourning, and under normal circumstances I would respect that. Unfortunately, the circumstances are far from normal.'

His amplified voice sounded even more sonorous than usual. While he spoke Lyn Metcalf's husband stared down at the table as though he wasn't aware of anyone else in the room.

'I will be brief, but what I have to say concerns all of us. It concerns everyone in this village. I would ask only for you to hear me out before asking any questions.' Scarsdale didn't look at any of the press when he spoke, but it was obvious who that last point was addressed to.

'Two women we all knew have now been killed,' he went on. 'As unpalatable as it may be, we can no longer avoid the fact that, in all likelihood, someone from this village is responsible. The police are obviously either unable, or perhaps unwilling, to take the necessary steps. But we can no longer sit back while women are being kidnapped and murdered.'

With deliberate, almost exaggerated solicitude, Scarsdale gestured to the man beside him. 'You all know the loss Marcus has suffered. The loss that his wife's family have suffered, having their daughter, their sister, ripped from them. Next time it could be your wife. Or your daughter. Or your sister. How much longer are we going to do nothing while these atrocities continue? How many more women must die? One? Two? More?'

He glared around, as if waiting for an answer. When none came, Scarsdale turned and murmured something to Lyn Metcalf's husband. The man blinked as if waking up. He looked blankly into the crowded hall.

'You have something to say, don't you, Marcus?' the reverend prompted, moving the microphone in front of him.

Marcus seemed to come to himself. He looked haunted. 'He killed Lyn. He killed my wife. He . . .' His voice faltered. Tears had started running down his face. 'He's got to be stopped. We should find him, and . . . and . . .'

Scarsdale put a hand on his arm, either to comfort or restrain. The reverend's expression was one of pious satisfaction as he slid the microphone in front of himself again.

'Enough is enough,' he said, in reasoned, measured tones. 'Enough . . . is . . . *enough*!' He slowly beat the table in emphasis. 'The time for doing nothing has passed. God is testing us. It's been our weakness, our complacency, that has allowed this creature masquerading as a man to conceal himself among us. To strike with impunity and contempt. And why? Because he knows he can.

236

Because he sees us as weak. And he doesn't fear weakness.'

The microphone jumped as he banged his fist on the table.

'Well, now it's time to *make* him fear us. Now's the time to show our strength! Manham has been a victim for too long! If the police cannot protect us, then we should protect ourselves! It's our duty to root him out!'

His raised voice merged into a howl of feedback. As he sat back the hall burst into commotion. Many of the people in the chairs came to their feet, applauding and shouting approval. As the cameras flashed and journalists shouted questions, Scarsdale sat centre stage and surveyed his work. For a moment he looked right at me. His eyes burned with fervour. And triumph, I realized.

Unnoticed, I made my way out.

'I just can't believe the man,' I said angrily. 'He seems to want to stir people up rather than calm things down. What's wrong with him?'

Jenny threw a piece of bread for a duck that had waddled up to our table. We were at a pub on the banks of the Bure, one of the six rivers that run through the Broads. Neither of us had wanted to stay in Manham, and although this was only a few miles away it could have been a different world. Boats were moored on the river, children played nearby, and the tables were full of people chatting and laughing. Textbook English pub, textbook English summer. It was a far cry from the oppressive atmosphere we'd left behind.

Jenny gave the last crumbs to the duck. 'He's got people listening to him now. Perhaps that's what he wants.'

'But doesn't he realize what he's doing? One man's already been put in hospital by idiots who got carried away, and now he's encouraging vigilantes. And using Marcus Metcalf to drum up support!'

I remembered how Scarsdale had been with him even during the search for his wife. I wouldn't have put it past our reverend to have been priming him even then, getting ready to exploit the tragic husband. I wished now I'd spoken to Marcus when Lyn went missing. I hadn't wanted to intrude on his grief, but I couldn't deny there might be a selfish aspect as well. Seeing him had been a painful reminder of my own loss, but by standing back I'd given Scarsdale a free rein to exert his influence. And he hadn't missed the opportunity.

'You think that's really what he wants? To stir things up?' Jenny asked. She hadn't been to the meeting; said she didn't feel she'd lived in the village long enough to take part in it. But I think it was also the prospect of the crowd that had kept her away.

'That's what it sounded like. I don't know why I'm surprised. Fire and brimstone makes more of an impression than turning the other cheek. And he's spent years standing in front of an empty church on Sunday morning. He's not going to miss his chance to say "I told you so" now.'

'Sounds like he's not the only one who's worked up.'

I hadn't realized how angry Scarsdale had made

me. 'Sorry. I'm just worried somebody might do something stupid.'

'There's nothing you can do about it anyway. You're not the village conscience.'

She sounded distracted. It occurred to me that she'd been quiet all evening. I looked at the line of her profile, the faint pattern of freckles across her cheeks and nose; the fine blond down on her arms, whitened by the sun against her tanned skin. She was gazing off into the distance, lost in some internal dialogue.

'Anything the matter?' I asked.

'No. I was just thinking.'

'What about?'

'Oh . . . just stuff.' She smiled, but there was a tension about her. 'Look, do you mind if we go back?'

I tried to hide my surprise. 'Not if you want to.'

'Please.'

We drove back in silence. There was a hollowness in the pit of my stomach. I cursed myself for making such a fuss about Scarsdale. No wonder she'd had enough. *Well, now you've blown it. Congratulations.*

The light was fading when we reached Manham. I indicated to turn off onto her road.

'No, not here,' she said. 'I . . . I thought you could show me where you live.'

It took me a moment to understand.

'OK.'

The word didn't come out right. I felt breathless as I parked the car. I unlocked the door to the house and stood back to let her in. The delicate musk

239

of her perfume made me light-headed as she passed.

She went into the small lounge. I could feel her nervousness, matching my own.

'Would you like a drink?'

She shook her head. We stood awkwardly. *Do something.* But I couldn't. In the half-light I couldn't see her clearly. Only her eyes, bright in the darkness. We looked at each other, neither of us moving. When she spoke, her voice was unsteady.

'Where's the bedroom?'

Jenny was hesitant to begin with, tense and trembling. Gradually, she began to relax, and so did I. At first memory tried to impose its own template of shape, texture and scent. Then the present took over, sweeping away everything else. Afterwards, she lay curled against me, breath soft on my chest. I felt her hands go to my face, explore the tracks of wetness running down.

'David?'

'It's nothing, just . . .'

'I know. It's all right.'

And it was. I laughed, hugging her, then tilted up her chin. We kissed, long and slowly, and my tears dried unnoticed as we moved together again.

Some time that same night, while we were in bed together, across the village Tina thought she heard a noise in the back garden. Like Jenny, she'd avoided the meeting in the village hall. She'd stayed in, a bottle of white wine and a block of chocolate for company. She'd intended to stay up until Jenny got home, eager to hear how the evening had been. But by the time she'd watched the DVD she'd hired she was yawning and ready for bed. It was as she turned off the TV that she heard something outside.

Tina wasn't stupid. There was a killer at large who had already murdered two women. She didn't open the door. Instead, snatching up the telephone, she turned out the light and went to the window. With the telephone poised, ready to connect to the police, she peeped cautiously into the back garden.

Nothing. The night was bright, the moon full and revealing. The garden, and the paddock beyond, was empty of menace. Even so, she watched for a while before she convinced herself it had been her imagination.

It was only next morning that she saw what had been left outside. In the centre of the lawn was a dead fox. It might almost have been arranged there, so carefully was it positioned. If she had known about the swan wings, or the mallard, or any of the other dead creatures the killer had used to decorate and elaborate his creations, Tina would not have done what she did next.

But she didn't know. Country girl that she was, she just scooped it up and deposited it into the dustbin. Judging from its wounds, it had probably crawled there after being savaged by a dog, she reasoned. Or perhaps been run over. She might still have mentioned it to Jenny, if only in passing. Who might then have told me about it. Except Jenny hadn't come home that night. Jenny was still at my house, and when Tina saw her again the topic of conversation was naturally about matters far removed from dead wildlife.

So Tina told no-one about the fox. It was only days later, when its significance was all too obvious, that she even remembered it.

And by then it was too late.

18

Two things happened over the next twenty-four hours. Of the two, it was the first that had most people talking. At any other time this was an event that would have been a source of scandalized gossip, subject to endless tellings and retellings before it became absorbed into Manham folklore, a chapter of village history to be chuckled and tutted over for decades. As it was, it was to have repercussions that were far more serious than any physical injuries it caused.

In a confrontation that many thought was years overdue, Ben Anders and Carl Brenner had a fight.

It was partly drink, and partly animosity, and partly the pressures of recent days. The two men had never made any pretence of liking each other, and the unnatural tensions in the village had the effect of rubbing raw far slighter grievances than theirs. It was almost closing time at the Lamb. Ben had just ordered a whisky to finish, after what he admitted was a pint or two more than normal. He'd had a hellish day at the nature reserve, having to give first aid to a birdwatcher who'd had a heart attack in the heat, as well as coping with the usual crises of the tourist season. When Carl Brenner came into the pub, 'cocky and full of himself', as Ben later put it, he'd turned his back, determined not to give a bad day a worse end by letting himself be goaded.

It didn't quite work out that way.

Brenner hadn't come in just for a drink. Fired up over Scarsdale's call to arms the night before, this was both a recruitment drive and an announcement of intent. With him was Dale Brenner, a swarthy cousin unlike him in looks, but a brother in habit and temperament. They were part of a larger group who, under Scarsdale's urging, had taken it upon themselves to patrol the village, day and night. 'Because the police are doing fuck all, so we've got to sort this bastard out ourselves,' was how Brenner put it, echoing the reverend's sentiment, if not his language.

At first Ben remained silent as the Brenners tried to drum up more volunteers. But then Carl, emboldened by alcohol and his new-found mission, made the mistake of confronting him directly.

'So what about you, Anders?'

'What about me?'

'You with us or not?'

Ben slowly finished his whisky before answering. 'So you're going to sort this bastard out, are you?'

'That's right. You got a problem with that?'

'Only one. How do you know he isn't one of you?'

Never blessed with the sharpest of minds, that had

244

obviously never occurred to Brenner. 'In fact, how do we know it isn't *you*?' Ben demanded. 'Digging holes, setting traps. Sounds right up your street.'

He admitted later that he was merely baiting the other man, didn't stop to think what a dangerous accusation it was. And it pushed Brenner further than he might otherwise have gone.

'Fuck off, Anders! The police know I had nothing to do with it!'

'This the same police you said a minute ago were doing fuck all? And you want me to join you? Jesus,' Ben sneered, letting his contempt show. 'Stick to poaching. It's all you're good for.'

'At least I've got an alibi! What about you?'

Ben levelled a finger at him. 'Watch it, Brenner.'

'Why? Have you or haven't you?'

'I'm warning you . . .'

Bolstered by the presence of his cousin, Brenner didn't back down as he usually did. 'So fucking what? I'm getting sick of you throwing your weight around. And you were quick enough to stick up for your doctor mate last week, weren't you? Where was he when Lyn went missing?'

'So now you're saying we both did it?'

'Prove you didn't!'

'I don't have to prove anything to you, Brenner,' Ben said, his tenuous grip on his temper slipping. 'So why don't you and the rest of your vigilante heroes take your pathetic patrol and shove it up your arse?'

They glared at each other. Brenner broke first. 'Come on,' he said to his cousin, and it almost ended there. But, unable to leave without an attempt to

245

save face, he couldn't resist one final jibe. 'Fucking coward,' he spat as he turned to leave.

That was the point when Ben's good intentions went out of the window. And so, very nearly, did Carl Brenner.

The fight that followed was short-lived. There were enough men in the pub to jump in before it got too far out of hand, which was probably just as well for Ben. Brenner by himself posed no threat, but as big as he was Ben might have struggled to take on his cousin as well. By the time they were dragged apart a table and several chairs had been smashed, and it would be several weeks before Brenner could look at himself again in a shaving mirror – far less shave – without wincing. Ben himself didn't emerge unscathed, suffering various cuts and bruises and dislocating one of his knuckles. All of which, he claimed, were well worth it.

But the truly serious damage wouldn't emerge for several more days.

I wasn't there when the fight happened. I had cooked a meal for Jenny, who was staying the night, and Manham's problems had gone from my mind. In fact, I was probably one of the last people to hear about it, as first thing the following morning I went to continue the grim task waiting for me at the mortuary.

Since Lyn Metcalf's body had been found, Henry had again been standing in for me while I went to the lab. I was doing my best to rush back in time for evening surgery, but the additional workload was taking its toll on him. He was looking tired, even though he'd reduced surgery hours to a bare minimum, running it almost on a skeleton basis when I wasn't there.

I felt guilty, but at least it wouldn't be for much longer. Another half-day at the lab and I would have done as much as I could. I was still waiting for most of the test results, but so far Lyn Metcalf's remains had yielded a similar story to those of Sally Palmer. There had been no real surprises, except the question of why the first victim's face had been so badly battered while that of the second had been left untouched. Also, with the decomposition less advanced, some of Lyn Metcalf's fingernails had still remained on the body. They'd been broken and torn, and the forensic lab had found hemp fibres attached to some of them. Rope, in other words. Whatever else had been done to her, it seemed she'd been tied up.

Other than the wound that had opened her throat and the horrific mutilation, Lyn's injuries had been mainly superficial cuts. Only the one to her throat had left its mark on the bone. Like the one I'd found on Sally Palmer, it had been caused by a large, sharp blade. Probably a hunting knife, and almost certainly the same one, although at this stage there was no way of proving that for certain. But it wasn't serrated. Which left me no wiser as to why the two women had been killed with one weapon, while another had been used on the dog.

I was still worrying at it as I went into the waiting area after the last patient had left. The evening surgery had been quiet, with barely half the number of patients as normal. Either people were loath to worry about more trivial complaints in the face of the larger tragedy, or there was another, even less palatable reason why so many had decided to avoid their doctor. Or one of them, at least. Requests to see Henry were higher than they had been for years, more and more people apparently preferring to wait rather than see me.

But I was too taken up by Jenny and my work at the lab to worry about it.

Janice was tidying the waiting room when I went in, straightening the mismatched old chairs and restacking the dog-eared magazines.

'Quiet night,' I said.

She picked a child's puzzle off the floor and put it back in the wooden box with the other toys. 'Better than a room full of sniffles and hypochondriacs.'

'Fair point.' I appreciated her tact. She knew as well as I did that my appointment list was shrinking. 'Where's Henry?'

'Having a doze. I think surgery this morning took it out of him a bit. And don't look like that. It's not your fault.'

Janice knew I was doing something for the police, if not exactly what. There was no way I could have kept it from her, and no real reason to. She might have liked to gossip, but she knew where to draw the line.

'Is he OK?' I asked, concerned.

'Just tired. Besides, it's not just the work.' She gave me a meaningful look. 'It would have been his anniversary this week.'

I'd forgotten. There had been too much else going on for me to keep track of dates, but Henry always became subdued around this time of year. He never spoke about it, any more than I did when mine came round. But it was there, all the same.

'It would have been their thirtieth,' Janice went on, keeping her voice down. 'Makes it even worse, I suppose. So in a way it's good that he's working more. Helps him keep his mind off it.' Her expression hardened. 'It's just a shame that—'

'Janice,' I said, warningly.

'Well, it is. She didn't deserve him. And he deserved better.'

The words came out in a rush. She seemed close to tears.

'Are you all right?' I asked.

She nodded, smiling tremulously. 'Sorry. But I just hate seeing him get upset over . . .' She broke off. 'And all this other business. It just wears everybody down.'

She started bustling over the magazines again. I went over and took them off her.

'Tell you what, why don't you go home early for once?'

'But I was going to vac up . . .'

'I'm sure we can stand to be a health hazard for another day.'

She laughed, more herself again. 'If you're sure . . .'

'Certain. Do you want a lift?'

'No! It's too nice an evening to be sitting in a car.'

I didn't insist. She only lived a few hundred yards

249

away, and most of that was on the main road. There was a point where being safety conscious became paranoia. Still, I watched through the window as she went down the drive.

When she'd gone I went back to the magazines she'd left and made a token attempt to finish straightening them. A few old copies of the local parish newsletter had found their way into the pile, left by patients too idle to throw them away. I dropped them into the bin, but as I did something on one of their pages caught my eye.

I retrieved it from the waste bin. Sally Palmer's face smiled brightly out at me. Below her photograph was a small piece about Manham's 'celebrity author', printed a few weeks before she'd been murdered. I hadn't seen it before, and it was unsettling to find it now, after her death. I started to read it and felt as if the air had been driven from my lungs. I sat down, read it again.

Then I went to phone Mackenzie.

He read the article in silence. He'd been at the mobile incident room when I'd phoned, and when I told him about the newsletter he'd come straight over. The back of his neck and hands were livid with sunburn as he read the story. When he'd finished he closed the paper without expression.

'So, what do you think?' I asked.

He rubbed at the peeling and reddened skin on his nose. 'It could be just coincidence.'

He was being the policeman now, professionally uncommunicative. And he might be right. But I doubted it. I picked up the newsletter and looked at the story again. It was only short, little more than a filler on a quiet news day. The caption read 'Country life gives wing to local author's imagination'. The quote that had inspired it was at the end:

> *Sally Palmer says living in Manham helps her to write her novels. 'I love being this close to nature. It helps my imagination take flight. It's the next best thing to having wings,' says the critically acclaimed writer.*

I put the newsletter down. 'You think it's a coincidence that someone stuck a pair of swan wings into her back a couple of weeks after she said this?'

Mackenzie showed signs of exasperation. 'I said it could be. I'm not prepared to say one way or the other just off the back of a flimsy item in a newsletter.'

'So how else do you explain the mutilation?'

He looked uncomfortable, like a man forced to recite a party line he wasn't convinced by himself. 'The psychologists think it might be a suppressed desire for transformation. Giving her angel wings after he'd killed her. They say he could be some religious nut who's obsessed with a higher state.'

'What do the psychologists say about the other dead animals? Or what he did to Lyn Metcalf?'

'They're not sure about that yet. But even if you're right, that' – he gestured at the newsletter – 'doesn't explain it either.'

I chose my words carefully. 'Actually, that was something else I wanted to talk to you about.'

He regarded me cautiously. 'Go on.'

'After I called you I looked through Lyn Metcalf's medical notes. And her husband's. Did you know they were trying to start a family? They were considering fertility treatments.'

It only took him a second to get it. 'Baby rabbits. Jesus,' he breathed.

'But how would the killer know about that?'

Mackenzie looked at me, debating something. 'We found a pregnancy testing kit hidden in a drawer in the Metcalfs' bedroom,' he said, slowly. 'There was a receipt in the bag, from the day before she went missing.'

I remembered bumping into her as she came out of the chemist's. How happy she'd looked. 'Had it been used?'

'No. And her husband claimed he didn't know it was there.'

'But you don't buy something like that unless you're planning to use it. So she must have thought she could be pregnant.'

Mackenzie nodded, his expression grim. 'And what would a pregnant woman say to someone who'd kidnapped her? "Don't hurt me, I'm having a baby." ' He passed a hand over his face. 'Christ. I suppose there's no way of knowing now if she was or not?'

'Not a chance. Not so early in the term and with the condition the body was in.'

He nodded, unsurprised. 'If she was, though – or

if she only thought she was – then catching this bastard's going to be even harder than we expected.'

'Why?'

'Because it means the mutilations aren't planned in advance. He's making it up as he goes along.' Mackenzie rose to his feet, looking tired. 'And if he doesn't know what he's going to do next, what chance have we got?'

After he'd gone I drove out into the country. I didn't have any destination in mind, just wanted to get away from Manham for an hour or two. I wasn't seeing Jenny that evening. We were both surprised by how suddenly things had developed between us, and after the intensity of the last two days we needed some time apart. I think we both wanted breathing space to stand back and consider this unexpected sea change in our lives, and where it might take us. There was an unspoken sense that neither of us wanted to spoil things by going too fast. After all, if this was what we both felt it to be, what was the hurry?

I should have known better than to risk tempting fate.

Before long I found myself on top of a low rise, offering views of the spreading landscape around me. I stopped the car and got out. I sat on a hummock of grass, watching the sun sink towards the waiting marshes. Light blazed golden from the pools and creeks that formed abstract patterns in the reeds. For a while I tried to concentrate on the murders. But it all seemed too far removed from me now. The colours of sky and land slowly deepened towards night, but I felt no compulsion to move.

For the first time since the accident I felt as if the future had opened up for me. I was finally able to look ahead rather than to the past. I thought about Jenny, and about Kara and Alice, searching myself for any trace of guilt, any sense of betrayal. There was none. Only anticipation. The pain of absence was still there, and always would be. But now there was also an acceptance. My wife and daughter were dead, and I couldn't bring them back. For a long time I'd been dead as well. Now, unexpectedly, I'd come alive again.

I sat watching the sun set until it was no more than a bright sliver on the horizon, the marsh landscape a uniform dark matt that soaked up the light. When I finally got up, stiff and aching after sitting for so long, I realized I didn't need any more time to think things through. And I didn't want to wait till the next day before I saw Jenny again. I reached for my phone to call her, but it wasn't in my pocket. It wasn't in the Land Rover either. I remembered putting it on my desk when Mackenzie came, and with my mind on other things I must have walked out without it.

I almost didn't bother going to get it. But I didn't want to turn up unannounced on Jenny's doorstep. Just because I'd resolved my own issues didn't necessarily mean that she had as well. And besides, I was still the village doctor. Manham might have its reservations about me at the moment, but I couldn't bring myself to be out of touch. And so, when I reached the village, I headed to the surgery for my phone.

The streetlights came on as I drove along the main street. Just before I reached the police trailer in the square I saw a group of men standing in the spill of light from one. One of Scarsdale's vigilante patrols, I guessed. They stared at me as I went past, their faces suspicious in the sickly yellow glare.

Leaving them behind, I turned off the main street and up the long drive leading to Henry's. The car tyres crunched on the gravel, my headlights splashing on the front of the house as I mounted the rise and dropped down the slope. The windows were dark, which didn't surprise me because Henry usually went to bed early. Not wanting to wake him, rather than use the front door I went round the back to let myself directly into the surgery.

I'd taken out my keys to unlock the French doors to my office before I noticed that the door to the kitchen stood open. If the light had been on I might have thought nothing of it. But the kitchen was in darkness, and I knew Henry would never have gone to bed without locking up.

I went across and looked inside. Nothing seemed disturbed. I started to reach for the light switch, but checked myself. Some instinct told me something was wrong. I briefly considered phoning the police. But what could I tell them? For all I knew Henry might just have forgotten to close the door after going out into the garden. My stock in the village was low enough as it was without word getting out that I'd made a fool of myself.

Instead, I went into the hallway. 'Henry?' I called, loud enough to be heard if he was up and about, not loud enough to wake him.

There was no reply. His study was at the far end of the hallway, around the corner. Unable to shake the idea that I was overreacting, I set off towards it. The door was slightly ajar, revealing that the light was on inside. I paused, listening for some sign of life or movement. But the thump of my own heart drowned out any lesser sounds. I put my hand on the door and started to push it open.

Suddenly it was wrenched from my hand. I was knocked aside as a bulky shadow burst from the room. Winded, I lunged for it and felt a waft of air pass in front of me. My hand clutched coarse, greasy cloth and then something crashed into my face. I staggered back as the figure bolted into the kitchen. By the time I reached it the back door was swinging back against its hinges. Without thinking I set off to go after him. And then I remembered Henry.

Pausing only long enough to close and bolt the door to the garden, I ran back to his study. As I reached it the hall lights came on.

'David? What the hell's going on?'

Henry was pushing himself down the hallway from his bedroom, looking dishevelled and startled.

'Someone was in here. They ran out when I disturbed them.'

Reaction was setting in now, the aftermath of adrenalin making me shaky. I went into the study. With relief I saw that the steel cabinet was still locked. Whoever had been in here hadn't got into our drug store, at least. Then I noticed the glass case where Henry kept his collection of medicinal relics. The doors were thrown open, the objects and bottles inside scattered.

Henry swore and started towards it. 'Don't touch anything. The police will want to check for finger-prints,' I warned. 'Any idea what might have been taken?'

He was peering uncertainly at the mess. 'I'm not sure . . .'

But even as he spoke I noticed one obvious absence. As long as I'd worked here there had been an antiquated bottle gathering dust on the top shelf, its green glass vertically ribbed in the long-outmoded warning for poison. Now it was gone.

Until then I thought the intruder had been looking for drugs. Even Manham had its share of addicts. But I doubted even the most desperate junkie would have taken a bottle of chloroform.

I was brought back by an exclamation from Henry.

'My God, David, are you all right?'

He was staring at my chest. I was about to ask what he meant, but then I saw for myself. I remembered the waft of air I'd felt as I'd grabbed at the intruder in the hallway. Now I understood what it was.

The front of my shirt had been slashed open.

19

After the commotion of the previous night, the next day started off like any other. That was what struck me, later. I should have known from experience that catastrophe doesn't announce itself in advance. But when it came now I was completely unprepared.

Like everyone else.

It was almost four o'clock before the police had finished at the surgery. They'd descended on it like a fury, taking photographs, dusting for fingerprints and asking their questions. Mackenzie had arrived looking tired and frazzled, like a man recently woken from a bad sleep.

'Go through it again. You're telling me someone broke into the house, took a slice at you and managed to get away, without anyone getting a look at him?'

I was tired and irritable myself. 'It was dark.'

'So there was nothing familiar about him?'

'No, sorry.'

'And there's no chance you could identify him again?'

'I wish there was, but I've told you, it was too dark.'

Henry had been equally unable to help. He'd been in his bedroom all the time, unaware of anything until he'd heard the commotion and emerged to see me returning from my abortive chase. If things had gone differently, Manham might have been waking up to hear of another murder. Perhaps even two.

Judging by Mackenzie's attitude as he questioned me, he thought that was the least we deserved. 'And you've no idea what else he might have taken?'

I could only shake my head. The drugs cabinet was undisturbed, and nothing was missing from the fridge where we stored the vaccines and other temperature-reliant medicines. But Henry was the only one who knew what was in the cluttered glass display case, and until the forensics team had finished with it he couldn't say for sure what was missing and what wasn't.

Mackenzie squeezed the bridge of his nose. His eyes were red-rimmed and angry. 'Chloroform.' He sounded disgusted. 'I don't even know if you've broken any laws having something like that on the premises. I didn't think doctors used it any more.'

'They don't. It was just a curio of Henry's. There's even an old stomach pump in there somewhere.'

'I wouldn't care about a stomach pump, but this bastard's dangerous enough as it is without a bottle full of bloody anaesthetic!' He stopped himself. 'How the hell did he get in here anyway?'

'I let him in.'

We both turned as Henry came through the doorway. We were in my office, one of the few downstairs rooms where we knew we wouldn't compromise any evidence, as I locked it every night. I'd insisted that Henry have a break from the questioning. The break-in had badly rattled him, and he hadn't improved after almost an hour of interrogation. He seemed a little recovered now, although his colour still wasn't good.

'You let him in,' Mackenzie repeated flatly. 'You said earlier you didn't know anyone was in the house.'

'That's right. But it's still my fault. I've been thinking back, and . . .' He took a deep breath. 'Well, I . . . I can't seem to remember actually locking the kitchen door before I went to bed.'

'I thought you said it was locked.'

'Yes, I assumed it was. I mean, I always lock it. As a rule, that is.'

'But not tonight.'

'I'm not certain.' Henry cleared his throat, his discomfort painful to see. 'Apparently not.'

'And what about the cabinet? Was that unlocked as well?'

'I don't know.' Henry sounded exhausted. 'The keys are in my desk drawer. He might have found them, or . . .' His voice trailed off.

Mackenzie looked as though he were trying hard to keep hold of his temper. 'How many people knew about the chloroform?'

'Lord knows. It's been here longer than I have. I never considered it a secret.'

'So anyone who came in here could have seen it?'

'It's possible, I suppose,' Henry conceded, grudgingly.

'This is a doctor's surgery,' I told Mackenzie. 'Everybody knows there's going to be dangerous substances here. Tranquillizers, sedatives, whatever.'

'Which are supposed to be locked away,' Mackenzie said. 'The bottom line is this man was able to just walk in here and start helping himself.'

'Look, I didn't bloody invite him!' Henry flashed. 'Don't you think I feel bad enough already? I've been a doctor for thirty years, and nothing like this has ever happened before!'

'But it happened tonight,' Mackenzie reminded him. 'The one night you forgot to lock the door.'

Henry looked down at his lap. 'Actually . . . it might not be the only time. There have been a couple of occasions recently when I've . . . I've got up and found the door still open. Only one or two. I generally remind myself to lock up,' he added, hurriedly. 'But . . . well, lately I seem to have been getting a bit . . . forgetful.'

'Forgetful.' Mackenzie's voice was toneless. 'But this is the first time anyone's actually broken in, is it?'

I was about to answer for Henry, say that of course it was. Then I caught his anguished expression.

'Well, I . . .' He crossed and uncrossed his hands. 'I'm not sure.'

Mackenzie continued to stare at him. Henry gave a lost shrug.

'The thing is, I suppose there have been a couple of times I thought the cabinet seemed . . . rearranged.'

'Rearranged? You mean things were missing?'

'I don't know, I was never very sure. It could have been my memory playing tricks.' He gave me a shame-filled glance. 'I'm sorry, David. I should have told you. But I hoped . . . Well, I thought if I made more of an effort . . .'

He lifted his hands, let them fall helplessly. I didn't know what to say. I felt worse than ever for forcing him to stand in for me recently. Apart from his disability, I'd always thought of him as being physically sound. Now, in the early hours of the morning, I saw signs I'd overlooked before. There were hollows under his eyes, and the skin around his silver-stubbled chin and neck hung loosely. Even taking into account the shock he'd had, he looked ill and old.

I caught Mackenzie's eye, willing him not to push too hard. Thin-lipped, he led me aside, leaving Henry to sit disconsolately with a cup of tea a young policewoman had made for him.

'You realize what this means?' Mackenzie said.

'I know.'

'This might not be the first time this has happened.'

'I know.'

'Good, because your friend over there could be looking at losing his licence. It'd be bad enough if it was just junkies, but this is a serial killer we're talking about. And now it looks as though he's been able to waltz in here and help himself for Christ knows how long!'

I stopped myself before I could say 'I know' again. 'He'd have to have some medical knowledge to know what to take. And how to use it.'

'Oh, come on! The man's a killer! You think he's going to worry about giving the right dose? And you don't need to be a brain surgeon to know what to do with chloroform.'

'If he'd been in here before why didn't he take the entire bottle?' I asked.

'Perhaps he didn't want anyone to know what he'd taken. If he'd not been surprised tonight we wouldn't have found out now, would we?'

I'd been unable to argue with that. I felt as culpable as if I'd been the negligent one instead of Henry. I was his partner, I should have been more aware of what was going on. Of what was happening to him.

Finally, the police had done as much as they could, and I'd gone home. The dawn chorus was already starting when my head touched the pillow.

Almost immediately, it seemed, I was awake again.

It was the first time in days that I'd had the dream. It had been as vivid as ever, but for once it hadn't left me with a renewed sense of loss. I felt saddened but calm. Alice hadn't been there, only Kara. We'd talked about Jenny. *It's all right*, she'd told me, smiling. *This is how it should be.*

It had seemed almost like a leave-taking; long-delayed but inevitable. Yet the memory of Kara's final words, delivered with the slight furrow of concern I knew so well, had left a lingering unease.

Be careful.

But of what I should be careful, I didn't know. I puzzled over it for a while before realizing I was only trying to analyse my own subconscious.

It was just a dream, after all.

I got up and showered. Although I'd only been in bed a few hours I felt as rested as if I'd just had a full night's sleep. I set off early for the lab so I could check on Henry on my way in. I was worried about him after what had happened the night before. He'd looked awful, and I couldn't help but feel responsible. If he hadn't been so tired from all the extra work I'd forced on him he might not have forgotten to lock the surgery door in the first place.

I let myself into the house and called him. There was no answer. I went into the kitchen but there was no sign of him there either. Trying to ignore the prickle of unease, I told myself he was probably still sleeping. As I turned to leave the kitchen I glanced out of the window and stopped dead. Across the garden I could glimpse part of the old wooden jetty where it jutted into the lake. Henry's wheelchair was on it.

It was empty.

I ran out of the back door, shouting his name. The entrance to the jetty was further down the garden, obscured by shrubs and trees. I couldn't see onto it until I reached the gate, and then I slowed, relieved. Next to the empty chair, Henry was perched precariously on the jetty's edge, trying to lower himself into the dinghy. His face was flushed with effort and concentration as his legs dangled uselessly over the boat.

'For God's sake, Henry, what are you doing?'

He flashed me an angry look but didn't stop. 'I'm going out in the boat. What's it bloody look like?'

He was grunting as his arms took the strain of his weight. I hesitated, wanting to help him but knowing better than to try. At least if he fell in now I was there to drag him out.

'Come on, Henry, you know you shouldn't be doing this.'

'Mind your own bloody business!'

I stared at him in surprise. His mouth was set but quivering. He carried on with his futile attempt for a moment longer, and then the struggle abruptly went out of him. He sank back against a wooden post, covering his eyes.

'I'm sorry, David. I didn't mean that.'

'Do you want a hand back into the chair?'

'Give me a minute to catch my breath.'

I sat down next to him on the rough planks of the jetty. His chest was still labouring, his shirt stuck to him with sweat. 'How long have you been here?'

'I don't know. A while.' He gave a weak smile. 'Seemed like a good idea at the time.'

'Henry . . .' I didn't know what to say. 'What the hell were you thinking of? You know you can't get into the boat by yourself.'

'I know, I know, it's just . . .' His expression darkened. 'That bloody policeman. The way he looked at me last night. Spoke to me, like I was some . . . some senile old fool! I know I made a mistake; I

265

should have checked the locks. But to have someone patronize me like that . . .'

He stared down at his legs, mouth tightening.

'It gets frustrating sometimes. Feeling helpless. Sometimes you feel you've just got to *do* something, you know?'

I looked at the flat, deserted expanse of the lake. There wasn't another soul to be seen. 'What if you'd fallen in?'

'Then I'd have put everyone out of their misery, wouldn't I?' He glanced up at me and gave a sardonic grin, looking more like himself. 'Don't look at me like that. I'm not planning on topping myself just yet. I've made a big enough fool of myself for one day.'

He pushed himself upright, grimacing with the effort.

'Help me back into that bloody chair, will you?'

I got my hands under him, supporting his weight as he levered himself back into the wheelchair. It was a sign of how tired he was that he made no objection when I pushed him back to the house. I was already late for the lab, but I stayed long enough to make him some tea, and to satisfy myself he was all right.

He yawned and rubbed his eyes as I stood up to leave. 'I'd better get myself ready. Morning surgery starts in half an hour.'

'Not today. You're in no condition to work. You need to get some sleep.'

He cocked an eyebrow. 'Doctor's orders, is it?'

'If you like.'

'What about the patients?'

266

'Janice can let them know it's cancelled this morning. If it's urgent they can call the out-of-hours service.'

For once he didn't argue. Now that the frustration had left him, he looked drained.

'Look, David ... You won't tell anyone about this, will you?'

'Of course not.'

He nodded, relieved. 'Good. I feel stupid enough as it is.'

'There's no need.'

I was at the door when he called me back.

'David ...' He paused, embarrassed. 'Thank you.'

His gratitude didn't make me feel any better. As I drove to the lab I was uncomfortably aware of how much extra pressure I'd placed him under lately. I'd been taking him for granted, not only in terms of the practice but in other ways as well. I wished now I'd made the effort to go out with him on the lake, or just spend more time with him. But I'd been so wrapped up with the investigation, and even more so with Jenny, that I hadn't spared much thought for Henry.

That would change, I resolved. I'd done nearly as much as I could in the lab. Once I'd given Mackenzie my findings it would be down to the police to try and make some use of what I'd told them, and I'd be able to make amends for my recent neglect. After today, I told myself, my life would be back to normal.

I couldn't have been more wrong.

After the turmoil of the past twelve hours it was almost a relief to get back into the clinical sanctuary of the lab. Here, at least, I was on surer footing. The results of the analyses had come back, confirming what I'd guessed already. Lyn Metcalf had been dead for approximately six days, meaning her killer had kept her alive for whatever unholy reason for nearly three before slitting her throat. That was the wound that had killed her. Like Sally Palmer, the desiccated state of her body revealed that she'd bled out. And the low iron content of the soil around the body again showed that her death had taken place somewhere else, her body taken to the marsh and dumped afterwards.

Also, as with Sally Palmer, there had been nothing found at the site to indicate who might have done this to her. The ground was baked too hard to yield footprints, and except for the rope fibres caught on her broken fingernails there was no trace evidence, no forensic clues left as to the killer's identity.

But that was for someone else to worry about. My own contribution was almost finished. I took final casts of the cervical vertebrae that had been cut by the knife, more certain than ever that the two women had been killed by the same weapon. After that there was nothing more to do but clean up. Marina asked if I wanted to have lunch to mark the occasion, but I declined. I still hadn't had a chance to talk to Jenny, and all at once I couldn't wait.

I rang her as soon as Marina had left. As I waited for her to answer my excitement was so keen it hurt.

'Sorry,' she said, out of breath. 'Tina's out and I was in the garden.'

'So, how are you?' I asked. I felt suddenly nervous.

I'd been so busy contemplating my own navel I'd not stopped to consider what conclusions she might have reached herself about our relationship.

'I'm OK, but how are you? Everyone's talking about what happened at the surgery last night. You weren't hurt, were you?'

'No, I'm fine. It was worse for Henry.'

'God, when I heard I thought . . . well, I was worried.'

It had never occurred to me that she might be. I wasn't used to having to consider anyone else. 'Sorry. I should have called earlier.'

'It's all right. I'm just glad you're OK. I would have called you, but . . .' I tensed as she paused. *Here it comes.* 'Look, I know we said we were going to take a couple of days, but . . . Well, I'd really like to see you. If you want to, I mean.'

I found myself grinning. 'I want to.'

'You're sure?'

'I'm certain.'

We both laughed. 'God, this is ridiculous. I feel like a teenager,' she said.

'Me too.' I glanced at my watch. Ten past one. I could be back in Manham by two, and evening surgery wasn't until four. 'I could come round now, if you like.'

'OK.' She sounded shy, but I could hear the smile in her voice. A two-note chime sounded in the background. 'Hang on a sec, someone's at the door.'

I heard her put the receiver down. I leaned on the edge of the workbench, an idiot grin still on my face as I waited for her to pick it up again. To hell with

269

giving ourselves space. All I knew was that I wanted to be with her right now, more than anything I'd wanted in a long time. I could hear the radio playing in the background as I waited. It was longer than I'd expected before I heard the phone being picked up again.

'Milkman?' I joked.

There was no answer. I could hear someone breathing at the other end. Deep and slightly rushed, as though after some exertion.

'Jenny?' I said, uncertainly.

Nothing. The breathing continued for one, two beats. Then there was a soft click as the other person hung up.

I stared stupidly at the receiver, then fumblingly redialled. *Answer. Please, answer*. But the phone rang on and on.

As I broke the connection and started to call Mackenzie, I was already running to the car.

20

It wasn't hard to guess what had happened. The house itself told the story. On the same rickety table where we'd had the barbecue was a half-eaten sandwich, already curling in the heat. Next to it a radio played indifferently. The door that led from the kitchen into the back garden stood wide open, bead curtain swaying from the passage of police officers. Inside, the coconut doormat had been kicked up against a kitchen cabinet, while the telephone receiver sat in the cradle where somebody had replaced it.

But of Jenny there was no sign.

The police hadn't wanted to let me in when I'd arrived. They'd already cordoned off the house, and a gaggle of children and neighbours stared solemnly from the street as the uniforms came in and out. A young constable, eyes darting nervously over the paddock and fields, blocked my path as I approached the gate. He refused to listen, but then the state I was in didn't exactly work in my favour.

It was only when Mackenzie arrived, holding up his hands to calm me, that I was let in.

'Don't touch anything,' he told me, unnecessarily, as we went into the house.

'I'm not a bloody novice!'

'Then stop acting like one.'

I was about to snap back at him before I caught myself. He was right. I breathed deeply, trying to control myself. Mackenzie was watching me, curiously.

'How well do you know her?'

Mind your own business, I wanted to tell him. But of course I couldn't. 'We've just started seeing each other.' I balled my fists as I saw two forensics officers dusting the telephone for fingerprints.

'How seriously?'

I just looked at him. After a moment he gave a short nod. 'I'm sorry.'

Don't be sorry! Do something! But everything that anyone could do was already being done. A police helicopter clattered overhead, while uniformed figures were already trudging through the nearby paddock and fields.

'Tell me again what happened,' Mackenzie instructed. I did, unable to take in that this was happening. 'You're sure about the time when she said someone was at the door?'

'Certain. I looked at my watch to see how soon I'd be able to get back.'

'And you didn't hear anything?'

'No! Christ, it's the middle of the afternoon. How could someone just knock on her door and drag her

272

away? The village is crawling with bloody police! What the hell were they doing?'

'Look, I know how you feel, but—'

'No, you don't! Somebody must have seen *something*!'

He sighed, then spoke with what I would later recognize as rare patience. 'We're talking to all the neighbours. But the garden's not overlooked by any of the other houses. There's a track leading across the paddock right up to the back here. He could have driven up in a van or car, then gone back the same way without anyone on the street seeing him.'

I looked out of the window. In the distance the mirrored lake lay still and innocent. Mackenzie must have guessed what I was thinking.

'There's no sign of a boat. The helicopter's still looking, but . . .'

He didn't have to explain. Less than ten minutes had passed between Jenny going to answer the door and the police arriving. But that was long enough for someone who knew this countryside to have disappeared, along with anyone else who was with him.

'Why didn't she shout for help?' I asked, quieter now. But it was the quiet of desperation rather than calm. 'She wouldn't have gone without a struggle.'

Before Mackenzie could answer there was a commotion outside. A moment later Tina rushed into the house, her face white and stricken.

'What's happened? Where's Jenny?'

I could only shake my head. She stared around, wildly.

'It was him, wasn't it? He's got her.' I tried to say

something, but I couldn't. Tina's hands went to her mouth. 'Oh, no. Oh God no, please.'

She started to cry. I hesitated, then reached out and touched her. She fell against me, sobbing.

'Sir?'

One of the forensics team had approached Mackenzie. He had a plastic evidence bag. In it was what looked like a wadded piece of dirty cloth.

'It was down by the hedge at the bottom corner,' the officer said. 'There's a gap there, big enough for someone to squeeze through.'

Mackenzie opened the bag, gave a cautious sniff. Without a word he held it out to me. The smell from it was faint but unmistakable.

Chloroform.

I didn't take part in the search. For one thing, I didn't want to be cut off from any news. With the area around Manham littered with dead zones where mobile phones became so much junk, I didn't want to risk being out of contact in some isolated stretch of marsh or wood. And I knew a search would be a waste of time. We weren't going to find Jenny by trudging randomly through the countryside. Not until whoever had taken her wanted us to.

Tina had told us about finding the dead fox. Even now she didn't realize its significance. She'd looked bewildered when Mackenzie had asked if she or Jenny had found any dead birds or animals lately. At first she'd said no, then mentioned the fox almost as an afterthought. I'd felt physically sick to think there had been a warning that had gone ignored.

'Still think it was a good idea to keep quiet about the mutilations?' I asked Mackenzie afterwards. His face reddened, but he said nothing. I knew I was being unfair, that the decision had probably been taken above him. But I wanted to hit out at something. Someone.

It was Tina who remembered Jenny's insulin. A forensics officer was going through Jenny's handbag, and seeing him Tina suddenly paled.

'Oh God, that's her pen!'

The policeman was holding Jenny's insulin injecter. It looked like a fat pen, but contained measured doses of insulin to keep her metabolism stable.

Mackenzie was looking at me for explanation. 'She's diabetic,' I told him, my voice cracking under this new blow. 'She needs to inject herself with insulin every day.'

'What if she can't?'

'Eventually she'll go into a coma.' I didn't say what would happen after that, but by the look on Mackenzie's face he understood well enough.

I'd seen enough. Mackenzie was clearly relieved when I left, promising to call me as soon as there was any news. As I drove home the thought that ran through my head time after time was that Jenny had come to Manham after surviving one assault, only to fall victim to an even worse one. *She came here because it was safer than a city.* It seemed so fundamentally unfair, as if some natural order had been violated. I felt as though I'd been split in two, the past superimposed upon the present so that I was reliving the nightmare of losing Kara and Alice all over again. Except this was a wholly different sensation. Then I'd been stunned by desolation and loss. Now I didn't know if Jenny was alive or not. Or, if she was, what she was going through. Try as I might, I couldn't help but think about the cuts and mutilations I'd seen on the other two women, the rope fibres snagged on Lyn Metcalf's shredded fingernails. They'd been tied up and subjected to God only knew what horrors before they'd died. And whatever they'd experienced would be happening now to Jenny.

I had never felt so scared in my life.

As soon as I walked into the house the walls seemed to press in on me. Torturing myself, I went up to the bedroom. I thought I could still detect Jenny's scent in the air, an agonizing reminder of her absence. I looked at the bed where we'd been only two nights ago, and couldn't stand being in the house any longer. I quickly went downstairs and back out again.

Without making a conscious decision, I drove to the surgery. The evening was full of birdsong and chlorophyll sunlight. Its beauty seemed cruel and mocking, an unneeded reminder of an indifferent universe. As I closed the front door behind me, Henry wheeled his chair out of his study. He still looked drawn and unwell. I could see from his face that he knew.

'David . . . I'm so sorry.'

I just nodded. He looked close to tears.

'This is my fault. The other night . . .'

'It's not your fault.'

'When I heard . . . I don't know what to say.'

'There's not much to say, is there?'

He rubbed the armrest of his chair. 'What about the police? Surely they've got some sort of . . . of lead or something?'

'Not really.'

'God, what a mess.' He passed his hand over his face, then drew himself up. 'Let me get you a drink.'

'No thanks.'

'You're having one, whether you want it or not.' He attempted a smile. 'Doctor's orders.'

I gave in, simply because it was easier than arguing. We went into the lounge rather than his study. He poured us both a whisky, handed me a glass.

'Go on. Straight down.'

'I don't—'

'Just drink it.'

I did as I was told. The spirit burned down to my stomach. Wordlessly, Henry took my glass and refilled it.

'Have you eaten?'

'I'm not hungry.'

He seemed about to argue, thought better of it. 'You're welcome to stay here tonight. Your old room won't take much making up.'

'No. Thanks.'

For want of anything else to do I took another drink of whisky. 'I can't help feeling I brought this on somehow.'

'Come on, David, don't talk rubbish.'

'I should have seen it coming.' And perhaps I had,

I thought, remembering Kara's warning in my dream. *Be careful.* But I'd chosen to ignore it.

'That's nonsense,' Henry snapped. 'Some things you just can't do anything about. You know that as well as I do.'

He was right, but knowing that didn't help. I stayed for another hour or so, the two of us sitting in silence for the most part. I nursed the rest of the whisky, refusing his attempts to pour any more. I didn't want to get drunk. Tempting as it was, I knew a fog of alcohol wouldn't improve anything. When I began to feel claustrophobic again I left. Henry was so obviously distressed at his inability to help that I felt sorry for him. But thoughts of Jenny didn't allow room for anything else for very long.

The police were going from door to door in yet another futile show of activity as I drove through the village. I felt an anger begin to burn as I watched them, methodically wasting yet more time. I carried on past my house, knowing I would find it no easier in there now than I had earlier. As I headed for the outskirts of the village I saw a group of men blocking the road. I slowed, recognizing most of their faces. Even Rupert Sutton was there, finally freed from his mother's apron strings, it seemed.

Standing in front of them all was Carl Brenner.

They all stared at the car, making no attempt to move as I leaned out of the window.

'What's going on?'

Brenner spat on the ground. His face was still bruised from the beating Ben had given him. 'Haven't you heard? There's been another one.'

I felt as if someone had physically punched me on the heart. If a fourth woman had been taken already it could only mean one thing: something had already happened to Jenny. Brenner went on, oblivious.

'The teacher from the school. He got her this afternoon.'

He said something else, but I didn't hear. Blood pounded in my head, deafening me as I realized he was delivering old news, not new.

'Where're you going?' he demanded, unaware of the effect of his words.

I could have told him. I could have explained, or invented some reason. But as I looked at him, jumped up with his new-found self-importance, I felt my anger swim into focus.

'None of your business.'

He looked taken aback. 'You going on a visit?'

'No.'

Brenner worked his shoulders uncertainly, like a boxer trying to summon his aggression. 'Nobody's getting in or out of here without telling us why.'

'What are you going to do? Drag me out of the car?'

One of the other men spoke up. It was Dan Marsden, the farmhand I'd treated after he'd been injured by one of the killer's traps. 'Come on, Dr Hunter, don't take it personal.'

'Why not? It seems bloody personal to me.'

Brenner had recovered his habitual aggression. 'What's wrong, *doctor*? Got something to hide?'

He made the word sound like an insult. But before

I could say anything Marsden took hold of his arm. 'Leave him, Carl. He was a friend of hers.'

Was. I gripped the steering wheel as they stared at me with raw curiosity.

'Get out of the way,' I told them.

Brenner put his hand on the door. 'Not until you—'

I stamped on the accelerator, flinging him off. The men standing in front of me leapt aside as the Land Rover surged forward. Startled faces flashed by, and then I was past them. Their angry shouts came after me, but I didn't slow down. It wasn't until they were out of sight that my anger faded to the point where I could think clearly again. What the hell had I been thinking? Some doctor I was. I could have injured someone. Or worse.

I drove aimlessly until I realized I was heading for the pub I'd visited with Jenny only a few days earlier. I braked hard, unable to bear even the thought of seeing it again now. When a car horn blared behind me I pulled into the verge, waiting until it was past before turning around and heading back.

I'd been trying to outrun what had happened, but I knew now I couldn't. I felt exhausted as I drove back into Manham. There was no sign of Brenner or his friends. I resisted the temptation to either go to Jenny's or phone Mackenzie. There was no point. I would hear soon enough if anything happened.

I let myself into my house, poured myself a whisky I didn't want, and sat outside as the sun sank from the sky. My heart descended with it. Half a day had already passed since Jenny had been taken. I could tell myself that there was still hope, that whoever had her hadn't killed his other two victims straight away. But there was no comfort there. No comfort at all.

Even if she wasn't already dead – a possibility that gaped terrifyingly in front of me – we had no more than two days to find her. If her insulin deficiency hadn't pushed her into a coma by then, the faceless animal would kill her as he had Sally Palmer and Lyn Metcalf.

And there was nothing I could do to stop it.

21

After a while, the darkness stopped being absolute. There were pinpricks of light, so small that at first she thought it was her imagination. When she tried to focus on them they disappeared. It was only when she looked off to one side that they became visible – tiny specks like a horizontal plane of stars on the edge of her vision.

As her eyes adjusted, she found she was able to make them out more easily. Not just specks. Slits. Cracks of brightness. Before long she was able to discern that they weren't all around her. The light was coming from a single direction. She started to think of that as Front.

With that to guide her, Jenny gradually began to impose form and shape on the darkness surrounding her.

Waking had come slowly. Her head hurt with a dull, senseless throbbing that made any movement agony. Her thoughts were scrambled, but a terrible sense of dread goaded her from sinking back into unconsciousness. She thought she was back in the car park, only this time the taxi driver had put her in the boot of the car. She felt hemmed in, unable to breathe. She wanted to shout for help, but her throat, like the rest of her body, wouldn't seem to acknowledge her commands.

Slowly, her thoughts had grown more coherent. She became aware that wherever she was, it wasn't the car park. That attack was in her past now. But the realization brought no relief. *Where was she?* The darkness confused and terrified her. As she struggled to sit up, something seemed to grab her leg. She tried to pull away, felt something snap taut, and then her fingers encountered the rough hemp of a rope around her ankle. With mounting disbelief, she followed it along its length until she came to a heavy iron ring set into the floor.

She'd been tied. And suddenly the rope, the darkness, the hard ground underneath her, all fell into awful alignment.

And she remembered.

It came back in fragments; a patchwork of memory that gradually merged together. She'd been talking to David on the phone. The doorbell had chimed. She'd gone to answer it, seen the figure of a man standing outside, obscured by the bead curtain in the doorway, and . . . and . . .

Oh, God, this couldn't be happening. Except it was. She called out, shouting for David, for Tina. Anybody. No-one came. With an effort, she forced herself to stop. *Deep breaths. Pull yourself together.* Shakily, she began to take stock of her situation.

Wherever she was, it was cool but not too cold. The air was foul, with a rank odour she couldn't identify. But at least she was still dressed, her shorts and sun vest undisturbed. She told herself that was a good sign. The pain in her head had subsided to a muted throb, and now the strongest sensation was thirst. Her throat was swollen and dry, making it painful to swallow. She was hungry, too, and with that thought came a far more chilling one.

She didn't have any insulin.

She couldn't even guess how long it was since her last shot. She had no idea how long she'd been here. She'd given herself her usual injection in the morning, but how long ago was that? If her next wasn't already overdue, it soon would be. Without insulin there was nothing to regulate her blood sugar, and she knew only too well what would happen when it started to rise.

Don't think about that, she told herself, sharply. *Think about getting out of here. Wherever here is.*

Stretching out her hands, she'd begun mapping the physical limits of her prison as far as the rope would allow. Behind her was a rough wall, but on the other three sides her hands met only air. Then, as she groped in the darkness, her foot kicked something. She gave a cry and stumbled away. When nothing else happened she crouched down and cautiously felt for the object again. It was a shoe, she thought, testing it with her fingers. A trainer, too small to be a man's . . .

She dropped it as realization swept over her. Not a trainer, but a running shoe. A woman's.

Lyn Metcalf's.

For a while fear threatened to overwhelm her. Ever since she'd felt the rope around her leg Jenny had been trying to hold back the knowledge that the killer must have selected her for his third victim. Now it had been brutally confirmed. But she couldn't afford to fall apart. Not if she wanted to get out of this.

Moving nearer the wall until the rope was slack, she explored the knots with her fingers. They might as well have been cast from the same iron as the ring itself for all the play in them. The noose wasn't tight enough to cause her pain, but it was too small for her to free her foot. Trying only rubbed the skin of her ankle raw.

After that she braced her untethered foot against the wall and heaved as hard as she could. Neither the rope nor the iron ring had budged, but she'd still pulled until her head pounded and flashbulbs popped and burst behind her eyes.

It was as they faded and she lay gasping for breath that she'd noticed the chinks of light. Light meant a way out, or at least something else beyond this black prison. But wherever it was coming from remained out of reach. Lowering herself to the floor, she moved to the furthest extent of the rope and stretched out. Tentatively, she put out her hand. It met something hard and unyielding less than a foot away. Jenny slowly ran her fingers over it, feeling the splintery texture of unplaned wooden planks.

The slivers of brightness were coming through cracks and gaps between them. One of them was right in front of her, slightly bigger than the rest. She edged closer. She flinched as her eyelashes brushed against the wood's rough surface, then carefully put her eye to the crack.

Through it she could see part of a long, deeply shadowed room. A basement or cellar, by the look of it, which would explain the subterranean dampness of the air. The walls were unpainted stone with the look of age about them. There were shelves filled with jars and tins, all of them dusty and old. Opposite her was a wooden workbench, with a vice and a variety of tools spread out on it. But that wasn't what made her breath catch in her throat.

Hanging from the ceiling, like obscene pendulums, were the mutilated bodies of animals.

There were dozens of them. Foxes, birds, rabbits, stoats, moles; even what looked like a badger. They undulated queasily, stirred by some faint draught like the surface of an inverted sea. Some were suspended by their necks, others by their hind legs, displaying blind stumps where their heads should have been. Many of the small corpses had rotted to skin and bone; empty eye-sockets staring blankly back at her.

Choking off a cry, Jenny pushed herself away from the planks. Now she knew what the foul smell was. And then the hairs on the back of her neck began to rise as something else occurred to her. She stood up and slowly felt above her head. Her fingertips brushed something soft. Fur. She snatched her hand back, then forced herself to reach up again. This time she felt the soft stir of feathers, swaying slightly from her touch.

There were animals hanging above her as well.

She let out an involuntary cry and ducked down to the floor, scrabbling along it till her back was against the wall. She broke down then, hugging herself as she sobbed. Gradually, though, the tears stopped. She wiped her eyes and nose. *Wuss*. Crying wasn't going to do any good. And the creatures above her were dead. There was no harm in them.

Gathering her resolve, she moved to the plank wall and put her eye to the crack once more. The room beyond was unchanged. No-one was there. And now she noticed something the shock of seeing the dead animals had made her overlook. Behind the workbench was a recess. What little light there was in the cellar was spilling from this; a dim, artificial glow. Just visible in it, rising out of sight, was a flight of steps.

The way out.

Jenny looked at them hungrily, then moved back from the crack and gave the planks an explorative push. Resting on her knees, she slammed both hands against them. The impact jarred her arms and drove splinters into her palms. The wooden wall didn't budge.

But the effort made her feel better. She drove her hands against it again and again, each blow exorcising a little more of the fear that threatened to paralyse her. Breathless, she moved back until the rope was slack enough to allow her to sit down. Her tethered leg had cramped, and the exertion had made her headache and thirst worse, but she felt a grim satisfaction. She held on to it, refusing to consider how little she had actually achieved. The planks weren't impassable. Given time she felt she could get through them. *Except you don't know how much time you've got, do you?*

Pushing that thought from her mind, she felt for the rope and began working at the knot.

22

Next morning when I turned on the news I heard that a suspect had been arrested.

I'd spent a largely sleepless night sitting in a chair for the most part, both hoping and dreading that Mackenzie would ring. But my phone had stayed silent. At five o'clock I'd got up and showered. I sat outside, watching numbly as the world came to life around me. After nearly an hour I went back indoors. I avoided putting on the radio, knowing what the main news story would be. Soon, however, the quietness of the house had become oppressive, and not listening was even worse. When the time came for the eight o'clock news bulletin I gave in and switched it on.

Even so, I wasn't expecting to hear anything I didn't know already. I'd been about to make myself a coffee, and as I filled the percolator the noise from the tap drowned out the first few seconds of the broadcast. But I heard the words 'arrest' and 'suspect', and frantically turned off the water.

'. . . identity hasn't been revealed, but police confirm that a local man was arrested late last night in connection with the abduction of schoolteacher Jenny Hammond . . .'

The newsreader then went on to the next item. *What about Jenny?* I wanted to yell. If they'd arrested somebody, why hadn't they found her? I realized I was still gripping the percolator. I banged it down and grabbed the phone. *Come on, answer*, I prayed, as I dialled Mackenzie's number. It rang several times, but just when I expected his voicemail to cut in he picked up.

'Have you found her?' I demanded before he could say anything.

'Dr Hunter?'

'*Have you found her?*'

'No. Look, I can't talk now. I'll call you back—'

'Don't hang up! Who've you arrested?'

'I can't tell you that.'

'Oh, for God's sake!'

'He's not been charged, and we're not releasing his name yet. You know how it works.' He sounded apologetic.

'Has he told you anything?'

'We're still questioning him.'

In other words, no. 'Why didn't you tell me? You said you'd call if anything happened!'

'It was late. I was going to let you know this morning.'

'What, you thought you'd be *disturbing* me?'

'Look, I know you're worried, but this is a police investigation—'

290

'I know. I've been involved in it, remember?'

'When I can tell you anything I will. But right now we're questioning a suspect, and that's all I can say.'

I fought back the urge to shout at him. He wasn't the type to respond to threats. 'The radio said it was a local man,' I said, fighting for calm. 'That means before long everyone in the village will know who it is, whether you like it or not. I'm going to find out eventually. It just means I'll spend the next couple of hours trying to guess what's true and what isn't.' All at once I felt I hadn't the energy to argue. 'Please. I need to know.'

He hesitated. I said nothing, giving him chance to convince himself. I heard him sigh. 'Hang on.'

The phone was muffled. I guessed he was moving out of earshot of whoever else was with him. When he came back on his voice was hushed.

'This is strictly confidential, all right?' I didn't bother answering. 'It's Ben Anders.'

I'd been prepared for it to be a name I recognized. But not that one.

'Dr Hunter? You there?' Mackenzie asked.

'Ben Anders?' I repeated, stunned.

'His car was seen near Jenny Hammond's in the early hours of the morning before she went missing.'

'And that's all?'

'No, that's not all,' he snapped. 'We found equipment for making traps in the back of it. Wire, wire cutters. Wood for stakes.'

'He's a nature reserve warden, he probably uses them at work.'

'So why was his car outside Jenny Hammond's house?'

I was still struggling to take this in. But my mind was starting to work now. 'Who saw it there?'

'I can't tell you that.'

'You had a tip-off, didn't you? An anonymous tip-off.'

'What makes you say that?' His voice had become suspicious.

'Because I know who made it,' I said, with sudden conviction. 'Carl Brenner. You remember I told you Ben thought he was poaching? They had a fight a few nights ago. Brenner lost.'

'That doesn't mean anything,' Mackenzie said, stubbornly.

'It means you should ask Brenner what he knows about this. I can't believe Ben's got anything to do with it.'

'Why not? Because he's a friend of yours?' Mackenzie was angry now.

'No, because I think he's been set up.'

'Oh, and you don't think that might have occurred to us? And before you ask, Brenner happens to have a solid alibi, which is more than your friend Anders has. Did you know he's an ex-boyfriend of Sally Palmer?'

The news wiped away anything I might have said. 'They had a relationship a few years ago,' Mackenzie continued. 'Just before you moved to the village, as a matter of fact.'

'I didn't know,' I said, dazed.

'Perhaps he forgot to mention it. And I bet he also

forgot to mention he was arrested for sexually assaulting a woman fifteen years ago, didn't he?'

For the second time I was lost for words.

'We were already looking at him even before we got the tip-off. Amazingly enough, we're not complete idiots,' Mackenzie went on, remorselessly. 'Now, if you don't mind, I've got a busy morning.'

There was a click as he broke the connection. I hung up myself. I didn't know what to think. Ordinarily I would have sworn Ben was innocent. I was still convinced the anonymous tip-off had come from Brenner. The man was small-minded enough to want to settle the score with Ben any way he could, regardless of the consequences.

Still, what Mackenzie had said had shaken me. I'd no idea that Ben used to have a relationship with Sally, far less that he'd a history of assault. True, there was no reason why he should have told me, and probably every reason for him not to under the circumstances. Now, though, I couldn't help but question how well I knew him. The world is full of people who've insisted the person they know can't be a killer. For the first time I wondered if I was one of them.

But far more worrying was the possibility that the police were wasting precious time on the wrong man. All at once my mind was made up. I grabbed my car keys and ran out of the house. If Brenner had lied to incriminate Ben, he had to be made aware of the cost to Jenny of what he was doing. I needed to know one way or the other, and if necessary convince him to tell the truth. If not . . .

If not I didn't want to think about what would happen.

The sun was already hot as I drove through the village. There seemed more police and press than ever before. The journalists, photographers and sound engineers huddled around in disgruntled groups, frustrated in their attempts to interview the closed-mouthed locals. I couldn't bear to think they were here because of Jenny. As I passed the church I saw Scarsdale in the graveyard. On impulse I pulled over and got out. He was talking to Tom Mason, wagging a bony finger as he delivered his instructions to the gardener. When he saw me approaching he broke off, his face folding into planes of displeasure.

'Dr Hunter,' he said, coldly, by way of greeting.

'I need a favour,' I told him, bluntly.

He couldn't quite conceal a glimmer of satisfaction. 'A favour? Quite a novelty, your needing to ask me for anything.'

I let him have his moment. There was more at stake here than pride, his or mine. He made a show of looking at his watch.

'Whatever it is, it'll have to wait. I'm expecting a phone call. I'm due on air for a radio interview shortly.'

Any other time I might have been irritated by his tone of self-importance, but now I barely noticed. 'This is important.'

'Then you won't mind waiting, will you?' He cocked his head as the sound of a phone ringing came from an open door at the side of the church. 'You'll have to excuse me.'

I wanted to grab him by his dusty lapels and shake him. I was even tempted to walk away myself. But Scarsdale's presence might help if I was going to appeal to whatever passed for Brenner's better nature. After the previous night when I'd almost knocked him down, I doubted he'd listen to me if I went alone. So I said nothing and waited as Scarsdale hurried inside.

The sound of garden clippers gradually penetrated my preoccupation. I looked over to where Tom Mason was carefully trimming the grass around a flowerbed and doing his best to pretend he hadn't heard the exchange. Belatedly, it occurred to me that I hadn't even acknowledged him.

'Morning, Tom,' I said, trying to sound normal. I looked around for his grandfather. 'Where's George?'

'Still in bed.'

I hadn't even known he was ill. It was yet another sign of how I'd let the practice slip. 'His back again?'

He nodded. 'Few more days and he'll be fine, though.'

I felt a stab of guilt. Old George and his grandson were Henry's patients, but home visits were my responsibility. And the old gardener was such a fixture in Manham I should have noticed he wasn't around. How many other people had I let down lately? And was still letting down, because Henry would be taking this morning's surgery without me yet again.

But fear for Jenny overrode anything else. The need to do something – anything – started to bubble over as the pompous drone of Scarsdale's voice drifted through the open doorway. I felt light-headed with impatience. The sunlight in the churchyard seemed too bright, the air sweetly nauseous with scents. Something was tugging at my subconscious, but whatever it was vanished as I heard Scarsdale hang up. A moment later he emerged from the church office, looking self-righteously pleased with himself.

'Now, Dr Hunter. You were asking for a favour.'

'I'm going to see Carl Brenner. I want you to come with me.'

'Indeed? And why should I do that?'

'Because there's more chance that he'll listen to you.'

'About what?'

I glanced at the gardener, but he'd moved away, engrossed in his work.

'The police have arrested someone. I think they could be making a mistake because of something Carl Brenner told them.'

'This "mistake" wouldn't involve Ben Anders, by any chance?' My expression must have been answer enough. Scarsdale looked pleased with himself. 'I'm sorry to disappoint you, but it's hardly news. He was seen being taken away. You can hardly keep something like that quiet.'

'It doesn't matter who it is, I still think Brenner gave the police false information.'

'May I ask why?'

'He's got a grudge against Ben. It's a chance to get his own back.'

'But you don't know for certain, do you?' Scarsdale's mouth pursed censoriously. 'And Anders is a friend of yours, I believe.'

'If he's guilty he deserves everything he gets. But if not the police are wasting time on a dead end.'

'That's for them to decide, not the village doctor.'

I tried to stay calm. 'Please.'

'I'm sorry, Dr Hunter, but I don't think you appreciate what you're asking. You're talking about interfering in a police investigation.'

'I'm talking about saving someone's life!' I almost shouted. 'Please,' I repeated, more quietly. 'I'm not asking for me. A few days ago Jenny Hammond sat in your church while you spoke about the need to do something. She might still be alive, but she won't be for much longer. There isn't . . . I can't . . .'

My voice broke. Scarsdale was watching me. Unable to speak any more, I shook my head, started to walk away.

'What makes you think Carl Brenner will listen to me?'

I took a moment to recover before I turned back to him. 'You started the patrols. He's more likely to take notice of you than he is me.'

'This third victim,' he said, carefully. 'You know her?'

I just nodded. He considered me for a while. There was something in his eyes I hadn't seen before. It took me a moment to recognize it as compassion. Then it was gone, replaced by his habitual hauteur.

'Very well,' he said.

* * *

I hadn't been to the Brenner house before, but it was the sort of local landmark that was hard to miss. It was a mile or so outside the village, set down a dirt track that was potholed all summer and reduced to dirty puddles and mud the rest of the year. The fields around it had once been drained farmland but were now steadily returning to the wild again. At their epicentre, surrounded by junk and debris, sat the house. It was a tall, dilapidated building that didn't seem to have a straight line or a right angle about it. Extensions had been added over the years, ramshackle constructions that clung to the walls like leeches. The roof had been repaired with a corrugated metal sheet. Next to it, incongruously modern, was a huge satellite dish.

Scarsdale hadn't said a word during the brief journey. In the confined space of the car his musty, faintly sour odour was more noticeable. The Land Rover bumped over the rutted track towards the house. A dog came running up to us, barking furiously, but it kept its distance when we got out of the car. I banged on the front door, dislodging flakes of old paint. It was opened almost immediately by a worn-looking woman I recognized as Carl Brenner's mother.

She was painfully thin, with lank grey hair and pale skin, as if the life had been sucked out of her. She was a widow, and given the nature of the family she'd had to bring up alone, it probably had. Despite the heat she was wearing a hand-knitted cardigan over a faded dress. She plucked at it as she blinked at us, saying nothing.

'I'm Dr Hunter,' I told her. Scarsdale needed no introduction. 'Is Carl in?'

The question seemed to provoke no response. Just when I was about to repeat it she folded her arms across her chest.

'He's in bed.' She spoke quickly, her manner aggressive and nervous at the same time.

'We need to talk to him. It's important.'

'He doesn't like being woken up.'

Scarsdale stepped forward. 'It shouldn't take long, Mrs Brenner. But it is important we speak to him.'

I felt a touch of irritation at the way he'd asserted control, but it was short-lived. All that mattered was getting into the house.

Reluctantly, she moved back so we could enter. 'Wait in the kitchen. I'll get him.'

Scarsdale went into the house first. I followed him into the untidy hallway. It smelled of old furniture and fried food. The smell of grease intensified as we went into the kitchen. A small TV was playing in one corner. A teenage boy and girl bickered at the table in front of empty breakfast plates. Scott Brenner sat nearby, one foot bandaged and propped up on a low stool, watching the TV while he nursed a half-drunk cup of tea.

They fell silent and stared at us as we walked in. 'Morning, Scott,' I said awkwardly. I couldn't remember the names of his teenage brother and sister. For the first time I began to have second thoughts about what I was doing, conscious that I was coming into someone's home to accuse him of lying. But I closed my mind to any doubts. Right or wrong, this was something I had to do.

Silence descended. Scarsdale stood in the centre of the room, as unperturbed as a statue. The teenage boy and girl continued to stare at us. Scott looked down at his lap.

'How's the foot?' I asked, to break the moment.

'All right.' He looked down at it, shrugged. 'Bit sore.'

I could see that the bandage was filthy. 'When was the last time the dressing was changed?'

He was growing red. 'Dunno.'

'It has been changed, hasn't it?' He didn't answer. 'It was a bad wound, you shouldn't just leave it.'

'I can't get anywhere like this, can I?' he said, upset.

'We could have arranged for a nurse to visit. Or Carl could bring you to the surgery.'

A shutter came down in his face. 'He's too busy.'

Yes, I thought, I bet he is. But I'd nothing to be self-righteous about myself. This was another reminder of how out of touch I'd become with the practice. There was the sound of someone coming downstairs, then his mother came into the kitchen.

'Melissa, Sean, you two get on out,' she told the teenagers.

'Why?' the girl demanded.

'Because I said so! Go on!'

They slouched out, sulking. Their mother went to the sink and began running water into it.

'Is he coming down?' I asked.

'He will when he's ready.'

That seemed to be as far as she was prepared to go. The only sound was the slosh of water and clatter of cutlery and plates as she bad-temperedly began to wash a pile of dishes. I listened for any movement from upstairs, but there was nothing.

'So what do I do, then?' Scott asked, staring worriedly at his foot.

It was an effort to drag my mind back. I was conscious of Scarsdale watching me. Impatience warred for a moment with obligation, then I gave in. 'Let me have a look at it.'

The wound wasn't as bad as it could have been, for all the filth of the bandage. It was healing, and there was a good chance he'd regain full use of his foot. The stitches looked as though they'd been put in by a clumsy student nurse, but the edges of the wound were starting to knit cleanly together. I fetched my kit from the car and set about cleaning and redressing it. I was almost done when the heavy thump of footsteps announced Brenner's arrival.

I finished off and stood up as he slouched into the room. He was wearing a pair of dirty jeans and a tight T-shirt. His upper body was pallid but powerful, corded with wiry muscle. He fixed me with a venomous look, then nodded at Scarsdale with something approaching grudging respect. He reminded me of a sullen schoolboy confronted by a stern headmaster.

'Good morning, Carl,' Scarsdale said, taking over. 'We're sorry to disturb you.'

His voice held an element of disapproval. Hearing

it, Brenner seemed to become conscious of his appearance.

'I've just got up,' he said, unnecessarily. His voice was still thick with sleep. 'Didn't get in till late last night.'

Scarsdale's expression said he would overlook it. Just this once. 'Dr Hunter wants to ask you something.'

Brenner didn't try to hide his hostility as he stared at me. 'Why should I give a f—' He caught himself. 'Why should I care what he wants?'

Scarsdale held up his hands, the patient peace-maker. 'I realize this is an intrusion, but he feels it might be important. I'd like you to hear him out.' He turned to me, signifying he'd done as much as he cared to. I was conscious of Scott and his mother watching as I spoke.

'You know Ben Anders has been arrested,' I said. Brenner took his time answering. He leaned against the table, folding his arms across his chest.

'So?'

'Do you know anything about it?'

'Why should I?'

'The police had a tip-off. Was it you?'

Belligerence was coming off him like heat. 'What's it got to do with you?'

'Because if it was I want to know if you really did see him or not.'

His eyes narrowed. 'You accusing me?'

'Look, I just don't want the police wasting their time.'

'What makes you think they are? It's about time people woke up to that bastard Anders.'

Scott stirred uneasily in his chair. 'I dunno, Carl, perhaps he's not—'

Brenner turned on him. 'Who fucking asked you? Shut it.'

'This isn't just about Ben Anders!' I said, as his younger brother flinched and ducked his head. 'For God's sake, can't you see that?'

Brenner pushed himself off the table, fists balled. 'Who the fuck do you think you are? You thought you were too good to talk to us when we stopped you last night, and now you come here telling me what I've got to do?'

'I just want you to tell the truth.'

'So now you're calling me a fucking liar?'

'This is someone's life you're playing with!'

He gave a savage grin. 'Good. They can hang the bastard for all I care.'

'I don't mean him!' I shouted. 'What about the girl? What happens to her?'

That took the grin off his face. He looked as though it had never occurred to him. He shrugged, but he was defensive now.

'She's probably dead already.'

Scarsdale put a restraining hand on my arm as I started towards Brenner. With an effort I made a last appeal.

'He keeps them alive for three days before he kills them,' I said, fighting to keep my voice steady. 'He keeps them alive so he can do God knows what. This is the second day, and the police are still trying to get Ben Anders to confess to it. Because someone said they saw him outside the house.'

I had to stop. 'Please,' I went on after a moment. 'Please, if it was you, tell them.'

The others were staring at me, stunned. No-one outside the investigation knew the victims had been kept alive. Mackenzie would be furious if he knew I'd told them. I didn't care. All my attention was focused on Brenner.

'I don't know what you're talking about,' he mumbled, but I could see the uncertainty in his face. He wouldn't meet anyone's eyes.

'Carl?' his mother said, hesitantly.

'I said I don't know, all right?' he snapped, suddenly angry again. He turned on me. 'You've asked your question, so now fuck off!'

I don't know what would have happened then if Scarsdale hadn't been there. He stepped quickly between us. 'That's enough!' He faced Brenner. 'Carl, I appreciate you're upset, but I'd thank you not to use language like that in my presence. Or in front of your mother.'

Brenner looked far from happy at the rebuke, but Scarsdale's conviction in his authority was absolute. The reverend turned to me.

'Dr Hunter, you have your answer. I don't think there's any reason for you to stay here any longer.'

I didn't move. I stared across at Brenner, more certain than ever that he'd incriminated Ben out of spite. Looking at his sullen features I wanted to batter the truth out of him.

'If anything happens to her,' I told him, my voice sounding like a stranger's, 'if she dies because you were lying, I swear I'll kill you myself.'

The threat seemed to soak up all the air in the room. I felt Scarsdale take hold of my arm and steer me towards the door. 'Come on, Dr Hunter.'

As I passed Scott Brenner I paused. His face was white and wide-eyed as he looked up at me. Then Scarsdale urged me into the hallway.

We went back to the Land Rover in silence. It wasn't until we were back on the road to the village that I felt able to speak again.

'He's lying.'

'If I'd known you would lose control of yourself I would never have agreed to come,' Scarsdale replied, heatedly. 'Your behaviour was disgraceful.'

I looked at him in astonishment. 'Disgraceful? He set up an innocent man without caring what might happen because of it!'

'You've no proof of that.'

'Oh, come on! You were there, you heard him!'

'I heard two men losing their tempers, that's all.'

'You're not serious? Are you telling me you don't think Brenner tipped off the police?'

'It's not for me to judge.'

'I'm not asking you to judge. Just come with me and tell them you think they should talk to him!'

He didn't reply straight away. When he did, it wasn't a direct answer. 'You said back there that the victims weren't killed straight away. How do you know that?'

Habit made me hesitate, but I didn't care who knew now. It didn't matter any more. 'Because I examined the bodies.'

His head snapped towards me in surprise. 'You?'

'I used to be an expert in that sort of thing. Before I came here.'

Scarsdale took a moment to digest the news. 'You mean you've been involved with the police investigation?'

'They asked me to help, yes.'

'I see.' It was clear from his tone that he didn't like it. 'And you chose to keep it a secret.'

'It's sensitive work. It's not the sort of thing you want talked about.'

'Of course. We're only locals, after all. I expect our ignorance must have amused you.'

Two points of colour had risen on his cheeks. He wasn't just displeased, I realized, he was furious. For a moment his reaction bewildered me, but then I understood. He'd enjoyed seeing himself in the ascendant role in the village, envisioned himself as Manham's leader. Now he'd found out someone else had been given a pivotal role all along, privy to information he was denied. It was a blow to his pride. And, even worse, his ego.

'It wasn't like that,' I told him.

'No? Strange that you should only tell me now, when you want something from me. Well, I can see now how naive I've been. I can assure you I won't be taken for the fool again.'

'No-one's been taking you for the fool. If I've offended you I'm sorry, but there's more at stake here than either of us.'

'Indeed there is. And from now on you can be sure I'll leave it in the hands of the "experts".' He said it with bitter mockery. 'I'm just a lowly minister after all.'

'Look, I need your help. I can't—'

'I don't believe we have any more to say to each other,' he said.

The rest of the journey passed in silence.

23

It was the noise that woke Jenny. At first the darkness disorientated her. She had no memory of where
she was, why she still couldn't see. She always slept
with the curtains open, so that some light fell into
the bedroom on even the darkest night. Then she
became aware of the hard floor, and the smell, and
with that awareness came crashing in on her.

She tugged on the rope again. Her fingernails were
already torn from working on it, and when she
sucked them she tasted blood. But there was no more
give in the knot for all her efforts. She slumped back.
Now other discomforts were beginning to make
themselves felt. Hunger, but more than that was
thirst. Before she'd slept, at the extreme edge of her
reach she'd found a tiny puddle of water that had
seeped through the floor and walls of her cell. It was
too shallow to drink from, but she'd taken off her
vest top and used it to soak up what moisture there
was. When she'd sucked it out it had been stale and
brackish, but still tasted wonderful.

Since then she'd found two other patches where water had soaked through, and done the same with both of them. But it had done little to slake her thirst. She'd dreamed of water, waking to a throat that was more parched than ever, and a feeling of lethargy she couldn't shake off. She knew that both were early signs of insulin deficiency, but that was something else she didn't want to think about. To give herself something to do she set about exploring the floor of her cell once more, hoping the wet patches might have replenished themselves.

That was when she heard the noise again. It came from the cellar beyond the wooden planks.

Someone else was down here.

She waited, barely daring to breathe. Whoever it was, they weren't here to rescue her. The sound of their moving about continued, but nothing else happened. Now she noticed that more light was spilling through the cracks in the wooden planks. The pulse of blood in her head almost drowned out everything else as she edged slowly towards them. Feeling her way with her hands, as quietly as she could she put her eye to the same gap as before.

After the pitch black of her cell, the brightness stabbed into her retina. She blinked away the tears until her sight adjusted. A bare light bulb was burning over the workbench, hanging on a long length of flex so that it was just above it. It was so low that it cast its light in a pool, illuminating only a small area and throwing everything else into unformed shadows. The dead animals suspended from the ceiling were lost in them.

The noise came again, and then Jenny saw a man emerge from the darkness. From her angle, close to the floor, her view was limited. There was a glimpse of jeans and what looked like an army jacket before he moved in front of the light. His silhouette gave an impression of size and bulk as he busied himself at the workbench. Then he was coming towards her.

She scurried away from the planks as his footsteps approached. They stopped. She stared into the blackness, paralysed. There was a loud scraping, then a vertical streak of light appeared. A moment later it flooded her cell as the planks were pulled back on a hinge. Jenny covered her eyes, blinded, as a dark shape towered over her.

'Get up.'

The voice was a low murmur. She was too scared to tell if it was familiar or not. She felt incapable of moving.

There was a sudden motion, then a quick, sharp pain. She cried out, clutching her arm. It was wet. She looked in disbelief at the blood on her hand.

'Get *up*!'

Clutching the cut on her arm, she scrambled to her feet. She stood shakily, pressing herself back against the wall. Her eyes were starting to adjust to the light, but she kept her head averted. *Don't look at him. If he knows you can recognize him he can't let you go.* But her gaze was drawn of its own accord. Not to his face, but to the hunting knife he held, the tip of its curved blade angled towards her. *Oh, God, no, please . . .*

'Get undressed.'

It was like the taxi driver all over again. Except this time was far worse, because she couldn't hope for rescue again.

'Why?' She heard the edge of hysteria in her voice, hated it.

She didn't have time to react as the knife slashed out again. There was a burn of cold on her cheek. Stunned, she put her hand to it, felt the wetness start to run out between her fingers. She looked at her hand, glossy with her blood, and then it started to hurt, a clean burning that took her breath away.

'Take your clothes off.'

Now she realized the voice was one she'd heard before. It seemed to echo down a well to her as she tried to identify it. *Don't pass out. Don't pass out.* The pain from her cheek helped her focus. She swayed but didn't fall. She could hear the man's hoarse breathing as he unhurriedly extended the knife. Its tip touched the skin of her bare arm, then turned so that the flat of the blade rested lightly against her. She shut her eyes as it slid like a feather to her shoulder, tracing the outline of her breastbone before coming to rest against her throat. Its point slowly drifted up until it reached the soft underside of her chin. The pressure relentlessly continued, forcing her to lift her head. When she couldn't move away any more it stopped, holding her poised on the needle-sharp tip, the full length of her throat exposed. Jenny struggled to keep still, her breath coming in ragged gulps. Then the knife was gone.

'Take them off.'

She opened her eyes, still avoiding looking at the

311

man in front of her. Her arms felt leaden as she took hold of her top, damp and filthy from where she'd used it to soak up the puddles, and drew it over her head. For a moment blessed darkness engulfed her. Then the T-shirt was over her face, and she was back in the stinking room.

For the first time she began to take in her surroundings. Her cell was little more than a partitioned part of the cellar, walled off by the screen of rough planks. Beyond the glow from the light bulb, the cellar was a shadowed mess of old furniture, tools and junk, almost too much to take in. At the back were the steps she'd seen earlier, dimly illuminated by some out-of-sight light source as they twisted upwards.

And hanging above it all were the mutilated bodies of the animals.

Now she could see that the entire cellar was full of them, shrivelled bundles of fur, bone and feathers, swaying in some unseen current. Then the man was blocking out the light as he came towards her. She couldn't keep her eyes from the knife poised in his hand. Hurriedly, she began to undress, desperate to forestall another cut. When she came to her shorts she froze, then pushed them down, letting them puddle around her tethered foot. She was covered only by her pants now. She kept her head down, as scared to meet his eyes as she would have been a rabid dog's.

'Everything.' The man's voice had thickened.

'What are you going to do?' Jenny whispered, despising herself for sounding weak.

312

'Just do it!'

Clumsy with fear, Jenny did as she was told. He bent down and swiftly slashed her shorts and pants, pulling them from her bound foot and impatiently casting them aside. She stifled a cry as he slowly stretched out his hand and, almost hesitantly, touched her breast. She bit her lip, turning her head away as she fought back tears. As she did she saw the bodies of the animals suspended from the ceiling.

Without thinking, she struck his hand away.

Her skin retained a tactile memory of the contact; a roughness of hair, the solidity of underlying bone. For a frozen moment nothing happened. Then his arm swung in a backhand blow to her face. Jenny crashed into the wall and slid to the floor.

She could hear him breathing as he stood over her. She cringed, waiting, but he didn't do anything else. With relief she heard him moving away. Her face ached where he'd hit her, but at least it was the other side to the cut. *Lucky*, she thought, numbly. *Lucky and stupid.*

There was a click and she was blinded once again as she was fixed by a piercing light. Shielding her eyes, she saw that he'd turned on a desk lamp that stood on the workbench. Caught in its spotlight, Jenny heard the scrape of a chair, the creak of it taking his weight as he sat down in the shadows.

'Stand up.'

Painfully, she obeyed him. Somehow, though, her brief revolt had wrought a subtle change. The fear was still there, but so now was anger. She drew strength from it, enough to straighten with

313

something like defiance. Whatever happened, she told herself, she was going to hold on to at least a semblance of dignity. Suddenly, that seemed hugely important.

All right, then. Do what you're going to do. Get it over with.

Naked and shivering, she waited for what would happen next. Nothing did. There were more sounds from the shadows. *What's he doing?* She dared a quick glance, enough to make out his indistinct figure just sitting there, big legs widely spread. And as the rhythmic, muted sounds continued, she finally understood.

He was masturbating.

The noises from beyond the pool of light became more urgent. She heard him give a choked cry. His boots scuffed against the floor, then fell still. Jenny stood unmoving, hardly breathing herself as she listened to his ragged breaths gradually quieten.

After a while he stood up. She could hear a rustling, then he was coming towards her. She kept her eyes on her feet as he stopped, so close she could smell him. He thrust something towards her.

'Put it on.'

She reached out to take it, but found herself staring at the knife. *Put it down*, she thought. *Put it down, just for a second. Then we'll see how brave you are.* But he didn't. The knife stayed in his hand as Jenny took the bundle from him. When she saw it was a dress she felt a faint flicker of hope, thinking he was going to let her go. But only until she recognized what she was holding.

It was a wedding dress. White satin and lace, yellowed with age. It was filthy and matted with dark, crusted stains, and Jenny gagged as she realized what they were.

Dried blood.

Jenny dropped it. The knife lashed out, neatly splitting the skin of her arm in a crimson line. It immediately began to well and run.

'Pick it up!'

Her limbs seemed to belong to someone else as she made herself bend down for the dress. She began to step into it before realizing that wouldn't work with the rope around her ankle. Hope flared briefly, but something made her stop before she could ask him to untie it. *That's what he wants*. She knew it, intuitively. *He wants me to give him an excuse.*

The room swam around her, but the insight gave her strength. Clumsily, she pulled the dress over her head. It smelled foul, a clotted odour of mothballs, old sweat and a faint trace of perfume. As the folds of heavy cloth covered her face she felt suddenly claustrophobic, terrified that the knife would slash at her again while she was trapped. She scrambled free, gulping for air as her head emerged.

But the man was nowhere near. He was in the darkness behind the light, busy with something on the workbench. Jenny looked down at herself. The wedding dress was creased and stiff. The blood from her cuts had smeared onto it, adding new stains to the dried ones already present. But it was finely made, the satin heavy and thick, with an elaborate panel of lace fleur-de-lis on its front. *Some bride*

315

wore this once, she thought, numbly. *The happiest day of her life.*

There was a ratcheting sound, like a clock being wound up. Still hidden by shadows, the man set a small wooden box next to the lamp. It was only when he lifted its lid that she realized what it was.

It was a music box. There was a tiny ballerina on a plinth in its centre. Jenny stared as the figure began to revolve, and a delicate chime tinkled crookedly into the fetid air. The mechanism was damaged, but the broken tune was still recognizable. *Clair de Lune.*

'Dance.'

Jenny was jerked out of her trance. 'What?'

'Dance.'

The instruction was so surreal it could have been another language. Only when the knife was raised was she shocked into motion. She began swaying from one foot to another in a drunken, tethered parody of dancing. *Don't cry, don't let him see you cry*, she told herself. But the tears still ran unchecked down her face.

She was conscious of the man watching her, half-hidden in the shadows. And then he was moving towards the steps. Jenny stopped dancing in bewilderment as he disappeared up them. For a moment she thought he was going to leave without walling her behind the wooden planks. But after only a few seconds footsteps started back down again. They were slow and measured, much more sluggish than when he'd gone up. There was something dreadfully ominous about their deliberate tread. *He's trying to scare you*, she told herself. *It's just another game, like the dress.*

She jerked her eyes away when the figure materialized at the bottom of the steps, and started to shuffle in time to the music once more. Keeping her head down, she heard him move slowly across the cellar. There was a scrape of wood and then the chair creaked again. She knew she was being watched, and her movements became stiff and uncoordinated under the physical pressure of his gaze. *Are you enjoying this?* she thought, fiercely, trying to fan her anger. It was the only way she could make the fear manageable.

The music was slowing, growing even more discordant as the mechanism wound down. As it died there was the scratch and flare of a match. For a moment the shadows jerked away from its yellow flame, and then darkness flooded back. But not before Jenny caught a glimpse of the face above it.

And all at once she understood.

The music had stopped without her noticing. She heard the box being rewound as the mingled smell of sulphur and tobacco smoke drifted across to her.

Crushed under a new weight of shock and despair, she continued her broken shuffle as the music chimed back into life.

24

The police released Ben Anders later that same day. Mackenzie phoned to tell me.

'I thought you'd want to know,' he said. He sounded tired and flat, as if he'd been up most of the night. He probably had.

I was in my office at the surgery, retreating from the emptiness of my house. I didn't know how I felt at the news. Pleased for Ben, yes. Yet there was also an unexpected sense of disappointment. I'd never really believed Ben was the killer, but on some level there must have been an element of doubt. Or perhaps it was just that as long as the police were questioning a suspect, regardless of who it was, there was a small hope of finding Jenny. Now even that had gone.

'What happened?' I asked.

'Nothing happened. We're satisfied he couldn't have been at her house on the afternoon she went missing, that's all.'

'That's not what you thought earlier.'

'We didn't know earlier,' he said, tersely. 'He wouldn't tell us where he was at first. Now he has, and it checks out.'

'I don't understand,' I said. 'If he'd got an alibi, why didn't he tell you straight away?'

'You can ask him that yourself.' He sounded irritable. 'If he wants to tell you, he will. As far as we're concerned, though, he's in the clear.'

I rubbed my eyes. 'So where does that leave us?'

'We'll carry on pursuing other leads, obviously. We're still looking at forensic evidence from the house, and—'

'Forget the official bullshit, just tell me!' Silence came down the line. I took a deep breath. 'Sorry.'

Mackenzie sighed. 'We're doing everything we can. I can't tell you any more than that.'

'Are there any other suspects?'

'Not yet.'

'What about Brenner?' At the last moment I decided not to mention seeing him that morning. 'I'm still certain he was the one who tipped you off about Ben Anders. Isn't it worth talking to him again?'

Mackenzie failed to conceal his impatience. 'I've already told you, Carl Brenner's got a alibi. If he was responsible for the false lead then we'll tackle him about it later. Right now I've got more important things to do.'

The despair I'd been trying to hold at bay was in danger of swamping me. 'Can I help?' I asked, knowing what his answer would be but hoping anyway.

'Not right now.' He hesitated. 'Look, there's still time. The other women were kept alive for three days. There's every reason to think he'll follow the same pattern now.'

Is that supposed to make me feel better? I wanted to shout. Even if Jenny were still alive, we both knew she wouldn't be for much longer. And the thought of what she might be going through in the meantime was unbearable.

After Mackenzie rang off I sat with my head in my hands. There was a knock on the door. I straightened as Henry came in.

'Any news?' he wanted to know.

I shook my head. I couldn't help but notice how tired he looked. Which wasn't surprising, really. Since Jenny had disappeared I'd given up any pretence of seeing patients.

'Are you OK?' I asked.

'Fine!' But he couldn't sustain the show of energy. He gave a wan smile and shrugged. 'Don't worry about me. I'm managing. Really.'

I wasn't convinced. There was a gauntness about him he couldn't conceal. But as bad as I felt about leaving him to run things by himself, right now all I could think about was Jenny, and what might happen in the next twenty-four hours. Anything else seemed too distant to contemplate.

Seeing that I was in no mood for company, Henry left me alone. I tried to go through my forensic reports on Sally Palmer and Lyn Metcalf, on the off-chance that I'd find something I'd missed. But that simply led my imagination in a direction I was trying hard to avoid. I turned my computer off in frustration. As I stared at the darkened screen I was struck with a conviction that there was something important I was overlooking. Something that was staring me in the face. For a moment it felt tantalizingly close, but even as I clutched for it I could feel it slipping away.

The need to do something pulled me to my feet. I grabbed my mobile phone and hurried out to the car. There was only one place I could think of to go.

But even as I set off the feeling that I was missing something obvious refused to die away.

Ben Anders lived in a large brick cottage on the edge of the village. It used to belong to his parents, and after they'd died he'd lived there with his sister until she'd married and moved away. He'd often said the place was too big for him, that he should sell up and buy somewhere smaller, but had shown no inclination to do so. When all was said and done, it was his home, too big or not.

I'd only been there a couple of times before, for an after-hours drink after the Lamb had shut, and as I parked outside the heavy wooden gate closing off the high stone wall, I thought it said a lot for the depth of our friendship that I'd never visited the place before in daylight.

I didn't even know if he'd be home. And, now I'd arrived, I half-hoped he wouldn't be. I'd come out here wanting to hear his version of why he'd been arrested, but I hadn't actually thought about what I was going to say to him.

But I put any doubts out of my mind as I knocked on the door. The house was built from pale brick, not pretty but with an attractive solidity to it. A big garden, tidy without being fussy. White windows, a dark green door. I waited, then knocked again. When there was no sign of life after a third attempt I started to turn away. I didn't leave, though. I don't know if it was just reluctance to go back to waiting or something more, but somehow the house didn't seem empty.

There was a path running around the side to the back. I followed it. Part way along there was a dark splash of something on the ground. Blood. I stepped over it. The back garden was like a well-kept field. At the bottom of it was a cluster of fruit trees. A figure was sitting in the shade underneath them.

Ben didn't seem surprised to see me. There was a bottle of whisky on the table next to him, a rough-hewn affair of unplaned timber. A cigarette burned itself to ash on the edge of it. Judging by the level in the bottle and the flush on his face, he'd been here for some time. He continued pouring himself another drink as I approached.

'There's a glass in the house if you want to join me.'

'No thanks.'

'I'd offer you a coffee. But, frankly, I can't be arsed to get up.' He picked the cigarette up, looked at it and stubbed it out. 'First one in four years. Tastes like shit.'

'I knocked.'

'I heard. Thought it might be the fucking press

again. Had two reporters round here already. Some loudmouthed copper gave them the wink, I expect.' He gave a lopsided grin. 'They took some convincing that I'd rather be left alone, but they got the hint eventually.'

'Is that where the blood on the path came from?'

'There was some spillage involved before they accepted my "no comment", yes.' Apart from his careful enunciation he didn't sound drunk. 'Bastards,' he added, his expression darkening.

'Hitting reporters might not be the best idea you've had.'

'Who said I hit them? I just escorted them off my property, that's all.' A shadow clouded his face. 'Look, I'm sorry about Jenny.' He sighed. 'Sorry. Shit, that doesn't come close, does it?'

I wasn't ready to acknowledge condolences. 'What time did the police release you?'

'Two or three hours ago.'

'Why?'

'Why what?'

'Why did they let you go?'

He eyed me over his glass. 'Because I didn't have anything to do with it.'

'So why are you sitting here getting drunk?'

'You ever been taken in for questioning for murder?' He gave a laugh. ' "Questioning" – there's a fucking joke. They don't question, they tell. "We know you were there, your car was seen, where did you take her, what have you done with her?" Not much fun, I can tell you. Even when they let you go they act like they're doing you a favour.'

He raised his glass in a mocking salute. 'And then you're a free man again. Except you know people are going to be looking at you and thinking, "No smoke without fire," and how they never trusted you anyway.'

'But you didn't have anything to do with it.'

I saw the muscles in his jaw bunch, but when he spoke his voice was still calm. 'No, I didn't have anything to do with it. Or what happened to the others, either.'

I'd not intended to interrogate him, but now I was here I couldn't seem to help it. He sighed and shrugged, easing the tension.

'It was a mistake. Someone told the police they'd seen my car outside Jenny's house. But they couldn't have.'

'If you could prove you hadn't been there why didn't you do it straight away? Why make it look like you were hiding something, for Christ's sake?'

He took another drink. 'Because I was. Just not what they thought.'

'Whatever it was, I hope it was important.' I couldn't keep the anger from my voice. 'Jesus, Ben, the police wasted hours with you!'

His mouth tightened, but he accepted the rebuke. 'I've been seeing a woman. No-one you know. She lives ... well, she doesn't live in the village. I was with her.'

I guessed the rest. 'She's married.'

'At the moment. Though now her husband's had the police calling at their house to ask if his wife can

324

verify she was in bed with me, I'm not sure she will be for much longer.'

I didn't say anything.

'I know, I know. I should have told the police earlier,' he burst out. 'Shit, I wish to Christ I had. I could have saved myself hours of fucking grief, and not be sitting here now wishing I'd done things differently. But when you get dragged out of the house and stuck in a police cell, things like that don't always occur to you at the time, you know?'

He rubbed his face, looking drawn. 'All because someone made a fucking mistake about seeing my car.'

'It wasn't a mistake. It was Carl Brenner.'

Ben looked at me sharply, a speculative light in his eye. 'I must be getting old,' he said after a moment. 'Shit, I never even thought about him.'

We were both moving away from the near-confrontation, tacitly accepting the stress talking on both sides. 'I went out to the house. Brenner wouldn't admit it, but I'd swear it was him.'

'He's not the sort to admit anything. But I appreciate your trying.'

'It wasn't just for you. I wanted the police to be out looking for Jenny, not sidetracked down a dead end.'

'Fair enough.' He considered his glass, then set it down without taking a drink. 'So what else did your inspector friend tell you?'

'That you used to have a relationship with Sally Palmer. And that you assaulted a woman fifteen years ago.'

He gave a sour laugh. 'It all comes back at you, doesn't it? Yeah, Sally and me got together a while back. No big secret, but we didn't advertise it. Not in a village like this. But it was nothing serious. Didn't last long, we stayed friendly afterwards. End of story. The other . . . well, let's say it was a youthful mistake.'

He must have read my expression. 'Before you get the wrong idea, I didn't assault anybody. I was eighteen and I'd started seeing a woman a good bit older than me. A married woman.'

'Again.'

'I know, it's a bad habit. I'm not proud of it. But at the time I thought it was a case of no-one missing a slice off a cut loaf, you know? I was young, I thought I was God's gift. Then when I wanted to end it, it got a bit ugly. She threatened me, we had a row. Next thing I knew she'd reported me for attempted rape.'

He gave a shrug. 'She withdrew the charges, eventually. But mud sticks, doesn't it? And in case you're wondering why you didn't know any of this, I don't broadcast my private life, and I don't apologize for it either.'

'I didn't ask you to.'

'OK, then.' He straightened, threw the rest of his whisky onto the grass. 'So that's it. My dark secrets. Now I can think about what I'm going to do to that bastard Brenner.'

'You're not going to do anything.'

He gave me a slow, dangerous smile that showed the effects of the whisky. 'I wouldn't put money on that.'

'If you go after him it's only going to muddy the water even more. There's more at stake here than some vendetta.'

Colour was mounting in his face. 'You expect me to just forget about it?'

'For now, yes. Afterwards . . .' The thought of what 'afterwards' might mean was like a blow to my stomach. 'When they've caught whoever took Jenny, you can do what you like.'

The heat went out of him. 'You're right. I wasn't thinking. Be something to look forward to, I suppose.' He looked thoughtful. 'Don't think this is just the grudge talking, but have you thought about why Brenner might have told the police he'd seen me at Jenny's?'

'You mean apart from getting you arrested?'

'I mean he might have had more than one reason. Like covering himself.'

'That crossed my mind, yes. But you're not the only one with an alibi. Mackenzie said he'd already checked him out.'

Ben studied his empty glass. 'Did he happen to say what his alibi was?'

I tried to remember. 'No.'

'Well, a pound will get you a penny it was his family who vouched for him. They're all as thick as bloody thieves. That's one reason we've never been able to get him for poaching. That and the fact he's a canny bastard.'

My heart had started beating faster as he spoke. Brenner was a hunter, a poacher known to be aggressive and antisocial. Given the killer's track record for trapping and mutilating animals as well as women, Brenner seemed an obvious match for the profile. Mackenzie was no idiot, but faced with neither evidence nor motive there was no reason for him to suspect Brenner above anyone else.

Not as long as he had an alibi.

I realized Ben had said something, but I'd no idea what. My mind was already racing ahead.

'What time is Brenner likely to go out hunting?' I asked.

25

Jenny had lost any sense of time. The fevered shaking that had gripped her after she'd finally been left alone had almost stopped. But what was more worrying was how sleepy she was starting to feel. It wasn't a normal tiredness. She had no idea how long she had been down here, but it must have been long enough for her to have missed two, perhaps three of her insulin injections. Now her blood sugar was starting to escalate out of control, and shock was making it worse.

Shock and blood loss.

In the darkness she had no way of gauging how much blood she'd actually lost. Most of the cuts had eventually crusted themselves shut, except the last one. The worst. The bloodied rag that had been her T-shirt was wrapped around her right foot. The cloth had a sticky feel to it now. A good sign, she hoped. It meant the wound wasn't bleeding so heavily any more. But it still hurt. God, it hurt.

It had happened after she'd taken off the filthy

wedding dress. As the music box had faltered into silence for a third time, Jenny had stopped too. She had swayed, dizzily, barely able to stay on her feet any longer. She sank to the ground, still wearing the bloodstained dress. She struggled to stay awake, but blackness slowly stole over her vision. She was dimly aware of movement around her, but it seemed increasingly distant. Time passed; then she'd felt herself being prodded roughly.

When she opened her eyes the first thing she saw was the knife.

She raised her head to look up at the man holding it. There was no reason not to any more. She knew now she wasn't going to get out of here alive, whether she could identify him or not.

Even so, she felt her stomach coil as she stared into his face and saw that knowledge confirmed.

He prodded her again with his foot.

'Take it off.'

Using the wall for balance, she rose unsteadily to her feet and fumbled the wedding dress over her head. He snatched it away and stood in front of her. She kept her head bowed, feeling him staring at her nakedness. Her heart thumped painfully. She could smell him, feel his breath on her flesh as he moved closer. *Oh, God, what's he going to do?* She couldn't keep her eyes from the knife he held at his side, willing him to set it down. *Just once. Just one chance, that's all I ask.* But he didn't. Slowly, he raised it, letting her see the blade before moving it towards her. She flinched as it pricked her arm.

'Keep still.'

She forced herself to stay immobile. The knife moved over her, pricking her flesh with its tip. Each time a pinpoint of blood would appear, a dark red bead that would swell before trickling down her skin. It hurt, but the anticipation was even worse. She could feel his breathing growing faster, smell the excitement radiating off him like heat. He shuffled even closer. Jenny gave an involuntary gasp and jerked back as one of his boots came down on her toes, and with that the floodgate opened to her panic.

'Get off me!' she yelled, lunging away blindly, forgetting about the rope around her ankle. It pulled her up short, yanking her leg so that she fell heavily. She twisted around as he stood over her. The look in his eyes sent a chill through her. There was nothing human in them, nothing sane.

'I told you to keep still.' His voice was terrifyingly calm. He reached down and took hold of her untethered foot. 'You shouldn't try to run away. I can't let you do that.'

'No! No, I wasn't . . .'

He wasn't listening. He was stroking her foot with the knife. His expression was rapt as he touched her big toe with the blade.

'This little piggy went to market.' His voice was soft, almost sing-song. He went onto the next toe. 'This little piggy stayed home. This little piggy had roast beef.'

Onto the third, then the fourth.

'This little piggy had none. And this little piggy . . .'

331

Jenny realized what was going to happen an instant before it did. White heat lanced up from her foot as the knife suddenly jerked. She screamed, trying to pull her foot away. He held on to it, watching her thrash and struggle, then let it drop. The severed toe lay like a bloodied pebble on the ground.

'This little piggy didn't try to run away any more.'

As he'd stood over her, knife blade dulled with her blood, she'd thought he was going to finish it. She wanted to plead with him, but some stubbornness held her back. Now she was proud of that much, at least. And she knew it would have done no good anyway. He would only have enjoyed it.

He'd left her then, dragging the planks back into place to shut her in the dark once more. She'd no idea how long ago that was. It could have been hours, minutes, even days. The agony in her foot had settled into a hot, bone-deep throb, and her throat was so dry it felt as though shards of glass were embedded in it. Yet it was becoming more of a struggle than ever for her to remain awake. She'd tried to work again on the rope around her ankle, but the effort was too much. In the darkness she couldn't tell if her vision was blurring, but she knew she was becoming hyperglycaemic, her blood sugar now dangerously high. And without insulin it was only going to get worse.

Assuming she lived long enough.

Jenny wondered why she hadn't been raped. The lust and hate had been obvious, but for some reason the assault hadn't come. Even so, she didn't delude herself. She thought about the face she'd glimpsed in the glare of the match. There was no mercy, no hope for her there. And she was all too aware that she wasn't the first woman to be brought down here. The cuts, the dress, the dancing – they seemed almost part of some incomprehensible ritual.

One way or another, she knew she wouldn't survive it.

26

It was late afternoon when I reached the Brenner
house. There was a haziness to the day, a faint mist-
ing of clouds beginning to encroach across the
previously pure blue of the sky. I stopped at the
bottom of the track, looking at the ramshackle building. It seemed even more run-down than I
remembered. There was no sign of life. I watched for
a moment or two longer, until I realized I was
putting off what I'd come here for. Shifting the Land
Rover into drive, I slowly bumped up the uneven
track.

Once I'd decided what I was going to try to do, the
hardest part was being patient. Every instinct in me
had cried out to act straight away, to drive out to the
house immediately. But I knew that any chance of
success depended on Brenner not being home. Ben
had suggested waiting till later, when the odds were
he would either have gone to the Lamb or be out
hunting. 'He's a poacher. He'll be busy either early
morning or late at night. That'd be why he was still

in bed when you called earlier. He'd probably been out working his snares till after dawn.'

But I couldn't stand the thought of waiting that long. Each hour that passed reduced the chances of finding Jenny alive. In the end I hit on a ridiculously obvious solution: I simply called the Brenner house and, without identifying myself, asked if Carl was in. The first time his mother answered. When she told me to wait and went to get him I hung up.

'What will you do if their phone stored your number and he calls back?' Ben asked.

'It doesn't really matter. I can say I want to talk to him. I can't see him agreeing to that anyway.'

But Brenner hadn't called back. I left it a while, then called again. This time it was Scott who answered. No, Carl was out, he told me. He'd no idea when he'd be back. I thanked him and broke the connection.

'Wish me luck,' I said to Ben, standing up to leave.

He'd wanted to come as well, but I'd refused. As much as I would have welcomed his company, it would have been asking for trouble. He and the Brenners were a volatile combination at the best of times, let alone when Ben had half a bottle of whisky inside him. And what I'd got in mind called for persuasion, not confrontation.

I'd considered telling Mackenzie what I was going to do, but quickly dismissed the notion. I'd no more to back up my suspicions now than I'd had when I spoke to him earlier. And Mackenzie had already made it clear he didn't appreciate my interference. He wasn't going to do anything without evidence.

Which was why I was going to the Brenner house.

I felt less confident now, though. My earlier certainty had ebbed as I parked outside. The same dog ran around the corner barking at the sound of the car. But it was bolder this time. Perhaps because I was alone it didn't retreat as it had before. It was a big mongrel with a torn ear. Bristling, it planted itself between me and the house. I took my first-aid kit out of the car and held it ready in case it attacked. The dog hackled as I walked towards it. I stopped, but it continued to growl.

'Jed!'

The dog gave me a last warning look as it trotted towards where Mrs Brenner had appeared in the doorway. Her narrow face was hostile.

'What do you want?'

I had my story prepared. 'I'd like another look at Scott's foot.'

She regarded me with suspicion. Or perhaps my nerves just interpreted it as that. 'You looked at it earlier.'

'I didn't have everything I needed with me then. I want to make sure it doesn't get infected. But if you don't want me to bother . . .'

I made as if to go back to my car. She sighed. 'No, you'd better come in.'

Trying not to show how relieved – and nervous – I was I followed her inside. Scott was in the living room, sprawled in front of the television on a grubby settee. His injured leg was stretched out along the cushions.

'The doctor's come to see you again,' his mother said as we walked in.

He pushed himself upright, looking surprised. And guilty, I thought. But again, that could have been my imagination.

'Carl's not back yet,' she said.

'That's OK. I was nearby and I thought I'd take another look at your foot. I've brought an anti-bacterial dressing for it.' I tried to seem relaxed, but my voice sounded horribly false to my ears.

'Was it you phoned for Carl earlier?' his mother asked, her hostility surfacing.

'Yes, I got cut off. I was on my mobile.'

'What did you want him for?'

'I wanted to apologize.' The lie came surprisingly easily. I went and sat on the chair nearest to Scott. 'But right now I'm more interested in your foot. Do you mind if I examine it again?'

He looked at his mother, then shrugged. 'No.'

I began to unwrap the bandage. His mother stood in the doorway, watching.

'I don't suppose there's any chance of a cup of tea?' I asked without looking up.

For a moment I thought she was going to refuse. Then, with a huffy sigh, she went into the kitchen. After she'd gone the only sound was the babble of the television and the whisper of the bandage as I unwound it. My mouth was dry. I risked a glance at Scott. He was watching me with a faintly worried expression.

'Tell me again how it happened,' I said.

'I stepped in a snare.'

'Whereabouts did you say it was?'

He looked down at his lap. 'Can't remember.'

I stripped away the bandage and dressing. Underneath, the stitches were as ugly as ever. 'You were lucky not to lose your foot. If it gets infected you still could.' He was past the danger stage, but I wanted to rattle him.

'It wasn't my fault,' he said, sullenly. 'I didn't step in it on purpose.'

'Perhaps not. But if there's nerve damage you're going to limp for the rest of your life. You should have had it looked at before this.' I looked up at him. 'Or didn't Carl want you to?'

His eyes flicked away from mine. 'Why shouldn't he?'

'It's common knowledge about his poaching. The last thing he wants is for the police to ask questions because his brother's stepped in a trap.'

'I told you, it wasn't one of ours,' he mumbled.

'OK,' I said, as though I didn't care one way or the other. I made a show of examining his wound, flexing his foot back and forth. 'But you didn't report it to the police, did you?'

'I told them when they came and asked me about it,' he said, defensively.

I didn't mention I'd been the one who'd told Mackenzie. 'What did Carl have to say about that?'

'What do you mean?'

'When the police came to see you. Did he tell you what to say to them?'

He suddenly pulled his foot away. 'What the fuck's it got to do with you?'

I tried to sound reasonable, even if I didn't feel it. 'Carl lied to the police, didn't he?'

He was glaring at me. I knew I'd gone too far. But I couldn't think how else to approach it.

'Get out! Go on, fuck off!'

I stood up. 'OK. But ask yourself why you're covering for someone who'd let you get gangrene rather than take you to a hospital.'

'That's bullshit!'

'Is it? So why didn't he take you straight away? Why did he come looking for me to patch you up when he could see how badly you were hurt?'

'You were closest.'

'And he knew a hospital would report it to the police. He didn't want to take you even when I said you needed stitches.'

Something in his face made me stop. I looked down at the clumsy stitches in his foot, and suddenly understood.

'He never did take you, did he? That's why you never had the dressing changed. You never went to hospital in the first place.'

Scott's anger had evaporated. He couldn't look at me. 'He said it would be all right.'

'So who put the stitches in? Him?'

'My cousin Dale.' He sounded embarrassed now that he'd been found out. 'He used to be in the army. He knows about stuff like that.'

That was the same cousin I'd seen with Brenner at the road block the day before. 'And did he bother to look at it again after he'd put them in?'

Scott shook his head, miserably. I felt sorry for him, but not sorry enough to stop.

'Does he help Carl with other things as well? Like the poaching?'

He gave a reluctant nod. I knew I was on the verge of something. Two men. Two hunters, one with an army background.

Two different knives.

'And what else?'

'Nothing,' he insisted, but his attempt at ignorance was feeble.

'They put you at risk. You know that, don't you?' I told him. 'What was so important they'd let you lose your foot over it?'

He was squirming now. I saw with dismay he was close to tears. But I couldn't afford to care about that.

'I don't want to get them into trouble,' he said, so quietly it was almost a whisper.

'They're in trouble already. And they weren't so worried about what happened to you.' I was about to push further, but instinct made me hold off. I waited, letting Scott wrestle with his decision.

'They've been trapping birds,' he said at last. 'Rare ones. Animals as well, like otters and things when they can get them. Carl thought there might be a market for live stuff as well as eggs. To sell to collectors. You know.'

'They're in it together?'

'Pretty much. But Carl does most of the trapping. He keeps them out on the marsh, in the old windmill.'

My mind was working so fast it seemed to be skidding. The windmill was completely derelict, isolated and long abandoned. Or apparently not.

I started rebandaging his foot again. 'That was

where you stepped in the trap,' I said, remembering their story when they'd stumbled into the Lamb that night. And how Brenner had cut him off from saying too much.

He nodded. 'When the police started searching for those women Carl was frightened they'd look there. He doesn't let me go out with him normally. He says I should get my own business and keep out of his. But Dale was away that week, so I had to help him move everything.'

'Where to?'

'All over. Different places. We brought most of them here, in the outhouses. My mum wasn't happy but it was only for a couple of days, until the police had searched the windmill. But then I stepped in the trap, and he had to take them back by himself.' He looked downcast. 'He went mad. But it wasn't like I did it on purpose.'

'So was the trap his?'

He shook his head. 'He said afterwards it must have been that nutter's who's been killing those women.'

I kept my face averted, feigning preoccupation with his foot. 'Has he got anything out there now?'

'Yeah. He's got nowhere else to put them. Dale won't risk moving them with all the cops knocking about.'

'And does Carl still go out there?'

'Every day. He's got to keep them alive until they can sell them.' He shrugged. 'Don't know how much longer he'll bother, though. They haven't been able to get rid of many yet.'

It was an effort to act normally. I kept my voice as casual as I could.

'So did you cover for Carl with the police?'

He looked confused. 'What?'

My hands were trembling as I finished bandaging his foot. 'When they were asking about the missing women. He couldn't tell them his alibi was being out poaching, could he?'

Scott actually smiled. 'Naw. We just said he'd been here all the time.' His smile faltered. 'You won't tell him I've said, will you?'

'No,' I said. 'I won't tell him.'

I'd told him too much already. I remembered what I'd said to Brenner earlier. *He keeps them alive for three days before he kills them.* Now he knew the police were aware of his timetable. Thanks to me Jenny might not have even that small chance of survival.

God, what had I done?

I stood up, fumbling to pack away my things as Scott's mother returned carrying a mug of tea.

'Sorry, I've got to go.'

Her mouth thinned with displeasure. 'I thought you wanted a cup of tea?'

'I'm sorry.'

I was already hurrying from the room. Scott was looking at me uncertainly, as if he was starting to regret what he'd said. All at once I was desperate to get away, half-expecting Brenner to suddenly materialize and try and stop me. I threw my first-aid kit into the Land Rover and quickly switched on the ignition, aware of Mrs Brenner staring at me from the doorway as I bumped down the track.

I was reaching for my phone as soon as I was out of sight. But when I tried to call Mackenzie the signal wavered in and out before dying altogether.

'Come on, come *on*!'

I shot out onto the road and turned towards the old windmill, willing the signal to reappear. As soon as it did I redialled Mackenzie's number.

His voicemail service answered. *Shit, shit!* 'Carl Brenner's family lied about his alibi,' I said without preamble. 'He's been—'

Mackenzie abruptly picked up. 'Tell me you've not been out to see him.'

'Not Brenner, his brother, but—'

'I told you to keep away!'

'Just listen!' I shouted. 'Brenner's been trapping birds and animals to sell with his cousin. Name of Dale Brenner, he's ex-army. They've been keeping them out at a ruined windmill, about a mile south of the village. Where Scott Brenner stepped in the trap.'

'Wait.' Now I'd got his attention he was all business. I heard muffled voices in the background. 'OK, I know where you mean. But that was checked, there's nothing in it.'

'They moved them all when you were searching around there for Lyn Metcalf, then put them back again. That's when Brenner's brother was injured. Brenner was so keen not to involve the police he wouldn't even take him to hospital.'

'He's a poacher, we already know that,' Mackenzie said, stubbornly.

343

'You didn't know his family lied to protect him. Or that you've got a hunter and an ex-army man trapping animals and keeping them in an abandoned building, and at least one of them doesn't have an alibi. Do I have to spell it out for you?'

The obscenity I heard him mutter told him I didn't.

'Where are you now?'

'I've just left Brenner's.' I didn't tell him I was on my way to the windmill.

'Where is he?'

'No idea.'

'OK, look, I'm at the mobile incident room. Get out here as soon as you can.'

That was in the opposite direction.

'What for? I've told you all you need to know.'

'And I'd like to hear about it in more detail. I don't want anyone going off half-cocked, do you understand?'

I didn't answer. I drove with the phone pressed to my ear, the road whispering by under the car wheels, each second taking me closer to where I was certain Jenny was being kept.

'Did you hear me, Dr Hunter?'

Now there was steel in Mackenzie's voice. I eased my foot off the accelerator. It was one of the hardest things I'd ever had to do.

'I heard you,' I grated.

And I turned round and went back.

The sky had developed an unhealthy sheen. A thin scab of clouds had formed over the sun, giving the light a jaundiced quality. For the first time in weeks, the breeze carried a hint of something other than overheated air. Somewhere, not too far off, was the threat of rain, but for the moment the increased humidity only made the heat seem worse.

Even with the windows down, I was sweating by the time I reached the police trailer that served as the incident room. There was more activity than usual around it. Mackenzie was standing at a table with a group of plain-clothed and uniformed police officers when I went in, poring over a map. The ones in uniform were wearing body armour. He broke off when he saw me.

His expression was far from fond as he came over. 'I'm not going to pretend I'm happy about what you did,' he said, jaw thrust out aggressively. 'I appreciate the help you gave us earlier, but this is a police investigation. There's no room for civilians blundering about in it.'

'I tried to tell you about Brenner but you wouldn't listen. What was I supposed to do?'

I could see he wanted to argue, but he checked himself. 'The superintendent wants to talk to you.'

He led me over to the group of officers at the table and introduced me. A tall, gaunt man with a no-nonsense air of command stuck out his hand.

'I'm Detective Superintendent Ryan. I gather you've got some new information, Dr Hunter?'

I ran through what Scott Brenner had told me, trying to stick to the bare facts. When I'd finished Ryan turned to Mackenzie.

'You know this Carl Brenner, I take it?'

'He's already been interviewed, yes. Fits the profile,

but he could account for himself both times when Lyn Metcalf and Jenny Hammond went missing. His family backed him up.'

'There's one more thing,' I interrupted. My heart bumped painfully, but they had to know. 'I told Brenner yesterday that you know the victims have been kept alive.'

'Jesus,' Mackenzie breathed.

'I wanted to make him see it was about more than him and Ben Anders.'

The attempt at justification sounded inadequate even to me. The policemen were staring at me with a mixture of disgust and hostility. Ryan gave a terse nod.

'Thank you for coming in, Dr Hunter,' he said coolly. 'You'll have to excuse us now. We've a lot to do.'

He was already turning away. Mackenzie steered me away. He held himself in check until we were outside.

'What the *hell* possessed you to tell Brenner that?'

'Because I knew you were questioning the wrong man! And believe me, there's nothing you can say that can make me regret it more than I do already.'

Some of the anger left him as he saw the truth of that. 'It might not make any difference,' he said. 'As long as his brother doesn't say anything, he still doesn't know he's a suspect.'

That didn't make me feel any better. 'Are you going to search the windmill now?'

'As soon as we can. We can't just go charging into a potential hostage situation.'

'It's only Brenner and his cousin!'

'Both possibly armed, and one with military training. You can't launch a raid without planning it first.' He sighed. 'Look, I know this is hard for you. But we know what we're doing, all right? Trust me.'

'I want to come with you.'

Mackenzie's face hardened. 'No chance.'

'I'll stay back with the cars. I won't get in the way.'

'Forget it.'

'She's diabetic, for God's sake!' Heads turned towards us at my raised voice. I made myself lower it. 'I'm a doctor. She'll need insulin straight away. She might be injured or in a coma.'

'We'll have an ambulance and paramedics standing by.'

I tried once more. 'I need to be there. Please!'

But he was already heading back towards the trailer. Almost as an afterthought he turned back to me.

'Don't get any ideas about going out there yourself, Dr Hunter. For your girlfriend's sake, we can do without any distractions.'

He didn't have to say what we both thought. *You've done enough damage already.*

'All right.'

'Do I have your word on that?'

I took a deep breath. 'Yes.'

His expression softened, if only relatively. 'Just try and stay calm. I'll call you as soon as we have any news.'

Leaving me standing there, he went back inside.

27

The summer when Jenny was ten her parents had taken her to Cornwall. They'd camped at a site near Penzance, and on the last day her father had driven them along the coast to a small cove. If it had a name she never knew it, only that the sand was fine and white, and the cliffs behind them had been full of nesting birds. It had been a hot day, and the sea had been deliciously cool. She played in the shallows and on the beach, then lay in the sun and read the book she'd been bought. It was *The Chronicles of Narnia*, by C.S. Lewis, and she'd felt very adult to be reading it on holiday.

They had stayed there all day. There had been a few other families in the cove, but one by one they had all gone until only Jenny and her parents were left. The sun had settled slowly into the sea, casting longer and longer shadows. Not wanting the day to end, Jenny had waited for one of her parents to finally stretch and announce that it was time to leave. But neither did. The afternoon stretched into evening, and still her parents seemed as reluctant to end the holiday as Jenny herself.

They'd put sweaters on when the temperature dropped, laughing at the goosebumps on Jenny's mother when she'd insisted on one final swim. The cove faced into the west, presenting them with a panoramic view of the sunset. It had been glorious, a vast smear of gold and purple, and the three of them had fallen silent to watch as it deepened into night. Only when the last rays of the sun had fallen behind the horizon did her father stir.

'Time to go,' he'd said.

And they had walked back along the beach through the thickening twilight, leaving just the lingering memory of the most perfect day of her childhood.

She thought about it now, conjuring the feel of the sun on her skin and the sand running through her fingers. She could smell the coconut of her mother's sun oil, taste the saline tang of sea on her lips. The cove was still out there, and somewhere in the universe Jenny could almost believe that younger version of herself still existed too, forever caught on the cusp of that never-ending day.

As she lay on the floor of her cell, the ache from her amputated toe had joined with her other wounds to form a rolling wave of pain that seemed to carry her along. But now even that seemed remote, as though she were observing it rather than experiencing it herself. She was drifting in and out of consciousness, finding it harder to distinguish delirium from brutal reality. On one level she knew that was a bad sign, that she was beginning the descent into coma. But perhaps that was better than experiencing whatever her captor had planned. *Hey, look on the bright side.* One way or another, Jenny knew she was going to die here.

It would be much better if it happened before he came back.

She wondered about her parents now, and what they would do when they heard. She felt sad for them, but only distantly. The thought of David brought a deeper sadness. But there was nothing she could do about that either. Even her fear had become diluted and blurred, like something viewed through water. The emotion that still burned brightest, with a feverish intensity, was anger. Anger at the man prepared to fritter her life away as easily as scattering dust.

During one moment of lucidity she tried working at the knot on her ankle, but it was a feeble attempt. There was no strength left in her fingers, and all too soon her body's shaking made even that impossible. She sank back, exhausted, slipping quickly into delirium again. Once she dreamed that she had the knife her captor had used on her. It was huge and bright, like a sword, and she sliced easily through the rope and felt herself soar weightlessly away, floating into freedom and sunlight.

Then the dream abandoned her, and she was back on the floor of the cellar, filthy and bloodied.

The grating noise seemed like another dream at first. Even the light that spilled on her melded seamlessly into images of blue skies, trees and grass. Only when something struck her face, splitting open the cut on her cheek with a sharpness like ice, did she become aware once more of where she was. She felt someone lift her shoulders off the ground, roughly shake her.

'David...?' she said, trying to make out the blurred figure bending over her. Or perhaps she just tried to say it, because the only sound that escaped her lips was a weak, dry groan. Her head snapped to the side as a rough hand slapped her again.

'Wake up! Wake *up*!'

The face looming in front of her swam into focus. *Oh. Not David.* The man's features were contorted with anger and disappointment. She felt like crying. So she wasn't going to die in time, after all. That seemed so unfair. But already she was beginning to drift away again. She barely noticed when he let her drop, even the pain of her head striking the hard earth only a minor irritation.

Suddenly she was jolted back into herself by a shock of freezing cold. For an instant her heart seemed to stop. She struggled to breathe, her diaphragm spasmed to stone. She clawed in one breath, then another, blinking away water to see him standing over her. He held an empty bucket, still dripping.

'Not yet! You don't die yet!'

He let the bucket fall, roughly seized hold of her foot. In a few swift motions the knot that had been holding her was untied. Still wheezing for breath, Jenny was hauled to her feet. He half-dragged, half-carried her to the far end of the cellar. There was a brick partition here. He dumped her behind it, onto a hard and unyielding floor. Through blurred vision, Jenny looked above her and saw a rusting tap jutting from the wall. And then she noticed something else, something that penetrated even the insulin-starved fog. Next to where she was lying was a circular iron drain, and with sudden intuition Jenny realized what was going to drain down it.

He'd brought her to the killing ground.

He reappeared now, carrying a sack. Untying its neck, he upended it, spilling out a bundle of feathers close to her head. Jenny found herself staring into the terrified yellow eyes of an owl.

He was smiling down at her now. 'Wise bird. For a teacher.'

Knife in hand, he reached down and grabbed hold of the owl by its feet. They were tethered, Jenny saw, but as he lifted the bird there was a sudden burst of movement. For a moment the owl seemed fastened to his hand. The knife clattered on the concrete floor as its wings beat wildly, then he dashed it hard against the wall. It fell to the ground in a soft explosion of feathers. He stared mutely at the wound on his palm, blood dripping from where its beak had ripped into his flesh. *Good*, a voice thrilled in her, as the room began to ripple out of focus. Then, as he sucked at the gouge, their eyes met. *Not yet. Just a little longer. Then I won't care what you do*, she thought, seeing the intent blossom in them.

But he was already coming towards her. 'You're on the owl's side, aren't you? Poor owl. Poor little owl.'

He stood over her, his expression thoughtful. Suddenly he tilted his head, listening. Through the grey fog clouding her vision, she saw surprise blank his face. A moment later, filtering through the cotton wool enclosing her, Jenny heard it as well. A heavy bang, coming from above them.

Someone was upstairs.

28

A hundred and fifty years ago, the old windmill had been the pride of Manham. It was a wind-powered pump rather than a corn mill, one of hundreds used to drain the marshes across the Broads. Now it was a decaying husk that bore no sign of its former glory. All that was left of its stately vanes was a gap in the crumbling masonry where they'd once been set, and nature had once more reclaimed the land around it. Over the years the waterlogged ground had been steadily taken over by scrub woodland, until now the crumbling tower was all but hidden.

But not unused.

I was able to piece together what happened from what Mackenzie told me later. The plan had been to launch raids on the windmill, the Brenner house and the cottage where Dale Brenner lived all at the same time. The intention was to seize both men without giving either them or their family chance to issue a warning. Even though it would take longer to set up, it was thought that would give the best hope of recovering Jenny alive. If everything went according to plan, of course.

I could have told them that nothing ever does.

Mackenzie went with the tactical teams that would target the windmill itself. The day was settling into dusk as the cars and vans carrying police officers in body armour neared the target. An armed response unit was among them, as well as paramedics and an ambulance, ready to rush Jenny and anyone else to hospital. Because the only route to the windmill was down a narrow and overgrown track, it was decided to park up on the edge of the woods and make the final approach on foot.

At the windmill they stayed in the treeline while teams were sent to cover doors and windows around the back. As he waited for them to get in place, Mackenzie studied the ruined building. An air of abandonment hung over it, and in the fading light its brickwork seemed to soak up the gathering dark. Then his radio hissed and a voice told him everyone was in position. Mackenzie looked at the officer heading the tactical teams. He gave a short nod.

'Go.'

At the time I was unaware of any of this. I was aware only of the agony of having to do nothing but wait. I knew Mackenzie was right. I'd seen enough botched police operations to know they had to be planned properly. That didn't make it any easier, though.

It was obvious I wasn't welcome at the police trailer, even if I had wanted to stay. But I couldn't bear the frustration of waiting there, trying to guess what was happening from the sombre faces. I went back to the Land Rover and called Ben. He'd be waiting to hear what had happened. My hands shook as I dialled his number.

'Look, why don't you come and wait over here?' he said. 'Help me finish the whisky. You don't want to be alone right now.'

I appreciated his concern, but declined. Alcohol was the last thing I wanted right now. Or company, come to that. I ended the call and stared out of the windscreen. The sky above Manham had dulled to the colour of burnt copper, and still darker clouds were rolling in. The air was pregnant with the promise of rain. With percipient timing, the heat-wave was finally ending. *Like a lot of other things*.

Abruptly, I jumped out of the car, intent on appealing to Mackenzie again, to try and persuade him to let me go with them. But I stopped before I reached the trailer. I knew what his answer would be, and I wouldn't be helping Jenny by getting in the way now.

And then the solution suddenly came to me. I might not be able actually to go with them to the windmill, but they couldn't stop me from waiting nearby. I didn't need to ask Mackenzie's permission for that. I could take some insulin with me, be ready when they found Jenny. It wasn't much of a plan, but at least it was better than doing nothing. I'd already lost Kara and Alice. I couldn't just stand by idly while Jenny's fate was decided.

I didn't carry insulin in my medical kit, but we

kept a supply in the fridge back at the surgery. I ran
back to the car and drove to Bank House, leaving the
Land Rover engine running as I dashed inside.
Evening clinic had finished, but Janice was still there.
She looked up in surprise as I burst in.

'Dr Hunter, I wasn't expecting . . . I mean, have
you heard anything?'

I just shook my head, in too much of a hurry to
answer. I rushed into Henry's study and tore open
the fridge. I didn't look around as Henry wheeled
himself in.

'David, what on earth are you doing?'

'Looking for the insulin.' I scrabbled through the
bottles and cartons. 'Come *on*. Where the hell is it?'

'Calm down, tell me what's happened.'

'It's Carl Brenner and his cousin. They've got
Jenny at the old windmill. The police are going to
raid it.'

'Carl Brenner?' He took a moment to absorb the
news. 'So why do you need insulin?'

'I'm going out there.' The insulin was staring me
in the face. I grabbed it and unlocked the steel
cabinet for a syringe.

'But won't they have an ambulance with them?'

I didn't answer, stubbornly continued looking on
the shelves for the disposable syringes.

'David, just think about it. They'll have properly
equipped emergency teams, with insulin and everything else. What good are you going to do charging
up there?'

The question pierced my frenzy. All the manic
energy that had been driving me seemed to leak

away. I looked stupidly at the insulin and syringes in my hands.

'I don't know.' My voice was hoarse.

Henry sighed. 'Put them back, David,' he said, gently.

I held out a moment longer, then did as he said.

He took my arm. 'Come and sit down. You look awful.'

I let him lead me to the chair, but didn't sit in it. 'I can't sit down. I need to do something.'

He was looking at me with concern. 'I know it's hard. But sometimes there just isn't anything you can do, no matter how much you might wish otherwise.'

My throat had constricted. I could feel tears pricking at my eyes. 'I want to be there. When they find her.'

Henry didn't speak for a moment. 'David . . .' He sounded reluctant. 'I know you don't want to hear this, but . . . well, don't you think you ought to prepare yourself?'

I felt as if something had punched me in the stomach. I couldn't breathe.

'I know how fond of her you are, but—'

'Don't say it.'

He nodded, tiredly. 'All right. Look, let me get you a drink.'

'I don't want a drink!' I stopped myself. 'I can't sit around and wait. I just can't.'

Henry looked helpless. 'I wish I knew what to say. I'm sorry.'

'Give me something to do. Anything.'

'There isn't anything. There's only one visit in the book, and—'

'Who is it?'

'Irene Williams, but it's not urgent. You'd be better off staying here—'

But I was already heading for the door. I went out without collecting the patient's notes, barely aware of the worried look Janice gave me. I had to keep moving, had to distract myself from the fact that Jenny's life was out of my hands. I tried to blank it from my mind as I drove to the small terraced cottage on the outskirts of the village where Irene Williams lived. A talkative woman in her seventies, she was waiting to have her arthritic hip replaced with stoic good humour. Normally I enjoyed visiting her, but this evening any small talk was beyond me.

'You're quiet. Cat got your tongue?' she asked as I wrote out her prescription.

'Just tired.' I saw I'd made the prescription out for insulin instead of painkillers. I screwed it up and wrote another.

She chuckled. 'Don't think I don't know what's wrong with you.'

I could only stare at her. She smiled, her false teeth the only youthful feature in her wizened face.

'You want to get a nice girl. That'd brighten you up a bit.'

It was all I could do not to run out.

Back in the safety of the Land Rover, I put my head on the steering wheel. I looked at my watch. Its fingers seemed to move with mocking slowness. It was still too soon to hear anything. I'd had enough experience of how the police worked to know they would probably still be talking, briefing the tactical teams and finalizing their plans.

I checked my mobile anyway. The signal fluttered weakly, but there was enough reception for any calls or messages to have reached me. Nothing. I stared through the windscreen at the village. It struck me then how much I hated Manham. I hated the flint buildings, hated the flat, waterlogged landscape. Hated the suspicion and resentment that crowded the attitudes of its inhabitants. Hated that a perverted killer had managed to live here unnoticed, until his sickness was ready to declare itself. Most of all, I hated the fact that it had given me Jenny and then taken her away again. *See this? This is what your lives could have been like.*

The almost feverish emotion faded as quickly as it came, leaving me sick and febrile in its wake. Dark clouds were blackening the sky like a spreading bruise as I started the car. There was nothing to do now but go back, and sit and wait for the phone call that terrified me. The thought of it was suffocating.

And then I remembered there was something else after all. That morning when I'd gone to see Scarsdale in the churchyard, Tom Mason had told me about his grandfather's bad back. It was a recurrent problem for the old man, the price of a lifetime spent stooped over other people's flowerbeds. Calling to see him would take up a few more minutes, provide another distraction until I could expect to hear from Mackenzie. With relief bordering on desperation, I turned the car around and headed for the Masons' house.

Old George and his grandson lived on the edge of the woods by the lake, in what had once been the lodge for Manham Hall. The family had been gardeners there for generations, and as a young man George had worked at the hall himself until it had been demolished after the war. Now the lodge was all that remained, a few acres of neatness and cultivation surviving among the encroaching woodland.

The gunmetal sheen of the lake was visible through the trees as I parked in the yard and went to knock on the door. It had a large, frosted glass panel that rattled slightly under my hand. When there was no answer I rapped again. As I waited the air vibrated with a rumble of thunder. I looked at the sky, surprised to notice how quickly the light had faded. The storm clouds rolling in overhead had brought a premature end to the day. It would be dark before much longer.

I belatedly realized something else. There were no lights on in the house, which there should have been if anyone was home. There were only the two of them, Tom's parents having died when he was a boy. So perhaps George had recovered enough to go to work after all. I started back towards the Land Rover, but only took a few paces before I stopped. Some awareness was nagging at me, a sense of something missed. The air seemed hushed with an eerie, pre-storm quiet. I looked around the yard, gripped by an uneasy feeling of imminence, that something was about to happen. Yet there was nothing I could see.

I jumped as something struck my bare arm. A fat raindrop had spattered on it. A moment later the sky was lit up by a flat sheet of lightning. For an instant everything was bleached to a dazzling white. In the pregnant silence that followed I became aware of a sound more felt than heard. It was drowned out a moment later by the bellicose crack of thunder, but I knew I hadn't imagined it. A low, almost subliminal hum that was all too familiar.

Flies.

And while recognition was dawning on me, several miles away, Mackenzie stood grim-faced, surrounded by cages of terrified birds and animals as a breathless police sergeant confirmed what he already knew.

'We've checked everywhere,' the man said. There's no-one here.'

29

It was difficult to pinpoint where the sound of flies had come from. But I knew it was from the house. The darkened windows stared blindly down at me, offering no help. I went to the nearest and peered through. Inside I could dimly make out a kitchen, but little else. I tried the next. A living room, the dead screen of a television set facing two worn armchairs.

I went to the door, raised my hand to knock again, then let it fall. If anyone had been going to answer they would have. I paused on the step, uncertain what to do.

But I knew what I'd heard. And I knew I couldn't ignore it. My hand went to the door handle. If it was locked the decision would have been made for me. I turned it.

The door opened.

I hesitated, knowing I shouldn't even be considering doing this. Then I caught the smell from inside the house. Fetid and faintly sweet, it was an odour I recognized only too well.

I pushed the door fully open onto a dim hallway. The smell was unmistakable now. Dry-mouthed, I took out my phone to call the police. It was no longer a question of jumping at shadows. Something – some*one* – had died in here. I'd actually started to dial before I realized there was no signal. The Mason house was in a dead zone. I swore, wondering how long I'd been out of touch, if Mackenzie had been trying to reach me.

That gave me another reason to go inside. But even if I hadn't needed to find a landline, I didn't have a choice. As little as I wanted to go into the house, there was no way now I could simply walk away.

The smell immediately grew stronger. I stood in the hallway, trying to get a feel for the house. At first glance it seemed superficially tidy, but there was a thick covering of dust over everything.

'Hello?' I called.

Nothing. There was a door off to my right. I opened it, found myself in the kitchen I'd seen through the window. Dirty dishes stacked in the sink, food left to congeal and rot on plates. A few fat flies were stirred into life, but not enough to account for the noise I'd heard earlier.

The lounge was similarly untenanted. The same dusty armchairs I'd seen through the window faced the dead television. I couldn't see a telephone. I came out and made my way to the stairs. The carpet running up them was old and threadbare, the top of them almost invisible in the gloom. I paused at the foot of the stairs, my hand on the banister.

I didn't want to go up there. But having come this

far I couldn't just leave. There was a light switch at the bottom. I flicked it, and jumped when the bulb popped and went out. Slowly, I made my way up. The smell became more pervasive with every step. And now it was joined by another, something cloying and tarry that pricked at my subconscious. But I didn't have time to wonder about it now. The stairs ended in another hallway. In the near-darkness I could make out an empty, dingy bathroom, and two other doors. I went to the first, opened it. Inside was a rumpled single bed, standing on unpainted floorboards. I came out and went to the second door. The tarry smell was stronger here as I took hold of the handle. When I turned it the door stuck, and for a second I thought it was locked. Then the resistance suddenly gave way and I pushed it open.

A black cloud of flies buffeted my face. I batted them away, almost gagging at the warm stench from the room. It was a smell I thought I'd become almost accustomed to, but this was overpowering. The flies were becoming less hysterical, beginning to settle again on a shape on the bed. Covering my mouth with my hands, I breathed in short gulps as I approached it.

My first feeling was relief. The body was badly decomposed, and though it was impossible to tell at a glance whether it had been male or female, whoever it was had obviously been dead for some time. Certainly a lot longer than two days. *Thank God*, I thought, weakly.

The flies covering it stirred irritably as I carefully moved closer. It was getting too dark for them to be active now. If I'd arrived at the house a little later, or lightning hadn't chosen that moment to disturb them, I might never have heard their tell-tale drone. The window was slightly open, I saw now. Not enough to allow the air in the room to clear, but wide enough for flies attracted by the perfume of decay to enter and lay their eggs.

The body was propped up on pillows, the arms lying limply outside the bedclothes. By the bed was an old wooden cabinet, on which was an empty glass and a motionless alarm clock. Next to them was a man's watch and a small prescription bottle of pills. It was too dark to read the label, but then another flash of lightning lit up the room. It picked out features like a silent snapshot: faded floral wallpaper, a framed picture above the bed, and in its momentary glare I made out the printing on the bottle. Coproxamol painkillers, for George Mason.

The old gardener's back may well have been bad, but that wasn't the reason he hadn't been in the village lately. I remembered what Tom Mason had said in the churchyard when I'd asked him where his grandfather was. *Still in bed.* I wondered how long ago old George had died. And what it said about Manham that no-one had noticed his absence.

I was careful not to touch anything as I turned to leave. This had more of the makings of a domestic tragedy than a crime scene, but I didn't want to disturb anything more than I already had. Someone else would have to determine what he'd died of and try to fathom his grandson's reason for not reporting it.

It was hardly the action of a sane mind, but then grief was a strange thing. He wouldn't be the first person to prefer denial.

As I went into the hall the tarry smell hit me again. And now, with the door open, there was just enough light for me to see the thick black smears along the edges of its frame. A strip of wadded-up newspaper, coated with the same material, still clung to the bottom of the door. I remembered the resistance when I'd first tried to open it. When I lightly touched the black stuff my fingers came away sticky.

It was bitumen.

And all at once I knew what had been trying to surface from my subconscious since that morning. Among the scent of flowers and cut grass in the churchyard had been another faint odour. I'd been too distracted to spare it much thought, but now I realized what it had been. Bitumen, clinging to either Mason or his tools after he'd used it to try and seal his grandfather's bedroom.

The same substance I'd found in the knife cut in Sally Palmer's vertebra.

I tried to calm down, to think this through. It seemed inconceivable that Tom Mason was the killer. He seemed too placid, too uncomplicated to be capable of planning the atrocities, let alone carry them out.

But we'd known all along that the killer had been hiding in plain sight. Mason had done that all right, patiently working in the churchyard or on the village green, blending into the background so effectively that no-one ever really noticed him. Always in his

367

grandfather's shadow, a softly spoken man who never made an impression.

Except he'd made one now.

I told myself I was jumping to conclusions. Until a few minutes ago I'd been convinced Carl Brenner was the killer. But Mason fitted the profile just as well. And Brenner didn't keep the decomposing body of his grandfather in the house. Or try to mask the smell with the same material that had been embedded in a dead woman's neck.

My hands were shaking as I took my phone out to call Mackenzie, forgetting that there was no reception. I swore and hurried downstairs. But as much as he needed to know what I'd found, I couldn't leave until I'd made sure Jenny wasn't here. I tore through the darkened house, opening every door to check inside. None of them held any sign of life, nor even a telephone I could use.

I ran out to the Land Rover, trying my mobile again in case some atmospheric fluke allowed a signal. It was still dead. A gust of thunder boomed overhead as I started the car. It was fully dark now, and raindrops were starting to burst on my windscreen. The yard wasn't big enough to turn the car round so I began to back up. As I did the headlights swept across the trees opposite, and for an instant there was a small, answering flash.

If the car hadn't been an automatic I would have stalled it as I stamped on the brake. I stared into the woods where the flash had appeared. But whatever had been caught in the headlights was invisible now. Mouth dry, I slowly edged forwards, turning the wheel back towards it. As the beam swung over the trees, something deep within them gleamed again.

It was the luminous yellow rectangle of a car registration plate.

I saw now that the track I'd driven up didn't stop at the yard but continued on into the woods. Although it was heavily overgrown it still looked used. But whatever was parked up it was too far away to see. If not for that momentary reflection I would never have known anything was there.

I needed to contact Mackenzie, but the track beckoned me. This was private land, several miles from where either of the bodies had been found. It wouldn't have been searched. And there had to be a reason for a car to be there. I hesitated, torn between two impossible choices. Then I rammed the Land Rover into drive and set off up the track.

Almost immediately I was forced to slow down as the branches closed in. I switched off my headlights, not wanting to broadcast my approach any more than I already had, but without them it was impossible to see. When I turned them back on the track seemed to disappear beyond their beam. The rain was drumming down now. I flicked on the wipers and peered through the smeared glass as the car bounced along the uneven track. My headlights again picked out the bright smudge of the registration plate, a beacon of brightness in the gloom. Then I could make out the vehicle itself. Not a car, but a van.

It was parked next to a low, tree-shrouded building.

I stopped the car. When I turned off the headlights everything outside vanished. I rummaged in the glove box for the torch, praying that the batteries still worked. A yellow beam sputtered into life when I turned it on. My pulse thudded in my ears as I opened the car door and quickly shone the torch around. No-one leaped out; its beam revealed only trees. Through them I could make out the solid blackness of the lake. The rain soaked me, drowning out any noise as I went to the back of the Land Rover and took out the heavy socket spanner from the toolbox. Reassured only slightly by its weight, I started towards the building.

The van parked outside was old and rusty. The back doors were fastened with a piece of string. When I untied it they swung open with a creak. Inside was a collection of gardening equipment: spades, forks, even a wheelbarrow. I looked at the spool of wire it also held and thought that Carl Brenner had told his brother the truth. The snare that had injured Scott hadn't been one of his.

Neither had any of the others.

As I was turning away the torch beam fell on something else. Lying on top of a collection of tools was a clasp knife. It hadn't been folded up, and the exposed blade was serrated like a miniature saw. It was crusted with black.

I knew I was looking at the weapon that had killed Sally Palmer's dog.

I jumped as there was a sudden flash of lightning. The thunder followed almost immediately, a raging bellow that shook the air. I checked my phone again, not really expecting there to be a signal. There wasn't. Leaving the van I went towards the low building, and felt something snag my thigh. I looked down to see a rusty wire fence running through the undergrowth. Hanging from it were dozens of dark objects. At first I couldn't make out what they were, then I shone the torch on the nearest shapes and saw a gleam of bone. The bodies of small birds and animals had been hung on the wire and left to rot.

Dozens of them.

The rain was drumming through the trees as I picked my way along the wire fence. After a few yards it simply stopped, the strands lying curled and broken in the grass. I stepped over them, continued to circle the building. It was a squat, featureless block, without doors or windows. In places its concrete walls had spalled away to reveal a skeleton of reinforcing rods. But it was only when I reached the far side and saw the deep-set door and single, narrow window that I understood what this place was. It was an old air-raid bunker. I knew quite a few country houses had them, little more than latter-day follies built at the start of the Second World War, most of them never used.

But someone had found a use for this one.

Moving as quietly as I could, I went to the door. It was steel, rusted to a dull red. I expected it to be locked, but it swung open when I pushed.

A waft of musty air greeted me. I stepped inside, my heart thudding. The torch revealed a single room, empty except for dead leaves curled on the floor. I shone the light around the bare walls, and then the beam fell on a second door, hidden away almost invisibly in a corner.

A noise behind me made me spin around in time to see the outer door swinging shut. I made a grab for it, but not in time. The bang was shockingly loud. As its echoes died I knew I'd just announced my arrival to anyone inside.

But there was nothing to do but go on. No longer worried about keeping quiet, I went to the second door. When I opened it I was looking at the top of a narrow flight of steps. Above them a feeble light bulb cast a sickly illumination.

I turned off the torch and started down.

The air was stale and fetid. I recognized the flavours of death in it, tried to shut my mind to what that might mean. The steps bent away, doubling back on themselves. After one final turn I emerged into a long, low cellar. It seemed much bigger than the concrete structure above, as though the shelter had been built on older foundations. The far end disappeared into darkness. A light bulb hung low over a workbench, its weak glow revealing a bewildering profusion of shapes and shadows.

I stood transfixed by the sight in front of me.

The entire ceiling was hung with animal and bird corpses. Foxes, rabbits, ducks, all suspended like some macabre exhibit. Many of them had rotted to mummified skin and bone, while others showed more recent putrefaction. All were mutilated. Lacking heads or limbs, they swung with hypnotic slowness in time to some faint draught.

I wrenched my eyes away and looked around the cellar. More images clamoured for my attention. A desk lamp stood on a workbench, aimed into an empty corner of the cellar. Picked out by its harsh light was a rope, one end trailing, the other tied to a metal ring. On the workbench itself was a selection of old tools and vices, given a hideous new significance in this setting. And then I saw an object that seemed even more obscenely out of place.

Draped over a chair, its front an intricate patterning of lace fleurs-de-lis, was an ornate wedding dress. It was soaked in blood.

The sight of it brought me out of my shock. 'Jenny!' I shouted.

From the shadows at the far end of the cellar there was an answering movement. A figure slowly emerged, and then George Mason's grandson moved into the light.

He wore the same harmless expression as always. But there seemed nothing harmless about him now. He was a big man, I realized, taller and broader than me. His jeans and combat jacket were stained with blood.

He wouldn't look directly at me, shifting his eyes instead between my chest and shoulders. His hands were empty, but I could see there was a knife sheath hanging under his stained jacket.

I gripped the socket spanner. 'Where is she?' My voice was cracked.

'You shouldn't be down here, Dr Hunter.' He sounded apologetic. As he spoke he was unhurriedly reaching towards the knife sheath. He seemed as

373

surprised as I was when he discovered it was empty.

I took a step towards him. 'What have you done to her?'

He was looking on the floor around him as if expecting to see the lost knife. 'Who?'

I turned the desk lamp so its light struck him. He raised a hand to shield his eyes. And as the light spilled into the corners behind him, I saw a naked shape half-hidden behind a wall.

My breath caught in my throat.

'Don't,' Mason said, squinting against the light.

I ran at him then. I raised the spanner, aiming to swing it into that docile face with all my strength, and as I did my arm snagged the animals hanging from the low ceiling. I was engulfed in a reeking avalanche of fur and feathers. Choking, I swept them aside in time to see Mason lunging at me. I tried to duck, but he was grabbing for the spanner. I still had the torch in my other hand. I swung it at him, catching him a glancing blow on his head. He yelled and lashed out, and I tumbled backwards, the spanner and torch flying from my hands to clatter to the floor. I fell against the workbench, and a spasm of fire shot through my back as it struck the corner of a vice.

The breath exploded from me as Mason's shoulder rammed into my stomach. I felt myself being bent backwards, the vice still digging into my spine. I looked into his face, and saw his placid blue eyes still untroubled as he eased his forearm up to my throat and began to push. I managed to wrench free one of my hands, tried to pull his forearm off my throat. He shifted slightly, leaning more of his weight on it, and reached for something on the workbench. I heard metal scrape on wood as he tried to take a chisel from a wooden block. I grabbed hold of his arm, but that left my throat unprotected. He gazed down at me as he increased the pressure, still groping for the chisel. Sparks of light were appearing in my vision. He glanced towards the chisel, and as he did I saw movement beyond him.

It was Jenny. She was moving with agonizing slowness towards what looked like a pile of feathers lying on the floor. As she struggled to pull something from beneath it, I forced myself to stare into Mason's calm face rather than at whatever she was doing. I tried to bring my knee into his groin but we were too close. Instead I raked my shoe down his shin. He gave a grunt, and I felt the weight on my throat ease fractionally. But from beside us there was a thud as the block containing the chisels fell over. I watched as Mason's fingers scrabbled like thick spiders' legs, tugging one of the chisels free inch by inch despite my hand pulling at his arm. A flicker of movement caught my eye. On the edge of my vision I saw Jenny trying to stand up. She was kneeling, leaning against the wall as she clutched something in front of her.

Then Mason had pulled one of the chisels from the block. Now instead of trying to hold his arm back I was struggling to push it away. I felt a growing panic as I realized how strong he was. My arm started to shake as he forced the chisel steadily nearer. Sweat dripped from his face onto mine, but other than that there was no sign of exertion in the bland features above me. He wore the same expression of gentle concentration as when he tended his plants.

Without warning he wrenched the opposite way, tearing his arm free. I clutched at it as he raised the chisel above my head, knowing I couldn't stop him. Suddenly he screamed and arched backwards. The arm that had pinned my throat was gone. I looked up to see Jenny swaying unsteadily behind him, naked and covered in blood. She was holding a huge-bladed knife, but it dropped from her fingers even as I looked. As it rang onto the floor Mason roared and swung his arm against her.

She fell bonelessly. I threw myself at him. We landed in a heap, and he cried out again. He pushed me off, tried to crawl away, and I saw the spreading stain of blood on his back. He was trying to reach the knife. I scrabbled over him, and as I did my foot kicked something hard. I looked down, saw the socket spanner. As Mason grabbed for the knife I snatched the spanner up and brought it down onto the stab wound in his back. He howled, and as he turned to face me I swung it at his head.

The impact hurt my hand. Mason dropped without a sound. I raised the spanner to hit him again but there was no need. Gasping, I waited until I was sure he wasn't going to move again, and then went to Jenny. She was lying where she'd fallen. I gently turned her over, feeling my heart miss when I saw the blood. She had cuts all over her body, some tiny, others deep slashes. The one in her cheek was almost to the bone, and when I saw what Mason had done to her foot I wanted to club him again. I almost cried with relief when I felt the pulse in her throat. It was weak and irregular, but she was alive.

'Jenny, Jenny, it's me, it's David.'

Her eyes fluttered open. '. . . David . . .' It came out as a whisper, and I felt my relief turn to ice when I caught the sweet chemical odour of her breath. *Ketoacidosis*. Her body had started to break down its own fats, producing toxic levels of ketones in her blood. She needed insulin, fast.

And I didn't have any with me.

'Don't talk,' I said, stupidly, because her eyes were already closing again. Whatever strength she'd found to stab Mason had been exhausted. The pulse in her throat seemed even weaker than before. *Oh God, not now, don't do this now.*

Ignoring the pain that flared through my back and throat, I picked her up. I was shocked at how light she felt. She weighed nothing at all. Mason still hadn't moved, but I could hear his rasping breaths as I carried her to the steps. Upstairs I kicked open the door and stumbled out into the trees. The rain was driving down now but it felt clean after the abomination of the cellar. Jenny's head lolled as I bundled her into the passenger seat of the Land Rover. I had to fasten the seat belt to keep her from falling over, then reached into the back for the blanket I kept as part of my emergency kit and draped it over her. I started the engine, scraping the side of Mason's van and snapping branches as I turned around and roared back down the track.

I drove as fast as I dared. Jenny had been two full days without any insulin, subjected to God only

377

knew what, and had obviously lost blood as well. She needed emergency treatment, but the nearest hospital was miles away, too far to risk driving in her condition. Tortured by the thought that I'd had the insulin actually in my hands at the surgery, I desperately ran through my options. There weren't many. Jenny might be already slipping into a coma. If she wasn't stabilized soon she would die.

Then I remembered the ambulance and paramedics Mackenzie had on standby for the raid on the old windmill. There was a chance they were still there. I reached for my phone, ready to call for help as soon as there was a signal. It wasn't in my pocket. Frantically, I searched the others. It wasn't there either. I fought down panic as I realized it must have fallen out during the struggle in the cellar. My mind stalled with indecision. *Go back or go on? Come on, decide!* Abruptly, I jammed my foot on the accelerator. Going back to look for it would have wasted too much time.

Time Jenny didn't have.

I reached the end of the track and shot the Land Rover out into the road. There was insulin at the surgery. Back there I could at least start treating her while an ambulance was still on its way. I put my foot down, peering through the windscreen into the night as the wipers struggled to clear it of the water sheeting down. Even with the headlamps on full beam it was raining so heavily I could only see a few yards ahead. I risked a glance at Jenny, saw enough to make me grip the wheel and go even faster.

It seemed to take an age to make it back to

Manham. Then the village was on me in a rush, suddenly leaping out of the rain. The roads were deserted in the storm, the press that had clogged the streets earlier nowhere in sight. I considered stopping at the police trailer that was still parked by the green, but immediately dismissed it. There was no time for explanations, and right now the priority was getting insulin for Jenny.

The house was in darkness as I roared down the drive. I had enough presence of mind to park at one side, leaving room for the ambulance to get right up to the door, then jumped out and ran around to the passenger side. Jenny's breathing was rapid and shallow, but she began to stir as I lifted her out and carried her through the rain.

'David . . . ?' Her voice was still a whisper.

'It's all right, we're at the surgery. Just hang on.'

But she didn't seem to hear me. She began to struggle feebly, her eyes unfocused and frightened. 'No! No!'

'It's me, Jenny, you're all right.'

'Don't let him get me!'

'He won't get you, I promise.'

But she was already slipping away again. I hammered on the door, unable to hold her and unlock it at the same time. After an eternity a light came on in the hallway. I barged inside as soon as Henry started to open the door.

'Get an ambulance!'

He hurriedly wheeled himself out of the way, his face startled. 'David, what . . . ?'

I was already rushing down the hallway. 'She's

going into diabetic coma, we need an ambulance now! Tell them the police might still have one on standby!'

I kicked open the door to Henry's office as he made the call from the hallway. Jenny didn't stir when I lay her on the couch. Under the mask of blood her face was white. The pulse in her throat fluttered weakly. *Please. Please hold on.* This was a desperation measure at best. She might have already suffered kidney and liver damage, and her heart could fail at any time if she wasn't treated soon. As well as insulin she needed salts and intravenous fluids to flush out the toxins that were poisoning her. I couldn't do any of that here. All I could do was hope the insulin kept her alive long enough for the ambulance to get her to hospital.

I tore open the fridge, fumbling in my haste as Henry pushed himself in.

'I'll get it. You find a syringe,' he instructed.

The framed photographs on top of the steel drugs cabinet rattled as I flung open the doors and rooted on the shelves for the syringes.

'What about the ambulance?'

'On its way. Here, you're in no state for this. Let me,' Henry said, peremptorily, holding out his hand for the syringe. I didn't argue. 'What in God's name is going on?' he asked, stabbing the needle through the seal.

'It was Tom Mason. He was keeping her out at an old air-raid shelter near the house.' I felt my heart twist at the sight of Jenny's unmoving form. 'He killed Sally Palmer and Lyn Metcalf.'

380

'George Mason's grandson?' Henry said incredulously. 'You're not serious!'

'He tried to kill me as well.'

'Christ! Where is he now?'

'Jenny stabbed him.'

'You mean he's dead?'

'Perhaps. I don't know.'

Right then I didn't care. I watched in an agony of impatience as Henry frowned over the syringe.

'Blast! The needle's blocked; it's not filling. Get me another, quick.'

I wanted to shout at him as I turned back to the drugs cabinet. The doors had swung to, and I wrenched them open so hard that one of the photographs standing on top fell over. I barely gave it a glance, but as I snatched up the syringes something belatedly registered.

I looked again, not at the picture that had fallen but the one next to it. It was the wedding photograph of Henry and his wife. I'd seen it any number of times, been moved by the captured moment of happiness. But that wasn't why I stared now.

Henry's wife was wearing a dress exactly like the one I'd seen in Mason's cellar.

I told myself I was imagining it. But the design, with its ornate panel of lace fleurs-de-lis on the front, was too distinctive to mistake. They were identical. No, not identical, I realized.

It was the same dress.

'Henry—' I began, then gasped at a sudden pain in my leg. I looked down to see Henry pushing himself away from me, an empty syringe in his hand.

'I'm sorry, David. I truly am,' he said, regarding me with a curious mix of sadness and resignation.

'What . . .' I started to say, but the words wouldn't form. Everything was starting to recede, the room around me growing indistinct. I sank down onto the floor, feeling suddenly weightless. As I lost my grip on the world, my last sight was an impossible one, of Henry standing up from the wheelchair and walking towards me.

Then he and everything else disappeared into blackness.

30

The slow ticking of the clock filled the room with a sound like dust falling through sunlight. Each leisurely stroke seemed to hang for an age before being followed by the next. I couldn't see it, but I could visualize the clock, old and heavy, its polished wood smelling of beeswax and age. I felt I knew it intimately, could anticipate the brass curve of its key when I came to wind it.

I could have listened to its stately cadence for ever.

A log fire burned in the grate, giving off a sweet pungency of pine. Tall bookshelves filled one wall, and lamps lit the corners of the room with a soft glow. A white bowl of oranges sat in the centre of the cherrywood table. There was a warm familiarity to the room, just as there was to the entire house, even though I knew I had never set foot here in my waking life. This was the place Kara and Alice inhabited in my dreams. This was home.

I was filled with a joy so overwhelming I felt I couldn't contain it. Kara sat opposite me on the sofa,

Alice curled like a kitten on her lap. Their faces as they looked at me were sad. I wanted to reassure them there was no reason to be. Everything was all right now. I was back with them again.

For ever.

Kara eased Alice down from her knee. 'Go and play outside, there's a good girl.'

'Can't I stay with Daddy?'

'Not now. Daddy and I have to talk.'

Alice gave a moue of disappointment. She came over and hugged me. I could feel the heat and reality of her small frame as I squeezed her.

'Go on, it's all right.' I kissed the top of her head. Her fine hair felt like silk. 'I'll be here when you get back.'

She regarded me solemnly. 'Bye-bye, Daddy.'

I watched her walk from the room. At the door she turned and gave a little wave, then she was gone. My heart was so full I couldn't speak for a moment. Kara was still looking at me from across the table.

'What's wrong?' I asked. 'Aren't you happy?

'This isn't right, David.'

I laughed. I couldn't help myself. 'Yes it is. Can't you feel it?'

Even through my joy I couldn't mistake Kara's sadness. 'It's the drug, David. That's what's making you feel like this. But it's false. You have to fight it.'

I couldn't understand her concern. 'We're together again. Isn't that what you want?'

'Not like this.'

'Why not? I'm here with you. That's all that matters.'

'This isn't just about us. Or you. Not any more.'

The first breath of a chill wind cooled my euphoria. 'What do you mean?'

'She needs you.'

'Who? Alice? Of course she does.'

But I knew it wasn't our daughter she was talking about. The happiness I'd felt was being buffeted now. Determined to hold on to it, I went over to the table and took an orange from the bowl.

'Do you want one?'

Kara just shook her head, watching me in silence. I held the fruit in my hand. I could feel its weight, see the dimpled texture of its skin. I could picture the spurt of juice that would come when I started to peel it, could almost smell the sharp orange zest. It would be sweet, I knew, just as I knew that eating it, tasting it, would somehow be an act of acceptance. And one from which there would be no going back.

Reluctantly, I put the orange back in the bowl. There was a heaviness in my chest as I went back to sit down. Kara's eyes were brimming as she smiled.

'Is this what you meant before? When you told me to be careful?' I asked.

She didn't answer.

'Isn't it too late?' I wanted to know.

A shadow crossed her face. 'Perhaps. It's going to be close.'

My throat felt constricted. 'What about you and Alice?'

Her smile was full of warmth. 'We're fine. You don't need to worry about us.'

'I'm not going to see you again, am I?'

She was crying silently, still smiling. 'You don't need to. Not any more.'

Tears were rolling down my own face. 'I love you,' I told her.

'I know.'

She came over and hugged me. I buried my face in her hair for the last time, breathing in the scent of her, not wanting to let go and knowing I had to.

'Take care, David,' she said. And as I tasted the salt tang of tears on my lips, I realized I could no longer hear the clock . . .

. . . and found myself in darkness, paralysed and suffocating.

I tried to breathe and failed. My chest felt wrapped with bands of iron. Panicking, I struggled to claw in a breath, managed one wheezing gasp, then another. I felt as though I was packed in cotton wool, muffled from the external world. It would have been so easy to give up and sink into it once more . . .

Fight it. Kara's words jolted me back again. The euphoria I'd felt earlier had turned to ashes. My diaphragm fluttered, protesting against each breath. But my breathing was becoming less laboured with every meagre inhalation.

I opened my eyes.

The world was canted over at a crazy angle. I struggled to focus as everything swam around me. I became aware of Henry's voice, drifting above my head.

'. . . didn't mean for this to happen, David, please

believe that. But once he'd taken her it was out of my hands. What could I do?'

Now I saw that I was moving. A wall was sliding by next to me. I realized I was in Henry's wheelchair, being pushed down the hallway. I tried to sit upright, succeeded only in flopping limply in the chair. The room spun around even more, but now everything was starting to come back.

Henry. The needle.

Jenny.

I tried to shout her name, but it came out as a moan.

'Shush, David.'

I twisted to look up at Henry, bringing on another violent bout of vertigo. He was leaning heavily on the chair as he laboriously pushed me down the hall.

Walking.

None of this made any sense. I tried to lever myself up but there was no strength in my arms. I collapsed back again.

'Jenny . . . the ambulance . . .' My voice was a slurred mumble.

'There's no ambulance, David.'

'I don't . . . don't unnerstand . . .'

But I did. Or at least I was starting to. I remembered how Jenny had roused when I'd brought her to the house, how frightened she'd been. *Don't let him get me!* I'd thought she was delirious, that she'd meant Mason.

She hadn't.

I tried to get up again. My limbs felt sluggish, as though I were suspended in aspic.

'Come on, David, stop it.' Henry sounded waspish.

I sagged back, but as we passed the staircase I made a lunge for the railings. The chair slewed around and almost spilled me out. Henry staggered, clutching for balance.

'God damn it, David!'

The chair had turned sideways on in the hallway. I held on to the railing, closing my eyes as everything began to spin again. Henry's voice, breathless and irate, floated down to me.

'Let go, David. This isn't doing any good, you know.'

When I opened my eyes again Henry was leaning for support against the wall in front of me, dishevelled and sweating.

'Please, David.' He sounded genuinely pained. 'You're only making this harder for both of us.'

I hung on determinedly. With a sigh he reached into his pocket and brought out a syringe. He held it up so I could see it was full.

'There's enough diamorphine here to drop a horse. I really don't want to have to give you any more. You know as well as I do what'll happen then. But I will if you force me.'

My mind sluggishly processed the information. Diamorphine was a painkiller, a heroin derivative that could cause hallucinations and coma. It had been Harold Shipman's drug of choice, used to send hundreds of his patients into a sleep from which they'd never woken.

And Henry had pumped me full of it.

Pieces of the puzzle were falling into place with terrible clarity. 'You and him . . . It was . . . you and Mason . . .'

Even now part of me expected him to deny it, to somehow offer a reasonable explanation. Instead he considered me for a long moment, then lowered the syringe.

'I'm sorry, David. I never thought it would come to this.'

It was too much to take in. '*Why*, Henry . . . ?'

He gave a crooked smile. 'I'm afraid you don't know me very well at all. You should stick to dead bodies. They're far less complicated than people.'

'What . . . what're you talking about . . . ?'

The lines of Henry's face deepened into a scowl of contempt. 'You think I've *enjoyed* being a cripple? Being stuck in this hole of a place? Patronized by these . . . these *cattle*? Thirty years of playing the noble doctor, and for what? Gratitude? They don't know the meaning of the word!'

A spasm of pain crossed his features. Supporting himself on the wall, he made his way stiffly to the old cane chair by the telephone table. He saw me staring as he sank into it with relief.

'You didn't really think I'd give up trying, did you? Always told you I'd prove the specialists wrong.' Out of breath from his exertions, he mopped the sweat from his brow. 'Trust me, it's no fun being helpless. Having your impotence publicly on display. Have you any idea how *demeaning* that is? How soul-destroying? Can you imagine being like you are now, all the time? And then to suddenly find yourself

389

presented with an opportunity to literally, quite *literally* have the power of life or death! To play God!'

He gave me a complicit grin.

'Come on, David, admit it. You're a doctor, you must have felt it sometimes. That little whisper of temptation?'

'You . . . you *killed* them . . .!'

He looked slightly put out. 'I never laid a finger on them. That was Mason, not me. I just let him off his leash.'

I wanted to close my eyes and shut all this out. Only the thought of Jenny, of what he might have done to her, prevented me. But as desperate as I was to find out, I was in no state to help either her or myself at the moment. The longer he talked, the more chance I had of the drug wearing off.

'How . . . how long . . .?'

'How long have I known about him, you mean?' Henry gave a shrug. 'His grandfather brought him to see me when he was a boy. He liked hurting things, making up little rituals around killing them. Only animals back then, of course. No concept of what he was doing was wrong, none at all. Quite fascinating, really. I offered to keep it quiet and supply tranquillizers to take the edge off his . . . proclivities, on the condition that I carried on monitoring him. My unofficial project, if you like.'

He raised his hands in mock submission.

'I know, I know, not very ethical. But I told you I'd always wanted to be a psychologist. I would have been a bloody good one, too, but coming here put an end to that. At least Mason was more interesting than arthritis and footrot. And I don't think I did too bad a job, actually. If not for me he'd have gone off the rails years ago.'

Fear for Jenny was tugging at me, but even a slight shift in the chair made the world spin and brought on a queasy wash of nausea. I began tensing the muscles in my arms and legs, trying to will some use back into them.

'Did he kill . . . kill his grandfather as well . . .?'

Henry seemed genuinely shocked. 'Good God no! He worshipped the old man! No, that was natural causes. Heart, I expect. But with George dead there was no-one to make sure Mason took his medication. I'd stopped seeing him in a professional sense years ago. Believe it or not, endless accounts of animal mutilations begin to pall after a while. I made sure old George had a supply of tranquillizers, but other than that I'm afraid I rather lost interest. Until he turned up on my doorstep one night and announced he'd got Sally Palmer locked in his father's old workshop.'

He actually chuckled.

'Turned out he'd had a thing about her ever since she hired him and his grandfather a year or two ago. Which wasn't a problem until the tranquillizers wore off and he started feeling his oats again. So he began stalking her. Probably didn't even know what he'd got in mind himself, but then one night her dog saw him and kicked up a fuss. So Mason cut its throat, belted her one to shut her up, and then carted her off.'

He shook his head, almost in admiration. I couldn't believe this was the same man I'd known for years, the man I'd believed was my friend. The gap between who I'd thought he'd been and this twisted thing in front of me was unbridgeable.

'For God's sake, Henry . . . !'

'Oh, don't look at me like that. It served the stuck-up cow right! Manham's "celebrity", slumming it with the yokels when she wasn't swanning off to London or somewhere. Condescending bitch! Christ, I couldn't look at her without being reminded of Diana!'

The mention of his dead wife threw me. Henry saw my confusion.

'Oh, I don't mean physically,' he said, irritably. 'Diana had far more class, I'll give her that. But they were two of a kind in other ways, believe me. Both arrogant; thought they were better than anyone else. Typical bloody women! They're all the same! Bleed you dry and then laugh at you!'

'But you loved Diana—'

'*Diana was a whore!*' he roared. 'A fucking *whore!*'

His face was contorted almost beyond recognition. I wondered how I could have missed such a depth of bitterness for so long. Janice had hinted more than once that the marriage hadn't been a happy one, but I'd dismissed it as jealousy.

I'd been wrong.

'I gave everything up for her!' Henry spat. 'You want to know why I became a GP instead of a psychologist? Because she got pregnant, so I had to

392

get a job. And shall I tell you what's really funny? I was in such a hurry I didn't bother finishing my training.'

He seemed to take a perverse pleasure from the confession.

'That's right. I'm not even a qualified doctor. You think I stayed in this shithole of a village from choice? The only reason I chose here in the first place was because the old sot who ran the practice was too addled to check my qualifications.' He gave a bitter laugh. 'Don't think the irony escaped me when I found out you'd been less than honest as well. But the difference between you and me was that once I'd come here I was trapped. I couldn't leave, couldn't walk into another job without risking being found out. You wonder that I hate this place? Manham's my fucking prison!'

He cocked an eyebrow at me, a twisted parody of the Henry I thought I knew.

'And did dear Diana stand by me, do you think? Oh, no! It was all my fault! My fault she miscarried! My fault she couldn't have any more children! My fault she started fucking other men!'

Perhaps it was the drug heightening my senses, but suddenly I knew where this was leading.

'The grave in the woods . . . The dead student . . .'

That brought him up short. He looked suddenly tired. 'Christ, when they found him, after all these years . . .' He shook off the memory. 'Yes, he was one of Diana's. I'd thought I'd been hardened to anything she did by then. But he was different from the usual oafs. Intelligent, good-looking. And so bloody *young*. He'd got his whole life, his whole career in front of him, and what had I got?'

'So you killed him . . .'

'Not intentionally. I went out to where he was camping, offered him money to leave. But he wouldn't take it. Bloody fool thought it was a real love affair. Of course, I set him right, told him what a round-heeled little bitch Diana really was. We argued. One thing just led to another.'

He gave a shrug, absolving himself of responsibility.

'Everyone assumed he'd just upped sticks and left. Even Diana. Plenty more where he came from, that was her philosophy. Nothing had changed. I was still the village cuckold, a laughing stock. And finally, one night when I was driving us back from a dinner party, I had enough. There was a stone bridge, and instead of turning onto it I put my foot down.'

All the animation he'd been showing seemed to drain out of him. He slumped on the chair, looking old and exhausted.

'Except I lost my nerve. Tried to turn at the last second. Too late, of course. So that was the famous accident. Just another bloody cock-up. And even then Diana got the laugh over me. At least she was killed outright, not left like this!'

He struck himself on the leg.

'Useless! Living in Manham had been bad enough before, but now I looked at all the people here, my *flock*, with their pathetic little lives still intact, all sneering behind my back, and I felt such . . . such *loathing*! I tell you, David, there were times when I wanted to kill the lot of 'em! Every one! But I didn't have the guts. Any more than I had to kill myself, come to that. And then Mason turned up on my doorstep, like a cat bringing a bird to its owner. My very own golem!'

There was an expression almost of wonderment on his face. He stared across at me with renewed intensity.

'Clay, David, that's what he was. Not an ounce of conscience or thought for consequences. Just waiting for me to mould him, to tell him what to do. Can you imagine what that was like? How bloody *exhilarating* it was? When I stood in that cellar and looked at Sally Palmer, I felt powerful! For the first time in years I didn't feel like a pathetic cripple. I looked at this woman who'd always been so patronizing and arrogant, crying and covered in blood and snot, and I felt *strong*!'

His eyes shone with an unholy light. But for all the madness of his actions, they were terrifyingly sane.

'I knew here was my chance. Not just to hit back at Manham, but to debase, to exorcize Diana's memory as well! She'd always prided herself on her dancing, so I gave Mason her wedding dress and the music box I'd bought her on our honeymoon. God, I hated that thing! I'd hear it playing "Clair de Lune" over and over while she got ready to meet whoever she happened to be fucking that day. So I told Mason to make the Palmer woman wear the dress, and then wait outside. And I went down there and watched her dance, so scared she could barely move. Watched her *humiliated*! That was all, but I can't tell you how cathartic it was! It almost didn't matter that it wasn't Diana herself!'

'You're sick, Henry . . . You need help . . .'

'Oh, don't be so bloody pious!' he snapped. 'Mason was going to kill her anyway. And once he'd blooded himself do you really think he was going to stop? If it's any consolation, at least he didn't rape them. He liked to look but daren't touch. I'm not saying he wouldn't have got round to it eventually, but in an odd way he was almost afraid of women.' The thought seemed to amuse him. 'Ironic, really.'

'He *tortured* them!' I shouted.

Henry shrugged, but he wouldn't meet my gaze. 'The worst of it happened after they were dead. The swan wings, the baby rabbits . . .' He gave a grimace of distaste. 'All part of Mason's ritual thing again. Even the wedding dress became part of it for him. After he'd done something once, it was set in stone. You know the only reason he kept them alive for three days? Because that's when he killed the first one. Lost his temper when she tried to escape, otherwise it could just as easily have been four or five.'

So that was why Sally Palmer had been beaten but Lyn Metcalf hadn't. Not out of any attempt to conceal her identity. Just the temper tantrum of a madman.

I gripped the arms of the chair as I remembered Henry's advice to me before the police raid on the windmill. *Don't you think you ought to prepare yourself?* He knew they were going to the wrong place, knew what was going to happen to Jenny. If I could have, I would have killed him there and then.

'Why Jenny?' I croaked. 'Why her?'

He tried for insouciance, but didn't make it. 'The same reason as Lyn Metcalf. She just caught Mason's eye.'

'Liar!'

'All right, I felt *betrayed*!' he yelled. 'I thought of you like a son! You were the only decent thing about this entire rotten fucking place, and then you met her! I knew it was only a matter of time before you left, started a new life. It made me feel so bloody *old*! And then when you told me you'd been helping the police, sneaking around behind my back, I just . . . just . . .'

He broke off. Slowly, so as not to alert him, I tried to shift my position in the wheelchair, trying to ignore the way it made the room swoop and tilt around me.

'I never wanted you hurt though, David,' he insisted. 'The night when Mason came round for more chloroform, the "burglary"? I was there in the study when you almost walked in, but I swear I didn't know he'd tried to cut you. Not until I saw you afterwards, when you thought I was just coming down the hallway. And the next morning, when you found me trying to get into the dinghy?'

He gave me a glance that held both apology and pride.

'I wasn't trying to get in. I was getting out.'

It was obvious now I thought about it. Both Henry's and Mason's houses bordered the lake, and unless anyone was actually looking for it, at night there was little chance of anyone noticing a small boat silently making its way across the water.

'I'd been to call him off,' Henry went on. 'Tell him I'd changed my mind. Took me hours, but he didn't have a phone so there was no other way. But it was a waste of time. Once Mason was set on something there was no budging him. Like leaving the bodies out on the marsh. I tried to get him to get rid of them properly, but he wasn't interested. He'd just look at you with that empty bloody stare and do it anyway.'

'So you let him take Jenny . . . And you went and . . . and watched her . . .'

He raised his hands, then let them fall, helplessly. 'I never expected it to turn out like this. Please believe me, David, I never wanted you hurt!'

He was searching my face, desperate for some sign of understanding. After a moment I saw the hope go out of his eyes. He gave a crooked smile.

'Yes, well, life never turns out how we want, does it?'

Suddenly, he slammed his hand down on the table.

'Dammit, David, why couldn't you have made sure Mason was dead? I might have taken my chances then, even with the girl! But now I don't have any choice!'

His frustration echoed around the hallway. He passed his hand over his face, then sat motionless, staring into space. After a while he seemed to rouse himself.

'Let's get this over with,' he said, dully.

As he started to push himself to his feet, I gathered all my strength and lunged out of the wheelchair at him.

It was a feeble attempt. My legs gave way immediately, dumping me onto the hallway floor as the chair clattered onto its side behind me. The sudden movement had set the room spinning again. I squeezed my eyes shut as it canted at a crazy angle, any hope of rebellion swiftly ended.

'Oh, David, David,' Henry said, sadly.

I lay there as the floor wheeled and swooped, helplessly waiting for the prick of the needle and the final blackness that would follow it. Nothing came. I opened my eyes, tried to focus on him through the vertigo. He was staring down at me with something like concern, the syringe held uncertainly in one hand.

'You're only making it worse. If I give you this it'll kill you. Please don't make me.'

'Going to anyway . . .' I slurred.

I tried to push myself up. There was no strength in my arms, and the sudden exertion had set my head pounding. I collapsed back to the floor as a haze began to creep into my vision. Through it I saw Henry reach down and take hold of my wrist. I had no strength to pull free, could only watch as he put the needle against the soft skin of my forearm. I tried to ready myself, determined to resist the drug even though I knew it would be futile.

But Henry didn't depress the syringe. Slowly, he took it away again.

'I can't, not like this,' he mumbled.

He tucked the syringe back in his pocket. The mist was spreading across my vision now, darkening the hallway. I felt consciousness drifting away again. *No!* I resisted but it slipped through my fingers no matter how hard I tried to hold on. The world disappeared except for a huge, rhythmic booming. I dimly recognized it as my heartbeat.

From a long way away, I felt myself being lifted. I became aware of a sense of movement. I opened my eyes, shut them again as a shifting kaleidoscope of colours and shapes brought a queasy wave of nausea. I fought it down, determined not to black out again. There was a bump, and then I felt cool air against my face. I opened my eyes to see an indigo night sky domed above me. Its stars and constellations seemed crystal bright, appearing and disappearing behind the torn clouds that raced across it on invisible winds.

I breathed deeply, trying to clear my head. Ahead of me was the Land Rover. The chair was bumping towards it unevenly, its wheels crunching over the driveway's gravel. Now my senses seemed to have been honed to an uncanny clarity. I heard the rustle of branches in the wind, smelled the loamy scent of wet earth. The scratches and mud splashes on the Land Rover seemed as big as continents.

The drive was on an incline, and I could hear Henry panting as he struggled to push me up it. He went around to the back of the car and stopped, gasping for breath. I knew I should try to move, but the knowledge didn't seem to extend to my limbs. When he'd recovered, Henry began making his way around the chair, supporting himself on it until he could transfer his grip to the car. He moved awkwardly, his legs wooden and rigid. He swung open the Land Rover's single rear door and lowered himself until he was sitting down on the back edge. He was drenched in sweat, his exhausted pallor visible even in the moonlight.

He looked up, chest heaving for breath. A weak smile touched his face when he saw me.

'You . . . you with us again?' Still sitting on the inside edge of the Land Rover, he leaned towards me. I felt his hands under my arms. 'Last leg, now, David. Up we get.'

Years of pushing himself about in the wheelchair had given him considerable upper body strength, and he used it now to lift me again. I thrashed weakly against him. He grunted, taking firmer hold. As he hauled me from the chair I grabbed hold of the car door. I clung on to it, so that it swung with me.

'Come, David, don't be stupid,' he gasped, trying to prise me off it.

I kept hold, grimly.

'Look, bloody let go!'

He wrenched me free, cracking my head against the edge of the door. The impact jarred me, and then I was being laid out on the hard metal floor in the back of the Land Rover.

'Oh, God, David, I didn't mean to do that,' Henry said. He took out a handkerchief, began to dab at my forehead. The cloth came away glistening darkly. Henry stared at it, then leaned against the doorframe and covered his eyes. 'Christ, what a bloody mess.'

My head hurt savagely, but it was a clean pain, almost refreshing after the drug-induced mist. 'Don't . . . Henry, don't do this . . .'

'Do you think I want to? I just want it to end now. That's not too much to ask, is it?' He swayed, wearily. 'God, I'm so tired. I was going to drive you down to the lake and finish this there. Take the boat over and see to Mason. But I really don't think I can manage that now.'

He reached behind me into the Land Rover's shadowy interior. When he straightened he was holding a length of rubber hosepipe.

'I salvaged this from the garden while you were out. Don't think Mason will be needing it any more.' The grim attempt at humour was short-lived. He seemed to sag. 'It'll be messier if they find you here, but there's nothing else for it. With a bit of luck everyone will assume it was suicide. Not perfect, but it'll have to do.'

The light was cut off as Henry slammed the Land Rover's back door. I heard him lock it, then he was moving around outside the car. I tried to sit up but dizziness swept over me again. I put my hand out to steady myself and touched something rough and solid. A blanket. I saw there was something underneath it and with a cold shock I realized what it was.

Jenny.

She was huddled on the floor behind the passenger seat. In the near-darkness only the blonde cap of her hair was visible. It was dark and matted. She wasn't moving.

'Jenny! *Jenny!*'

There was no response as I pulled the blanket from her head. Her skin was icy. *Oh God, no, please God.*

The driver's door suddenly opened. Henry grunted as he eased himself into the seat.

'Henry . . . Please, help me.'

My voice was drowned out as he started the engine. It settled into a dull grumble. Henry cracked open the driver's window slightly, then twisted round to look at me. In the darkness it was difficult to make out his face.

'I'm sorry, David. Truly. But I can't see any other way.'

'For God's sake!'

'Goodbye, David.'

Awkwardly, he levered himself out and slammed the door. A moment later something snaked through the gap at the top of the window.

It was the rubber hose. And now I understood why he'd left the engine running.

'Henry!' I called, fear giving strength to my voice. I caught a glimpse of him passing the windscreen, heading back towards the house. I squirmed around and tried to open the rear door, even though it was locked. It didn't budge. I thought I could smell the exhaust fumes already. *Come on! Think!* I began dragging myself towards the cab, where the rubber pipe was jutting through the window. The impassable barricade of the driver and passenger seats rose up before me. I tried to use them to pull myself up and felt the fog closing in on me. I collapsed weakly into the back again. *No! Don't black out!* I turned my head, saw the still unmoving shape of Jenny, and fought off the rising blackness.

I tried again. There was a slim gap between the seats. I succeeded in hooking my arm through it and managed to heave myself partway up. I could feel unconsciousness hovering behind my eyes, threatening to engulf me again. I paused, my heart hammering painfully, until it had passed. I heaved myself further up, clenching my teeth as the Land Rover seemed to yaw and pitch under me. *Come on!* Now I was wedged partway through the gap, my chest resting on the utility box fixed between the seats. The car keys hung in the ignition, but they might as well have been a mile away. I groped for the window control, knowing even that was too far. Head spinning, I looked at where the dark mouth of the rubber pipe gaped obscenely. I'd no idea if I could reach it before I was overcome by the fumes. And even if I did, what then? Henry would simply put it back, assuming he didn't just lose patience and use the rest of the diamorphine on me.

But I couldn't think of anything else to do. I grabbed hold of the handbrake and used it to haul myself further into the gap between the seats, and as

I did I saw Henry framed in the windscreen in front of me. He was leaning heavily on the wheelchair, his exhaustion evident as he slowly pushed it back towards the house.

I was still gripping the handbrake. Without pausing to think, I let it off.

I felt the Land Rover shift slightly. But even though the driveway sloped down towards the house it didn't move. I threw my weight forward, trying to break the inertia that held the car in place, but it had no effect. My gaze fell on the automatic transmission. It was nestling in park as the engine idly pumped its exhaust into the cab.

I strained forward and pushed the lever into drive.

The Land Rover rolled forward smoothly. I was still wedged between the seats, and through the windscreen I saw Henry hear its approach. He looked back, his mouth opening in surprise. Even as the car gathered speed on the slope there seemed ample time for him to get out of its way. But perhaps he'd already used up all his reserves, or his wasted legs simply couldn't respond quickly enough. For a moment our eyes met, and then the Land Rover struck him.

There was a thud and Henry disappeared. I felt a sickening bump, then another. Off balance, I groped for the handbrake as the house suddenly loomed up in the windscreen, but I was too slow. With a loud bang the car jolted to a halt. I was pitched forward and lay stunned across one of the seats. The engine continued to rumble. I reached up and turned off the ignition. Then, taking out the key, I managed to fumble open the door.

Cold, fresh air flooded in. I gulped it greedily as I tumbled onto the drive. I lay panting on the sharp gravel for a moment while I gathered my strength. Then, rolling over onto all fours, I used the Land Rover to pull myself up. Supporting myself on it in much the same way Henry had done, I made my way around to the back.

He lay a few yards away, a dark shape lying unmoving next to the broken wheelchair. But there was no time to think about him. I managed to get the key into the lock and open the door, then climbed into the back to Jenny.

She hadn't moved. My hands were uncoordinated as I tore the blanket from her. *Please, please, be alive.* Her skin was pale and cold, but she was still breathing, the tell-tale acetone odour treacherously sweet. *Thank God.* I wanted to hug her, give her some of my warmth, but she was in urgent need of far more than that.

I slid out of the car and stood up. It was easier this time, the adrenalin and desperation helping counter the waning effect of the drug. The front door to the house was still open, a rectangle of light spilling from it. I lurched into the hallway. Bracing myself against the wall, I staggered towards the telephone table that Henry had supported himself on earlier. I almost fell over the chair next to it, but managed to stay upright. Knowing if I sat down I might never get up again, I remained standing as I pawed for the phone. I couldn't remember Mackenzie's number, and my fingers were thick and uncooperative as I dialled 999.

A sudden spasm of dizziness shook me as the operator answered. I closed my eyes against it as I began to speak. I made an effort to concentrate as I gave the details, aware that Jenny's life depended on my making sense. I took care over enunciating the words 'emergency' and 'diabetic coma', but then I could hear myself starting to ramble. When the operator started asking more questions I let the phone drop back into the cradle. I'd intended to go to the fridge for the insulin, but as I clung to the sideboard, struggling to stay upright as my vision came and went, I knew I wouldn't be able to make it. And even if I did, I daren't attempt injecting her in the state I was in.

Rolling like a drunk, I went back outside. A sudden tiredness threatened to overwhelm me as I lumbered over to the Land Rover. Jenny was lying on her side where I'd left her, her face terribly still and white. Even from where I stood I could hear that her breathing had grown worse. It was wheezing and uneven and far, far too fast.

'David.'

Henry's voice was a mere whisper. I turned to look at him. He hadn't moved, but now his head was turned towards me. His clothes glistened, dark and wet with blood. The pale gravel around him was stained with it. In the half-light I could see that his eyes were open.

'Said you were . . . dark horse . . .'

I started to turn back to Jenny.

'Please . . .'

I didn't want to look back. I hated him, not just

407

for what he'd done, or even what he'd turned out to be, but for what I now knew he wasn't. Still, I hesitated. Even now, looking back, I'm not sure what I might have done.

But at that moment Jenny stopped breathing.

The sound of it simply cut off. For a moment I just stared at her, unable to move as I waited for the next breath to follow. None did. I scrambled into the back of the car.

'Jenny? *Jenny!*'

Her head fell back as I turned her over. Her eyes were partly open, half-moons of white lined with achingly beautiful lashes. I felt frantically for a pulse. There was nothing.

'No!'

This couldn't be happening, not now. Panic almost paralysed me. *Think. Think!* Adrenalin helped clear my head as I rolled Jenny onto her back, then snatched up the blanket and wadded it up under her neck. I'd practised CPR during training, but never used it. *Come on!* Cursing my awkwardness, I tilted her head back, clamped her nose and jammed clumsy fingers into her mouth to clear her tongue. My own head swam as I lowered it to her lips, breathed my own air into her – once, twice – then put my hands on her breastbone and began to rhythmically press and count.

Come on, come on! I begged, silently. I breathed into her mouth again, went back to pumping her lungs. Repeated it. She lay limp and unresponsive. I was weeping now, my vision blurring as I continued to work on her, trying to will her heart back to life. Her body remained slack and lifeless.

Useless.

I forced the knowledge from my head, breathed into her mouth once more, then counted as I pressed rapidly down on her chest. I did it again. And again.

She's gone.

No! I raged, denying it. Blinded by tears, I continued to work on her. The world was reduced to thoughtless repetition. *Breathe, press, count. Breathe, press, count.*

I lost track of time. I wasn't even aware of the approach of sirens or the headlights that splashed through the car. Nothing else existed except for Jenny's still and cold body, and my desperate rhythm. Even when I felt hands on me I refused to give it up.

'No! Get off me!'

I tried to fight them, but I was pulled back, out of the Land Rover and away from Jenny. The driveway outside the house was a confusion of flashing lights and vehicles. As the paramedics ushered me towards an ambulance, the last of my strength crumbled. I collapsed onto the gravel. Mackenzie's face appeared in front of me. I could see him mouthing questions, but paid him no attention. There was a flurry of activity around the Land Rover.

Then, out of the confusion, I heard the words that almost stopped my own heart.

'It's no good. We're too late.'

Epilogue

The grass cracked underfoot like broken glass. The early-morning frost bleached the colour from the landscape, turning it into a monochrome wilderness. A lone crow wheeled across the white sky, its wings motionless as it skated across the cold air. It beat them once, twice, then disappeared among the skeletal limbs of a tree; one more black shape among the tangle of bare branches.

I pushed my gloved hands further into my pockets, stamping my feet as the cold seeped through the soles of my boots. In the far distance, reduced to little more than a speck of colour, a car was heading away on a winding, hair-thin ribbon of road. I watched it go, envying the driver's journey towards the warmth of life and houses.

My hand went to rub the white line on my forehead. The cold was making it ache. Its sensitivity was a lingering reminder of the night I'd gashed it on the doorframe of the Land Rover. In the months since then the wound had healed to leave only a thin scar. It was the less visible scars that made their presence more keenly felt. But I knew that even those would eventually scab over and heal.

Given time.

Even now it was difficult to look back on what had happened in Manham with any degree of objectivity. Flashbacks to that night of the storm, of descending into the cellar, driving Jenny through the rain, and of what followed, came with less frequency now. But they still left me winded by their impact when they did.

Mason had still been alive when the police found him. He survived for three more days, regaining consciousness only long enough to smile at the policewoman guarding his hospital bed. For a while I'd been concerned that there might be charges, English law being what it is. But the obviating circumstances of self-defence, coupled with the grim evidence of the cellar itself, had been enough to brush aside the greyer areas of legality.

If any more evidence was needed, it was supplied by the journal the police found at the back of a locked drawer in Henry's desk. It contained a detailed account of his patronage of Manham's gardener, an unofficial case study that amounted to a posthumous confession. His fascination with his subject was all too apparent, from Mason's early sadism – as an adolescent he had been responsible for the cat mutilations Mackenzie had told me about – to their final twisted partnership.

I hadn't read it myself, and didn't want to, but I'd spoken to one of the police psychologists who had.

He'd failed to hide his excitement over what was, after all, a unique glimpse into not one but two damaged psyches. It was, he told me, the stuff professional reputations were made from.

As a frustrated psychologist himself, I thought Henry would appreciate the irony.

About my partner himself, my feelings were still unresolved. There was anger, certainly, but also sadness. Not so much for his death as the waste of his life, and all the other lives he'd also caused to be wasted. It was still difficult to reconcile the man I'd regarded as my friend with the bitter creature who'd revealed himself at the end. Or to know which of them was the true Henry.

The fact was my friend had tried to kill me, yet at times I wondered if the truth was more complex. The post-mortem had revealed he'd died not from his injuries, although they would probably have proved fatal by themselves. He'd been killed by a massive overdose of diamorphine. The syringe he'd had in his pocket had been empty, the needle embedded in his flesh. It could have been accidental, a fluke caused when the Land Rover had run him down. Or, as he lay in agony afterwards, he might have injected himself deliberately.

But that still didn't explain why he hadn't given me a lethal dose in the first place. It would have been a far easier way of staging my suicide, and certainly far more effective.

It was only at the inquest that I found out something that made me question how committed he had really been. When the police examined the Land

Rover, one end of the rubber pipe was still jutting through the window. But instead of being connected to the exhaust, the other was simply trailing on the floor.

It might have come off when the car started moving. It might have snagged loose on Henry's body as the wheels went over him. But I couldn't help but wonder if it had ever been fixed to the exhaust in the first place.

It was asking too much to believe Henry had planned it to happen as it did, but I liked to think he might have had second thoughts. If he'd truly wanted to kill me he'd had ample opportunity. And I kept coming back to how he made no attempt to move out of the way of the Land Rover. Exhaustion, perhaps; his weakened legs unable to react in time. Or perhaps as he saw the car bear down on him he simply made a decision. By his own admission he lacked the courage to take his own life. Perhaps at the end he simply chose the easiest route, and let me do it for him.

But that might be reading too much into it, bestowing on him a benefit of the doubt he doesn't deserve. Unlike Henry, I don't claim any insights into human psychology. That remains a far murkier field than mine, and no matter how much I want to believe some redeeming spark existed in him, there's no way of knowing for sure.

As with so many other things.

I'd had quite a few visitors after I'd been discharged from hospital, some calling out of duty, some curiosity, a few out of genuine concern. Ben

Anders was one of the first, bringing with him a fine old malt whisky.

'I know grapes are traditional, but I thought grain would do you a damn sight more good,' he'd said as he opened it.

He'd poured us both a glass, and as I'd raised mine slightly in answer to his silent toast, I almost asked him if the older woman he'd had an affair with all those years ago had been a doctor's wife. But I didn't. It was none of my business. And when it came down to it I didn't really want to know.

A more surprising visitor was the Reverend Scarsdale. It had been an awkward visit. The old differences still remained, and neither of us had much to say to the other. But I was touched he'd made the effort, even so. As he rose to leave he'd looked at me gravely. I thought he was about to say something, vocalize some sentiment that would bypass the antagonism that always seemed to exist between us. In the end, though, he'd simply nodded, wished me well, and gone on his way.

My only regular caller was Janice. Without Henry to care for, she'd tearfully transferred her attentions to me. If I'd eaten all the meals she'd brought I would have put on half a stone in the first two weeks, but I'd no appetite. I would thank her, pick at the solid English cooking, and when she was gone throw it away.

It was some time before I found the courage to ask her about Diana Maitland's affairs. She'd never made any secret of her disapproval of Henry's late wife, and that hadn't changed now he was dead.

Diana's unfaithfulness had been an open secret, but Janice was indignant when I asked if it had made her husband a laughing stock, as he'd believed.

'Everyone knew, but we turned a blind eye to it,' she said, reprovingly. 'For Henry's sake, not hers. He was too well respected for anything else.'

If it hadn't been so tragic, it would have been funny.

I didn't go back to work at the surgery again. Even after the police had departed from Bank House it would have been too painful to return. I arranged for a locum to be brought in until either a permanent replacement was found, or people registered with other practices in the area. Either way, I knew my days as Manham's doctor were over. And there was a noticeable reserve now among my former patients. In many of their minds I was still the newcomer who had, for a time, been a suspect. Even now my involvement with events meant I was still regarded with something like suspicion. Henry had been right, I realized. I didn't belong there.

I never would.

One morning I woke and knew it was time to move on. I put my house on the market and began setting my things in order. On the evening before the removal van was due to take my things away, there was a knock on the door. When I opened it I was surprised to find Mackenzie outside.

'Can I come in?'

I'd stepped back, led him into the kitchen and begun trying to find a pair of mugs. As the kettle boiled he asked how I was.

'OK, thanks.'

'No ill effects from the drug?'

'Don't seem to be.'

'Sleeping all right?'

I smiled. 'Sometimes.'

I poured the tea, handed him a mug. He blew on it, avoiding looking at me.

'Look, I know you didn't want to get involved in this in the first place.' He shrugged, looking uncomfortable. 'I suppose I feel a bit bad about dragging you into it.'

'No need. I was involved anyway. I just didn't realize it.'

'Even so, given how it turned out . . . well. You know.'

'That wasn't your fault.'

He nodded, not convinced he couldn't have done more. But then he wasn't the only one who felt that way.

'So what are you going to do now?' he asked.

I shrugged. 'Look for somewhere to live in London. Other than that I'm not sure yet.'

'Do you think you'll do any more forensic work?'

I almost laughed. Almost. 'I doubt it.'

Mackenzie scratched at his neck. 'Don't suppose I can blame you.' He fixed me with a look. 'I know you probably don't want to hear this from me. But don't decide anything yet. There are other people who could use you.'

I looked away. 'They'll have to find someone else.'

'Just think about it,' he said, getting up to leave.

We shook hands. As he turned to go I nodded at the mole on his neck.

'I'd still get that looked at if I were you.'

Next day I left Manham for good.

But not before I'd made another kind of farewell. The night before I'd had the dream for what I knew would be the final time. Everything about the house was as familiar and peaceful as it had always been. Yet now there was one crucial difference.

Kara and Alice had gone.

I'd wandered through the untenanted rooms, knowing this was the last time I would visit them. And knowing that was as it should be. Linda Yates had told me you have dreams for a reason, although 'dream' still seems too inadequate a description for what I experienced. But whatever the reason for mine, it no longer held. When I woke up my cheeks were wet, but there was nothing wrong with that.

Nothing at all.

The ringing of my phone brought me back to the present. Breath clouding in the cold air, I reached into my pocket for it. I smiled when I saw who was calling.

'Hi,' I said. 'You OK?'

'Fine. Am I disturbing you?'

I felt the familiar warmth spread through me at the sound of Jenny's voice. 'No, of course not.'

'I got your message that you'd arrived. How was the journey?'

'OK. Warm. It was getting out of the car that was the problem.'

417

I heard her laugh. 'So how long will you be away?' she asked.

'I don't know yet. But no longer than I have to.'

'Good. The flat seems empty already.'

I grinned. Even now there were times I couldn't believe we'd been given a second chance. But mostly I was simply grateful that we had.

Jenny had almost died. Had died, in fact, though the pronouncement that had so scared me had been about Henry, not her. But another few minutes and it would have been too late for Jenny as well. It was sheer chance that, in the confusion after the abortive raid on the windmill, no-one had thought to stand down the ambulances and paramedics. When I'd made the phone call from Henry's they had only just set off for the city, and been swiftly turned back. If not for that, the stuttering life I'd unknowingly pumped back into Jenny's heart would have snuffed out before help arrived. As it was, her heart had stopped again just after she arrived at the hospital, and again an hour after that. But each time it had been started again. After three days, she'd regained consciousness. After a week she'd been transferred out of intensive care.

The fears of brain and organ damage, of blindness, that I'd known were a possibility and that her doctors thought likely, never materialized. But while her body had begun to mend itself, for a time I'd worried about what deeper, less physical trauma might remain. Gradually, though, I realized there was no need. Jenny had retreated to Manham because she'd been afraid. Now the fear was gone.

She'd been face to face with her nightmare and survived it. And, in a different way, so had I.

One way or another, we'd both been brought back to life.

The crow flapped out of the tree as I reluctantly put away my phone. The clatter of its wings was loud in the crystalline silence. I watched it fly across the frozen Scottish moorland. But as bleak as it was, even now there were green shoots starting to push through the frozen earth, forerunners of the spring to come.

I turned as a young policewoman approached, feet crunching on the frost. Above the dark coat, her face was white and shocked.

'Dr Hunter? Sorry to keep you waiting. It's over here.'

I followed her to the waiting group of officers, shook hands as introductions were made. They moved aside to let me approach the reason for the gathering.

The body was lying in a hollow. I felt the familiar detachment start to take over as I took in its position, the texture of skin and blown wisps of hair.

I stepped closer and set to work.

THE END

Acknowledgements

The idea for *The Chemistry of Death* stemmed from an article I wrote for the *Daily Telegraph* Magazine in 2002. It was on the National Forensic Academy in Tennessee, which provides intensive and exceptionally realistic forensic training to US police officers and crime scene investigators. Part of the course takes place at the unique outdoor facility known colloquially as the Body Farm. Founded by forensic anthropologist Dr Bill Bass, it's the only one of its kind in the world, using real human cadavers to research the process of decomposition and ways of determining time since death – both vital tools in murder investigations.

My visit there proved a sobering yet fascinating experience, without which Dr David Hunter might never have existed. Thanks are therefore due to the National Forensic Academy and the University of Tennessee's Anthropology Research Facility for their co-operation in allowing me to write the original article.

A number of people provided invaluable help with research for this novel. Dr Arpad Vass of the Oak Ridge National Laboratory, Tennessee, fielded endless questions on the intricacies of forensic anthropology and made time in a busy schedule to read the manuscript. In the UK, Professor Sue Black of the University of Dundee was similarly helpful, and never too busy to return a phone call. The press office of Norfolk Constabulary, the Broads Authority and Norfolk Wildlife Trust Hickling Broad also deserve thanks for answering what must have seemed like suspiciously odd questions. Needless to say, any inaccuracies or technical errors are mine rather than theirs.

Thanks also to my wife Hilary, Ben Steiner and SCF for their input and comments, my agents, Mic Cheetham and Simon Kavanagh, not just for their hard work but for keeping the faith, to Paul Marsh, Camilla Ferrier and all at the Marsh Agency for a sterling job, and my editor Simon Taylor and the team at Transworld for their enthusiasm.

Finally, I would like to thank my parents, Sheila and Frank, for their unfailing support. Hope it's been worth it.

Simon Beckett

Simon Beckett's thrilling new novel is

WRITTEN IN BONE

Here's the first chapter to whet your appetite . . .

Chapter 1

Given the right temperature, everything burns. Wood. Clothing.

People.

At 250° centigrade, flesh will ignite. Skin blackens and splits. The subcutaneous fat below it starts to liquefy, like grease in a hot pan. Fuelled by it, the body starts to burn. Arms and legs catch first, acting as kindling to the greater mass of the torso. Tendons and muscle fibres contract, causing the burning limbs to move in an obscene parody of life. Last to go are the organs. Cocooned in moistness, they often remain even after the rest of the soft tissue has been consumed.

But bone is, quite literally, a different matter. Bone stubbornly resists all but the hottest fires. And even when the carbon has burned from it, leaving it as dead and lifeless as pumice, bone will still retain its shape. Now, though, it is an insubstantial ghost of its former self that will easily crumble; the final bastion of life transformed to ash. It's a process that, with few variations, inevitably follows the same pattern.

But not always.

The peace of the old cottage is broken by a footfall. The rotting door is tugged open, its rusted hinges protesting the disturbance. Daylight falls into the room, then is blocked out as a shadow fills the doorway. The man ducks his head to see into the darkened interior. The old dog with him hesitates, its heightened senses already alerting it to what's within. Now the man, too, pauses, as though reluctant to cross the threshold. When the dog begins to venture inside he recalls it with a word.

'Here.'

Obediently, the dog returns, glancing nervously at the man with eyes grown opaque with cataracts. As well as the scent from inside the cottage, the animal can also sense its owner's nervousness.

'Stay.'

The dog watches, anxiously, as the man advances further into the derelict cottage. The odour of damp envelops him, moss and mould the building's only inhabitants. And now another smell is making itself known. Slowly, almost reluctantly, the man crosses to a low door set in the back wall. It has swung shut. He puts out his hand to push it open, then pauses again. Behind him, the dog gives a low whine. He doesn't hear it. Gently, he eases open the door, as though fearful of what he's going to see.

But at first he sees nothing. The room is dim, the only light coming from a small window whose glass is cracked and cobwebbed with decades of dirt. In the mean light that bleeds through, the room still retains it secrets for a few moments longer. Then, as the man's eyes adjust, details begin to emerge from the gloom.

And he sees what's lying in the room's centre.

He sucks in a breath as though punched, taking an involuntary step backwards.

'Oh, Jesus Christ.'

The words are soft, but seem unnaturally loud in the still confines of the room. The man's face, which had been pale before, now seems leeched to the point of luminosity. He looks around, as if fearful he'll find someone there with him. But he's alone.

He backs away, as if reluctant to turn away from the object on the floor. Only when he is through the doorway, and the warped door has creaked shut, cutting off his view of what lies on the other side, does he turn his back.

His gait is unsteady as he goes outside. The old dog greets him, but is ignored as the man reaches inside his coat and fumbles out a pack of cigarettes. His hands are trembling, and it takes three attempts for him to ignite the lighter. He draws the smoke deep into his lungs, a nub of glowing ash chasing the paper back towards the filter. But by the time the cigarette is finished his trembling has steadied.

He drops the cigarette stub onto the grass and treads it out before bending down and retrieving it. Then, slipping it into his coat pocket, he takes a deep breath and goes to make the phone call.

I was on my way to Glasgow airport when the call came. It was a foul January day, brooding grey skies and a depressing mizzle driven by cold winds. The east coast was being lashed by storms, and although they hadn't worked their way this far inland yet, it didn't look promising.

I only hoped the worst would hold off long enough for me to catch my flight. I was on my way back to London, having spent the previous week first recovering, then examining a body from a moorland grave out on the Grampian Highlands. It had been a thankless task. The crystalline frost had turned the moors and peaks to iron, as breathtakingly cold as it was beautiful. The mutilated victim had been a young woman, who still hadn't been identified. It was the second such body I'd been asked to recover from the Grampians in less than a year. As yet it had been kept out of the press, but no-one on the investigating team was in any doubt that the same killer was responsible for both. One would kill again if he wasn't caught, and at the moment that wasn't looking likely. What made it worse was that, although the state of decomposition made it hard to be sure, I was certain that the mutilations weren't post-mortem.

So all in all, it had been a gruelling trip, and I was looking forward to going home. For the past eighteen months I'd been living in London, based at the Forensic Science department at King's College. It was a temporary contract that gave me access to lab facilities until I found something more permanent, but in recent weeks I'd spent far more time working out in the field than I had in my office. I was ready for a break, and when my phone rang I thought it might be my girlfriend Jenny, calling to make sure I was actually on my way home.

But the number on the caller display wasn't hers, or any I recognized. When I answered, the voice at the other end was gruff and no-nonsense.

'Sorry to disturb you, Dr Hunter. I'm Detective

Superintendent Graham Wallace, at Inverness Force HQ. Can you spare me a few minutes?'

He had the tone of someone used to getting his own way, and a harsh accent that spoke of Glasgow tenements rather than the softer tones of Inverness. I glanced through the rain-smeared taxi window. The signs for the airport showed we were almost there.

'Just a few. I'm on my way to catch a flight.'

'I know. I've just spoken to DCI Allan Campbell at Grampian Police, and he told me you'd finished up here. I'm glad I've caught you.'

Campbell was the Senior Investigating Officer I'd been working with on the body recovery. A decent man and a good officer, he found it difficult to separate himself from his work. Which was something I could appreciate.

I made sure the partition separating me from the taxi driver was closed so I wouldn't be overheard. 'What can I do for you?'

'I'm looking for a favour.' Wallace clipped the words out, as though each one was costing more than he liked to pay. 'You'll have seen about the train crash this morning?'

I had. At my hotel before I'd left I'd watched the news reports of a West Coast commuter express that had derailed after hitting a minibus on the line. From the TV footage it looked bad, the train lying mangled and twisted by the track. No-one knew yet how many people had been killed.

'We've got everyone we can up there now, but it's chaos at the moment,' Wallace continued. 'There's a chance the derailment was deliberate, so we're having to

427

treat the whole area as a crime scene. We're calling in help from other forces but right now we're running at full stretch.'

I thought then I could guess what was coming. Although the news reports hadn't said as much, if some of the carriages had caught fire it would make victim identification both a priority and a forensic nightmare. But before that could even begin, the bodies would have to be recovered, and from what I'd seen that was still some way off.

'I'll do what I can. But I'm not sure how much help I'd be at the moment.'

'It isn't the crash I'm calling about,' he said, impatiently. 'We've got a report of a fire death out on the Western Isles. Small island called Runa, in the Outer Hebrides.'

I hadn't heard of it, but that was hardly surprising. All I knew about the Outer Hebrides was that the islands were one of the most remote outposts of the UK, miles from anywhere off the northwest coast of Scotland.

'Suspicious?' I asked.

'Doesn't sound like it. Might be suicide, but more likely to be a drunk or vagrant who fell asleep too close to a camp fire. Dog walker found it at an abandoned croft and called it in. He's a retired DI, lives out there now. I've worked with him. Used to be a good man.'

I wondered if the *used to be* was significant. 'So what else has he said about it?'

There was a beat before he replied. 'Just that it's badly burnt. But I don't want to pull resources away from a major incident unless I have to. A couple of the local boys from Stornoway are going out there by ferry later today, and I'd like you to go with them and take a look.

See if you think it's low priority, or if I need to get an SOC team out there. I'd like an expert assessment before I press the panic button, and Allan Campbell says you're bloody good.'

The attempt at flattery sat awkwardly with his bluff manner. I'd also noticed the hesitation when I'd asked about the body, and wondered if there was something he wasn't telling me. But if Wallace thought there was anything suspicious about the death, he'd be sending a scene-of-crime team up there rather than me, train crash or not.

The taxi was almost at the airport. I had every reason say no. I'd only just finished working on one major investigation, and this sounded fairly mundane; the sort of everyday tragedy that never makes it into the newspapers. I thought about having to tell Jenny that I wouldn't be back today after all. Given the amount of time I'd already spent away recently, I doubted it would go down well.

But even as I thought about that, I knew I'd already made my decision.

'How do I get there?' I asked.

**Read the complete book –
coming in August from Bantam Press**

The following article by Simon Beckett about the National Forensic Academy first appeared in the *Telegraph* magazine in 2002.

The white-suited figures have been working in the Tennessee woods for several hours. Earlier that morning they located what appeared to be a grave, following a tip-off to police that a serial killer has buried at least one of his victims here. They have started to expose the remains of a body, when a shout from one of the team alerts them to an un-welcome development. 'OK,' one of them says, peering into the grave, 'looks like we got two.'

The scenario is fictional: no serial killer, no tip-off. But the bodies are real. If it seems a particularly grisly form of make-believe, that is only a reflection of the even grimmer reality it attempts to re-construct. If this were a real murder, the forensic evidence collected here could help capture the killer. Mishandled, it could enable the killer to escape detection. The exercise is part of a new training programme run for police officers and crime scene investigators by the National Forensic Academy (NFA) in Knoxville, Tennessee. Open to international as well as American students, it aims to deliver training that is as close to the real thing as possible; not only does it blow up real cars for its bombs and booby-traps section and burn down houses for its arson module, it is also the only course in the world that uses real corpses in some of its reconstructions.

'We try to cover every serious crime,' says Jarrett Hallcox, the NFA's programme coordinator. 'There's nothing better than experiential learning. It's hard to get a police officer to sit in a classroom unless you tie him down. But if you see a car explode, you'll remember what you've picked up a lot better than if you're just told about it.'

Funded by the Department of Justice, the NFA is a part of the Law Enforcement Innovation Centre, a partnership between the University of Tennessee and the Knoxville Police Department. Using specialist instructors from organizations such as the FBI as well as civilian experts, its 10-week residential course provides a mix of lab work, classroom-based studies and field exercises to instruct its students in all aspects of crime-scene processing, from blood pattern analysis and gunshot residue to terrorist crime scenes and weapons of mass destruction. And murder.

The training is the first of its kind in America. High-profile cases such as the OJ Simpson murder trial (where doubts about the prosecution's evidence contributed to Simpson's acquittal) highlighted the need for the proper collection, identification and preservation of evidence. But while courses in individual forensic disciplines such as fingerprinting and crime-scene photography already exist, until now there has been nothing offering a comprehensive approach, far less any sort of national standard. While police and civilian crime-scene examiners in Britain have to undergo training approved by the Association of Chief Police Officers (generally at the National Training Centre for Scientific Support in County Durham, although the Met has its own school), in America requirements – and standards – vary from state to state.

'Right now the way crime scene investigators are being trained, it's kind of like the Wild West,' says

Hallcox. 'Everybody's just shooting their guns off, hoping to hit something. In more rural departments you could be thrust into a job and have no formal training. And you can see the evidentiary problems when that case goes to court.'

The academy opened its doors a year ago, and if a need for such training was already recognized, six days before the start of its inaugural class it was underlined in a far more potent way than anyone could have predicted. 'September 11 was a wake-up call,' says Hallcox. 'We were in the final stages of preparing, and then that happened. The instructors for our second week – which is photography taught by the FBI evidence response team – were called away to Pennsylvania to cull the plane wreckage.' With the world's largest crime scene suddenly present in New York, forensic examination acquired a new significance.

The NFA has three classes scheduled for this year (from 2003 it will be running four), and demand for the 16 places on each has been high. The $6,500 fee is generally paid by the student's own police department, and includes accommodation and use of a laptop computer as well as technical and photographic equipment for the duration of the course. At the end of it, in order to graduate, students have successfully to process mock crime scenes set up by an FBI evidence response team.

The academy is based in the Law Enforcement Innovations Centre's headquarters, a large brick building that, incongruously, also houses the Boys and Girls Club of Greater Knoxville. On the Monday morning of their sixth week, the students of the third class begin to drift into the classroom at 8am. There's a uniform of sorts: dark blue NFA polo shirt (the academy's logo is a skull, a fingerprint and a gun emblazoned on a shield), combat trousers and black boots. The students are predominantly police officers; bulky, beef-fed men for the most part. But not all of them.

'I'm here to enhance the skills I already have, in addition to learning new ones,' says Jennifer Rhinebarger, one of the four women in the class. A civilian crime scene investigator – or 'criminalist' – for the police department in Plato, Texas, she already has more than 400 hours of forensic training that took her five years to accumulate. Even so, she still regards the NFA as something not to be missed. 'All the instructors they have are nationally and world renowned in their fields, and you can't learn from anybody better.'

So far the class have covered aspects such as crime-scene management, latent fingerprint process-ing and forensic sketching. But the coming week is the one they've been most anxiously anticipating: body recovery. Although other countries may have their own version of the NFA's training (the National Training Centre in County Durham also uses mock crime scenes in its nine-week course), they cannot compete with this, so extreme are the lengths to which the academy goes to ensure its reconstructions are realistic. The theory is that the more lifelike the recreations are, the better prepared the students will be when they encounter the genuine thing. For the blood-spatter analysis, expired human blood from blood banks is used rather than pig; to replicate arson, houses earmarked for demolition rather than custom-built sets are torched. But it is the body recover exercise that sets the NFA apart. 'That's our calling card. It's what makes us unique,' says Hallcox. 'There's several places where you can go and excavate pig remains, but nowhere other than right here can you find a research facility where you can excavate human remains.'

It is run in association with the University of Tennessee's outdoor Anthropological Research Facility. Known colloquially as the 'Body Farm', it was started in 1980 by Dr William Bass to document and investigate the process of decomposition, and especially to find ways of establishing the all-import time-since-death of human remains. It is the only anthropological facility in the world to use human bodes in its research. While some are 'unclaimed indigents' supplied by the medical examiner, the majority of bodies are donated, either by the individual themselves or their families. Last year alone, the facility received nearly 50: an egalitarian mix of university professors, lawyers, nurses and vagrants.

With the exception of the FBI, which spends a week each year at the site for its own in-house training, only the NFA is allowed to use it for body recovery exercises. The class will spend the next three days here, carrying out two exercises. The first is called surface recovery, and involves processing a mock crime scene where there are scattered skeletal remains. The second, and more difficult, will be to excavate a buried body.

The day before they begin, Dr Bass himself instructs the class in what to look for when dealing with a crime scene involving human remains. He has worked on dozens of crime scenes during his career, and though officially retired is still very much a part of the facility. His Snoopy tie and informal delivery helps counter the undeniable grimness of his subject, but there is no disguising the underlying seriousness. 'There are no stupid questions,' he tells them. 'You don't want to assume too much when you're dealing with a crime scene.'

For the next two hours the students are presented with slides from crime scenes Bass has worked on, along with lessons drawn from each. 'You always, always X-ray burn material, and you always X-ray maggot-covered material. There could be a knife underneath.' The class listens impassively as he describes the length of time it might take a body to decompose fully, or 'skeletonize'; the effect on vegetation of volatile fatty acids from a corpse; and the fact that, as a body decomposes, the skin will slough off hands 'like a glove'. Easily mistaken for a leaf when the body is outdoors, this grisly remnant is often overlooked by investigating officers, who thereby miss one of the best means of identifying the victim (in what sounds like a grisly recipe, Bass tells them that if the skin is soaked overnight in warm water, fingerprints can still be taken from it).

Early next morning the class gather in the car park outside the Body Farm gates. Spread over two acres of wooded hillside, the facility is hidden behind a high wooden and chain-link fence topped with razor wire. There is nervous banter as the students liberally douse themselves with insect repellent (everything in Tennessee seems to bite or sting) and don protective white overalls, gloves and overshoes. Ominously, masks are also available in case anyone cannot handle the smell.

The general feeling is one of anticipation, but also apprehension, even among the more seasoned hands. 'I've been around some dead bodies and stuff, but I've never done anything like this,' says Sammy Liles, a police lieutenant from Martin, Tennessee, An affable bear of a man, like most of his classmates Liles will be expected to pass on what he's learnt to his fellow officers when he returns to his department. But despite 13 years of experience, he admits to being nervous about what is ahead. 'This is what it's all about. This is actually hands on. You can look at all the slides and read all the books you want to, but until you get your hands dirty, you just don't know.'

The students are given a preliminary talk by Jackie Fish, the NFA's project manager, reminding them to respect the fact that all the bodies they will see are still individuals whose rights must be respected. With a final admonition to watch out for poisonous snakes and spiders and toxic plants, the gates are opened and they are allowed in.

It is a macabre setting. Two bodies are immediately visible lying in the open, but they are part of other projects being carried out at the facility, and nothing to do with today's exercise. (The facility researches such aspects as the time it takes for hair to slough off a body, the role of insects in decomposition, even the differing effects that light and shade will have on the process of decay.) The NFA students have been warned what to expect. Still, there is an understandable hush as the students are led up the hillside where they are to spend the rest of the day.

The class has been split into two groups, each of which will have its own crime scene. These are already cordoned off with yellow police tape. Scattered among the trees and bushes in each area are human bones, the positions of which have been carefully recorded by the instructors so that every piece can be accounted for. As an additional test, trace evidence such as shell casings has also been included without the students' knowledge.

'Y'all ready for the walk through?' Detective Brian Kiersey asks his group. The 43-year-old from Collierville, near Memphis, is one of the most experienced members of the class, having been a police officer for the past 20 years. Although he has worked on several homicide investigations, the recovery process is as new to him as it is the rest. Unlike some of them, however, he is actively looking forward to it. 'I'm looking at it as a police officer who's been in court before and had to testify as to my processing of certain crime scenes. You can't redo it, and if you screw up you can't go back. I hate that.'

The students form a line and slowly work their way through the crime scene, marking anything they find with a miniature orange flag. This is harder than it sounds; not only is there a thick leaf cover on the steep and uneven terrain, but also it is often difficult to distinguish small bones from stones and pieces of wood. 'I found some vertebrae up by that tree,' says Kiersey during a water break. Even in the shade of the trees it is already hot and humid, making the overalls unbearable.

By the end of the exercise, the location of everything the students have found has been noted, the whole procedure carefully photographed and each piece of evidence placed into a brown paper evidence bag, ready for sending to the crime lab if this were a real investigation. One group missed three small bones out of the 30 scattered in their crime scene, the other only one. Not 100 per cent scores, perhaps, but not bad for what amounts to a novice class.

But everyone is aware that the real test will come the next day. For the burial recovery the class is again split into groups. Using long metal probes to test for tell-tale softer ground, the two graves are soon located. After examination with a metal detector, a grid of string is pegged over each site so that the position of everything found within it can be logged, and then the excavation starts.

All that is missing are the bodies.

It is a dirty, painstaking business, requiring an archaeological thoroughness. Most of the digging is done with hand trowels, and every inch of soil has to be carefully sieved. Anything that looks remotely like evidence is recorded and bagged. Even samples of maggots and insect eggs are taken and stored in small jars – these can reveal a wealth of information, such as how long the body may have been here.

With the temperature now in the 90s, tempers are

growing short. One student thinks she may have found tissue. 'Tissue as in skin?' another asks. 'Well, it ain't Kleenex,' comes the retort.

It is several more hours before the first groups discover what they are looking for. 'Its got a sock on it,' the student says, carefully brushing away the soil form the leg bone she has exposed. A few minutes later its partner is unearthed. Unfortunately a third is discovered; true to the serial kill scenario, the instructors have thrown a curve-ball at the students by placing two bodies in the same grave.

The second group, meanwhile, are having their own problems: they are more than two feet down and while they have found a .22 bullet, so far there is no sign of a body. Which means it is either deeper than they were expecting, or they have digging in the wrong place.

It takes until the following afternoon before the bodies are fully uncovered. Having been placed here several months before, the remains are mainly skeletal, with items of rotting clothing still attached. Everything is photographed, and sketches made of the bodies' positions. After the remains have been carefully removed, the class's final duty is to replace them with new ones (actually several months old) from the facility, ready for the next NFA class. As a final touch, a note saying 'Good luck' is put into a plastic film container and buried as well.

Tired, sweaty and dirty, the main emotion among the students is relief that it is over. But none of them doubts the value of what they have just been though. 'It's amazing. It's great because you can actually look at these remains and visualize what they've been telling us about for the last two weeks,' says Jennifer Rhinebarger.

Despite his earlier nerves, Sammy Liles agrees. 'It's been hot and tiring, but it's given you a real-life experience of working a crime scene with a body,' he says. 'I was afraid of the gruesomeness of it, but it wasn't nearly as bad as I expected. I enjoyed it for the most part, if you can say that. I wouldn't want to do it for a living. But I'm glad to say that I've come, I've seen, I've experienced.'

As realistic as it is, however, it is still only training. The bodies were donated, the crime scenes staged, not real. But a grim reminder of the reason – and the need – behind it is delivered that same week, with the news that a five-year-old girl has been abducted and murdered by a paedophile serial killer in California. A man is swiftly arrested, but it is nevertheless a sobering example of what is at stake.

It is admittedly early days for the academy – after only three intakes they are still fine-tuning the course. But there are already signs that it is beginning to make a difference. 'We're getting feedback all the time,' says Jackie Fish, the NFA's project manager. 'The students who've been here have gone back to their agencies and already started training or setting up evidence recovery teams We're getting success stories, and it's only going to get better and better.'

Expectations are clearly high, as is indicated by the additional $1 million of funding that the National Institute of Justice has recently provided to create a

National Forensic Science Institute in Tennessee, of which the NFA will be only a part.

The hope is that the academy will eventually become a model for crime scene training across America. Given the scale of the task, that might not happen for some time – getting 50 notoriously in-dependent states to toe the federal line will not be easy. But Hallcox believes that the effort needs to be made. 'It's not glamorous like in these television shows, where they show up in their dresses and make-up. These people are down on their hands and knees, culling through the muck and the guck, because someone has to do it. Because there's evil in the world.'

WRITTEN IN BONE
Simon Beckett

'I took the skull from its evidence bag and gently set it on the stainless steel table. 'Tell me who you are . . .'

On the remote Hebridean island of Runa, a grisly discovery awaits the arrival of forensic anthropologist Dr David Hunter.

A body – almost totally incinerated but for the feet and a single hand – has been found. The local police are quick to record an accidental death but Hunter's instincts say otherwise: he's convinced it's murder. Indeed it appears Runa might not be such a peaceful community after all – and a burned corpse but one of its dark secrets.

Then an Atlantic storm descends, severing all power and contact with the mainland. And as the storm rages, the killing begins in earnest . . .

Powerful, unpredictable and shocking, *Written in Bone* is a nerve-shredding crime thriller from a brilliant British storyteller.

'Beckett cranks up the suspense . . . unexpected twists and a gory climax'
Daily Telegraph

9780553817508

BANTAM BOOKS

SWEET GUM
Jo-Ann Goodwin

'This ingenious, amoral thriller crackles with surprises
. . . it's almost as ghoulish as they come, with a truly
stomach-churning finale'
Mail on Sunday

Evil haunts the alleys and archways of North London:
'the Meatman' is about to begin his grisly work.

But for now things are looking up for the firm's young
fixer Eugene Burnside. The Faron Brothers have
earmarked Eugene for bigger and better things – and
everyone knows the Farons are 'the Firm'.

On the domestic front, things are not so sweet. Little
sister Simone is a star turn at Sweethearts lap-dancing
club – not a great career choice in Eugene's view. While
she shimmies and grinds nights, mum Gladys is left in
charge of Simone's six-year-old son. Eugene's worried:
he's not a nice child – disturbed isn't the half of it.

Then a Sweetheart's girl goes missing. The Meatman's
murderous odyssey has begun . . .

'A modern parable . . . a nightmare vision . . . it's
bloodcurdling stuff'
Independent on Sunday

'Oozes gore and throbs with the stench of decay . . .
Goodwin has first-hand knowledge of the underworld.
She is also a fine writer'
Daily Telegraph

'Far more profound than your average mortuary
slab read . . . her skill at characterization is equal
to Zadie Smith's'
Scotland on Sunday

9780552773737

BLACK SWAN

THE LAST SECRET OF THE TEMPLE
Paul Sussman

A two thousand year-old mystery – a pulse-pounding race against time . . .

Jerusalem, 70 AD. As the legions of Rome besiege the Holy Temple, a boy is given a secret that he must guard with his life . . .

Southern Germany, December 1944. Six emaciated Nazi prisoners drag a mysterious crate deep into a disused mine. They too give their lives to keep the secret safe: murdered by their guards . . .

Egypt, Valley of the Kings, the present day. A body is found amongst some ruins. I appears to be an open-and-shut case but the more Inspector Yusuf Khalifa of the Luxor police uncovers about the dead man, the more uneasy he becomes. And his investigation turns out to be anything but routine. Khalifa doesn't know it yet, but he is on the trail of an extraordinary long-lost artifact that could, in the wrong hands, turn the Middle East into a blood bath. It's a dangerous path he's taking – and what's more he's not alone.

From ancient Jerusalem, the Crusades, Cathar heretics and coded medieval manuscripts to the Holocaust, hidden Nazi treasure and the murderous present-day, this is a thrilling rollercoaster ride of an adventure.

'The intelligent reader's answer to *The Da Vinci Code*: a big, fat, satisfying archaeological puzzle'
Independent

9780553814057

BANTAM BOOKS

THUNDERSTRUCK
Erik Larson

The true story of Dr Crippen and the miraculous invention
that helped catch a killer and transform the world . . .

The Edwardian age: A time when shipping companies
competed to build the biggest, fastest vessels, the rich vied
with one another with their displays of wealth, and science
dazzled the public with visions of a world made wondrous.

The Murderer: Wanted for what would become one of the
twentieth-century's most infamous murders, Dr Hawley
Crippen fled England on a ship bound for America
accompanied by his unsuspecting mistress disguised as a boy.

The Detective: A veteran of the Ripper case, Inspector
Walter Dew found himself strangely sympathetic to the
murderer and his young lover.

The Inventor: Guglielmo Marconi drove himself to the brink
in his obsessive struggle to perfect his visionary creation, but
his 'wireless' would play a pivotal role in catching the killer.

Written with riveting attention to detail, narrative drive and
an uncanny ability to bring a bygone era to life, this true
story culminates in one of the most spectacular criminal
chases of all time, as one luxury liner pursued another across
the Atlantic, and recalls an extraordinary and largely
forgotten chapter from history.

'Meticulously researched . . . a fascinating read'
Daily Express

'Larson has an exceptional mastery of historical detail and a
real flair for suspense'
Observer

'Shines a vivid electric light on the birth of the modern age
. . . Larson is a great master of narrative'
Mail on Sunday

'Larson has done it again . . . as in his last book, *The Devil
in the White City*, he has taken an unlikely historical subject
and spun it into gold'
New York Times

9780553817089

BANTAM BOOKS